CAROL O'CONNELL

one of the most poetic yet tough-minded writers of the genre."

—*San Francisco Chronicle*

MALLORY

the most interesting fictional detective I've come across in years."

—*San Jose Mercury News*

CAROL O'CONNELL

unges deep into the minds of all her characters."

—*The Denver Post*

MALLORY

s a rare literary accomplishment—an authentic female antihero."

—*St. Petersburg Times*

DEAD FAMOUS

"A palpable neo-noir grit . . . O'Connell devilishly fills in the pieces so that the reader's perspective undergoes constant shifts." —*Publishers Weekly* (starred review)

"Stark and chilling. Mallory is tough as nails, a female equivalent of Burke, Andrew Vachss's legendary loner." —*BookPage*

And more praise for the Mallory novels by Carol O'Connell

CRIME SCHOOL

"Mallory has become the fictional personification of New York City. O'Connell is that rare mystery/thriller writer who finds complex characters to be as important as intricate plots . . . [a] fascinating series." —*The Denver Post*

"Easily one of the most original and striking crime fiction protagonists to appear in the last few years . . . Multi-layered, serpentine in plot, *Crime School* is a rich, evocative novel." —*St. Petersburg Times*

"A standout among modern mysteries." —*San Jose Mercury News*

"Like the best work of James Lee Burke and Barbara Vine, O'Connell's character-driven procedural transcends genre pigeonholing." —*Kirkus Reviews* (starred review)

"Breathtaking . . . Searing suspense." —*Booklist* (starred review)

"O'Connell delivers all the best parts of suspense fiction—plot twists, chilling details, and a rapid pacc—while simultaneously delving into the psyche of her protagonist. She displays not only the dark horrors of the criminal mind but also what lurks in the hearts of those who try to protect us." —*Library Journal*

continued on next page . . .

MALLORY'S ORACLE

"*Mallory's Oracle* is a joy . . . exciting, riveting . . . Mallory is a marvelous creation." —Jonathan Kellerman

"A classic cop story . . . one of the most interesting new characters to come along in years." —John Sandford

"An author who really involves you, and makes you care." —James B. Patterson

"Wild, sly, and breathless—all the things that a good thriller ought to be." —Carl Hiaasen

THE MAN WHO CAST TWO SHADOWS

"Even more satisfying than *Mallory's Oracle*. And that's high praise indeed." —*People*

"Beautifully written." —*Harper's Bazaar*

"The suspense is excruciating." —*Detroit Free Press*

KILLING CRITICS

"Darkly stylish . . . highly original . . . This is great fun." —*Chicago Tribune*

"A tight, twisting mystery." —*Newsday*

"[A] crafty page-turner." —*People*

STONE ANGEL

"Mallory makes a hard-edged, brilliant and indomitable heroine. *Stone Angel,* as much Southern novel as mystery novel, is rich in people, places and customs vividly realized, with mordant humor, terror and sadness." —*San Francisco Chronicle*

"O'Connell conjures up a world of almost Faulknerian richness and complexity. In *Stone Angel,* her imagination truly takes wing."
—*People*

SHELL GAME

"An intricate whodunit." —*Chicago Tribune*

"One of O'Connell's best." —*Milwaukee Journal Sentinel*

"The plot's hairpin twists and turns are dazzling."
—*Library Journal* (starred review)

"Rich, complex, memorable . . . another superb effort from one of our most gifted writers." —*Booklist* (starred review)

Also by Carol O'Connell . . .

JUDAS CHILD

"Breathtakingly ambitious suspense . . . A brilliant twist . . . mesmerizing." —*Minneapolis Star Tribune*

"More than enough darkness and tension to make fans of Mallory take notice . . . Solidly crafted . . . a compelling tale."
—*Chicago Tribune*

"Her most stunning novel yet . . . more chilling, twisted, and intense with each page . . . [a] soul-shattering climax."
—*Booklist* (starred review)

TITLES BY CAROL O'CONNELL

Dead Famous
Crime School
Shell Game
Judas Child
Stone Angel
Killing Critics
The Man Who Cast Two Shadows
Mallory's Oracle

dEAd fAMOUs

CAROL O'CONNELL

BERKLEY BOOKS, NEW YORK

DEAD FAMOUS

A Berkley Book / published by arrangement with
the author

PRINTING HISTORY
G. P. Putnam's Sons hardcover edition / September 2003
Berkley mass-market edition / September 2004

Cover design and art by Tony Greco.

For information address: The Berkley Publishing Group,
a division of Penguin Group (USA) Inc.,
375 Hudson Street, New York, New York 10014.

ISBN 0-425-19797-2

BERKLEY®
Berkley Books are published by The Berkley Publishing Group,
a division of Penguin Group (USA) Inc.,
375 Hudson Street, New York, New York 10014.
BERKLEY and the "B" design
are trademarks belonging to Penguin Group (USA) Inc.

PRINTED IN THE UNITED STATES OF AMERICA

10 9 8 7 6 5 4 3 2 1

This book is dedicated to the walking wounded, in and out of uniform, all around the town, and to those who came from far away to help us. Though New York City is the prime character in my novels, the event of September 11, 2001, does not appear in these pages, not even in passing, no mention at all. There will be readers who find that odd, for it changed the very landscape, but one does not have to draw a tragedy literally in order to draw from it. Some New Yorkers still stop and raise their eyes to the sound of overhead planes, but then they move on down the sidewalk. Life goes on. It's a very tough town—unbreakable.

ACKNOWLEDGMENTS

Many thanks to Dianne Burke, researcher extraordinaire, for her wide-ranging technical support; Bill Lambert, Arizona firearms aficionado; Richard Hughes, for valuable insight on a psychological disorder; radio station personnel from coast to coast; the Chelsea Hotel; the FBI Firearms Tactical Institute; and special thanks to the Federal Bureau of Investigation for being good sports. They never sent me hate mail for things done to them in previous novels. This time, in an effort to be evenhanded, I have also taken broad shots at the news media and the American Civil Liberties Union. As a card-carrying member of the ACLU, I would be proud to receive their hate mail. However, I believe they are equally blasé in the area of satirical pounding.

dEAd fAMOUs

PROLOGUE

JOHANNA COULD HEAR CAT'S PAWS MADLY THUDding on the bathroom door, and the animal was crying in a human way—so frightened. Or was he merely hungry? She had fed the poor beast, but how long ago? No matter. The cat's cries receded, as though her front room had decamped from the hotel suite, floating up and away with utter disregard for gravity.

And time? What was that to her?

The whole day long, Johanna had not moved from her perch at the edge of a wooden chair. She sat there, wrapped in a bathrobe, as the sun moved behind the window glass, as shadows crawled about the room with a slow progress that only a paranoid eye could follow. One of the shadows belonged to herself, and the dark silhouette of her body was dragged across the wallpaper, inch by inch, extending her deformity to a cruel extreme.

Inside her brain was the refrain of a rock 'n' roll song from another era. "Gimme shelter," the Rolling Stones sang to her, and she resisted this mantra as she always did, for there were no safe places.

Perhaps another hour had passed, maybe three. She could not say when night had fallen. Johanna unclenched her hands and looked down at a crumpled letter, as if, in absolute darkness, she could read the words of a postscript: *Only a monster can play this game.*

1

THE BLACK VAN HAD NO HELPFUL LETTERING ON the side to tell the neighbors what business it was about on this November afternoon. Here and there, along the street of tall brownstones, drapes had parted and curious eyes were locked upon the vehicle's driver. Even by New York City standards, she was an odd one.

Johanna Apollo's skin was very fair, the gift of Swedes on her mother's side. And yet, from any distance, she might be taken for a large dark spider clad in denim as she climbed out of the van, then dropped to the pavement in a crouch. Dark brown was the color of her leather gloves, her work boots and the long strands of hair spread back across the unnatural curve of her spine. Her torso was bent forward, her body forever fused into a subtle question mark as her face angled toward the ground, hidden from the watchers at their windows. They never saw the great dark eyes—the beauty of the beast. And now the neighbors' heads turned in unison, following her progress down the street. Dry yellow leaves cartwheeled and crackled alongside as she walked with a delicacy of slender spider-long legs. Such deep grace for one so misshapen—that was how the neighbors would recall this moment later in the day. It was almost a dance, they would say.

And none of them noticed the small tan car gliding into Eighty-fourth Street, quiet as a swimming shark. It stopped near the corner, where another vehicle had just taken the last available parking space.

The young driver of the tan sedan left her engine idling as she stepped out in the middle of the street. Nothing about her said *civil servant*; the custom-tailored lines of her designer jeans and long, black leather coat said *money*. And the wildly expensive running shoes allowed her to move in silence as she padded toward a station wagon. She leaned down and rapped on the driver's window. The pudgy man behind the wheel gave her the grin of a lottery winner, for she was that lovely, that ilk of tall blondes who would never go out with him in a million years, and he hurried to roll down the window.

Oh, happy day.

"I want your parking place," she said, all business, no smile of hello—nothing.

The wagon driver's grin wobbled a bit. Was this a joke? No man would give up a parking space on any street in Manhattan, not *ever,* not even for a *naked* woman. Was she *nuts?* He summoned up his New Yorker attitude, saying, "Yeah, lady—over my dead body." And she raised one eyebrow to indicate that this might be an option. The long slants of her eyes were unnaturally green—unnaturally cold. A milk-white hand rested on the door of his car, long red fingernails tapping, tapping, ticking like a bomb, and it occurred to him that those nails might be dangerous.

Oh, shit!

One hand had gone to her hip, opening the blazer for just a tease, a peek at what she had hidden in her shoulder holster, a damn cannon that passed for a gun.

"Move," she said, and move he did.

Kathy Mallory had a detective's gold shield, but she rarely used the badge to motivate civilians. Listening to angry tirades on abuse of police power was time-consuming; fear was more efficient. And now she drove her tan car into the hastily vacated parking space. After killing the engine, she never even glanced at the black van.

It was her day off and this covert surveillance was the closest she could come to an idea of recreation.

The routine of the van's driver was predictable, and Mallory was settling in for a long wait when a large white Lincoln with rental plates rounded the corner. This motorist was less enterprising, settling for double-parking his car across the street from the vehicle that so interested Mallory—until now. The driver of the rented car became her new target when he craned his neck to check the black van's plates. His head was slowly turning, eyes scanning the street, until he located the deformed figure of Johanna Apollo walking down the sidewalk in the direction of Columbus Avenue.

Mallory smiled, for this man had just identified himself as another player in the mother of all games.

The company uniform was stowed in Johanna Apollo's duffel bag along with the rest of her gear. She never wore it when meeting the clients. The moonsuit was far more unsettling than the sudden appearance of a hunchback at the door.

A man her own age, late thirties, awaited her on the front steps of a brownstone built in the nineteenth century. He wore a flimsy robe over his pajamas, and, though his feet were bare, he seemed not to mind the cold. When Johanna lifted her head to greet him, his face was full of trepidation, and then he nearly smiled. She could read his mind. He was thinking, *Oh, how normal,* so glad to see her conventional human face. He adjusted his spectacles for a better look at her warm brown eyes, and he took some comfort there, even before she said, "I'll be done in an hour, and then you can have your life back."

That was all he wanted to hear. Relieved, he sighed and nodded his understanding that there would be no small talk, not one more chorus of *I'm so sorry,* false notes in the mouth of a stranger.

Johanna followed him into the house and through another door to his front room. It was decorated with period furniture and smeared with the bloody handprints of an intruder. She recognized the spots on the wall as a splatter pattern from the back-strike of a knife. The chalk outline sketched on the rug was that of a small, lean victim who had died quickly, though her blood was spread thin all about the room, giving the impression that the attack had gone on forever. She wondered if anyone had told the husband that his wife had not suffered long. Johanna turned to the sorry man beside her. It was her art to put disturbed people at ease; she did it with tea.

"You don't have to stay and watch. Why not wait in the kitchen?" She pulled a small packet of herbal tea from the pocket of her denim jacket. "This is very soothing."

The client took the packet and stared at it, as though the printed instructions for steeping in hot water might be difficult to comprehend. He waved one hand in apology to say that he was somewhat at sea today. "My wife usually handles these—" Suddenly appalled, he lowered his head. His wife had usually handled the messes of their lives. How could he have forgotten that she was dead? His hands clenched tightly, and Johanna knew that he was silently berating himself for this bizarre breach of etiquette.

The murder was recent, and she would have guessed that even without the paperwork to release the crime scene. Judging by the growth of stubble on the man's face, only a few days had passed since his wife's death. Unshaven, unwashed, the widower walked about in a stale ether that the bereaved shared with the bedridden. His head was still bowed as he edged away from her and ambled down a narrow passageway. Upon opening a door at the far end of this hall, he raised his face in expectation, perhaps believing that he would meet his dead wife in the kitchen—and she would make him some tea.

Johanna knelt on the floor and opened her duffel bag. One hand passed over the hood and the respirator. No need for them today. She pulled out a protective suit and gloves for working with blood products in the age of AIDS—even the blood of children, nuns and other virgins. Her employer had given her the basic vocabulary of the job: *fluids* and *solids* and *hazardous waste,* though she had never seen the common debris of brains and shattered bone, feces and urine as anything but human remains. She had also been encouraged to remove photographs of the victim before she began, and this was another trick to dehumanize the task. But Johanna never disturbed the wedding portrait on the wall, and the bride with downcast eyes continued to shyly smile at the chalk outline of her own corpse.

Johanna sponged the stains on the cream-white wall and charted a thief's progress around this room, going from drawer to pulled-out drawer. She knew where he had been standing when a policeman had barreled through the door with a drawn gun. The bullet had been pried out of the wall, but the hole remained. The thief must have had the knife in his hand, and the officer must have been very young, untried and nervous.

She filled the hole with a ready-mix plaster. A small brush and a few deft strokes of tint made it blend into the paint. Below this patch were red drops of *hazardous waste* from a murderer. He was wiped away with one wet rag, and, though no one would ever know, she placed it in a separate bag so the blood of the innocent woman would not mingle with his. Next, she replaced the contents spilled from the drawers, then went on to the problem of a torn lampshade and resolved it with a bit of mending tape. Last, she pulled out a hair dryer and moved it across the wet areas where she had spot-cleaned the rug, the couch and the drapes. Some of her services went beyond the job description, but she wanted the widower to find no trace of murder, no damp ghost of a stain that he might commit to memory.

No more than an hour had passed, as promised, and now the client inspected her work. She watched his fearful eyes search the wall for the bullet hole, but there was no sign of it anymore. And, by his wandering gaze, she could tell that he had forgotten the exact location of that scar in the plaster and his wife's chalk silhouette on the floor. The room seemed so normal, as though no violence had ever taken place here—and his wife had never died—so said his brief smile as he wrote out a check.

Four months ago in another city, her first crime scene had required less work, and she had been her own client on that unpaid job. The armchair had absorbed most of the FBI agent's blood, and so it had been a simple matter of furniture disposal after mopping up the puddle on the floor and the red drops spattered on the wall. In that room, death had been a drawn-out affair, for Timothy Kidd had not struggled enough to spend all his blood at once, and there had been ample time for him to be afraid.

However, that event had occurred in a previous life lived by another version of herself, though the dead man did remain with her as a constant presence, a haunt. And so it was neither odd nor coincidental to be thinking of Timothy when she emerged from the building to find an unpleasant reminder of his death.

Marvin Argus was waiting for her on the sidewalk. His trench coat flapped open in the wind, exposing a dark gray suit with a slept-in look. She guessed that he had taken the red-eye flight from Chicago to New York, and there had been no time for a change of clothes after landing, that or his fastidious grooming habits were deteriorating. Perhaps there had been some urgency in tracking her down today.

No, that was not it.

Argus had found time to carefully style his sparse brown hair so that no strand could escape the gelled fringe of bangs covering his receding hairline. The effect was juvenile and so at odds with his forty-year-old face.

"Hel*lo,* Joh*anna.*" He smiled to show her all of his perfect teeth, acting as if this meeting might be a happy chance encounter and not an ambush, not a defiance of the court order to keep him at a distance.

Did he seem a little jittery—just on the verge of a tic or a twitch? She looked through him, then passed him by on her way back to the black van.

He walked alongside her, keeping his tone light, fighting down all the high notes of runaway anxiety. "You're looking well."

"Still alive, you mean, and you're wondering why."

"No, seriously, I think physical labor agrees with you," he said. "But I suppose this new line of work is your idea of penance."

Much could be read into that clumsy little barb, perhaps some desperate situation coming to a head. Johanna's bent posture had made her a student of footwear, and now she gleaned more from his shoes than his words. The black leather was, as always, fanatically shiny, but both laces had been broken and repairs effected with knots. The man was coming undone.

Good.

She raised her face to his, not bothering to hide her contempt. "You don't look well, Argus. You seem a little shaky today. Under a lot of stress?" Did that sound like a taunt, like getting even? She hoped so. "And you're losing weight."

He dismissed this with a wave of one hand, saying, "Long hours." He drew back his shoulders in an effort to appear larger and less the nervous rabbit. Eyebrows arched, he folded his arms to strike a condescending pose, exuding an arrogance that invited every passerby to punch him in the face.

"I met your boss today." Argus staged a pause. "We had a long talk about you."

"Really?" That was unlikely, for Riker was tight with his words. And so she could surmise that this lie was an implied threat. Yes, Argus would want her to worry about what he might have shared with her employer. She stared at him, wondering, *How frightened are you?*

"That guy Riker, he's a heavy drinker, isn't he? Yeah," said Argus. "Couldn't help but notice. You can tell by the eyes, all those red veins." He was still pressing what he believed was his advantage over her. A few seconds of silence dragged by before he realized that she was not at all threatened, and neither was she inclined to banal conversation. The man looked up at the sky, unwilling to meet her steady gaze anymore.

"He tried to grill me on your background." The old familiar pomposity was back in his voice. "I could tell Riker was an ex-cop by his interrogation style. They never lose that, do they? On or off the job, they can never have just a normal conversation. I figure he doesn't know the first thing about you, Johanna. That or you fed him some fairy tale—and he *knows* it." Argus smiled, awaiting praise for this insight. Failing in that, he flicked imaginary lint from the sleeve of his coat. "Of course, I didn't tell him anything. Not who I was or what I—"

"So you lied to him. You think Riker didn't pick up on that?" She swung her body up into the driver's seat and slouched deep into worn upholstery that received the hump on her back like a cupped hand. She faced the windshield.

Marvin Argus rushed his words. "Does your boss know—"

"I told Riker my history was none of his damn business." She slammed the door and put the van in gear.

Argus reached up and gripped the door handle, as if that could prevent her from driving away. He yelled to be heard through the rolled-up window. "Johanna! About Timothy! Did *you* believe him—while he was still *alive?*"

If the man had held on to the van another moment, he would have lost his hand when she pulled into the street. Johanna pressed the accelerator pedal to the floor and sped toward the broad avenue at the end of the street. She passed through a red light amid the screech and squeal of braking cars and a cabdriver's hollered obscenities.

Marvin Argus had grown smaller in her rearview mirror, only insect high when she rounded the corner.

The young detective slouched down behind the wheel of her tan car and watched the black van speed away. Her eavesdropping device was picking up a clear conversation between the van's driver and the radio dispatcher for Ned's Crime Scene Cleaners. The vehicle was heading for the company parking lot in Greenwich Village.

Mallory reached out for the small silver camera on her dashboard. It contained a photographic record of the hunchback's meeting with the driver of the white Lincoln. After downloading the new images into her laptop computer, she admired the array on the glowing screen. No public record had such clear likenesses of Johanna Apollo. The blurry portrait on a Chicago driver's license had been, in Mallory's view, deliberately sabotaged by the subject, who had moved in the moment the picture was taken. A perusal of prep school and college yearbooks had been of no help either, for the camera-shy hunchback had always been absent on the days when school photographs were taken.

The last photograph was the best of the lot, for the wind had swept the hair away from Apollo's body. With one red fingernail, Mallory traced the outline of the hump that rode the woman's back, bending her spine and bowing her head. This was the soft spot.

Mallory smiled.

With a tap of keys, her computer returned to another file and an official portrait of the man in the double-parked Lincoln. Not content with running the rental plate and billing for his car, she had spent the past hour acquiring a dossier on the renter, Marvin Argus from Chicago, who now smiled at her from the glowing screen. His brow was fringed with ludicrous bangs, but she did approve of the double-breasted blazer and the tie.

Argus was the solid connection that she had been waiting for—living proof.

The detective closed her laptop and set it on the passenger

seat where her partner used to ride. Riker had been a constant fixture in her life since she was ten years old, but now he would not return her phone calls. And he was never home to her when she came knocking on his door, looking for a word with him alone. But that would change when he read her report on the hunchback. It mattered nothing to Kathy Mallory that this case belonged to federal investigators, that it was well outside the purview of a New York City cop. This was a national contest, and anyone with the stomach for it could play the game on the radio five nights a week.

Marvin Argus slid behind the wheel of the white rental car and drove off. Detective Mallory's vehicle eased up the street at a discreet distance, then crept into the southbound stream of traffic on Central Park West, following the man from the FBI.

Riker's gray eyes were hooded, always had been, and his constant squint gave him the air of a man who was damn suspicious all the time. Mixed with this message was the attitude and posture of an easygoing soul, and the total effect said to everyone, *I know you're lying, but what the hell.*

The man who ran Ned's Crime Scene Cleaners was not named Ned. Ned was his brother. Riker did have a first name and even a middle name—Detective Sergeant, though no one had called him by that moniker for the past six months, not since acquiring the scars of four gunshot wounds. He had spent most of his medical leave in charge of a glorified janitorial service. His brother, niece and sister-in-law were away on an extended visit to the fatherland. They had not intended to stay away so long, but distant relations had held the small family hostage, dragging them up and down the Rhine, in and out of German castles and other tourist traps—poor Ned. Riker had been placed in charge of the business and left to consider his brother's offer of a partnership.

He could not picture himself filling out the forms for his separation from NYPD, though this was common enough for cops at the age of fifty-five. His younger brother had left the force three years ago, and maybe it was time to follow suit. True or not, he believed his hair had gone grayer since leaving the hospital. And there was one more hint that the good years were gone; his wounds hurt him each time it rained—just like Dad's arthritis.

Riker planted his elbows in the mess of papers that littered the desk, causing the top layer to avalanche to the floor. The office window gave him a view of gray bricks, a sliver of sky and a parking lot enclosed by a chain-link fence—a view of the future? Could he really do this job for a living?

At least he had been liberated from suits and ties. That was something.

He wore the jeans and flannel shirt of a working man, though he never traveled with the cleaning crews anymore. His last time out with a new trainee, he had nearly wrecked a van. That was the day he had discovered his one remaining infirmity, a sorry little secret that he had chosen not to share with his doctors.

Most of his time was spent in the office, where he was daily nibbled to death by forms, federal, state and local, for the management of hazardous waste, quarterly taxes, payroll deductions and other mind-numbing bits of paper. And all the while, he listened to a police scanner on the pretext of noting addresses for sudden deaths and potential customers. At midday he followed his brother's custom of buying lunch for homicide cops, the real source of new business. He had eaten two lunches today, one in a Brooklyn precinct and one in the Bronx, so he had missed the hunchback when she had reported for work. And, in another sense, he simply missed Jo when she was not around.

He walked to the front window, called there by the sound of a dying muffler on the worst vehicle in the small fleet of three. He leaned both hands on the sill and winced as the van limped into the parking lot on one soft tire—more money out the window.

The woman he knew as Josephine Richards cut the engine and climbed out.

Lady, what long legs you've got.

Those mile-long gams were a subject of much discussion around the office. On the day of her hire, he had seen in her the makings of a Vegas showgirl spliced with a carnival freak. Over the past four months, he had become comfortable with her looks, her face in particular; it was saved from being ordinary by big brown eyes, warm and velvety, that held a man's attention. Oh, and her mouth—some might call it too wide, too large; he called it generous. Oddly enough, of all the employees, she was the easiest to look at. And he would not be a complete man if he did not occasionally speculate about the legs beneath the blue jeans. They strolled, graceful and naked, through his fantasy life at least once a day.

Jo looked so tired as she crossed the lot, bent forward, eyes to the ground.

He could have made her workdays easier by giving her the lightest jobs, but he never deferred to her handicap. That would have ruined his new mythology of himself: it was said that he was so mean only silver bullets could kill him; conventional lead had failed every time. And legend had it that, during his seven hours of surgery, the doctors had removed what passed for his heart, a hard little knot of a thing mistaken for a wayward prune pit. It was also rumored that he had once kicked Jo's cat clear across a room, and he would have kicked the poor animal through a window but his aim was off that day.

Riker had started these rumors himself, and none had taken hold. The employees insisted upon believing him to be a decent, likeable sort, a peg higher than a cat killer. In truth, he had only extended one hand to Jo's cat to stroke it. He had taken no revenge for the savage mauling of claws that had followed this friendly overture. And Riker was a man of such sweet nature that he never failed to ask after the health of Jo's pet whenever the lady walked in the door, as she did now.

He yelled, "Is that fleabag, shit-for-brains cat of yours dead yet?"

"Not yet!" Jo called out from the reception room as she

set off the buzzer beneath the floor mat. A moment later, she stood on the threshold of his private office, saying, "Mugs is just fine."

He shook his head to convey regret, then settled into the chair behind his desk and hunted through the pile of papers. "I got a note here—a name and a phone number. Some guy dropped by today—a real flake."

And, with only that description, she said, "Marvin Argus? I don't need the number." She tossed a set of keys on the desk. "The van needs a new tire."

Of course, this was sarcasm. They both knew that the van needed a whole new van. She signed her name in the logbook, then checked her watch before adding the time, five-thirty, and handed him two checks totaling an even thousand dollars.

"Not bad, Jo—for less than half a day. You can put in more time if you want."

"Don't start." Her eyes were fixed on a clipboard as she made note of all the supplies she had used and the containers of hazardous waste to be disposed of. Bent over her paperwork this way, she seemed almost normal, and he half expected her to straighten up at any moment.

"Hey, Jo, just try it out for a week or so. What's the harm?"

She met his eyes and wordlessly told him, *I'm tired of discussing this, okay?* Aloud she said, "I don't need more hours."

The lady only worked on murder scenes. She had no interest in cleaning up the debris of landlords whose tenants had died of natural causes, leaving a stinking mess beyond the sensibilities of ordinary cleaning services. Early on, he had wondered about this woman's penchant for murder. Forays into her mind-set had always proven fruitless, and he could not shake the idea that Jo had racked up many hours in interviews with other cops. He also wondered why she paid extravagant rates to live in a hotel instead of finding some cheaper, more permanent address. It would have been an hour's work to run a background check, but where was the fun in that?

"Stay awhile." He smiled and gestured toward the chair beside his desk.

Whenever Jo sat down with him at the end of a day, he always had the sense of some ritual examination taking place. He could swear that her brown eyes were looking deep inside of him, visually probing his innards, body and brain—just checking to see that everything was where it ought to be and working well. And now came her brief smile that pronounced him A-okay. He felt so safe in Jo's eyes. When she was not scheduled to work, the structure of his day collapsed.

She leaned forward in the chair, arms braced on her thighs. In this posture, she seemed not at all deformed, merely tired. Jo's head tilted to one side, suddenly wary of Riker as he reached into a drawer and brought out the good stuff—a bottle of cheap bourbon instead of the usual beer cans. She also seemed suspicious of the clean coffee cups, a rarity so late in the day, for Miss Byrd, the receptionist and dishwasher, only worked mornings. Oh, and now the *pièce de résistance*—goat cheese. Outside of work, all they had in common was this weird cheese addiction inherited from Nordic mothers. And, with these offerings, he telegraphed a bribe in the making.

"Given any more thought to that radio show?" He handed her a cup and waited out the silence.

Many times she had declined the offer to plug his brother's business on the hottest radio program in America. Riker had actually given up on this gift-from-God advertising, but the request from the star of shock radio had raised some interesting questions. "I know this guy Zachary's got a real smart mouth. Now *I* could probably never hold my own in an interview with him." He widened his smile. "But you're smarter than me."

Was she buying this flattery?

No, she merely took this as an obvious statement of fact—and it was.

He poured a shot of liquor into her cup. "All you gotta do is mention the name of the company three times, then hit the road. What could be easier?" He opened the package of cheese and pushed it across the desk—all for her. Was there a more generous boss in the entire—

"No." Johanna sliced off a hunk of cheese with the letter opener that passed for a paring knife after hours. "Get someone else to do it."

"I tried. I told the producer I got five guys with more experience. Then Ian Zachary phones me himself. Says he only wants *you.* I call that odd." It could not be the novelty of a hunchback that so enticed the talk-show host; this was radio, not television. "The guy wants a *woman* crime-scene cleaner, but he hasn't tried any competitors yet, and they've got more broads than we do. Me, I never heard the guy's act. You ever tune into his show?"

"Every night," she said.

It surprised him that she would admit to being a shock-radio listener, but then, he had always suspected her of being dead honest at core—even though he was ninety-nine percent sure that she had lied on her job application. But this only enhanced the ongoing mystery of Jo. It was a little taste of police work, The Job, the only one that had ever mattered.

A chill breeze of outside air ruffled the papers on the desk. Every muscle in Riker's body tensed, and his hand went to that place where he had once carried a shoulder holster. The feeling of cold panic was not unreasonable, not *this* time, for the intruder in the next room had neatly stepped over the doormat, avoiding the concealed buzzer that loudly announced each exit and entry.

Paranoia was a contagious thing. Jo was also staring at the office door.

Kathy Mallory appeared on the threshold. The young detective wore a long, black duster in the best tradition of the Old West—a gunslinger with a subscription to *Vogue* magazine.

You spooky kid.

Riker smiled, always glad to see his partner on these rare occasions when she stopped by to discover that they had nothing to say to one another anymore. He had missed her so much—and he wished that she would never come back again.

Poor Jo was startled into spilling her drink. Stunning Mallory, straight and tall, always had an adverse effect on her. By luck or design, his partner only visited when Jo was in the office, and that was a pity. It was almost an assault to put Mallory in the same room with her.

Jo rose from the chair, making exit apologies with her mouth full of goat cheese, not wanting to spend one more second in the younger woman's company. Perhaps it was the way Mallory looked at her with the eye of a predator that had not fed recently. When the office door had been softly shut, Mallory waited a beat until she heard the buzzer and then the close of the outer door. She turned on Riker.

"Hey, Kathy." His greeting was met with a cold glare to remind him of the rules: it was always Mallory now and never Kathy anymore, not since she had joined NYPD. As if he could throw away all of her puppy days—watching Kathy grow, though his old friend's foster daughter had never been a real child, not in terms of innocence. After a little girl had lived on the streets awhile, homeless and eating her dinner from trash cans, childhood was over. But Riker had done his small part to make certain that she never went hungry again. He had a favorite memory of taking Kathy to a baseball game when she was eleven years old. He had bought her enough hot dogs and soda to bring on projectile vomit.

Food was love.

In that same spirit, he pushed the remaining goat cheese in her direction. It was all that he had to offer her these days. "Mallory," he said. "Hungry?"

She leaned over his desk to drop a computer spit-out on top of his mountain of bills and forms, time sheets and invoices. Without even glancing at her offering, he guessed that she had made good on a threat, and this was the background check on Jo.

"Her name isn't Josephine Richards," said Mallory. "That's an alias."

"Yeah, yeah. Big surprise." Riker picked up the sheet, and, without reading it, he wadded it into a ball. "You might've noticed—" He dropped it into a wastebasket. "I don't need any more paper today. But thanks anyway."

She glared at the pile on his desk and the other pile that had slopped to the floor, all the paperwork that was burying him alive. He could see that she was longing to create order out of the chaos, to align every sheet and envelope, every paper clip and pencil at right angles. Mallory was freakish about neatness, and that was her most benign personality trait.

With a slow shift of strategy, she settled into a chair. Her head rolled to one side, eyes closing to languid slits of green, calm and drowsy. Riker had seen Jo's cat do this, and he knew it was a trick to lull him into a false idea that he was safe from attack.

"You haven't been reading your personal mail," she said. "I bet you're wondering how I know that."

Riker did not like to repeat himself, so this time he only waved one hand to say, *Yeah, yeah.* Letters from One Police Plaza had been stacking up unopened in his new SoHo apartment for months. He could guess that most of them required his immediate attention. One clue was a slew of stamped messages on the outside of last month's envelopes, words in red ink and capital letters, *OPEN IMMEDIATELY.* The heaviest one had been pushed under his door, and it had borne a more expansive wording in Mallory's machine-perfect penmanship: *Open this IMMEDIATELY, you bastard!*

"Well, I'm not much of a reader," he said. "Haven't touched a newspaper in six months." Riker preferred to spend his time cocooning in the company of a quiet bartender. "But I do open *some* of my mail." He held up both hands. "See? Paper cuts." This was what came of handling dangerous utility bills in the evening hours after the lights had been turned off for nonpayment due to apathy.

His partner was not amused, and he could hardly blame her. The young cop deserved a better explanation for her abandonment. Regardless of the circumstances, she took every desertion so personally. She had yet to forgive her foster parents for dying. Helen Markowitz had been wheeled away into surgery, then returned to her family as a corpse. Unfair. And Lou Markowitz, Riker's oldest friend, had died in the line of duty. Kathy Mallory was not about to stand for any more defections.

"Your leave time expired." Her voice was a bit testy, and this was akin to Jo's cat switching its tail. "You never showed up for the physical or the psych evaluation." And that was an accusation. "They ran you out of the department on a medical discharge." She leaned forward, a prelude to a lunge. "If you'd bothered to open your damn mail, you'd know that they pensioned you off." She slammed her hand on the desk and sent papers flying to the floor. "Is that what you wanted?"

Riker shrugged as if this meant nothing. It meant the world to him.

She held up an envelope, and by its thickness, he guessed it was a twin to the one on his kitchen table at home. "This is the form to appeal your discharge. I've got Lieutenant Coffey's signature. Now I need yours." After pulling out the sheets and unfolding them, she pointed to a red *X* so large that he could find his signature line without the bifocals he never wore in public. Mallory had often pointed out to him that his refusal to wear eyeglasses was an absurd vanity in a man with a shabby wardrobe, scruffy shoes and a bad haircut. And she had also meant well on that occasion.

She handed the heavy document across the desk. "Sign it," she said to him, *ordered* him. "Then I'll set up new dates for your exams."

He could not even *touch* it. "I'll read the form tonight, okay?"

No, that was obviously not okay, but she let the bundle of sheets fall from her hand to the desk, then leaned down to retrieve the crumpled ball he had tossed in the wastebasket. "Now, back to your hunchback, Johanna Apollo."

So that was the lady's real name.

Mallory tossed the wadded paper at him, and he caught it in one hand. Was she testing his reflexes—wondering if he could pass the police physical? Or had she guessed that he was most afraid of the psychiatric test?

"Are you listening to me?"

"Yeah, I hear you," he said.

She rose from her chair, braced both hands on the edge of the desk and stared him down, settling for no less than his complete attention. "But you never listen to the radio, do you, Riker?"

2

JOHANNA APOLLO'S EYES WERE DOWNCAST AS SHE crossed the avenue, moving toward the Italianate row houses along St. Luke's Place. She lacked a hunchback's gooseneck aspect, for she rarely raised her head to cope with the curious faces of strangers. Instead, she studied their feet, and, based solely upon the science of shoes, made personal judgments on her more upright fellowman. A cab stopped up ahead, and the trendy loafers of a soulless yuppie stepped out onto the pavement to cross paths with the dusty work boots of a blue-collar man who could not afford the rents in this Greenwich Village neighborhood. In her previous life, Johanna had often mused that she should have cultivated foot fetishists, for they would have had more to talk about.

Behind her, she heard the hesitation steps of clicking high heels, some woman in a pedestrian dilemma of political correctness: how to get past the cripple on a sidewalk made narrower by lines of garbage cans? Impatience won out, and the shoes of an office girl walked abreast of her, hurrying to pass the leisurely hunchback. Without raising her head, Johanna knew the girl would be young. These were the dangerous spiked heels of an on-the-job man hunter, seeking fun or rescue in that other sex. The shoe design was flirty and flimsy, not made for the dead run at a moment's notice—like now. Two rats slithered out of a mound of trash bags torn open by sharp little teeth. The office girl's feet turned skittish, skipping to the side, followed by a sudden breathy surprise when she collided with a garbage pail and knocked it over.

"Turn at the corner," said Johanna, raising her eyes to the younger woman's face. "The vermin aren't your worst problem." She pointed toward the ragged man standing in the center of the sidewalk on the next block.

And now that the beggar had an audience, his arms raised slowly, then flapped up and down in the manner of demented pump handles. Bunny was what he called himself, but Johanna knew him by all his street names: Bum, Fool, and You Crazy Son of a Bitch. He was waiting for his tribute money, but first—a little fun, another fright night.

The office girl obediently turned at the corner to take another route to the subway station. Johanna did not. As she closed the distance between herself and the homeless man, she raised her face once more and sighed, resigned to the trial ahead.

Behind a fringe of matted hair was the pug nose of a boy and a grin that insisted on innocence. Bunny's face belied the adage that the homeless life aged people well beyond their years. Though he was in his thirties, she always saw him as a child. Closer now, Johanna stared at one blackened ankle. It was too late to save his foot. Soon the skin would slough away, and he would die from massive infection. Ah, but his shoes said more—the cold wind leaking in, life leaking out, tired leather parting with the sole and showing a peek at sockless, gangrenous toes. By the shoes alone, she knew that he had been defeated in two great themes of the ancient Greeks: man against nature, and man against himself. He stank of disease and soiled underwear.

Bunny's hand struck out and batted the air an inch from her face. She had dodged the first shot and neatly evaded the second, yet she was falling, her feet slip-sliding on marbles that crashed to the sidewalk from Bunny's outstretched hand.

She hit the ground and felt the searing pain of her elbow smashing into cement. The agitated man stood over her, waving his arms, though this was hardly frightening. His hands were arthritic claws after too many winters without the protection of gloves. He could barely make a fist, and any damage he might do unto others would hurt Bunny more. Nevertheless, she raised her hands in surrender. "I've got money," she said, and these ritual words appeased him, as they always did.

She rose to her feet, careful to avoid the other marbles around her work boots. And now she must keep Bunny still, or he might fall and break a bone. Such an injury could mean death for a man in his shape and circumstance. She handed him the same ten-dollar toll she paid each time they met. "Well, Bunny, you learned a new trick tonight. The marbles. That was very smart."

He had finally found a means to keep people from running away at the first sign of madness. But she knew this trick was well beyond his reasoning ability. It was also a bad joke, the cliché of lost marbles, lost mind. And whose sick bit of humor was this? Had some neighborhood child taught him the new stunt? It hardly mattered. He would forget it in a few hours' time. Short-term memory also had a way of outrunning Bunny.

"You're quick. That's what *he* says." Bunny tapped his head in a knowing way and made a sly face as he looked down at the fallen marbles. "He gave me those. Says I gotta play it smart to catch— Oh, oh, ooooh." He laughed and shifted his weight from foot to foot in a bob and a weave, so excited. "I got a message for you." His eyes closed and his teeth clenched in fierce concentration. And now he had it, and his eyes opened wide. "It's a message from Timothy Kidd. He says it's real cold in hell, and ain't *that* a surprise."

Johanna's mouth rounded in a silent *No!*

"Where did you hear that name?" Was there a siren of alarm in her voice? Yes, but it was well beyond the pitch of Bunny's impaired perception. He had no empathy with the fears of others. "*Tell* me—where did you hear that name?"

Bunny kept tapping his skull. "In here. He lives with me."

It was useless to pursue this little horror, impossible to distinguish between Bunny's real and imagined people, though she knew the messenger was a living human being, someone who had spent a great deal of time with the homeless man. Only constant repetition over days and days would have made that sentence remain in his mind; it was so crowded in Bunny's head, where so many people talked to him all the time.

Johanna pulled a newspaper from one of the trash cans and used it to sweep the marbles off the sidewalk so he would not trip and hurt himself. Should she call the police? And tell them what? From NYPD's point of view, it was the rest of the citizenry who needed protection from Bunny. She shook her head, giving up on the idea of asking them to look after the homeless man. From now on, she would take a different route home from work, and perhaps that would keep Bunny from harm. As the last marble rolled off the curb, her injured elbow throbbed with pain, and this was only the first leg of her gauntlet. There was still the cat to deal with at the other end of her odyssey.

At the West Fourth Street station, she boarded a subway car crammed with passengers who made space to accommodate her. Johanna was that rare straphanger who was offered a seat by men, women and, most humiliating—children. During the short ride home, she observed the egalitarian meeting of the city's shoes, real leather and faux, sneakers and oxfords.

Out of the subway, tired and sore, she made her way down Twenty-third Street, heading toward her hotel. The Chelsea was a bastard castle, Victorian and Gothic, striped with long rows of wrought-iron balconies and crowned on the twelfth floor with tall chimneys and dormer windows set into a pitched gray roof. All told, the redbrick giant had two hundred windows overlooking the street. It was not the tallest building in this neighborhood of lesser architecture, but certainly the grandest.

Grandeur ended as Johanna passed through the front door.

The lobby was rimmed with nineteen-sixties track lights surrounding the crystal chandelier of a more distant period, and the statue of a fat pink girl perched upon a swing was also suspended from the high ceiling. Abstract pieces of sculpture sat on the marble floor beside contemporary and antique furniture, and the walls were covered with the large canvases of an ever-changing art show. The eclecticism was so extreme that nothing—not a live elephant—*nothing* would seem out of place here. And then there were the tenants, permanent and transient: the Chelsea was a haven for certifiable creative types, artists and the like, and proudly advertised itself as haunted by a history of suicide and murder. In the past four months of residence, Johanna had encountered no earthbound spirits other than the ghosts she had checked in with, ten of them, including Timothy Kidd.

She crossed the dark carpet, eyes fixed on a parade of luggage on wheels and the out-of-town shoes of visitors. Only one pair was familiar, spit-shine black and memorable for the broken laces and the knotty repairs. They were ten steps in front of her, when she raised her head to see the FBI agent, Marvin Argus, approach the front desk. Johanna waved at the clerk, begging him in dumb show not to give her away as she rounded the corner and pushed the elevator button. The door slid open, and she slipped inside.

Moving through the Chelsea in any direction was like a trip through time and other places. She rode upward in a small box with midcentury gas station decor. Its doors opened onto the seventh-floor foyer and an ornate staircase from her exchange-student days in Paris. Turning left, she opened a fire door of wood and glass and passed into a silent corridor leading to her rear apartment and its tall windows with southern plantation shutters. The last skirmish of the day lay before her as she fitted a key into her lock. The moment she cracked the door open, a white furry paw appeared, claws extended and swatting air, so anxious to get at all comers and rake them till they bled.

Johanna lived with New York City's only attack cat.

She guessed that her apartment had been cleaned late in the day, for Mugs was still angry and up for a fight. The formidable hotel maid always came armed with a water pistol to keep the cat at bay. Johanna had no such defenses, only denim jeans to protect her legs from the needle-sharp claws. She edged past the animal. Mugs followed her down the short hallway to the spacious front room with an armchair in front of the fireplace—so inviting—but before she even removed her coat, she quickly entered the kitchen. The cat would be hungry, and food would buy her a small respite from his attentions. On the days when she was feeling fragile, Mugs was locked in a bathroom, but most of the time he roamed free, rubbing up against her legs, purring, then clawing her when he felt the agony of close association. A nerve along the cat's spine had been damaged long before she found him, and any physical contact caused him excruciating pain. Yet Mugs came looking for love each time she walked into a room.

While he was distracted by his bowl of gourmet cat food, she inspected the doors to a maple armoire, one of the few pieces of custom-made furniture that she had brought with her from Chicago. The cat hair in the lock opening had not been disturbed in her absence. She inserted the key, and the paneled doors opened to rows of shelves, cubbyholes and a desktop littered with newspaper clippings on the men and women who had died in fear and violence and those who were still in the game. Her journal lay open to a blank page, and she penned a few lines about Bunny's message from the late Timothy Kidd. Then she tidied up the desktop, sorting papers for the jurors who had survived. Material on the dead was consigned to the drawers below the desktop, and Timothy had a drawer all to himself.

She was so in tune with him tonight, almost paranoid enough. Johanna slowly revolved, taking in the entire room. Everything was in neat order, no objects added or taken away, no obvious signs of trespass. The only disturbance was a pile of mail knocked to the floor, and she credited this to the cat's revenge on the maid and her water pistol. All was as it should be, but she could never lose the sense of something tall and wobbly teetering on the verge of a crash. Even within the perfect silence of these thick walls, peace was a rare thing. She lived every day in a heightened state of readiness—waiting.

Mugs padded away from his empty bowl and paused to stretch on the way to his basket, where he completed three turns on a red pillow, never fewer, never more, then curled up for a postprandial nap. His eyes closed on an expression of sweetness which lured strangers into the deception that he could be petted and stroked. Johanna lay back in a reclining chair, dry-mouthing pain pills and watching the evening news on television.

All the major networks had developed the macabre murder spree into a miniseries format, replete with original theme music for the Reaper's segment. The serial killer, not trusting his name and fame to the vagaries of tabloid reporters, had christened himself with the crude sketch of a scythe drawn in blood on the walls of every crime scene. It was also his habit to write the score in blood, keeping the tally of murdered jurors current. His last message had figured nine down—

"—and three to go," said the smiling broadcaster on the screen.

His guest for the evening was a retired federal judge railing against the incompetence of the FBI to stop this assault on the American judicial system. *"If we cannot guarantee the safety of every juror, then the law becomes impotent."*

The broadcaster listened with mock sympathy, then broke in on the judge's tirade to complain that *"It's been nearly a month since the last murder—"*

And his story was getting stale. Tonight's program gave Johanna no new information. It was rather like a tired rerun, repeating old encounters with the bereaved friends and families of the dead. Some of these people had become inadvertent players, giving up clues to the whereabouts of runaway jurors, and others had taken money for this information. Several family members had settled for fame as payment, becoming media personalities over the past six months, always good for an interview on a slow news day.

Johanna closed her tired eyes for a brief nap, one of the most underrated luxuries of life. Soon she would be delivered from angst and pain. Her concept of heaven was not a place of eternal peace, but a small window in time, a few tranquil moments between consciousness and sleep, blessed sleep.

Mallory's present was tucked under one arm as Riker strolled past the old men's social club, a small gathering that convened in Ned's parking lot every night. Four old fellows with their folding chairs sat in a circle with a jug of wine to fortify them against the cold air. They nodded to him in passing, then turned up the volume of a portable radio and rocked their chair legs to a Spanish rhythm. Riker's feet weighed less and less, then nothing at all, walking him back to a warmer season.

The summer of his seventeenth birthday, he had left his father's house and run two thousand miles. He had made it all the way to Mexico, past the tourist traps of the borderland and farther south along roads that had no names or signposts, only piles of sand to trap the rusty old Volkswagen van. He had bought the vehicle for next to nothing, a necessary expense: in those days, he would go nowhere without the giant amplifiers for his electric guitar. Every ten miles, he had climbed out of the van to dig his bald tires out of foreign sand, every ten miles all the way to Cholla Bay. He had found that place under a sky of a billion brilliant stars. Until that moment, he had not known that they were up there, for the stars of city skies had been stingy and few. By the close of that summer, the Brooklyn boy, barefoot and sun brown, had learned some new words and another kind of music that went into his blood, swimming backward to the heart, and lying there in wait for a day like today.

He had spent the best part of his life trying to forget that place—or was it a time?—when he had been happy. Riker walked on in dreams of Mexico, knowing that he would never get back to Cholla Bay. Happiness had not been on his wish list when he had decided to become a cop.

Could he ever make his way back to the police force?

The Latin beat of the old men's social club was blocks behind him when he stopped to look up at the sky.

No stars.

He turned left instead of right, taking a different route home, one that would lead him by a bar where he could run a tab, drink all night and clear his head of music.

It seemed that only seconds had passed before Johanna Apollo started awake. Mugs's front paws were kneading her chest as he licked her face with a sandpaper tongue. She looked past the cat to the clock on the mantelpiece. So much time had been lost, hours and hours. She rose from her chair to switch off the television set, and Mugs was dumped from her lap to the floor. Deeply offended and tail held high, he returned to his basket pillow.

Johanna reached out to the radio by her chair and tuned in to the familiar voice of Ian Zachary. The game master was recapping the life-and-death plight of twelve human beings. The surviving jurors had fled from Chicago, where their verdict had been so unpopular that three of them had been put to death within the city limits. The rest had peeled away from their government bodyguards after a fourth juror had died while under the protection of the FBI. The fifth kill had occurred on an isolated farm in Kansas. Other jurors had gone to hide among family in small towns, and now only three of them remained alive and at large. One of the shock-jock's callers had sighted a live one hiding in San Francisco, but no contest prize had been awarded for lack of photographic evidence. The game had strict rules.

"Who's next?" asked Ian Zachary, called Zack by his fans. The Englishman's voice was deep-throated, and the tenor was seductive. "Come on, all my idiot children, retard bastards every one of you, *talk* to me. Daddy loves you."

Riker unlocked the door to his apartment, flicked on the light switch and stepped over the notes pushed under his door by well-wishers who could never find him at home or in his favorite cop bar. He spent his evening hours supporting a different saloon in a neighborhood where he would not encounter detectives from Special Crimes Unit. One of the notes on his floor was an invitation in Charles Butler's handwriting. His old friend and new landlord had not yet grasped the fact that Riker preferred to drink his dinner alone, ungrateful as that might seem.

This SoHo apartment was bigger than anything he could afford, and Charles had insisted on chopping off more than half the rent. Riker knew it was a better place than he deserved, and so he compensated for this by turning every surface into a trash magnet. His dirty laundry had been scattered to four corners and the ashtrays filled to overflowing.

He entered the generously proportioned sit-down kitchen, a collection dump for his unopened mail. He had no other use for this room except as an additional storage area for the empty Chinese take-out containers, pizza cartons, crushed beer cans and bottles. With one hand, he swiped a pile of envelopes from the table, then set down his gift from Mallory, a radio. She had accurately guessed that his own had worn out and that this damage had gone unnoticed for years. The television had also been broken, or he had assumed as much since the screen had been cracked by a bullet. The TV set had been left behind in his old apartment in Brooklyn, where he had lain bleeding and shaking, hearing the distant scream of sirens and believing that he would die. He believed it still, though all the bloody holes in his body had been neatly closed and stitched.

He walked through the rooms turning on all the lights.

It was not yet midnight, and there was still time to catch the last twenty minutes of Ian Zachary's program. He returned to the kitchen and set up the antenna per Mallory's advice for the best reception. She had already tuned in the station for him, and then, distrustful brat, she had fixed the position of the dial with tape. Contrary to her style of complex electronics, this was a very simple appliance, only a few knobs to work. He could tell that a good deal of thought had gone into Mallory's selection of this model; she had wanted something that a drunk could easily operate. Plugging it in was a problem; his hand wavered back and forth, always missing the wall socket. Finally, he rammed the plug home, turned on the radio and recognized the voice of a transplanted Englishman dabbling in American slang. This was the man who had telephoned him six times to request an interview with Jo.

"No, you *imbecile!"* yelled the talk-show host. "The Reaper is *not* an escaped mental patient. He only kills on the weekends. That means he's a working stiff with a regular job and a leisure-time avocation of justice."

"You mean *murder!"* This second voice revealed a genuine Bronx pedigree. "I'm tellin' you the guy's a nutcase. So I figure—"

"The Reaper's *not* crazy," said Ian Zachary. "He's a man on a mission to cull the brain dead from the judicial system. And you don't win any prizes for your damn opinion, fool. I want hard information—*facts* and *proof*."

Zachary tapped a button to cut off the caller, then lowered his voice to speak to the wider audience. "All right, this is *my* fault. Too many big words. We'll review the rules one more time, people. While I go to the next commercial break, get out your damn crayons so you can take notes." He looked up at the window separating his dark studio from the well-lit booth of his sound engineer. The young woman behind the glass gave him a cutthroat signal to say he was off the air.

His eyes darted to the next booth window, the one where the light never shone, though he doubted that it was always empty. His producer, an abject coward, had yet to show his face, but that was not to say that the man did not occasionally look in on the radio show. Zachary used the reflective dark glass as a mirror, and his fingers combed back unruly strands of long black hair to expose a widow's peak. This was a sign of the black arts in his grandmother's lexicon. And his ears tapered down to the skin, no lobes, another granny omen that he would turn out badly. Yet he had evolved into God or God the Son. The station manager told him so every day when the man answered each telephone call with the words, *Oh, God, it's you, oh, Jesus freaking Christ.*

But women liked him.

His full lips and a bad-boy smile promised the ladies a roller-coaster ride of a real bad time. Women were also attracted to the hazel eyes that changed color depending upon ambient light or his mood: dark as bullet holes if he was angry; greenish brown when he was merely sardonic; and sunshine brought out the bits of blue, though he was only awake in the daylight for staff meetings and pretaped interviews. Ian Zachary had a preference for vampire hours, and his skin tone bordered on prison pallor. Slouching deep in his chair, lean and languid, he propped his cowboy boots on the console. His black shirt and jeans had designer chic and the tightness of a second skin. He was that new creature—Cool Goth.

A polar opposite was that lump of girl in the control booth. She obviously cut her own hair over the bathroom sink, and her shapeless clothes were more appropriate to the prairie town she hailed from. This homely youngster with thick ankles and prissy thin lips was his new sound engineer, call screener, personal assistant and whipping girl. Zachary had chosen her from a lineup of less ugly mutts with more experience. He had found her fragile personality . . . appealing.

His new pet sat in her cage of glass and steel, electronics and blinking ruby call buttons. Each red light represented a fool who actually believed he had a chance of getting on the air, though only one would make the cut in the final segment. On his own side of the window, best described as a cave, darkness was alleviated only by the glow of his control panel and the screen on his laptop computer. In the next room, his engineer sat shell-shocked beneath fluorescent lights that faded her freckles and leached the healthy farm-girl glow from her skin. After hours of being ridiculed on the air, her eyes were no longer bright, and gone was that smile of eagerness to do good on the first day of her brand-new job.

Zachary checked the digital clock on his panel as it counted down the seconds before live air. The commercial break was almost done. "Babe?" All employees of both sexes were called babe. What was the point of remembering names when so many did not last an entire shift? "Prep the next caller. We'll take the moron with the lisp."

She looked down at her phone board, suddenly frightened, and then she shook her head to tell him that the lisping caller's light had gone dark. Zachary left his chair and crossed the room, walking toward her window, saying, "No, babe, don't tell me you lost *that* one." Ah, but she had. This incompetence was the downside of hiring the tender mental cases. He returned to his panel to check the screen for the most overt flaws of call-in fans. "Okay, babe, we'll take the next one—that guy who squeaks like a girl." And if the next caller did not squeak as promised, he was going to fire the engineer as a finale to the show.

He sat back in his chair, glaring at her until she cued him to pick up line six. The commercial interlude was over. He hit the button for the next caller, saying, "So you're Randy from SoHo."

"Hi," said a small reedy voice almost lost in the dark. "I'm waiting to talk to Zack."

"You're talking to me *now,* you fool. When you hear my voice, that means you're on the air. My idiot engineer never mentioned that?" He heard a sudden intake of breath, then dead silence from the stagestruck Randy of SoHo.

"Don't be afraid," said Zachary to the caller. "Daddy loves you, you useless twit. What've you got for me? It better be damn good. If you're as lame as the last one, I'll have to fire the little girl who screened you." He imagined the caller's sweaty hands worming round a telephone receiver. "That's right, you geek. Her job is hanging on you. Randy? Still there, sport? Yes, I hear you breathing. And now, for the listening pleasure of my audience, I'll describe my engineer's reaction to her impending redundancy while we all do a slow countdown from ten. If Randy can't get his little dick up in time to save her, she's history. *Ten.* Did I mention that she was young? Oh, yes, fresh off the farm—just a little lost girl a thousand miles from home. *Nine.* She's wearing shiny new shoes and an outfit she bought for her first trip to New York City. She must've thought we all dressed like Catholic schoolgirls."

He swiveled around to face the plate glass. "She's just sitting there so pale and still—so exposed. Can you see her? Every pimple, every pucker of cellulite? Oh, and that hairy patch on one knee, a spot she missed with her razor this morning. *Eight!* She *seems* quiet. But you just *know* inside her head, she's running round in circles, flapping like a duck and *screaming.*"

Her shoulders slumped as she died a little. They all did that. She was probably wondering if she should risk a nervous laugh. Could she risk *not* laughing? What if he was serious? He could see all of this flashing through her mind.

"Well, people, so far, this isn't much fun. She's about as animated as a corpse."

Stupid, boring cow.

"*Seven.* Randy? You think her parents are listening tonight? Of course they are. *Six.* She would've told all her friends and relatives to tune in for her first big break in show business. Five seconds to go, people. Will our hero on the phone make it in time? *Four.* Will the little girl lose her job and take the next bus back to the farm?"

She snapped.

Finally.

"Our girl's not dead yet. Her chair is spinning round and round. Her eyes are glazing over as she stares at the ceiling. Looking for flights of angels, babe? Her chair just came to a dead stop. Her head is slowly swiveling. Oh—*scary.* I swear to God, people, it's like a scene from a horror movie. Her eyes are bulging, going medieval on me. She's raising a fist—extending her middle finger—a suggestion that I commit a physically impossible sexual act on myself. *Wait.* There's more. She could've let it go at that, a simple elegant gesture that pretty much said it all. But she just mimed a well-known slang word for the anal orifice. I'm guessing that's my new name. Is that right, babe?"

She mouthed the words, *Die, you bastard.*

He liked that. He liked it a lot. Ah, and now the angry tears. She was shredding all the careful notes written at the start of the day, making confetti of pages lined with her schoolgirl penmanship.

"Uh, Zack?" Randy the timid caller had found his voice. "I got a photograph of a live juror right here in Manhattan. So . . . what do I win?"

3

JOHANNA APOLLO RAISED HER FACE TO THE LOW-riding sun as she strolled toward Bleecker Street. The morning air was cold, but early risers got company vans with four good tires. This would be the happy side effect of changing her hours and her route to avoid any more contact with Bunny. His habits were nocturnal and his home was a patch of sidewalk on another block.

Every retail store in Greenwich Village was still locked behind burglar gates, but the bagel shop in Father Demo Square was open for business, and she stopped to buy coffee. She was unable to abide the swill at work, believing that the coffee grounds were strained through Riker's old socks to save money on filters. Exiting the shop with a steamy paper cup in hand, she turned on Bleecker and, halfway down the block, she saw the shoe by the curb—Bunny's shoe. There was no mistaking this mangle of tortured leather for anyone else's. Another pedestrian passed her by, a true New Yorker, ignoring the evidence of violence, the blood in the shape of heel marks and red toe prints from one bare foot—and more blood later on down the sidewalk. The widely paced red tracks along the pavement were those of a loping man.

Johanna followed the trail of lost blood, running fast, then faster, full-out, losing her paper cup somewhere along the way. And then—breathless and stunned—she came to a stop before the open gate of a playground.

Dead stop.

Bunny was seated on the small wooden board of a child's swing, and his back was turned to the gate. From any distance, he might pass for a man at rest. Johanna walked toward him, her footsteps slowed by shock as she rounded the swing and saw his stark white face. A loose link in one of the chains had snagged the shoulder of his coat and prevented his body from falling. His throat was slashed open, and blood drenched his breast.

How could he have traveled so far with that gaping wound?

It must have taken great will beyond anything she had imagined him capable of—and focus—and all the strength that he had. Buzzing flies lighted on the gross tear in his skin. Others walked across his closed eyes. His hands were folded in his lap and fingers interlaced.

Bunny, did you pray?

What had drawn him here? She knew that his illness had begun when he was painfully young. A playground might be the last memory of joy, some old association with a time when his mother still loved him. During all of the telephone calls to Bunny's mother, Johanna had listened to the voice of an automaton, a woman sucked dry by the incredible labor of raising a child who had early lost his mind.

His most pitiable wound was the one bare foot blackened with disease and unprotected. In other respects, it was like revisiting Timothy Kidd's murder. There could be no doubt that this homeless man was killed because he had met the messenger, the one who had taken such pains to imprint Timothy Kidd's name on his poor, cracked brain. She brushed the matted hair from Bunny's eyes, and a score of fat black flies took wing. Johanna's skin turned clammy as her breakfast marched back up her throat. She fell to her knees.

This death was a personal message. There could be no other point in slaughtering this poor lunatic. Bunny would have been so useless to a police lineup, unable to differentiate between a suspect and a shopping cart. The killer could not have guessed that she would be the one to find the body, but after all the months of noisy street encounters, it was predictable that the police, with only the description of a hunchback, would come knocking on her door.

Johanna stared at the glint of metal near the dead man's feet. This bloody knife, honed to a razor edge, had not been dropped by Bunny. His arthritic hands were no good at articulating small objects. Only in death would his fingers be pliant enough to press them to the metal. So Bunny's murderer must have come this far with him, walked alongside him on the death march, keeping a discreet distance to avoid the splatter of vagrant blood.

And saying what?

Oh, all the things that would terrify the homeless man as he struggled toward this place. And what had kept him on his feet all the way to the playground? Perhaps he had come looking for a parent he had lost years ago, the one who had called him her honey bunny. Had he believed that this woman would heal his gaping wound and calm his banging heart with motherlove? How disappointed he must have been not to find her here.

Bunny, did you cry?

Johanna looked up at his face and whispered, "I'm sorry." She was sorry that his life had been hell on earth, that he had died in pain and in such frightening company, sorry that she had not protected him. Johanna lost all track of time as she knelt in the dust, stuttering her apologies to a bloodied corpse. And now she heard the march of little feet and larger mother shoes and the giggle of soft voices approaching the playground. The children were coming.

Riker never wanted to remember his dreams, intuiting that scary country as best left alone. This morning he had been tricked by a fake awakening, a dream inside the dream, wherein he had opened his eyes to see the scary boy astride his chest, riding him like a belly-up horse, pressing down on him with the heavy weight of crazy. Then came the sensation of lightness from great blood loss and trauma to the body and the brain.

He woke up dying.

And then came the real awakening. The ringing telephone jangled his raw nerve endings, though the sound had to travel down the hall from his front room. The bedside phone had been broken long ago, deliberately and violently. He opened his eyes, wondering if this was his wake-up call from Miss Byrd. He was prepared to roll over and go back to sleep, for the receptionist only rang twice. He waited out the next ring, then five more.

Not Miss Byrd.

Riker's most persistent caller was Mallory. She always rang exactly twenty times to punish him for his long silence. He rolled the covers back. His feet hit the floor wearing both of yesterday's socks, but only one shoe. Shoelaces were sometimes difficult for him. Their knots asked too much of him when he was falling-down drunk or hungover. Sometimes a week would go by when he was entirely shoeless for only the time it would take to shower and shave.

The phone was still ringing as he made his way to the kitchen, where he prepared his faster-than-instant coffee, using hot water from the tap. Alternately inhaling black liquid and cigarette smoke, he counted off the twentieth ring—ah, silence—and waited for the rush of caffeine and nicotine to kick in. And now his heart beat faster. The pump was started. The day had begun.

The phone rang again.

One fist sent it flying into the wall, then crashing to the floor, and a familiar voice—but not Mallory's—was yelling with great alarm, as if the caller had also been injured by the fall. "What's going on? Riker! Talk to me!"

As he reached for the phone, the caller asked, "Are you okay?"

No. No, he was not.

The most senior employee of Ned's Crime Scene Cleaners was a retired teacher of the ruler-wielding, knuckle-smashing, authoritarian school. Everyone on the payroll called her *Miss* Byrd, never Frances. None of them would cross that line of respect (call it fear) drawn in youth, for each of them had been hostage to at least one imperious Miss Byrd during their formative years.

Her gray eyebrows delicately arched as she glared at the front door. It had been left unlocked. Well, this was just one more sign of Riker's dereliction of duty. It never occurred to her that he might have come to work at this early hour, for Ned's brother was not a morning person. She had long suspected the man of drinking on the job, and this was proof; he had grown careless about locking up. Upon entering the reception area, she counted up the office machines, wall hangings and furnishings. All was as it should be, no signs of a thief, no thanks to Riker. The door to the private office was ajar, and, in the habit of thoroughness, she entered the room, then froze midstride.

Well, this was *outrageous.*

Seated behind the desk was Riker's rude young friend from the police department, the only visitor who had ever ignored Miss Byrd's attempts to prevent her from entering the boss's office unannounced. She was a lovely child to be sure, but such uncivilized eyes, so cold and showing no deference whatever for her elders.

It was Miss Byrd's habit to put everyone in their place by the use of diminutive first names, as though kindergarten had never ended. Of course, Riker foiled her in this regard; only the first letter of his name appeared on the payroll roster. However, this young woman posed no such problem, for she was much talked about by the crew.

"Kathy! What are you *doing?*" The tone implied that the girl should cease and desist immediately. "Kathy, do you *hear* me?"

"It's *Mallory,*" the younger woman corrected her, "*Detec-*

tive Mallory." She regarded Miss Byrd with grave suspicion, then said, "You're overpaid, Frances."

Miss Byrd sucked in her breath as she grappled with the novel experience of hearing her Christian name spoken aloud. And then she roughly guessed what lay in store for her. Yesterday's mountain of papers was now arranged in neat stacks around the edges of the desk, and an open account ledger had pride of place on the blotter.

Mallory ran one long red fingernail along a column of payroll figures. "Riker thinks you only work part-time. That's what you told him, isn't it, Frances? Before his brother left for Europe, you were working eight-hour days every week. But now you get the same paycheck for half a day. Interesting." She gestured to a chair beside the desk. "Sit down, Frances."

And Miss Byrd sat.

The young detective casually leafed through a few stacks of statements and tax forms, bills and letters, dragging out the moment, while the senior woman held her breath.

"Riker has the strange idea that you're a receptionist," said Mallory. "Nobody told him that you were the company office manager. He thinks all this paperwork is *his* job." She closed the heavy account book with a loud slam to make Miss Byrd jump, though she never raised her voice when she said, "Payroll fraud is a serious crime, Frances."

Miss Byrd's mouth was suddenly dry. She had never worried about the cleaning crew ratting out her fiddle of the hours, for she knew all the secret vices of every employee. However, now she felt queasy. Her voice cracked when she said, "You're going to tell Riker, aren't you?"

"Well, that depends on you, Frances. His brother Ned's due back on Monday. That's not much time to fix all this damage. I suggest you brown bag your lunch. Dinner, too. You won't be getting out much." Mallory moved a stack of papers to reveal the steel box that belonged in a locked drawer of Miss Byrd's own desk. "And here's another odd thing. Riker didn't know about the petty cash fund. He's been drumming up business, buying lunch for homicide cops out of his own pocket. You'll want to correct that error on his final paycheck."

The older woman's head wobbled in a lame version of a nod.

The detective pushed the account ledger across the desk. "You'll be putting in an eighty-hour week—for *free*. I'll stop by to check up on you, and when I do, there shouldn't be any problem with these figures. I want them to match the bank statements and—"

"I *never* stole money from the accounts. I was dead honest with—"

"With his brother? Yes, I know. I looked at *all* the accounts. But Riker's hopeless with paperwork. So now you've got a huge backlog to deal with. The bank statements don't agree with his deposits and debits. And the payroll deductions are all wrong, *months* of errors. He botched every one of them. That's more paperwork. Did I say eighty hours? You might have to camp out here every night. During the day, you'll be busy setting up the jobs and working as the dispatcher."

"But that's Riker's—"

"That's right, Frances. You'll be running the whole shop, doing your own job *and* Riker's. He's taking time off for a little police work. You don't have a problem with that, do you? No? Good. And get this place cleaned up. It's a mess."

After the detective had stalked out the door, Miss Byrd let out a long sigh in a hoarse, dry whistle as her body went limp. In the next moment, her heart lurched and fluttered like a goldfish when she felt a hand curl round her shoulder, cold steely fingers, not human—Mallory's.

The cop reached out with her free hand to run one finger down the dirty glass pane and through the painted name of the company. "Do you do windows, Frances?"

"I do now," said Miss Byrd.

A detective from the Greenwich Village copshop stood by the curb collecting notes from a patrolman. Flynn was his mother's son, tall and dark-skinned with features of Africa. Only the ten freckles across his nose came down from his Irish side. He smiled as his erstwhile drinking buddy lumbered toward him. "Hey, you're lookin' great, man!"

Untrue. Riker had not shaved this morning, nor had he taken the time to select the least dirty clothes from a wardrobe of flannel shirts and faded jeans, and his leather jacket was unzipped, exposing the worst of his stains. Hung-over and dragging, he stopped to thank Flynn for the phone call to tell him that one of his employees might need a friend.

Riker moved on toward the playground at the other end of the block. Though this was not his own precinct, there was no trouble getting past the men in uniform posted at the entrance. They stood aside for him, all but saluting as he passed through the gate. He was royalty now that he had been shot. Apparently, these men had not heard the news of his separation from NYPD via a stack of unopened mail. Even the medical examiner's men paused to slap him on the back, mumbling their greetings as they rolled a gurney toward the waiting meat wagon. Though the corpse was concealed in a zippered bag, Riker knew that Flynn had revised his earlier call of suicide, upgrading this case to murder. No lesser offense would merit the attentions of Crime Scene Unit. He watched one CSU investigator overturn a trash barrel and sift through the contents while others walked with their eyes to the ground, stopping now and then to collect small objects and map their locations on a sketch pad.

Jo was seated on a bench near a sandbox, bent forward, her long hair covering her face. Riker sat down beside her and gingerly encircled her with one arm. The hump on her back was a mystery to him, and it crossed his mind that he might hurt her if he held her tight. She raised her face to show him her red and swollen eyes. She had been crying, but now she seemed oddly calm. Shock could do that. The case detective was walking toward them. Flynn was a first-rate cop and a decent one. Riker trusted him to go light and easy with Jo.

The detective sat down on the other side of the bench and leaned forward to catch her eye. "Ma'am? I understand you knew the victim pretty well."

"Everybody knew that freak," said Riker. "He's been a pest in this neighborhood for—"

"Let the lady talk." Flynn turned back to his witness, prompting her. "Ma'am? What can you tell me about this guy?"

"I know his mother lives in Vermont," said Jo, "but she hasn't seen him in years."

Riker was stunned to hear her rattle off the long-distance telephone number for a homeless bum's next of kin. And now she gave another number that she had memorized, that of a local attorney who could supply more current information.

Detective Flynn's pen hovered over the notebook. "A vagrant with a *lawyer?*"

"New York City versus Bunny's Foot." She was quoting a tabloid headline that had been pinned to the bulletin board at Ned's Crime Scene Cleaners as homage to a neighborhood celebrity.

Flynn nodded. "I remember that case."

Even Riker knew this story, though he never read newspapers anymore. His only tie to the world was office gossip. According to his crew, an ACLU lawyer had defended the homeless man's right to die rather than lose his diseased foot to a surgeon's saw, thus nicely defeating the city's criteria for hospitalizing a vagrant as a danger to himself. The court, weary of drawn-out appeals by the American Civil Liberties Union, had decided that Bunny was legally entitled to a slow painful death on the street, though that initial plan had gone awry this morning.

Detective Flynn flipped through the pages of his notebook. "There's just a few things we need to clear up. We canvassed the block where this man spent most of his time.

According to the neighbors, you match the description of a woman who went round and round with this guy three nights a week. So this freak attacks you on a regular basis, but you don't even cross the street to avoid him. Can you explain that, ma'am?"

No, apparently she could not. Jo closed her eyes.

Flynn moved closer, trying to connect with her. "So when this bastard used you for a human punching bag, did he lead with his left or his right?"

"He was right-handed," said Jo, "and he never hit me."

"I know. He just *threatened* you," said Flynn. "He *scared* you, and you gave him money. That's what the neighbors say. Are you right- or left-handed?"

"Hold it," said Riker. "I can give you at least twenty people who wanted this bum out of the neighborhood—*permanently*. Just walk along that street and count the houses. The tenants must've filed a hundred complaints with you bastards."

"Hey." Flynn splayed one hand to say that the lady was not a serious suspect, and would Riker please shove his head up his butt so they could get on with this interview.

"Back off," said Riker. "Her lawyer's the same guy who defended the bum." He was making this up as he went along. "And now that you know the lady has counsel, that ends the interview."

"She's a witness, not a suspect," said Flynn, "I can question her all damn day long."

"Wrong. She was a suspect the minute you asked her what hand she used to hold the murder weapon. I think a judge is gonna see it that way, too. You like the idea of getting your ass reamed out in court? No, I guess not." Riker gently raised Jo from the bench. She was docile and made no resistance to going with him. "Now, if you don't plan to book her—with squat for evidence—I'm taking the lady home."

Flynn had a bewildered look about him as his eyes turned skyward. Riker, a fourth-generation police, had chosen the wrong side; and, though the sun was where it ought to be, the world was definitely out of order this morning. After clearing the playground gate, Riker turned back to see the detective hovering over a crime-scene technician, watching the man dust the bench for fingerprints—Jo's prints.

Long after Riker had left her hotel suite, Johanna Apollo sat in a patch of direct sunlight and never felt the warmth. It was a spider's business that called her attention to the window. Hours ago, the little spinner had begun a delicate web stretching across the sill. The ambitious project was complete, but horrific in light of the arachnid's nature. The web's pattern was flawed, strange and twisty, with ugly knots in the silk and gaping holes where a fine network of threads should be. Before the web was half done, all attempt at weaving symmetry had been abandoned. Johanna flirted with the idea that the tiny creature had lost its mind. She glanced at the cat curled on his red pillow, as if he might be the cause of the spider's affliction, but Mugs was in a mood of rare calm and watching her through half-closed eyes. He was the sane one this morning.

Or was it afternoon?

Johanna turned back to the problem of the spider spinning chaos. It was said by some that the observer influenced the outcome of the thing observed.

The telephone rang. It was jarring, frightening, this ordinary thing, this common sound. Her answering machine picked up the call. She recognized the voice of a veterinary surgeon reminding her that Mugs's checkup had been rescheduled. The cat padded toward her and sat down at her feet. Odd, but he seemed unwilling to touch her. Was he sensing something unhealthy in the air—something not quite sane?

Johanna would not look at the spiderweb again. Half the day had been lost before she rose from her chair and felt the hundred needles of limbs gone to sleep. She walked to the closet to fetch the plastic pet carrier. Even before she pulled it out, the cat was backing into a corner, baring his teeth and hissing the sentiment, *No! No way! You can't put me in there, not again!*

After a cab ride across town and uptown to Sixtieth Street, Johanna and the screaming Mugs entered the animal hospital. Behind the front desk, the teenage receptionist suddenly tensed every muscle in her young body, bracing for a touch of hell in the afternoon. The pet carrier in Johanna's hand was shaking with rage. And the poor beast's last howl conveyed the message, *I'll kill you all!*

4

THE NETWORK'S CONFERENCE ROOM HAD TWO walls of glass, a fabulous view that only obscene amounts of money could buy, and entirely too much light, though, during the daylight hours, Ian Zachary saw everything through the darkest of polarized lenses. He sat down at the head of a table lined with chairs to accommodate thirty media executives. He sat alone.

The producer of the shock-radio program had not arrived, but then Needleman never showed up for staff meetings. Yet Zachary continued to attend each week, lured here by the prospect of finally meeting the invisible man. Beyond the idiosyncrasy of extreme shyness, he could find no fault with the producer. This one was the best of the best, seducing guests with promises that their reputations would not be destroyed on the radio, promises never kept. So far, the man's only failure was Johanna Apollo.

Zachary's personal slave, the most recent in a long line of disposable employees, entered the room carrying a covered tray. She wore a secretive smile as she set it down before him. And there were other warning signs. The girl had not combed her hair today, but that was only mildly interesting. It appeared that she had misplaced her shoes, for she was walking barefoot through corporate America. And were those the same clothes she had worn last night? Yes. He smiled with genuine affection for her, his best find in months. It was a pity that she could not last much longer. His genius lay in the ability to spot fracture lines in a damaged psyche. He had known what she was on the day of her hire; he had seen it in her eyes, a bit too wide, too bright. The less astute personnel director had mistaken the girl's manic chatter for enthusiasm.

Her smile turned ghoulish as she lifted the silver tray cover to reveal a generous serving of steak tartare. "Mr. Needleman said this was your favorite."

"My producer? You *talked* to him?"

"Yeah, he called me this morning." She sat down at the table and lowered her head until her nose was only inches from his food, then watched his plate with great concentration.

"The bastard never calls *me*." And now he also stared at his lunch. "So you pissed on it, right?" When she raised her face to his, he saw deep disappointment in her eyes. "Sorry." He pushed the tray away. "I spoiled your fun."

She rallied with a triumphant smile. "Mr. Needleman gave me the call-in figures for last night. He said the listener response was over the moon."

Evidently, the producer had also told her that she was the inspiration for most of those calls. The fans had wanted to know if she had been fired or not, for the show had ended abruptly with the last caller's find of a live juror in Manhattan. Bless Randy of SoHo. Whenever the juror death rate remained stagnant for too long, Zachary worried that the game would become stale, that he would lose the high ratings of his shock-radio audience. Sometimes he had to skate by on his talent for torturing the hired help. The sound engineer had proved a huge success as his new whipping girl, and she knew it.

"So now you think you're bulletproof, don't you, babe?" He shook his head. "No way." He could kill her with words any time he wanted to. She would break and fold before tonight's show was over. Or maybe not.

The girl picked up a fork and began to eat the red meat, which obviously had not been pissed on. "Jerk-off," she said.

And his new term of endearment for her was "You crazy bitch."

She looked up from the lunch plate, responding to this name, and grinned as another thought occurred to her. "That window in my booth, is *that* bulletproof?"

"Absolutely unbreakable." Zachary had insisted upon that specification before he would sign with the New York media giant. Thick glass on the booth windows was a necessary precaution, a lesson learned the hard way when his show had been based in Chicago. One memorable night in his old studio, the security door had held up through a pounding—but the engineer's window had not. A crazed woman had broken the glass to get at him. She had nearly bled to death, clumsy fool, after cutting herself on the shards. And all the while, he had taped a play-by-play account of the action to the rhythm of a security guard banging on his door. The ambulance crew had provided the climax, asking for Zachary's autograph while strapping a bleeding woman to a gurney bound for a hospital psychiatric ward.

His most current crazy bitch was stuffing food in her mouth with her fingers. The concept of silverware was quite beyond her now.

"Maybe I'll take over the show," she said, "when they take you off the air."

"They? Who? The FCC?" He shrugged. "They can *try*."

In fact, lately he had wondered why they did not try harder. He missed his daily visits from frustrated bureaucrats who had failed to shut him down. Perhaps they were afraid of more formidable attorneys. Or had they simply tired of losing every legal action to the American Civil Liberties Union?

"Maybe the network will get rid of you," she said. "Sooner or later, somebody's going to sue you for—"

"I get sued all the time." He leaned back in his chair, hands clasped behind his head, warming to his favorite subject. "Usually it's the outraged relatives of dead jurors, looking to make some fast cash. The network accountants crunched the numbers. Given the current advertising revenues coast to coast, it's cheaper to pay off the families."

"Then the Reaper will get you."

"Oh, I doubt it. He couldn't find the jurors without me and my fans. He's probably my most loyal listener."

"What if he's saving you for last?"

He nodded, as if considering this. In reality, he was wondering why her cognitive reasoning remained unimpaired, and he made a mental note to work on that.

"If you die," she said, "I could be your replacement. I could be bigger than you."

"Well, you can *dream*." Zack smiled at his newest candidate for induced psychosis. He had to admire her stamina. She was the only one who had remained with him after that moment when her mind had gone elsewhere. "You crazy bitch."

Johanna Apollo almost dropped the pet carrier. Kathy Mallory was a jarring sight on any occasion, but this was such a gross invasion. The uninvited visitor stood at the end of the narrow foyer, somewhat annoyed by Johanna's intrusion into her own hotel suite.

Riker appeared at the young woman's side. "Hey, Jo."

Johanna entered the living room and set the pet carrier on the floor at her feet. "How did you two get in here?"

"Same way we got into this thing." Riker stood before her open armoire and nodded to the tall blonde. "She has a way with locks."

Mallory strode toward the front door, causing Johanna to move out of the way or be trod upon. One foot in the outer hall, the younger woman's face was turned toward the glass door that gave a view of the elevator. She called back over one shoulder, "Hurry it up. We've only got a few minutes."

"Get out now," yelled Riker.

"I'll call from the lobby." Mallory dropped a cell phone and kicked it to the end of the foyer, and then the door closed behind her.

Riker picked up the phone and pocketed it, then resumed his chore of ransacking the armoire. Johanna stared at the empty shelves and cubbyholes. Her red suitcase lay open on the floor, and it was filled with file holders and loose papers. She was being robbed.

"I didn't have time to wait for you, Jo. I'm one jump ahead of the cops."

"But Mallory's a cop. *You're* a cop."

"Not anymore. They pensioned me off." He pulled out a drawer and upended it, sending the contents into the suitcase. "And Mallory was never here. Remember that, Jo—when Flynn comes."

After replacing the drawer, he hit the wood hard with the heel of his palm to bang it shut, then moved on to the next one. She could not tell if this was done in anger. For as long as she had known him, he had slammed every drawer and door, though that quirk did not fit with his easygoing nature. This was a man with a great deal of unresolved anger, and he no doubt believed that he was hiding it well.

"If you've got anything else that's incriminating," he said, "go get it. I have to take it out of here before—"

"Incriminating? You can't believe I—"

"Jo, if I was still a cop, I'd lock you up—*right now!*" He hunkered down to open the bottom drawer filled with wine bottles, all the same vintner, the same year. This was Timothy Kidd's drawer. Riker looked up at her. "Is the hotel maid pilfering your bottles?"

"Something like that." It was nothing like that, but only now did she see her error, and it was too late to call the words back.

Riker's eyes strayed to the wine rack on the other side of the room. He had once commented on the high cost of her vintages, for the price labels had never been removed, and now he was checking the stickers on the bottles in the drawer, a lesser wine trove than the one in plain sight and reach of the hotel staff. Gallant man, he never called her on that lie. He simply closed the drawer on the wine, then dropped Timothy's file into the suitcase. "The cops got a warrant to search your rooms."

"Since when does an innocent bystander—"

"They upgraded you to a suspect." He closed the suitcase and stood up, the better to scrutinize her face, perhaps looking there for tells of guilt. "This is what Flynn told the judge who signed the warrant. Back in Chicago, you destroyed evidence before the cops could secure the scene of another homicide—same cause of death, same weapon he found this morning at the playground." He was staring at the contents of her suitcase. "And now it looks like murder is a hobby with you." Riker leaned down and picked up a newspaper clipping for one of the Reaper's kills. "If Flynn saw this, he'd put you in a lockup. Oh, and he knows you're not on good terms with Bunny's lawyer, but that was my lie, not yours. So just say as little as possible. Don't give him a reason to arrest you." He turned back to the gutted armoire. "Get me some stuff to put in this closet."

She understood. Her rooms should not have the appearance of hastily removed evidence, and now she helped him load in papers and items from other drawers in the kitchen and her bedroom. When they were done, the armoire had the messy look of a catchall closet that had not been recently disturbed.

"Is there anything else in this apartment? Anything Flynn shouldn't see?" He stared at her, and she wondered if he knew she was holding out on him. It was so hard to tell with Riker. Suspicion was built into the very shape of his eyes.

"Jo, there's nothing you can hide from a police search. The toilet tank, the light fixture, stuff taped behind a drawer—they know every damn hiding place."

Johanna glanced at the cat's pillow basket, a hiding place that would only be secure while the cat was loose. "No," she lied. "There's nothing else."

He looked down at the growling pet carrier that was rocking in place on the floor. "Keep Mugs locked up. Flynn might get pissed off and shoot him." The cell phone beeped in Riker's pocket. "That's Mallory. They're coming, Jo. Take a deep breath and try to act surprised, okay?" He picked up the red suitcase and crossed over the threshold.

Johanna put out one hand to prevent him from slamming the door. "Riker? Why take the risk? If you get caught with . . ." Her words trailed off as he passed through the fire door leading to the staircase and the elevators. He was taking her on faith and going against his old religion of a police.

Riker disappeared down the stairs as the elevator opened. Johanna quickly closed the door to her suite, then released Mugs from the pet carrier. She rushed to the cat's basket and unzipped the pillowcase. Reaching toward the back of the pillow, she retrieved a packet of letters and concealed them in her jacket pocket.

The knock at the door was a *bang, bang, bang.* A man's voice yelled, "Police! Open up!"

Mugs waited to greet them, scratching the rug, warming up to shed some blood. The cat had had a bad day at the animal hospital, and the next one to enter this room would pay for that. Johanna cracked the door by a few inches, and the cat's front paws slipped into that narrow opening to snag anything within reach.

Detective Flynn stared at the frenzied animal. "Let's do something about the cat, okay?"

"I have to get my gloves," said Johanna, as Mugs desperately tried to widen the crack in the door so he could maul his first pair of pant legs. "Unless—you'd rather—"

"Make it fast."

She held the door shut with one shoe as she donned a pair of gloves from her pocket. She picked up the cat, minding the place along his spine that caused him pain. "You can come in now."

Flynn opened the door wide, and Mugs growled.

"I'll just put him in the pet carrier," said Johanna.

"That can wait, *Doctor.*" Flynn entered the room leading a parade of three men in suits and a woman in uniform.

The detective handed her a photograph, and Johanna looked down at the image of herself at the playground in the company of police.

"Bunny's social worker identified your picture," said Flynn. "She told us you were the *psychiatrist* who recommended Bunny's hospitalization and surgery. Odd you never mentioned that when I questioned you."

"I was upset. I didn't—"

"The social worker says you used the same alias you gave us—Josephine Richards. But we couldn't find any shrinks by that name. So we pulled your prints from the playground bench. That's how we tracked you down to Chicago. Those cops remember you very well, Doctor—you and that dead FBI agent. But they call you Johanna Apollo." And now for his finale, there was a flourish of folded papers as Flynn handed her a search warrant.

She stared at this document, all too familiar from past experience with the Chicago police. "Can I put the cat away before you start?"

"Not yet." Flynn nodded to another man. "Check that thing out."

The younger man walked over to the pet carrier and turned it upside down to shake it. After a look inside, he pronounced it "Clean. No false bottom."

Mugs leaped out of Johanna's arms, but he did not attack. Perhaps the cat was overwhelmed by this embarrassment of riches, so many potential victims in one place. He stood beside her, eyeing the company of police as they spread across the room, pulling out drawers and sofa cushions. His ears flattened back, and he showed every sharp tooth in his mouth when he hissed.

"Mugs, it's all right," she said, then read the warrant with some relief. It included no search of her person, no discovery of the letters in her jacket.

"Mugs," said the female officer. "That's his name?"

"Yes." Johanna turned to look at the other woman's sensible black shoes, tightly laced and double knotted beneath the cuffs of uniform trousers. "It's short for Huggermugger." And now she looked up to the young face beneath the tri-cornered cap.

The police officer hunkered down for a closer look at the animal, not minding the warning of the arched back and bristling fur. This woman was definitely a cat person, for she engaged the animal's eyes, then imitated his slow blink. Mugs began to purr as he walked toward her. "Huggermugger. Cute name."

"More like a warning. Don't—"

"It's all right. Cats *like* me." Mugs rubbed up against the woman's thigh, then turned on her, biting her hand and drawing blood.

Johanna gathered up the cat before it could make another strike. "Sorry, so sorry."

"What the hell's wrong with him?" The policewoman was staring at the holes in her flesh as they pooled up with blood.

"Old nerve damage." Johanna pushed the cat inside the plastic pet carrier, using both gloved hands to corral the whirlwind of fur and flying claws that tried to prevent the door from closing. The cat's small face appeared at the wire window of his jail. Mugs growled as loud as any dog. Johanna glanced at the woman's injured hand. "I can fix that for you." She led the wounded officer into the bathroom. "This won't take long."

As she opened a cupboard below the sink, Johanna listened to the activity in the next room, sounds of drawers opening, objects hitting the floor, the cat alternately growling, hissing and screaming. She pulled out her first aid kit and found the bottle of antiseptic. "This might sting." She took the officer's hand in hers and irrigated the tiny holes. "These tooth marks aren't deep. There won't be any scars." When she was done with the bandaging, she reached into the back of the closet where she kept a physician's gladstone bag. Inside it she found a block of paper, each page bearing the medical icon of a caduceus beneath her name. "I'm prescribing a topical antibiotic and another one in pill form. Animal bites are easily infected." Done writing, she tore off the two sheets and handed them to the officer.

"I thought you were a shrink." The young woman stared at the prescriptions, dubious now, maybe wondering if this was illegal.

"I was a psychiatrist," said Johanna, "so I also have a medical degree. I'm sorry about the cat. I did try to warn you about the—"

"Can't you do anything for him? An operation or something?"

"There was an operation. A veterinary surgeon severed the damaged nerve so Mugs wouldn't feel the pain anymore. But he'd lived with it for too long before I found him. Now he only feels the phantom nerve, but the pain is very real to Mugs. The cat's quite insane. Perfect pet for a shrink, wouldn't you say?"

"And you still keep him."

Johanna suspected that this cat lover's approval was genuine. "Yes, I keep him. No one else would have him." She turned to leave the bathroom.

"Not yet, Dr. Apollo." The policewoman handed her a second warrant, this one for a personal search. "Sorry," she said, as she pulled on a pair of plastic gloves.

So this would be a *very* personal search. Johanna could even guess the order of violation: first oral, then vaginal, then anal.

"You'll have to remove all your clothes." The officer touched the collar of the denim jacket. "I remember this." She looked down at Johanna's legs. "And those are the same jeans you wore this morning, right?"

Johanna nodded as she removed her jacket, then pulled her sweatshirt over her head, catching sight of herself in the bathroom mirror. The deformity was more grotesque in the fleshy knotted muscles curving into a hump. The younger woman turned away, not enjoying this moment. Johanna removed her jeans, eyes fixed on the floor. She felt the heat rising in her face, the deep red flush of humiliation, as she unhooked her bra.

"You can keep the underwear on." The policewoman removed her gloves in a giveaway act of compassion. There would be no cavity search today.

"Thank you," said Johanna.

The officer gave her a curt nod. "But if anyone asks—"

"Understood. I'll tell them you were very thorough."

"I don't know why that detective even ordered it. Flynn says we're only looking for documents. Letters, records."

Johanna nodded. These were the sort of things she had destroyed on the day when Timothy Kidd was murdered.

The policewoman searched a pocket of Johanna's jacket where the bundle of letters had recently rested. All she found was spare change, a subway token, and some folding money, all of which she handed to Johanna. "We're taking your clothes with us. You'll get a receipt for everything." She nodded toward the robe hanging from a hook on the bathroom door. "Why don't you put that on?"

Johanna wrapped the robe about her and watched her work boots and socks disappear into a plastic bag. Barefoot, she followed the policewoman into the front room, where Mugs was in the hissing mode, and men were testing couch cushions for suspicious lumps. Drawers had been pulled out and emptied on the floor. One man had climbed on top of a table, scratching the finish with his shoes as he reached up to unscrew the overhead light fixture.

Detective Flynn stood by the armoire desk, where financial records had been piled to cure its recently raided appearance. His low whistle gave away the discovery of her stock portfolio and an income in the highest tax bracket. Now there would be questions about her most recent employment and the unhealthy interest in crime scenes. She was a woman of means. No need to work for her living. And she lived in a hotel suite, while these people rented small, cramped apartments on the wages of civil servants.

Yes, she would have a great deal to answer for.

The policewoman guided her to a kitchen chair that had been dragged into the front room for no other purpose than to deny her comfort. Johanna sat down on the hard wood, wrapping the robe closer about her person. The searchers circled around her in their travels, never making eye contact, treating her as a floor lamp or an incidental table in their way. Detective Flynn pulled up another straight-back chair, though his was padded with embroidered upholstery. He turned it around to straddle it and rest his arms on the back. He seemed so relaxed while Johanna shifted in her own chair. She understood why he had requested a full cavity search, a probe of every orifice in her body. That kind of trauma was most efficient in tearing down a suspect's ego. She also realized that it was nothing personal.

This time it would be different from her interview with the Chicago police. This New York detective would not invite her to visit his station house. The hotel room was an excellent choice for an interrogation, no lawyers around to prevent them from stripping her to a flimsy bathrobe and rattling her with ongoing violations of her life, her personal letters and—

The uniformed officer stood in the narrow hallway that led to the bedroom. She sought out Johanna's eyes to beg some explanation for the child-size pair of dancing shoes, black patent leather with metal cleats at toe and heel. The concept of a tap-dancing hunchback was too difficult for this young woman.

Johanna only shrugged to say, *Old dreams. I guess you had them, too.*

She had been eleven years old when thoracic kyphosis had become so apparent that it could no longer be put off to bad posture. Dancing classes had been cancelled for the remainder of childhood. It was too hard to tap dance in a heavy brace that could not fly with her across the long, mirrored classroom, and no one could do the Buffalo Shuffle in body armor.

The policewoman put the lid on the old shoe-box dream and returned to the bedroom to continue the search.

Johanna faced Detective Flynn. Everything about this man, his posture and his eyes, informed her that his power was unlimited, all but saying to her, *Give up—you're lost—*

you're mine. She shrank in size. She had no substance in this room. It belonged to them now, the searchers. She was the visitor here.

A man with plastic gloves was examining the drawer of wine bottles, and she ceased to breathe for a moment. Through the open bathroom door, she could hear the sounds of the medicine cabinet being ransacked. They would find all the pain medication, the pills to help her sleep and others to keep her awake. What would they make of the large store of pet tranquilizers? They would note her brand of toothpaste, examine the underwear in her hamper, attracted by spots of blood, and follow the scent of menstruation to the tampon in the trash basket. Would the searcher be delighted with this find—this perfect sample of DNA? Would he fold this treasure away in an evidence bag?

And what would the tag say? Lady on the rag?

Her toes curled as her bare feet drew back under the chair. "What do you want?"

Flynn was looking past her, as if the pictures on the wall were more interesting to him. "Most people go their whole lives and never stumble on a murder victim." He turned his eyes to hers, and his voice doubled in volume. "You found *two* dead bodies, lady! An FBI agent back in Chicago and that poor homeless bum this morning." He leaned far forward, startling her, and she recoiled. "That would've been enough to get my attention, but both of 'em had their throats slit. The Chicago cops tell me you made a little bonfire in your office wastebasket before you called 911. You destroyed all your patient records. And all the while, there's a man bleeding to death in your waiting room."

"He was dead when I found him."

"You're pretty cool under pressure, Doctor."

No, she was more vulnerable now.

"So, Dr. Apollo, you wanna cut the crap and—"

"Sir?" A man in uniform waited for the detective to acknowledge him before he said, "You have to stop the interview. There's a guy downstairs in the lobby. He says—"

"Hold it!" Flynn put up one hand in the manner of a traffic cop, and the other man fell silent. The detective turned on Johanna. "You called a damn lawyer, didn't you? You *knew* we were coming. Who tipped you off, Doctor? Was it Riker?" Not waiting for an answer, he fired his next question at the man in uniform. "Chase down that bastard Riker and drag him in. *Now!*"

"Wait," said Johanna. "About that man in the lobby." She dipped one hand into the pocket of her robe where she had put the money taken from her blue jeans. "I've got at least fifty dollars here. I'm betting he's not an attorney. Put up or shut up, Detective."

But Flynn was already satisfied that no one had tipped her off to the search warrant, for the anticipated visitor was standing in the open doorway and flashing his FBI credentials for all to see.

"Hel*lo,* Joh*anna.*" Special Agent Marvin Argus made a slow turn to acknowledge the others in her company and deigned to grace them all with his most condescending smile.

One night's sleep and he was back in arrogant form with all the old confidence that so annoyed her. Johanna's politics were pacifist, and yet she wanted to smack this man each time they met. Everyone did. He was from the Chicago bureau, and all the people in this room would be strangers to him, yet there was overt hostility in every face that turned his way—and a bit of confusion as well. Argus might be their first encounter with a male-heterosexual princess.

"So which one of you is Flynn?" He grinned at the angriest man in the room, the detective who sat with Johanna. "You? Well, this is my case now. Check with your lieutenant if you like. I won't be offended. But this interview is definitely over. And all the evidence your guys collected? That's mine."

No one paid any attention to Johanna as she rose from her chair and walked toward the pet carrier. This was where she had hidden the packet of dangerous letters in a sleight of hand while locking the cat inside. With no sane regard for the possible discovery of this evidence, she opened the carrier's

loor, and Mugs flew out. No, he *shot* out of that small open-
ng, all but flying across the room, as if she had deliberately
aimed him at Special Agent Marvin Argus.

Only a few more minutes passed before she had her life
back again, her possessions and her peace. She closed the
loor on the departing invaders, then turned to the cat, who
lelicately sniffed the abandoned bags of papers and cloth-
ng. Mugs had won the hearts of all the police. And the
bleeding FBI agent had not been offered any first aid for his
vounds.

Oddly enough, it had been a profitable afternoon—reassuring and informative. The New York detective might have
been a formidable opponent, but now Flynn was officially
off the case. And the Chicago police had been miserly in
haring information with him. He had tied her to only two
murders, a very modest body count.

5

RIKER WAS ONE UNHAPPY MAN AS HE ENTERED the Greenwich Village restaurant. He was responding to a summons from a revered icon of NYPD, a retired captain who continued to police his children, keeping track of all their transgressions. Brother Ned was the good son, who so seldom required this personal attention. All the blackest marks belonged to Riker.

Dad still harbored grudges from a teenage-runaway episode also known as the Mexican Rebellion. After a summer-long flight from the old man's tyranny, Riker had returned home to Brooklyn. Covered in road dirt and ragged, he had sported long hair and a boy's first beard, a defiant combination that had guaranteed him some fireworks. But the old man had met him at the door in cold silence and never said a word to him all that day. Years later, Riker had chanced upon an open drawer in his father's desk. It was usually locked, for this was where the old man had kept his only valuables, the badge and the gun. And there Riker had also found a third object, the single postcard mailed home from Mexico, the only shred of proof that his father had missed him, worried over him and possibly loved him.

The retired captain was seated in a corner booth. The bartender hovered over the table and personally poured out the single-malt whiskey, not trusting this special customer to a waitress. Into his late seventies, Dad had retained his ramrod posture and all his hair, thick and white. The old man did look sharp in his dark suit and tie so like the silk threads he had worn as a police detective. Drawing closer, Riker saw his father's lips move, probably rehearsing a lecture that would amount to only a few spoken words; the central point would be driven home by the famous glare of disappointment.

Riker knew he would not be forgiven for the clumsy error of getting shot, nor for the greater mistake of not fighting a medical discharge. And there was one more possibility for this meeting. Had Dad discovered that one of his sons had been busy committing criminal acts today? The old man's information network was uncanny. Already planning lies of protection to cover Mallory's part in foiling a search warrant, Riker rounded a pillar, and now he could see that the old man was not alone. His drinking companion was also dressed in a suit, and one of the stranger's pant legs was torn.

Mugs? Oh, yeah.

Riker owned a pair of jeans with those same distinctive claw marks. A bandaged hand was more evidence that this man, probably a detective, had paid a recent visit to the Chelsea Hotel. Damn Johanna. He had warned her to play nicely with the police. The man's face was shielded by a potted fern, but Riker could assume he was a cop from Flynn's Greenwich Village precinct.

"Sir?" This was all Riker said by way of a greeting to his father, a man with no use for long sentences. A grunt of acknowledgment would have been more to Dad's liking.

He was introduced to his father's guest by name, rank and no wasted words, "Special Agent Marvin Argus, FBI." This was the same man who had come looking for Jo yesterday afternoon. At the time, Riker had not taken Argus for a federal agent. He had never met a fed with a girly fringe of bangs plastered to his forehead.

The FBI man shifted his seat in the booth, making room

for Riker to sit beside him. "So you're the hero cop. I heard you left the force."

"That's not final," said Riker's father, hoping to put an end to this interminable babble. Dad leaned forward, glaring at the agent with a silent suggestion to *just get on with it.* The old man's tense body language put his son on notice that he was here under duress, that everything about this meeting stank. And just as clear was Dad's dislike for this agent from the Federal Bureau of Investigation. Riker wondered how many old favors had been called in to get his own father to act as a lure for this meeting.

"I'd like to talk about your employee, Johanna Apollo," said Agent Argus. "Oh, sorry—you know her as Josephine Richards. Hey, I never got your first name."

Ignoring this question and declining the space the agent had made for him, Riker elected to sit with his father on the other side of the table. And now that the lines were clearly drawn, he could see the agent backing up in his mind and rethinking his tactics.

Dad almost smiled. Almost.

Argus's grin was forced. "You probably think I'm here about that homicide at the playground. Well, you'd be wrong." He toyed with his cuff links while waiting in vain for some show of interest. Riker's father rapped one knuckle on the table, and the agent all but snapped to attention, saying, "I'm investigating the murder of an FBI agent, Timothy Kidd. Johanna's also connected to that one. But you already knew that."

You're guessing.

Riker shook his head in denial. "I don't know squat. The lady's a very private person." In a lighter tone, he said, "So, she killed a fed, huh?" He turned to his father to see if this also warranted a near smile.

Sit up straight, said Dad's cold gray eyes, *and not one more smart-ass remark.*

And Riker did sit up a bit straighter, force of habit from correction sessions at the dinner table every damn night of his childhood. Over the years, he had learned to decipher the words behind the old man's every glance in his direction. With a more sober attitude, he turned back to the FBI man, asking, "What do you want?"

"A little of your time." Argus leaned back against the booth's red leather cushion. "Let me tell you about this dead agent, a real sweet guy. And just between us?" He paused to flash a quick smile, still trying to curry intimacy. "Timmy was always a little spooky. Toward the end, he definitely had a few screws loose. But I think you would've liked him. One damn fine investigator—as good as it gets."

And now Riker learned that the deceased Timothy Kidd had possessed a heightened ability to ferret out nuances of guilt, to translate volumes of words from nothing said, finding patterns in chaos and in other people's unspoken thoughts. In the weeks before his death, the exquisite brain of this acute paranoid was electrified and wired up to everything that moved and everything that did not.

"Ah, Timmy," said Agent Argus. "Crazy bastard. He could read warning signs written on thin air. And he was one smart son of a bitch, smart enough to mask his symptoms for a long time. He got past the Bureau's psych test with no sweat. But down the road a bit, his reports started leaning toward fantasyland. The chief of his field office didn't report it—didn't want to lose a good man to the shrinks. Well, we fired his chief for incompetence, and then we tried to help Timmy with his—problem. If we'd only gotten to him sooner, he'd probably be alive today."

Riker understood that this confession of Bureau screwups was supposed to bring them closer together, cop to cop, but he was very fussy about his male bonding, and Marvin Argus did not make the cut.

Dad seemed at the verge of spitting on the FBI man, finding Argus's diatribe distasteful. Cops did not behave this way. Their messes were kept in the family.

"Well," said the agent, "we found Tim a psychiatrist with an IQ higher than his. That was so he couldn't put anything past her. Dr. Johanna Apollo was the highest-paid shrink in Chicago, and now she's a crime-scene janitor." The man staged a smug pause. "Yeah, I thought you'd find that interesting. She called Tim a gifted paranoid. Of course, that was *after* he was murdered. We think she's withholding information."

"So you want me to spy on her," said Riker. And now he waited for the pitch. A job offer was predictable, a carrot for the Judas goat.

Argus waved off this suggestion. "I need your help. Tim was brilliant, but you weren't such a bad cop yourself. I know your record in Special Crimes Unit. You did good work. Damn shame to retire that kind of talent. The Bureau needs a guy like you on this case." He flashed a smarmy grin, man to man. "It's not like I'm asking you to get in bed with a hunchback."

Riker's hands balled into fists.

Marvin Argus dropped the smile and shut his mouth, probably noting a sudden change in the atmosphere, a three-second warning that he had crossed a line that could get him decked. The agent's tone was more serious when he said, "I want to be very clear about this. A maniac played a game that scared the hell out of Timmy, and this freak might want to play with you, too. You could wind up dead."

Riker nodded his complete understanding. The agent was setting him up to look like a coward in his father's eyes if he dared to turn down the job. Argus clearly had no talent for sizing up other men. Dad's hands were tensing, fingers curling and uncurling. Riker and his father were in accord this time; they both wanted to slap this man senseless.

"Now, about that dead vagrant," said Argus. "The one the cops found this morning. I understand Johanna had confrontations with him all the time. She only had to walk a block out of her way to avoid him, but she never did. Yeah, that made you curious, didn't it? That's why you dug up her history—and found an identical murder, Timothy Kidd's."

Was this more guesswork or would that background check track back to Kathy Mallory?

Agent Argus, the mind reader, said, "We had two standout hits on our data bank this morning—from two *different* precincts. One search was done by Flynn, the catching detective on the bum's homicide, and he got zilch. But Johanna's alias raised a red flag at the Bureau. Now the *second* search didn't use her alias. And there was no password either. The hacker bypassed the lockout and raided the store. Nice work, Riker. I'm impressed. I guess you were visiting your old station house in SoHo. It was easy enough to sit down at an empty desk with a computer."

And now it was certain that Marvin Argus could trace nothing back to Mallory, who rarely left tracks. She had not used a police computer for her early morning hacking. And apparently Argus had no idea how many times she raided federal databases in an average week.

Riker, a renowned computer illiterate, shrugged. "Yeah, I was the hacker. Good catch, Argus." He turned to his father, checking for signs of trouble in the old man's face, and discovered that Dad actually sanctioned this illegal act, this promising sign that his son was still thinking like a cop.

Drumming the wood surface with two fingers, Argus called his attention back across the table. "Figure it out yet, Riker? Three days a week, Johanna Apollo goes round and round with this crazy bum. She's dodging blows, getting used to the idea of being attacked. And why? Because she'll never know the moment when our agent's killer comes for her. Tim didn't. And Johanna screwed up last night. That vagrant tripped her, and she took a bad fall."

If Jo's fall had been mentioned in any of the witness statements, Detective Flynn would have pressed that point during the brief playground interview. Riker knew the man's style: rattle the suspect up front and never let up on the pressure. So how would Argus have this detail? Had he been shadowing Jo, using a living woman for bait to catch a serial killer? And Argus had yet to mention the Reaper. That was curious, too.

"So your suspect is one of the doctor's patients," said Riker. "And you figure he wants to kill her before she can give up his name?" That was one obvious scenario for the FBI surveillance.

Marvin Argus's smile said, *Now you're catching on.* And by that smile, Riker knew that he was being misled.

The FBI man lightly slapped the table with his palm. "So this is the deal. We need a guy on the inside, someone who has Johanna's confidence. If you're really tight with her, she might let something slip—something useful."

A snitch is the lowest form of life on earth, said the mere lift of Dad's head. And now the old man's eyes were asking if his son could sink that low; could he travel from the rank of detective first grade to a bottom feeder in the space of a day.

"It's for Dr. Apollo's own good," said Argus. "She left the witness protection program."

"Here's where you're messing up," said Riker. "This killer watches you watching her. He's probably laughing his tail off every day. All those hours of FBI manpower, all for nothing. You'll never catch him that way."

"There was no surveillance on Johanna. We didn't know where she was before that raid on our computer."

"Oh, can it, Argus. You as good as told me the feds were watching her the night before Bunny's body was found." Riker hoped it would drive the agent crazy trying to figure out where the stumble had been made. Rising from the table, he nodded farewell to his father rather than say good-bye, for that would have been more familial affection than Dad could stand. Next, he turned to the FBI man, saying, "Keep the job. I'm not your boy."

On his way out of the bar, Riker glanced back to see the trace of a smile on the old man's lips—finally.

When the door had swung shut behind him, and he stood on the sidewalk again, an old sedan rolled by with the loud fart of a backfire. Though Riker knew the difference between the bang of a car and the bang of a gun, anxiety paralyzed him. His feet would not carry him away, and all his muscles constricted at once. He felt a great pressure on his chest—no air—and he could not fight down the panic of suffocation. People passed him by on the sidewalk, and he could not call out to them, nor even wave at them; his arms were leaden and fallen to his sides. The pedestrians saw nothing amiss—just a man frozen in place, sweating on a cool day. Only his eyes were in motion, silently begging each passerby, *Help me!* No one paused to see that his chest was not moving, lungs not breathing in and out—that he was *dying*.

The paralysis passed off. His lungs filled with oxygen. His feet obeyed him. And he walked down the sidewalk with a surefootedness that belied his idea of himself as a cripple.

When he greeted Riker at the door to the reception area, Charles Butler wore the vest, but not the jacket to his tailored suit, and this was his idea of casual attire. Strands of light brown hair curled past his collar, for though he possessed eidetic memory, he never seemed to remember a barber's appointment. But that was not his most outstanding characteristic. The man had once described himself as the bastard child of Cyrano and a pop-eyed frog. Though his eyes were heavy-lidded, the whites overwhelmed the small blue irises, giving him an air of constant astonishment, as though every word said in his company was absolutely fascinating. Oh, and that *nose*—what a magnificent beak. He sat behind an eighteenth-century desk. Most of the furnishings at Butler and Company were antiques, except for the couch that was custom-made to accommodate very long legs. Charles stood six foot four in his socks, but just now he slouched low in his chair, for he thought it rude to hover over visitors of normal height, even while sitting down. Among his other quirks was a monster IQ and an equally staggering generosity.

Riker had never believed the reason for the low rent on his own apartment one flight below. His old friend and new landlord still maintained the fiction that he felt more secure with a police presence in his building, even though Charles had the size and strength to pound the average human right into the ground. But that was not his nature. He was the most pacific of giants. Also, there was already one cop in residence; the building superintendent was a retired patrolman. And then there was his silent partner, Mallory, and her expertise in electronic burglar alarms and state-of-the-art locks. This might be the most secure building in New York City. So the cheap rent was a gift of charity disguised in a lie told by a man so hobbled by honesty that he could not run a bluff without blushing.

However, Riker had had nowhere else to go.

Returning to his old apartment in Brooklyn had never been an option. The prospect of entering that place one more time had been the stuff of nightmares, waking and sleeping. And so, upon his hospital bed, he had handed his keys to the moving men with instructions to steal what they liked—but to leave the rainy-day stash of good bourbon intact. That rainy day had come.

"Has Mallory been by?"

"Not today," said Charles. "She's been rather busy lately."

"You mean with her *real* job?"

"Well, yes. When she does come by, it's usually late in the evenings. Hence the term *moonlighting.*"

Kathy Mallory's second source of income was unauthorized, for cops were forbidden to use investigative skills in the private sector, but Riker well understood her interest in this place. Down the hall, she kept a private office where she housed her favorite toys. Most of them required a judge's warrant to operate or even to possess them. Fortunately, Charles Butler was a committed Luddite, who would not recognize the electronic equivalents of lock picks, and who no doubt believed that she used all her equipment to run the background checks on their odd clientele.

Mallory's boss at Special Crimes Unit was equally deluded. Lieutenant Coffey was still pretending that she had followed his direct order to sever all ties with Butler and Company. Instead, she had submerged her financial interest in the small firm of elite headhunters, becoming an invisible partner. And now this office was a warrant-proof squirrel hole, the perfect place to leave the suitcase of files and notes removed from Jo's hotel suite. If Detective Flynn had discovered Riker's interference, he would have papered the city with warrants to find his missing evidence, and he would have started with Riker's apartment. But this was no longer a problem. As Mallory had predicted, the FBI had hijacked Bunny's homicide, and feds were less diligent than Flynn.

"I suppose you'll want your property back." Charles stood before the open door of a closet and pulled the red suitcase down from a high shelf, handling this heavy luggage as if it weighed nothing at all. It would have been normal and natural to ask why Riker had stashed it here instead of in his own apartment downstairs, but Charles had been hanging with Mallory for too long, and he had learned to regret asking questions. Instead, he said, "Mrs. Ortega will be sorry to have missed you. She asks about you all the time."

That was odd and touching news, for Charles's cleaning lady, under normal circumstances, would rather be shot dead than admit concern for Riker. He was her favorite target for caustic remarks. "Tell her I said hello."

"I will," said Charles. "It seems that we see less of you now that you live in the same building. Are you getting enough heat and hot water? Any problems I should be aware of?"

"Naw, everything works great." Riker was rising, reaching for the suitcase, more than ready to take his leave. He had the sense that his friend was checking him for unplugged bullet holes and other signs that he was not quite mended. But then he realized that he did have a use for a man with a Ph.D. in psychology. "You know, there is one thing you could help me with—if you've got a few minutes."

"Of course." Charles inadvertently smiled like a loon, and he was all too aware of this unfortunate characteristic. His skin was deeply flushed with every happy expression, an apology of sorts for his foolish face. "My time is yours."

Riker settled back into the armchair. "It's about paranoia." He noticed the sudden concern in his friend's eyes, then hastily added, "Not me. This is another guy. You test people for oddball gifts. What about paranoia? We're talkin' wigged out, full-blown, to the nth degree. Could you see that as a useful talent?"

Charles, bless him, gave every stupid idea polite consideration. A few moments passed, and then he said, "Well, that's the sort of thing I'd try to fix with a psychiatric referral. Encouraging paranoia would be unethical. And there's really no market for mentally ill employees." He considered his own clients to be merely eccentric.

But Riker had other ideas. The job applicants of Butler and Company had rare talent and high intelligence prized by think tanks and government projects, and they were frequently a hair away from crazy, neatly explaining this man's vast expertise in abnormal psychology.

Head tilted to one side, Charles was having second thoughts, or perhaps he simply disliked disappointing a friend. "Well, I suppose it might have *some* applications. If your man worked in a dangerous environment, extreme paranoia could give him an edge in staying alive."

Riker had anticipated that much. New Yorkers who were not the least bit neurotic were listed on police blotters as the dead and wounded. A mild case of paranoia was considered a sign of good mental health, for it made people wary of strangers and dangerous streets. But Agent Timothy Kidd had been the king of paranoia, and he had not managed to stay alive in Chicago, a town with a lower homicide rate.

"Okay, suppose my guy is an FBI agent tracking a serial killer? Would paranoia give him an edge in dealing with suspects?"

"Bit of a stretch," said Charles. "But it *might*—if it shows in his outward behavior, and that's usually the case. His overt suspicion would increase the pressure on the person he was interviewing. The suspect might exhibit more enhanced reactions, involuntary facial expressions and nervousness—all the giveaway signs of a lie. A full-blown paranoid could pick up on all of that, consciously or unconsciously. However, here's another aspect to consider. A paranoid is working with more perceptions than the average person, taking in details and information that you or I would rightly deem irrelevant. That's the downside to your theory. They frequently detect patterns that simply aren't there."

"So flaming paranoia could never help him *find* a suspect?"

"I wouldn't think so. Everyone would seem suspicious to him. I imagine his illness would only clutter up the landscape and make things more difficult."

Then why had Marvin Argus gone to such trouble to spin the lie of a gifted paranoid?

Riker rose from his chair and picked up Jo's red suitcase. At least he had a satisfactory answer to the only question that had really mattered. Unlike Agent Argus, Charles Butler would not, could not, lie to him, and he had the man's assurance that Mallory had not visited this office today, that the contents of the suitcase were unrifled and still intact. And this oversight of hers, this failure to plunder Jo's papers behind his back, had sealed his theory that Mallory was playing him.

6

SO MUCH FOR THE WORLD-CLASS SECURITY FEAtures of his new address. When Riker unlocked the door to his apartment, he knew immediately that there had been a break-in. His laundry was no longer scattered about the room, but neatly gathered into a wicker basket. His other clue was the small, wiry woman cleaning his windowpanes.

"What're you doing?"

"As any fool can see," said Mrs. Ortega, "I'm robbin' you blind." She turned around to glare at him with dark Spanish eyes that silently asked if he had any more stupid questions. She also managed to convey that she was a woman on a mission, and *he* was the intruder here.

"Did Charles let you in? Or was it Mallory?"

"I got the super to open the door," said Mrs. Ortega. "I told him I was your cleaning lady." She looked down at her apron lined with pockets of plastic bottles, rags, brushes and other tools of the trade. "Great disguise, huh?"

She dropped a wet rag on the windowsill and walked over to the wicker basket. "Riker, there's something I just gotta know. I think I've figured out your system, but tell me if I'm wrong. You throw your socks into a different corner every night so you can rotate dirty laundry instead of washing it. Have I got that right?" She eyed the red suitcase he carried. "And now you're running away from home. I understand." The wave of her hand included the entire front room, its litter and streaks of—whatever that was on the walls. "Overwhelming, isn't it, Riker? Easier to pack up and leave."

He set the suitcase down by the door. "Okay, no more cleaning. Not today." He wanted to read all of Johanna's papers, and that left him no time to deal with Mrs. Ortega. Well, not *much* time. "I got cold beer in the fridge. Want one?"

"Don't mind if I do." She followed him into the kitchen, where his unopened mail covered most of the floor tiles. She swept a slew of envelopes from the seat of a chair and sat down at the table. "Maybe I should just ream this place out with a blowtorch and start over from scratch." She accepted a beer from his hand, stared at it with grave suspicion, then wiped the top of the can with a clean rag before opening it.

"Well, this room's not so bad," he said.

"Oh, yeah?" With the toe of one shoe, she nudged an open pizza carton on the floor. The remaining slice had grown enough mold to qualify as a houseplant. "You know why you don't have cockroaches, Riker? Those genius bugs, they know it's not safe to eat here."

"So you noticed I'm probably not the type to hire a cleaning lady. Now why are you doing this to me?"

"I got a philosophy," she said. "I'm gonna write a book—*Zen and the Art of a Clean House*—that's my title. You put a house in order, and you put your life in order. All this stuff is weighing you down, Riker. You might as well drag it around on your back, the dirt, the mess, the busted coffeemaker that probably hasn't worked in twenty years. But that ain't the worst of it."

He followed the point of her finger, looking through the doorway to the room beyond, where dust balls, having acquired tenure, roamed free and fearless across the open floor. One windowpane she had cleaned; all the rest were fogged with a yellow grime of nicotine. And a layer of dust colored everything else in gray.

"That's what the inside of your head looks like," she said. "Scary, huh?"

This tough little woman had a bad attitude, a penchant for heavy sarcasm, and she had touched him in all the soft places of the heart. He understood that she wanted to fix him, to make him better by cleaning him up. But Mrs. O. was not so talented. She could not scour away the image of a skinny psychotic teenager sitting upon his blood-soaked chest, pressing the muzzle of a gun to an eyeball, then pulling the trigger only to discover that he had spent all his bullets on Riker's prone body. Even now, with every loud noise he ceased to breathe, and he relived his dying.

"What's all this crap?" Mrs. Ortega leaned down to sort through the pile of mail, passing over advertisements and bills to examine the letters from the city of New York and NYPD. Selecting one, she held it up to the overhead light. "This one's got a check in it. I can tell. It's a blackout envelope. That's so you can't see what's inside."

Riker shook his head. "You're wrong. My paychecks were direct deposit." And then one day, the deposits had ceased, and he had never even picked up a phone to ask why.

She slapped a worn five-dollar bill on the table. "I say it's a check. I'm never wrong."

He laid five singles alongside her money. "Okay, you're on."

Mrs. Ortega slashed open the envelope, then waved a slip of paper in his face. "It's a disability check from the city." Now she looked through the rest of the mail at her feet. "And here's another one—and another one. Jesus, you're rich."

"This is a mistake." Riker shook his head as she emptied the envelopes one by one and lined up the checks on the table. "The city screwed up. These have to go back."

"Why?"

"Because I'm not disabled."

"Oh, yeah? Wanna bet?"

When Mrs. Ortega had pulled her rolling cart of cleaning supplies out onto the sidewalk, she heard the rattle of money in a beggar's ratty paper cup. She had passed by this bum half an hour ago on her way to Riker's apartment. And now she could tell by the sound of coins that his proceeds had been slim, and that alone was enough to arouse her curiosity. Considering the locals, all damn liberal idiots in her opinion, this youngster would have to *work* at driving off donations.

She might despise panhandling on principle, but she was even less tolerant of incompetence. Since Riker had sent her away before she could make inroads on his mess, Mrs. Ortega guessed she had a little time left over for charity work.

A man from the neighborhood stopped to give the beggar money, then had a change of heart and moved on. And now the cleaning woman knew how to fix the young man in the dark glasses and the red wig.

"Still here?" Her eyes were on the paper cup, and she counted up the paltry sum of two nickels and four pennies. "It ain't goin' so good, is it, kid? Well, I'm not surprised." She walked around him, taking his measure. "I'll tell you what you're doin' wrong. When that guy was gonna give you a dollar, you smiled. You looked at that bill and smiled. That's why he got pissed off and stuck it back in his pocket. In the future, try to remember this." Mrs. Ortega tapped the cardboard sign hung round the beggar's neck to label his affliction, his need for alms. She raised her voice, as if he might also be hard of hearing. "You're supposed to be *blind,* you *moron!*"

He cringed and pressed back against the wall, then raised his white cane, as if to ward off a blow, and that puzzled Mrs. Ortega. This conversation had been conducted on the decibel level of a standard New York street confrontation, and she had not even threatened him. Yet now he was reduced to a shivering geek show.

In a rare moment of weakness—call it mercy—she paid him a compliment. "That white cane is a good prop. Yeah, that's a keeper."

She stepped back to reassess him. He should definitely lose that stupid red wig. It was too long for the boy, even a weird boy. It was a girl's wig, for Christ's sake. Where the hell did this pansy come from? Puffed up with great xenophobic pride, she decided that he could not be a native of *her* New York. And it was on her mind to tell the boy that he should change the sign on his neck to say that he was crazy as well as stupid. But, having already done her bit for community service, she moved on down the sidewalk with her cart and never looked back. She never saw him raise his eyes to stare at Riker's second-floor window.

Papers covered every stained inch of the carpet, and this created the illusion of an improvement in Riker's front room. His deli sandwich disappeared in absentminded nibbles as he read another page of Dr. Johanna Apollo's neat handwriting.

Among the personal notes was a journal logging every meeting with Bunny, the homeless homicide victim, noting signs of physical and mental deterioration. The last entry was Bunny's message from the late Timothy Kidd, and a note on the use of a hapless vagrant as a living telephone for a serial killer. Riker marked this final entry with a paper clip, then put the journal to one side. One day it might be used as evidence in a trial.

Next he read the transcripts of several interviews with the Chicago police, all the details and conversation that Jo could recall. The case detective had hammered her so hard, accusing her of withholding evidence. Another group of interviews had been conducted by FBI agents and would be better described as debriefings. Curiously, the murder of their own man was never mentioned—only the dead man's theories about a serial killer. Agent Kidd had made contact with the Reaper. In Jo's words, "He saw the Reaper in a liquor store." Following an interruption from her interrogator, she admitted that "Yes, paranoia was at the heart of Timothy's theory."

Riker paused in his reading to digest the fact that the murdered agent was always Timothy to Jo. Only her FBI interrogators called the murder victim Agent Kidd.

He read the rest of her story: "Timothy entered the liquor store as another customer was leaving with a bottle of wine. This was a man he'd never met, yet the customer was obviously surprised to see him—a total stranger. Timothy gave the man a few seconds' head start, then followed him back into the street. But the man was gone. There was no sound of a car starting its engine. He must have run at top speed to get clear of that block so fast."

The FBI agent had returned to the store to interview the clerk. All he learned was that the departed customer had been overjoyed to see one particular wine in stock. In the clerk's words, "He thought he'd already bought the last bottle on the planet." According to Jo's best recall of Kidd's conversation with her, "Timothy said it was an oddball wine you'd never see in a food critic's column, though it was surprisingly good." And then Jo reminded her interrogators that the body of a dead juror had been found in that area on the following day.

Riker looked up from his reading. If Agent Kidd knew the taste of that wine, then he had gone to some trouble to track down another bottle of a scarce vintage. Though Jo's notes provided no such detail, Riker could name the wine and even the year. The bottom drawer in Johanna's armoire was stocked with ten bottles, all the same label, same vintage, but different store stickers and prices. He reached into a pile of bills from distributors and liquor stores in distant states. One reiterated the details of Jo's reward of a hundred dollars over retail cost. She had also been collecting this particular vintage, and the FBI only had her version of a *man* as the stranger in the liquor store.

He placed the receipts in another pile that he had mentally labeled with the query *To burn or not to burn?*

At the conclusion of her last interview, the FBI had dismissed her with thanks, then placed her in the Federal Witness Protection Program. By Jo's account, the feds had disregarded Timothy Kidd's Reaper sighting, for who would believe an insane story like that one?

Riker would. No one was more paranoid than a cop with the scars of four bullet wounds. He studied Jo's map of Chicago. Red circles marked the sites of three homicides, and one was four blocks away from the liquor store. He raised his eyes to the ceiling and played out the murdered FBI man's scenario on that blank white screen. Agent Timothy Kidd walked into a liquor store, and his mere presence startled another customer, a man he had never met. Most Chicagoans would be strangers to the Washington-based agent. Why, Kidd wonders, why does this customer appear to know him on sight? According to Jo's interview, the agent had visited only one crime scene in Chicago, and that one had belonged to the Reaper's second victim. Freaks sometimes returned to the sites of their murders to watch the ongoing show of cop cars and meat wagons, lights and cameras. Who but a haunter of crime scenes would have recognized Timothy Kidd as the law? And who but a guilty man would panic and run?

This was thin support for the identification of a prime suspect, but if it had been the Reaper in the liquor store that night, the most serious mistake he made was that flicker of recognition for an FBI agent who was also a world-class paranoid.

Good job, Timothy. Score one for the neurotics.

Riker had no conceit that the Bureau had not arrived at the same conclusion, so why was a serial killer still at large? Nowhere in Jo's files was there any mention of the suspect's name, nor even a description, and he was not surprised by that. It was the kind of thing that a smart cop, even a fed, would not confide in a civilian. Yet Agent Kidd had told her the name of the wine.

Unaware of time passing, crossing over from day into night, Riker did not recall turning on the lights so that he could continue to read every scrap of text, every news clipping and note. Before his alarm clock sounded, he was well versed on the Reaper murders, and it was time for Ian Zachary's show.

He turned on the radio, the source of the game clues.

"You crazy bitch!"

The sound engineer looked up from her computer screen. "Pick your words carefully, jerk-off, or I'll wipe all your calls."

Did she know they were still on the air? Yes, she did. Somewhat impressed, Ian Zachary lowered his voice as he spoke to his radio audience. "Crazy Bitch will take the next call after this word from our sponsor."

He pressed the button for the security lock. At the sound of the buzzer, a delivery boy entered the studio bearing a gift from a fan, Randy of SoHo. After the messenger had left the room, Zack continued his involuntary habit of checking the dark window of the producer's booth, looking for signs of movement within. Might Needleman be looking in on him tonight? Zachary considered the possibility that the producer was not shy, but brilliant, and playing a nervous game within the game. However, the more plausible theory was that his mysterious producer was a spy from the Federal Communications Commission. A federal court was still in the process of defining that fine line between entertainment and conspiracy to murder via public airways. The issue had been further complicated by all the newspapers and major television networks following the lead of Ian Zachary and his fans, reiterating every crackpot theory and juror sighting. The defense attorneys had argued that the Reaper had multiple sources for the same information, thus clouding the issue of cause and effect.

Upon ripping open the envelope from the local fan, he discovered that last night's caller had indeed snapped the picture of a surviving juror. Zachary glanced at the clock, then flipped the switch to open a line to the sound booth. "Oh, Crazy Bitch?"

She extended her middle finger to confirm that he was back on the air.

"Well, people," he said to his listening audience, "we have an official winner in the photo contest. Randy from SoHo, I assume you're listening tonight. So, Crazy Bitch, will you tell our contestant what he's won?"

Zack hit the time delay button to cut off a stream of obscenities from the sound booth. "That girl's really losing it. So, my friends, I propose a new contest. Pick the hour and the minute that she cracks. Something dramatic, maybe drool and speaking in tongues, pulling out patches of hair—mine or hers, your option. Five hundred dollars. Crazy Bitch will take the first ten callers. We won't have time for more players. I have a feeling that tonight's the night."

Oh, shit. Couldn't you wait another hour?

He overrode her own controls and cut to a commercial break five minutes ahead of schedule. The lights of her squirrel cage had gone out; and now he faced two black windows. She was taking a cue from Needleman and hiding in the dark.

Not for long, babe.

It was time to sweep out her idiot remains, the living body but not the mind—that was already lost.

Fun's over.

He raised the lights of his studio, for all the good that did. The lighting had been designed to suit his love of dark, cave-like environs. With the slight increase of illumination, he could barely make out her black silhouette in the booth. He walked toward his own lean ghost reflected in the darkened glass, enjoying this vision of himself, for he appeared to be strolling on thin air, neatly surpassing that tired old biblical trick of walking on the water.

At the top of her volume dial, Crazy Bitch screamed, *"Showtime!"*

He ripped the earphones off his head. *The pain, Jesus.* "Are you *crazy*?" he yelled at her—and how crazy was that? "Are you trying to break my eardrums?" Another silly question. Of course she wanted to hurt him. And his eyes were the next target. All the lights in her booth switched on at once. The desk lamp and track lights had been redirected at him, and he was blinded. The pain was passing off, but his vision was scorched with patches of hot white lights, and the earphones were still clutched in his hands when he heard the tinny distant sound of her voice at a normal decibel level, singing to him, "Oh, *jerk*-off?"

He lifted the microphone element to his lips and whispered, "You incredible *bitch.*"

She parried by extending her middle finger close to the glass. Her tone was actually sweet when she said, "We have a first-time caller on line three. He claims he's one of the surviving jurors."

"Good one," said Zack, all injury and hatred forgotten. What did it matter if this was a hoax? He had an audience of feebleminded, motivated believers. He ran to his panel and tapped the third light on his phone board. "Daddy loves you," he said to the caller, and he was sincere, for this one had drama potential. "Talk to me."

A man's angry voice responded, "You're an idiot!"

"The caller seems a bit confused," said Zack. "To recap for new listeners or anyone just tuning in, this man was on the jury of celebrity-blinded morons. He was so starstruck, he ignored all the evidence of guilt. We're talking blood and fingerprints, people. *DNA* and eyewitnesses. Out of three hundred million Americans, only the twelve jurors thought the defendant might be innocent. A verdict of sheer stupidity. No wonder the Reaper wants them all dead. Who doesn't? So, listeners, does our serial killer have a point? Is it time to clean out the gene pool?"

"Stop it!" yelled the caller. "You *can't*—"

"Or, as our hero the Reaper would say—is this juror too stupid to go on living? And now the most important question, the one that's worth hard cash. When will *this* one die?" Zack looked down at the photograph in his hand. It was a good likeness. "I didn't get your name. Who are you?"

"It's MacPherson, and you know damn well who I am!"

Yes, you fool.

The rules his lawyers had carefully laid out were tricky, but now that the juror had identified himself on the air, the man was fair game.

"McPherson? Still there?" Yes, he heard the sudden intake of breath. There was no more doubt. He had the genuine article on the line. "Any . . . last words?"

"How can you *do* this to me?" Frustration made the caller's voice crack.

Better and better.

"You and your fans," said MacPherson, "you did everything but draw that maniac a map to my damn *house!*" His voice was stronger, getting louder. "What the hell's *wrong* with you, man? I was one of the jurors who *set you free!*"

"Yes," said Ian Zachary. "So what's your point?"

7

CHARLES BUTLER, AN AVID COLLECTOR OF ANtiques, entered the only visually chilly room on the premises of Butler and Company. The furnishings of his business partner's office were twenty-first-century cold steel. It was a place of hard edges, mechanical clicks and whirs, and long shelves lined with electronics and technical manuals surrounding three computers on workstations. The single charming aspect of eighteenth-century arched windows had been neatly killed off with stark white metal blinds. Only one wall provided him with relief from severity; it was covered with cork from baseboard to ceiling and served as a gigantic bulletin board. This morning it added a rare human aspect to Mallory's private domain. It appeared as though Riker had taken all the papers from Johanna Apollo's suitcase and hurled them at the wall, pages sticking there of their own accord, and pushpins later added as an afterthought. Each crookedly hung sheet would be an affront to Mallory's pathological neatness.

And so Charles was unprepared for her response, and it gave him pause. She never smiled this way to convey any happiness. The young police detective paced the length of her cork wall, pausing sometimes to read a note or a newspaper article in its entirety. Her standard uniform of jeans, T-shirt and blazer only varied by color and material, smoky silk and cashmere today. Charles had long ago recognized this as the sign of a highly efficient brain with no spare time to waste upon wardrobe decisions. Her long black coat was slung over one arm. She had not yet committed to going or staying awhile.

Please stay.

They needed to talk about what she had done to Riker. While she scrutinized her wall, Charles was busy censoring his comments on this subject, culling the words *outrageous, dangerously irresponsible* and the like. But then he found himself altogether out of words. He stared at his shoes and said nothing. As her friend and foremost apologist, he would always excuse her most questionable behavior. By secondhand stories and deduction, he knew the darkest things about Mallory's childhood on the street, and he had paid dearly for that knowledge; on occasion, it still cost him sleep and peace of mind. She had lost everything that mattered to a little girl before she had even reached the age of reason, and yet a remarkable creature had emerged from devastating trauma. How prescient was the poet Yeats, for he had written his finest lines for Kathy Mallory long before she was made: *All changed; changed utterly. / A terrible beauty is born.*

"So now it begins," she said.

How he hated the sound of that. Charles faced the paper storm on her cork wall. "Riker finished this about an hour ago. I don't think he'd been to bed yet."

"Good," said Mallory. "I've got him hooked."

On any other day, Charles would have done headstands for the pleasure of her smile. However, this morning, he could only wish that she would stop, drop it, and not relish this mad game so much. He walked up behind her in the role of conscience and softly said, "You know this isn't wise. A psychotic shot Riker, and now you throw him in the path of a serial killer, *another* lunatic."

"That's what makes it so perfect. Another jury of idiots."

She stepped back to take in the entire sprawl of Riker's mess on the cork wall. "This case looks a lot like the horse that threw him."

Indeed, there was a clear parallel of jury verdicts and violence. If a teenage killer had not been found innocent, despite a plethora of incriminating evidence, then Riker, the prosecution's star witness, would not have been ambushed in his own home. And now another jury had come to an equally insane verdict in the Zachary trial, but, this time, the result had been a mass slaughter.

"However," said Charles, "this murderer is a bit more organized, more dangerous than the boy who shot Riker." He tapped the crime-scene photograph of a dead FBI agent, another parallel, for the Reaper also had a law-enforcement victim. In this case, it was an interesting departure from the juror killings. "What happens when this maniac recognizes Riker as a player? Given any thought to that?" Though he faced the wall, he was aware of Mallory's eyes on him, perhaps calculating that her only mistake was bringing him into the game.

One hand went to her hip as a warning. "You have a better way to fix Riker?"

"No." Sadly, he did not. Though one of his Ph.D.s was in psychology, he only applied it to assessing the stability of gifted clients, the better to find the right niches for them. He had never treated anyone as a patient, never even thought of opening that sort of practice. But Mallory, with no such background, was attempting shock therapy on a trauma victim in a very fragile state of mind. Charles made his own appraisal of the wall and pronounced it horrific. "You said you were going to feed him this case a piece at a time." A teaspoon of murder as medicine—that had been her stated intention. "This is too much."

"I know that," said Mallory. "But I didn't know about Dr. Apollo's stash, not until we tossed her hotel room. So what's the damage? Is there anything in her papers that would give Riker the whole picture?"

"Well, obviously he knows about the relationship with

Agent Kidd. But there's nothing here to tell him precisely how Dr. Apollo fits into the game."

"And I don't see that woman making any confessions." Mallory sat down at a workstation topped by a glowing monitor.

He watched as she downloaded photographs from a camera to a computer. The array of images appeared on the screen. Sometimes he wondered why she made so many portraits of Johanna Apollo. In most of them, the woman's deformity was covered by long tresses of dark hair and only mildly apparent in the forward curve of her upper body. His favorite was a close-up of the doctor's face. A man could make friends with those warm brown eyes. The most recent picture was a full-body shot. The wind had ripped aside the sheltering curtain of hair to reveal the hump. Somehow he knew that this would be Mallory's last portrait of Dr. Apollo. She had finally achieved the full exposure of vulnerability. And Charles felt suddenly protective of this woman he had yet to meet.

"You don't like her, do you, Mallory? Please tell me she's not a suspect."

"The only players I don't suspect are the dead ones."

"You never did tell me how you got caught up in this business. When did you first—"

"The day I met Riker's hunchback," she said. "I ran a background check on her alias, and the documentation was just too perfect, too neat. That's always a good marker for the FBI's witness protection program." Mallory was looking past him now and suddenly distracted. She rose from her chair and stepped close to the cork wall, honing in on the only sample of Riker's messy handwriting. She read this margin note aloud. "'Jo's wine.' What's *that* about?" A more careful perusal of the board offered her no enlightenment. "Damn Riker. He's holding out on me."

Johanna Apollo slung her duffel bag over one shoulder, and this was Mugs's cue to cry. There was a touch of betrayal about the cat's eyes, for she was obviously abandoning him. She would not be there to defend him when the maid arrived with the water pistol. Johanna was in no position to complain about the hotel staff defending themselves from a mauling, though she gave them hazardous-duty pay in the form of lavish tips. Also, Mugs preferred open warfare to being confined to his pet carrier. Nothing could drive him quite as crazy as being locked up in that box. She bent low to pat him where there were no memories of damaged nerves to make him scratch her. He pressed his head into the cup of her palm and cried again. In this moment, he managed to communicate a desperation, a message that he was already having a bad day, and he would be lost if she left him behind.

Upon entering the bathroom, she opened a box from her store of pet tranquilizers. She disliked drugging Mugs, though sometimes it was a mercy. If the maid arrived and found him docile and drowsing, it would not be necessary for the woman to shoot him with the water pistol in self-defense. After breaking open a capsule, Johanna poured half of it into his water bowl.

Next, lest Marvin Argus return with his own search warrant, she unlocked the armoire, retrieved a packet of letters and folded them into the pocket of her denim jacket. And last, she counted up her wine bottles, a neurotic ritual worthy of Timothy Kidd.

Mallory tidied up Riker's careless pushpin style, moving sheets of paper to hang at exact right angles to the architecture. No, on second glance, Charles decided that she had actually improved upon that, for now he realized that the building had settled out of alignment over the past century. He put more trust in Mallory's internal plumb line that ran infallibly to the center of the earth.

"So you spent some time with Riker," she said. "Notice any changes, anything odd?"

"No, in most respects, he seems his old self. Quite relaxed I'd say, no tics or twitches that I was aware of. He does have a tendency to slam doors, a very un-Riker-like thing to do. But that's been going on ever since the—"

"He's angry."

"No," said Charles. "He was rather affable."

"He's angry at *me*." And the slow shake of her head said that she had no idea why—only that this was true.

He understood her rationale. Underlying anger could explain Riker's monkish behavior since his release from the hospital. "Perhaps it's not *you*—not something quite so personal." And here he had the good sense to stop, for she disliked being challenged. Her arms were folded against him, and her eyes narrowed, reminding him that—true or untrue—she was *never* wrong.

"Why don't I refer him to a psychiatrist?" said Charles. "Therapy is what he needs."

"A talking cure? I don't have time for that." She amended this pronouncement, adding, "*Riker* doesn't have time. His apartment is a pit. Mrs. Ortega says it should be condemned."

"Well, that's because she never saw his old apartment in Brooklyn. I'm sure it can't be in worse shape." Ah, he had made another error, finding a logical explanation that disagreed with her own. He turned his eyes away from hers, hoping to avoid another ocular argument.

"The mess is twice as bad," she said. "So you haven't been down there yet?"

"No." He had not been invited. But now he gathered that Mallory had been visiting Riker's apartment, and not by invitation. She passed through locked doors too easily, so adept at breaking and entering—invading. He wondered how to broach the subject of Riker's need for privacy and security now more than ever. Empathy would be the wrong approach. She had none.

"I don't see anything wrong with his reflexes," she said. "You agree?"

"I didn't find any signs of physical disorder." He rattled off the items noted in every covert examination of Riker. "Motor skills, eye movement, speech patterns, reasoning ability—everything spot on." He knew it was frustrating her that there were no technical manuals on the subject of rebuilding Riker.

"Then it's the psych evaluation that has him freaked."

"Well, that makes my case for getting him to a therapist. The sooner we get him into treatment—"

"No time," she said, somewhat testy now, for she disliked repeating herself. "It's budget-cutting season, and Commissioner Beale is cleaning house. The little bastard has the soul of a cost accountant. He'd love to get rid of a senior detective with Riker's pay grade." She turned back to the board, back to the game. "Dr. Apollo was on two murder scenes. She had insider information from Agent Kidd."

Charles could see where this was going. "It might be a mistake to develop her as a suspect. Think about it. You say Riker hired her three months ago. Well, that's when he started shaving again. Oh, and his first haircut since the shooting—same time frame. Granted, that's not much to work with, but suppose he genuinely cares for this woman?"

Oh, Mallory, if a cat could smile. What great satisfaction he saw in her eyes.

"So he *does* have feelings for her. And you *knew* that." Oh, of course she did. What was he *thinking*? Dr. Apollo was Mallory's hostage. "So that's how you got Riker to play the game. Tell me, Mallory, how did you set him up? Did you whisper something scary in his ear? What did you say? No, let me guess. Oh, incidentally, Riker, this woman, this one bright spot in your otherwise miserable existence, she's in deep trouble. Maybe she'll die. Something like that?" Suddenly very tired, he leaned back against the cork wall. "I know you didn't tell him that Dr. Apollo was *your* favorite suspect. Then he'd have to choose up sides, wouldn't he? And it might not be your side."

Annoyed, she turned her back on him, not liking his tone one bit.

Well, tough.

Disregarding two facts—that he loved his life and she carried a gun—he reached out, grabbed her by the shoulders and spun her around. Well, that opened her eyes a bit wider.

"So I'm right," he said. "You planted a threat in that poor man's mind. You might as well have put a gun to Johanna Apollo's head. What about the effect on Riker? Did you give that any thought at all?" He was angry, close to shouting. Oh, what the hell. He yelled at her, "Clearly, you don't know what you're doing!"

Though—actually—she did.

He could see that now. Her cat's smile came stealing back, forcing him to admit that he had also been sucked into the game. And his own fears for Riker, hostage number two, would bind him to Mallory until it was played out. His hands fell away from her shoulders. His two-minute experiment with insurrection was over.

Hostilities forgotten—as if she had ever taken him seriously—she leaned down to tap the keyboard of the nearest computer, saying, "If Riker's afraid of the psych evaluation, he can fake it." She brought up a file with a questionnaire. "The test is in two parts, written and oral."

Charles recognized the screen image as the cover page of a personality profile. Many other pages would follow. The lengthy test would repeat and reword questions as traps for false replies. Mallory split the screen to display another document with recommended responses.

"All he has to do," she said, "is memorize this one. The city's too cheap to order new tests. This is going to be so easy. After a little coaching from you on the oral evaluation, he'll be back at work."

"This won't help him, Mallory. It's not that simple." He could read the look on her face. This was desertion from the ranks. "Getting his job back and getting him back on the job—that's two separate problems."

"He's already on the job," said Mallory. "He took this stuff out of Apollo's place so we wouldn't lose it to the feds."

"No, he's protecting his friend, Johanna—" Charles lost his train of thought. He was staring at the computer monitor and a dateline that corresponded to Mallory's last psychiatric evaluation, a mandatory test following the shooting of a suspect. He had always wondered how she navigated these examinations, missing all the traps set to catch her own peculiar bent of mind. This electronic cheat sheet forever killed his idea of her as an innocent savage. She knew exactly what she was. And Mallory was now twice wounded in his eyes, for she must realize that she would never be quite—

"Do you ever listen to the radio, Charles?"

"If you mean Zachary's program, no." He preferred newspapers to television and radio accounts of the Reaper, and he believed his view was less biased for that.

Mallory had moved on to another computer in the row of three terminals. She tapped the keyboard again, and the speakers announced the Ian Zachary show. "I have them all in my audio file. This is shock radio."

Charles was left alone to listen to the archived programs, and soon he had the gist of the game and the man who ran it—*another* sociopath.

Johanna had returned from her last stint at cleaning up crime scenes, and Mugs was still drowsy from his long nap. He slowly followed her into the bathroom and sat down at her feet, not having the energy to rub up against her legs for a fresh spate of agony, love and slashes—a proper hello.

The blood of the last job had never touched her skin, yet she washed her hands. It was a fight not to wash them a second and third time, though the cat would be the only witness to her compulsive behavior. She could not say when this urge had begun. Perhaps when she had opened her mind to Timothy's paranoia, a second neurosis, a hitchhiker sickness, had also entered in. She looked at herself in the mirror, then looked beyond her image to the shower curtain surrounding the bathtub. Though there was not even the shadow of an interloper, she pulled the curtain aside.

No one there. Of course not. And no one in the closets. She checked them all.

After changing into a suit, she wrapped her shoulders in a

stylish shawl, then pulled it over her head to form a hood. The bulk of material hid the line of her deformity quite well. Mugs was slow to react to this signal that she was going out again. Thanks to the drug, there was no sign of panic in his eyes. He padded alongside her as she walked to the door, and he did not cry this time. There was only mild curiosity in his eyes as he watched her leaving him once more.

8

IT WOULD BE GENEROUS TO SAY THAT THE DINING area was eight feet wide and twelve deep. There were four tables, small as postage stamps, and Riker was the only patron who did not take his foil-wrapped food and run. He was hoping to avoid his meal for as long as possible. The counterman was back in the kitchen having a protracted discussion with the cook. The subject of their argument was the simulation of a cheeseburger from their store of strict vegetarian ingredients. Riker had no plans to eat their concoction. He had ordered lunch for the sole purpose of renting a view of the hotel across the street. Having given up any hope of coffee, he opened the beverage cabinet and passed over all the health food juices to select a bottle of water.

He kept one eye on the front wall, all glass and neatly framing the Chelsea Hotel. When Jo had returned home from her last crime-scene cleanup, she had been followed by two men in suits. Federal shadows? In plain sight? This was not Riker's idea of a covert surveillance detail. Neither would those two men fit the protocols for bodyguards, for they had followed Jo at the distance of half a block. And now Marvin

Argus stepped out on the sidewalk. Nervous little bastard, his movements were jerky as his head snapped left and right. Finally the agent's gaze settled on the restaurant window.

Riker lifted his water bottle in a salute.

Special Agent Argus crossed the street in an unseemly hurry, and pushed through the glass door to greet Riker with all the suspicion this encounter deserved. Taking the only vacant chair at the table, the FBI man was forced to sit with his back to the window. "You just happened to be in the neighborhood?"

"I knew I'd find you here." And this was only half a lie. "I figured you'd stake out Jo's hotel."

Argus smiled, so willing to believe that this visit was on his own account. "So you've given my offer some more thought." He splayed both hands to say he was waiting for the decision. "And?"

Riker had never been susceptible to prompting. He drank his water, dragging out the silence and listening to the fast nervous tap of Argus's shoes under the table. He set the plastic bottle down very slowly. "Did Timothy Kidd ever give you a name for the Reaper? It's not like I think you'll tell me who the guy was. All I wanna know is—did Kidd give you a solid suspect before he died? Did he get that close?"

Argus was startled. His eyes shifted to one side, a hint that he was preparing another fairy tale. In this moment, when Riker was not being watched, he glanced at the door to the Chelsea Hotel. The FBI man held his silence as the counterman appeared with a fake cheeseburger. Riker gave it the sniff test, and it failed. "Try again, pal. This isn't even close."

The man walked away with his rejected offering, and another backroom discussion with the cook ensued, guaranteeing Riker at least fifteen minutes of privacy. He rapped his knuckles on the table to remind the fed that he was waiting for the next lie.

"Timmy had a suspect." Argus pretended interest in the beverage cabinet by the table. "But he named the wrong guy. Poor bastard. He was really past it by then, seeing things that weren't there." The agent turned back to Riker, watching his face in earnest now. "I could give you more details, but first I'd need a little something from you. Just a little—"

"How did you rule out Kidd's prime suspect?"

"The alibi was me and my crew. The next juror died at three in the morning. We were watching Timmy's suspect round the clock, covering all the exits of the apartment building."

"How many men were on that detail?"

"What? Four agents. All day, all night. I'm telling you, the suspect's alibi was solid."

Riker did the math of twelve-hour stints, partners split between two exits and no one to keep each agent company and awake in the graveyard hours. He recalled the drowsiness of that late shift, the first night of a detail when no amount of coffee—

Agent Argus was turning round to look at the hotel as Jo walked out the front door and down the sidewalk, and Riker said, "I know who the Reaper is." The window was forgotten, and he had all of the agent's attention. "I'm betting it's the suspect Kidd gave you. One of your guys screwed up and went to sleep on the job." Riker rose from the table, hoping to convey that he was suddenly fed up with this man's company—and that was true. "You had the bastard's name and address all this time." He laid down the cash to cover his uneaten lunch and walked quickly to the door, never glancing back to catch Argus's reaction.

The slow hydraulic pump above the restaurant door prevented him from slamming it. Standing out on the sidewalk, he watched Jo's gray shawl in the distance. She was so changed in this disguise, he had almost failed to recognize her. But even without eyeglasses, he knew that long-legged walk; he knew it better than any man on the planet; he had spent that much time speculating on the shape of the limbs beneath her jeans. In the short skirt she wore today, her legs more than lived up to the fantasy.

There was no need to close the distance as he followed her down Seventh Avenue, then underground and onto a southbound train. He already knew where she was going. According to his source, the woman was good at spotting and dodging her shadowers. This, of course, was Mallory's rationale for sometimes losing Jo's trail. But no one had ever shaken off Riker, not once in all his years on the force.

It was a cold day, yet Victor Patchock was perspiring profusely. He blamed this on the cheap red wig and the press of the surrounding subway passengers. He had no fear of getting caught by the cop in the brown leather jacket. Riker was so intent on following his own prey that he never looked back at his stalker, a smaller man lost among the taller riders.

The train stopped at the Franklin Street station in Tribeca. Victor had lost sight of the detective. With swipes of both hands, he wiped the sweat from his eyes, and the white cane dropped from his slippery fingers. He bent low to retrieve it, and the dark glasses slid down his wet nose and fell to the floor, where they were trampled by departing feet. He snatched up cane and glasses, holding each in a tight fist. And now his vision was blurred not by sweat but tears. He turned his crying face to another passenger, and the man stepped backward *slowly* in that New York drill of no sudden movements while encountering a lunatic. For the moment, Victor, the faux blind man, had truly lost his sight as he fought his way to the door of the train, colliding with those who were boarding. Tears falling, his mouth wide open in a silent scream, he waved his cane in the air, and the crowd magically backed away as he rushed off the train, stepping onto the platform, which might well have been a dark hole for all he knew. He made his way toward what he hoped was the exit, looked up and saw a bright patch of daylight.

Victor scrambled up the stairs, stumbling on every second step, and out onto the sidewalk, breathing deep and blinking like a mole. He opened one fist to see the twisted frames of his sunglasses, then put them on, lopsided as they were. He fancied himself to be all but invisible now and fearless. And then he spotted Riker—and he was terrified.

Riker walked the streets of Tribeca, craning his neck to look up at the buildings, unabashed at playing the gawking tourist. He loved this town, terrible and wonderful. Each time he turned a corner, he walked into another state of mind. Though he might flirt with Mexico, he could never leave this great, grand, bitch city; it had him by the balls. His immediate surroundings lacked the hustle of the Financial District or any other distinctive marker. Tribeca was a shifty character among New York neighborhoods. There was no quirky definition to the façades; her face gave no clue to her intentions. Between the sprawling yuppie lofts and the hole-in-the-wall bodegas, anything might be going on.

Riker glanced over one shoulder—just checking his back. He was vaguely unsettled by the blurred shape of a dark coat disappearing round a corner, but this was beyond squinting distance for a man who would not wear eyeglasses in public. He caught only the impression of a splash of bright red and a long slice of white on black. Was this another stalker, one of the people who followed him day in and day out?

No. This feeling was only nerves, nothing more; this was his mantra as he headed toward a renovated warehouse, home to a slew of small commercial ventures. The sign in one third-floor window advertised classes in self-defense. If the feds had ever followed Jo this far, that would have been their first guess for her business at this address. After entering the building, he followed Mallory's instructions, emerging from the elevator on the third floor. There was a sign on the fire door at the end of the hall, large block letters that even he could read told him that there was no access from the stairwell side. Clever Jo had picked this location well. No covert surveillance crew would have dared to use the elevator and risk a hallway encounter with her.

According to Mallory, the offices that did not advertise their businesses were rented on time-shares and paid for in cash—always a good sign of criminal activity. Neither the tenants nor a tax-evading landlord would readily share information with local police or government cops. And any verbal inquiries by a tall blonde with memorable green eyes would have gotten back to Jo and put her on guard. Mallory must have been so pissed off.

On his way down the hall, he looked in on the karate class of women slamming one another to floor mats. They were playing roles of victims and attackers, and deeply bowing with entirely too much courtesy. He wondered if these students understood that their training would only help them if a real rapist agreed to strike the classroom poses. Then the guy would have to wait for the women to kick him in the right place. And maybe, given a good-natured pervert, time would be allowed for a second shot if they missed the testicles on the first try.

He continued on down the hall and found a young man in conversation with an elderly janitor. The pair stood in front of the room that was Riker's own destination.

"You're late. They've already started," said the old man with his cluster of keys in hand. He unlocked the door for the other visitor, not wanting to disturb a meeting in progress by using the buzzer. Riker followed the other man through the door, nodding his thanks to the janitor, as if he had also come here by invitation.

In order to find out which of the many doors led to Jo's rented rooms, he guessed that Mallory, poor kid, had probably been forced to plant illegal eavesdropping equipment in every office on this floor. He could never ask her about that, but it was a safe bet.

Upon entering the small reception area, he could hear Jo's voice behind a closed door. She was welcoming the new arrival. Instead of following the other man into the next room, Riker settled into a shabby chair with worn upholstery and pretended to read a magazine plucked from the only table. More people entered this waiting room, and now he knew that Mallory had been right about the members of this select group, for he recognized these two visitors.

The little girl tugged on her mother's hand, wanting to stop awhile by Riker's chair, saying, "I remember you."

"Mr. *Riker!*" The child's mother was more enthusiastic with her own greeting. Fortunately, her voice was too soft to carry above the conversation in the next room. The woman reached for his hand and pumped it up and down, grinning widely, so happy to see him. "*Thank* you. Thank you so much." She caressed her child's curly dark hair. "Not the same little girl you met the night—the—"

The night your husband cracked half the bones in your face? The night you killed the bastard with a kitchen knife?

The damage was still visible in the broken planes of the mother's cheek and nose. Riker remembered her injuries well. The catching detective had called him to this woman's home while the blood was still wet on her kitchen floor and droplets streamed down the walls. An assistant DA had made the call of justifiable homicide, and the confessed killer, the victim's own wife, was not charged. The crime scene had been released to the cleaners that same night, for the mother and her child were poor. They had nowhere else to go.

Riker knew that feeling.

Jo, his new trainee, had been his helper on that pro bono job. And he well remembered this little girl, the witness to an assault on her mother and the death of her father. What a difference. Once she had been a painful reminder of Kathy Mallory at the same age—same look about the eyes.

Back in the days when he was still allowed to call his partner Kathy, the former street kid had been more determined to hold on to her own emotional wounds, insisting that her history belonged to her alone, and, as a child, she had dealt with it alone—and so quietly, without tears or complaint, without recovery or repair. But this little girl before him now was making a comeback, a return to humanity. Her eyes were no longer adult and wary when she smiled for him. Jo had done a good job. What a pity that there had been no talented Dr. Apollo to heal young Kathy.

And while he was admiring this less damaged child, the

mother expressed her thanks to Ned's Crime Scene Cleaners for the generosity of providing a therapy group. Mallory had uncovered the function of these rented rooms weeks ago, but Riker had only learned of it today. And now one mystery was solved: Jo's work on homicides was her introduction to the survivors, trauma victims all.

Mallory must have been so disappointed to find no money motive here, that far from working a fiddle on the side for profit, Dr. Apollo was applying her old trade free of charge. But trust a cop to come up with a sinister reason for acts of charity. The young detective had damned the doctor with the filthy crime of atonement. And now he remembered the gist of Mallory's final caustic remark: for her next act, Johanna Apollo would be washing the feet of lepers—expiating what sin?

Mother and child disappeared into the next room, and Riker listened to the healing balm of Jo's conversation on the other side of the door. He closed his eyes to be alone with that voice that also spoke to him.

Mallory slid her lock picks into the back pocket of her jeans, then opened the door to Riker's apartment. As always, her first impulse was to open a window, but Riker might notice the missing smell of stale smoke and the sweet rot of leftover food. Other emotions were in play: revulsion, and the almost unbearable desire to create order out of this unholy mess. But intuition and distrust held sway and led her to the fireplace, and there she found the evidence against him. There were no signs of a burnt log in the grate, only the flat ashes and remnants of papers.

A few of Dr. Apollo's notes? One of these pages might have explained Riker's cryptic line about the wine.

Well, this was not the plan—not *her* plan. Riker was running a different game. There could be no other explanation for this travesty of ashes. It was like cheating at chess—also Riker's game, or once upon a time it was. There was no chess set in this apartment. She had looked for it on previous expeditions, recalling the set he had thrown away and wondering if he had bought a new one. Evidently he never played anymore, and Mallory sometimes wondered if she might be the cause of that.

As the foster child of Helen and Inspector Louis Markowitz, most of her baby-sitters had been cops. The Markowitzes' early experiments with civilians had all ended badly; tender old ladies and teenage girls had proven no match for a ten-year-old semireformed street thief. Out of all her cop wardens, Riker had had the most staying power. He had taught her to sit still for hours—he had taught her to play chess. The child had loved the game, but hated losing, and she had devised schemes of distraction to cheat him. One night, his hand had been faster than hers. He had captured her tiny fist, which had barely concealed a stolen chessman, the pawn that had previously blocked her hopes of bringing down Riker's queen.

"Is this fun for you, kid?" Those had been his last words to her that night. She had watched him pick up a letter opener and gouge the cheap plastic pawn with a *K* for Kathy. He set it on his mantelpiece, then tossed the other chessmen into the trash can along with the board and never mentioned it again—no punishment, no lecture, nothing but silence. And he never ratted her out to her foster parents.

Secrets had such power.

Every night for a week, that ruined pawn on Riker's mantel was the last thing young Kathy thought about before she went to sleep. Guilt was not in her vocabulary; she was simply mystified. This puzzle followed the little girl all through the days. She bought a new chess set, actually paid for it instead of stealing one. Every day after school, she carted her chessmen and her board to Special Crimes Unit and sat for long hours in the squad's lunchroom—waiting. After three days, Riker finally came in to play.

She lost, lost every game, game after game, for a week. And then she won. And *then,* while Riker was still at work, she broke into his apartment and stole that defaced pawn from his mantelpiece. She had it still. It was in the back of her closet, hidden in the small box of a child's treasures: shoplifted items and baseball cards.

During her years as a cop, what sometimes passed for conscience was an echo of Riker asking, "Is this fun for you, kid?"

Yes. Yes it was. She loved to win, and she did not cheat the pieces of evidence that worked against her cases. She won because she was *good*—and because she was not above unlawful entry, robbing data banks and lying like crazy. But she never destroyed evidence.

Mallory stared at the ashes in Riker's fireplace.

Well, the man was not in his right mind, and she blamed Dr. Apollo for this. Yes, it was the doctor's fault. Mallory fixed this thought in her mind and pushed away the idea that she was cheating the pieces to hold Riker harmless and blameless.

At the end of the hour, when the last of the patients had filed out, Riker entered the next room to catch the psychiatrist unawares amid a clutter of wet tissues, ashtrays and paper coffee cups. This was Jo transformed. Earlier, he had only glimpsed her from a distance and only the back of her shawl. Most of his observation time had been devoted to the long expanse of nylon stockings below the short skirt—oh, and the high heels, stilettos, his personal favorites. But now he was staring at her wine-dark lipstick, and it shocked him. Until this moment, he had only seen her face naked.

"Hey, Jo."

She was folding metal chairs and leaning them against the wall when she turned to see him standing near the door. Guilt was there to read in her face and her body language. Her head lowered and her hands folded in prayer, as if asking forgiveness for her crimes. His partner would have loved this moment, but Riker was not enjoying his role this afternoon. He was at war with himself. Always inexplicably happy to be in the same room with Jo, he was also unsettled by suspicion, a symptom of Mallory's poison.

Aw, lady, what have you done?

He kept his silence, waiting for Jo to speak. There was a rhythm to an interrogation and it came as naturally to him as breathing. He was already predicting her opening gambit and laying plans to stun her and knock her sensibilities loose from their moorings.

"So you've read everything," she said. "And now you want an explanation." She slowly settled down on a chair, head bowed in the time-honored posture of the police interview.

How many times had she been through this before?

His face was somber as he walked toward her. "You know who the Reaper is."

Jo shook her head.

"That wasn't a question, lady. Agent Kidd told you. That's what brought you to New York. The Reaper's here, isn't he?"

"Timothy never told me."

"Then you worked it out on your own."

"You'd have to be as paranoid as Timothy to—"

"Been there," said Riker. "The Reaper was the guy he met in the liquor store. I believe his story." And now he saw shock in her eyes—and something else. Fresh guilt? Yes, and he nodded to say, *I can read your damn mind.* Aloud, he said, "But you didn't believe him, did you, Jo? Not then. Not till he died."

"And now you know all my secrets." She smiled to pass this off as banter. "I failed him—*badly.*"

"What about Bunny, that poor homeless bastard? What was that all about? Did you use him for a sparring partner? Is that how it started? Just a little practice for the main event?"

"That's not fair."

"Yeah, life sucks." He stood before her, not bending one bit, forcing her to look up at him as he was looking *out* at her—as if across a great gulf. "And what about Mugs? I think that cat keeps you in a constant state of alert. Hard to tell when he'll go ballistic, isn't it? Good practice for a scary situation. Or is Mugs your burglar alarm? Wouldn't take much to set him off."

"And sometimes a cat is just a cat. I love Mugs, I do."

"Then don't take chances, Jo. Live a long life. 'Cause if you die, you know what'll happen to that cat. If you're not around to protect him, he'll get kicked in the teeth by the next cop he mauls. Nobody's gonna take him to the vet and put him down with a nice painless needle. Whoever finds him first is gonna stomp him into the rug. Or maybe Mugs will get away with just a few missing teeth and some cracked ribs."

She rose from the chair, then picked up a plastic bag and collected a fallen tissue from the floor, clearly announcing the end of this conversation.

Not so fast, Jo, not quite yet.

"I won't be coming back to work." She avoided his eyes, and her voice became more formal, as if he were a stranger, just one more cop to deal with. "I left my resignation with Miss Byrd."

"Yeah, I heard. So you'll want your suitcase back."

"Yes." She walked about the room, bending low to pick up the cups and to empty the ashtrays into a plastic bag. "If you don't mind, could you drop it off at my hotel?"

"No, I don't think so." His voice was flat, giving away nothing, as he pulled one of Ned's business cards from his wallet. "You'll have to come and get it." He scrawled his address on the back of the card, then left it on the metal chair. "My place, seven o'clock. I'll cook. You bring the wine."

Jo walked everywhere in grace, and so the stumble gave her away. Knowing his preference for cheap bourbon and beer, she would probably bet her stock portfolio that he did not own a corkscrew, and now her thoughts must go to the wine in the bottom drawer of her armoire.

Riker ambled across the floor, taking his own time. He paused at the far end of the room and turned around to stare at her. All the trappings of a cop fell away for a moment, and he was only a man, as easily killed as any other. And she *could* kill him—with words, a look. He wanted to say something to her, something—personal. Ducking his head a bare inch, as if expecting a hail of laughter for this foolish unspoken idea, he held her glance a moment longer before turning back to the door. These days he left every room with a bang—not so loud as a paralyzing gunshot—just a satisfying slam that rattled every door in its frame.

9

RIKER COULD NOT SAY HOW HE HAPPENED TO FIND himself so far uptown in the neighborhood of wealth. From long habit, his feet knew the route of subway stairs and sidewalks leading to this Park Avenue apartment building. A liveried doorman greeted him with genuine affection, and another fiver traveled from Riker's pocket to his, though there was nothing new to report. Even at this posh address, betrayal was cheap and affordable.

Riker stepped back to the curb and looked up at one lighted window. A pale woman hovered there—expectant. This was the mother of the boy who had ambushed him. Her face was so much like her son's, though she lacked that wild-eyed look of crazy all the time. Her eyes were only fearful—of him. That much detail could not be seen on such a high floor; he simply knew this to be true.

And the woman knew.

If her child came home again, Riker would kill him.

As if reading his thoughts, the woman shrank back from the window, and Riker bowed his head in the manner of a shamed terrorist who has brought his bomb to the wrong door. He carried himself away from this innocent woman and walked on down the broad avenue—a man waiting to explode.

Mallory's small tan car pulled up in front of the Park Avenue building. The wealthy tenants, a man and a woman, withdrew to the safety of the lobby, preferring to communicate via the doorman, their conduit to the outside world. Over the past six months, they had grown skittish and shy of being waylaid by reporters, and they had come to fear police. Their faces were pale from infrequent forays into the sunlight.

As Mallory left her car and approached the doorman, she glanced at the couple on the other side of the glass entryway. They were staring at her, discussing her. Then they caught her eye, and now they fled across the lobby toward the elevator. She wondered if they knew about the doorman's profits and how easily he sold their private lives.

"Mallory." The doorman moved toward her, edging sideways like a crab, wanting no one from the building's interior to see the folding money that he anticipated. "You told me Riker wouldn't be back." He feigned a sigh. "Ah, those poor people. I don't think they can handle any more of this."

"I said I'd take care of it." She handed him a bill much larger than any of Riker's shabby bribes, instantly renewing this man's friendship and allegiance. He pocketed his money, then gave her a broad smile that said, *Screw those poor people. What can I do for you today?*

"What did Riker want?"

"Same old thing. He asked if they'd left the building in the last few days. Oh, yeah, and did they have any new visitors."

"And you said?"

"They don't go nowhere. They don't see nobody." He looked over one shoulder to be sure that the lobby was clear of prying eyes. "The missus, she feels sorry for Riker. But the mister's really steamed."

"But no threats, right? They didn't call in a complaint?"

"Naw, they don't want any more trouble with the cops. The truth, Mallory? They were more afraid of their own kid than Riker. Poor bastard. I told 'em the guy's a little nuts, but not the dangerous kind of crazy. Not like that son of—" He stopped abruptly, correctly intuiting that she would do him some damage if he continued with this line of prattle.

"He's not crazy," she said. "Don't you put that idea in their heads one more time."

Mallory felt no compassion for the parents of Riker's shooter. Those *poor* people had spent a million dollars on lawyers so their son would be free to ambush a cop. "You tell them I don't want to hear about any harassment complaints. Make that real clear."

Had that sounded sufficiently menacing? Yes. The doorman was back-stepping.

She wanted fear to be the strong point of his translation when he carried her message back to those millionaires with their psychotic genes and good lawyers. They had always known what kind of monster they had raised, yet they had not locked the boy away. And now they had no right to whine about the damaged man who sometimes haunted Park Avenue.

In honor of Johanna's visit, the dirty laundry had been stashed in his bedroom, where yesterday's socks joined the pairs previously scattered about the front room. While Riker waited, he began to see his apartment through Mrs. Ortega's eyes. He regretted tossing out the cleaning woman before she could do much more than leave her little footprints in the dust. A man could lose a corpse beneath the mound of black plastic garbage bags piling near the door. How much time had passed since he had last been inspired to carry out trash on collection night? Weeks? A month?

He looked at his watch, then dismissed the idea that Mrs. Ortega might make an emergency house call. After closing the doors to the kitchen and bathroom, two problems were solved. And now he rationalized away the rest of the mess in the front room. The state of this litter pit would take the lady by surprise. She would never see the first shot coming.

And the walls were thick. If she screamed, no one would hear it.

Mallory passed through the stairwell door, and entered the squad room of Special Crimes Unit, a large space with a haphazard arrangement of desks and one wall banked with tall, grimy windows overlooking the narrow SoHo street. Six men were working overtime tonight, filling in the gap left by Riker's forced departure and her own unauthorized sabbatical. The detectives sat amid the clutter and litter of their caseloads, files and notes and coffee cups, shouting questions at one another, barking deli orders to a police aide and holding telephone conversations.

All noise and motion ceased.

The men lifted their heads in the unison of chorus girls with shoulder holsters. Their eyes were trained on the squad's lone female as she crossed the room to her desk, the only desk at perfect right angles to the wall. Three days ago, this had been the most fanatically neat work space on the planet. No more. The locks on the drawers had been pried open, leaving scratch marks on the metal. The contents had been pawed over and jumbled, some of it strewn across her blotter, and the rest was on the floor. Case files and notebooks lay open, and her penchant for compulsive neatness was exposed in the spill of a drawer stocked with cleaning supplies.

But Mallory did not implode.

And hope died all around the room, for the show was obviously over and hardly worth the wait. The frozen tableau came back to life as talking and shouting resumed and papers shuffled.

Mallory turned to Detective Janos, a man with the large and solid build of a refrigerator that could talk and quote Milton. He had a brutal face that appealed to parents and parole officers alike, one that could frighten their charges into good behavior, and his was the most compassionate face in the squad room tonight. But sympathy was not what Mallory wanted.

He rose from his chair and slowly ambled toward her ruined desk, shaking his head to convey the commiserations of *Ain't it a shame?* and *What's this world coming to?* His voice was incongruously soft when he said, "I know what it looks like, kid, but nothing was taken." He hunkered down to retrieve a can of metal polish that had rolled under her chair.

"This is Coffey's work," said Mallory. Lieutenant Coffey might as well have gouged his name into the metal alongside all the other scratches. No one else would have dared to desecrate her personal space.

Janos shot a glance at the window that ran the length of the lieutenant's private office. The blinds were drawn, and the door was closed. "I wouldn't go in there right now if I were you. The boss just got rid of two vultures from Internal Affairs. They found out that Riker was working full-time for his brother Ned."

"He doesn't work there anymore. I took care of that."

"But he *did* work there." Janos, the quintessential gentleman, was on his knees, picking up the case files and notes strewn at her feet. "And the whole time Riker was working, he collected checks for full disability."

"He never cashed those checks." Mallory snatched the papers from his hands before he could put them into the wrong drawer. "And Riker only took a job after the department stopped his payroll deposits."

"Oh, the lieutenant knows that," said Janos, gathering pens and paper clips into his large meaty hands. "And that's what he told IA. Then he told 'em Riker was railroaded into a pension and showed 'em a copy of the appeal forms. And then he says, 'Where do you bastards get off harassing a decorated cop, a *wounded* cop?' So the boss holds up four fingers, and I'm thinkin', naw, that's three too many. But then he yells, 'Four bullet wounds! Count my fingers, you *morons!*' I thought that was a real nice touch. And then the bastards left—real fast. Case closed."

Mallory stared at her violated desk. "But that's got nothing to do with why Coffey popped all these locks. Right?"

"I'm getting to that."

Janos dumped his collection of small objects into her top drawer with no regard for the correct compartments of the plastic desk organizer. Mallory bit back a rebuke and quickly slotted the paper clips, pens and pencils into the proper square and rectangular wells.

"The district attorney sent one of his twits over here to hassle you," said Janos. "He wanted the package you promised. The trial's tomorrow, and he's a little antsy about it."

And that would be all the evidence she had been asked to develop for a pending court case. It had taken only a few hours to gather it, and she had done that three days ago but never turned it in.

"Coffey tried to reach you." The large detective rose to a stand, holding her feather duster delicately between his thumb and forefinger. "But you don't answer your beeper anymore."

"I'm on comp time." She snatched the feather duster and dropped it into its proper place. She planned to close this lower drawer quietly, not wanting to give the other men the satisfaction of a slam.

"But, Mallory, you never actually did the paperwork for time off."

She slammed the drawer, causing heads to turn, and she never bothered to lower her voice. "If I put in for all the extra hours I've racked up since Riker's been gone—"

"The city would go broke paying you off. I *know.* But the boss thinks you spent the last three days attached to the DA's office. Now he finds out they've never seen your face, not once."

"So you sat there and watched him bust my desk open."

"What could I do? I already told him I hadn't heard from you this week. How was I gonna explain all *your* evidence wrapped up nice and neat in *my* top drawer? So I had a patrol cop run your package downtown. Record time, sirens all the way. The assistant DA was still in the squad room when his office called to tell him they had everything they needed for court. Well, now this jerk has to apologize to Lieutenant Coffey. The boss *loved* that. So that's one point on your side."

"But it's not the real reason he broke all my locks."

"I'm guessing . . . no." Janos waved one hand, as if hoping to pluck just the right words from the air. And now he frowned—preparing her for the worst. It was his style to break all bad news in a slow and maddeningly gentle fashion. "You see, right before the DA's man showed up, the boss got this phone call. You know an ex-cop named Rawlins? He works for Highland Security. Maybe the lieutenant thinks you're working a second job on the side?"

"He knows better," said Mallory. Jack Coffey understood that her only illegal sideline was Butler and Company. "What else?"

"It has something to do with that shock-jock, Ian Zachary." Janos threw up his hands. "That's all I got." He looked up at the ceiling. "Well, almost. I know it's tied to that private dick, Rawlins. The guy's phone call really irritated the boss."

The translation of that soft-sold comment was Mallory's vision of Jack Coffey going ballistic with a crowbar. She could see him ripping into her desk, venting all his animosity with vandalism.

"I got an idea this is serious trouble." Janos nodded toward the lieutenant's private office. "So act real polite when you go in there. Don't say anything to get on his bad side, okay?"

Yeah, right.

Riker parted his curtains to look down at the street. Jo was walking alone, coming from the direction of the subway, and there were no feds in sight. Mallory was right. Jo could lose her federal watchers at will. That would also explain why she traveled on trains when she could afford cabs and limousines. It was harder to track someone underground, so many ways to lose a subject in a string of cars and all the station stops.

The intercom buzzed.

He pressed the talk button, not waiting to hear her voice. "Hey, Jo, come on up." He tapped the next button to admit her to the building, then opened his front door by a crack and listened for the rising elevator. He watched her step out into the hallway. It was a cold evening, and she wore a down jacket shaped like a dark blue hand grenade riding above her long blue-jeaned legs. In less than fifteen minutes, he would look back on this moment and recognize it as a warning.

He opened the door a little wider, then backed up to the wall. She entered slowly, head turning from side to side, so suspicious of an unlocked apartment, but she never looked behind her. He stepped out from the wall and punched her arm.

"So, Jo—did that hurt?"

"What?" She whirled around, stunned, as one hand covered her upper arm where he had hit her with a closed fist. "You *know* it hurt. Why would—"

"Good. Every civilian should take a body blow just once in their lives. Then they wouldn't freeze up, always anticipating the first punch, first pain." He stepped toward her, and educable Jo stepped back. "Let me take your jacket," he said. "It'll hurt more without all that padding."

"You *jerk*."

"Oh, all the women say that." And this was actually true. "So what are your physical limitations, Jo?"

"My what?"

"If you take a punch to the back, would that cause permanent damage?" He raised his fists, and her eyes rounded, but this time she did not back away from him. "All right, Jo, use your hands to deflect the shots. Stay alert. Here comes another one." His fist feinted toward her face, missing it by a bare inch. "Feel the air? Now imagine a bloody nose."

"Why, Riker?" She only stood there, so exposed, making no move to protect herself. Jo had disabled him with nothing more than large brown eyes full of absolute trust. "You've never hit a woman in your life, have you? This is not who you are."

"And who are you, Jo? You're a refugee from a witness protection program, and you keep shaking off your bodyguards." He had no more heart for this, and she knew it. His arms fell to his sides, and his voice had lost its edge. He was all but pleading now. "I only want you to have a sporting chance to stay alive."

Who else would teach her how to break a man's nose with the palm of her hand? Without guidance, how would she ever learn to pluck out the jelly of an eyeball with one finger? His resolve returned. This was the only way to keep her alive. His hands were rising.

"I won't do this, Riker. Not with you."

"I'm not giving you a choice, Jo. But I'll make it easy." He opened his arms wide to expose his chest as an easy target. "Your turn. Take your best shot."

She walked toward him, slow and deliberate, smiling to tell him that all was forgiven. And then—

Lieutenant Coffey was a man of average height, and even his hair and eyes were in that middling range of brown. He was young for a command position, only thirty-six, but he had compensated for that by prematurely aging to fit the job, acquiring worry lines that gave his otherwise bland face more character.

He glanced at his watch. It was just after seven o'clock, and he had no hope of escaping his office anytime soon. Two of his key people were missing; how was he going to fill that hole without more budget-breaking overtime? In his desk drawer was a letter from the commissioner asking why he had not yet replaced Detective Sergeant Riker. How long could he ignore that instruction? When would Riker sign the appeal forms? And was Internal Affairs planning another assault? Would Highland Security keep silent about the latest fiasco? Would the acid eventually eat through his stomach lining, and when, God, when was this ugly day going to end?

Jack Coffey's eyes rolled up to the ceiling, but no answers were written there.

The door was opening. There had been no knock, and that always irritated him. But could his mood be worse? Ah, and now he was graced with a visit from his only female detective. If not for Mallory, he might look years younger. If he fired her today, he might keep the hair that was left around the bald spot at the back of his head, and the tension headaches would go away.

She stood on the threshold, arms folded, glaring at him. "I want a new desk," she said. "A *brand-new* desk."

The lieutenant smiled against his will. This preemptive strike telegraphed that Mallory knew she was in trouble. He pointed to a chair. "Sit."

He was hardly surprised that she remained standing. She paused awhile to peruse his paperwork, reading upside down in a violation of his personal space. Was this payback for her broken desk? *Now* she sat down. Mallory had only one basic strategy—*offensive* in every sense of that word.

"I got an interesting phone call today." He tapped his pencil on the desktop, and this was the only giveaway that he was angry, for his voice was remarkably calm. "It was an ex-cop who runs Highland Security. The guy's name is Rawlins. You know him?"

"I've talked to him," she said.

How predictable that she would answer that question truthfully, for what was the point of getting caught in a *little* lie? Mallory was a big believer in truth administered in small doses to improve upon a falsehood.

Done with chitchat, Coffey dropped his pencil. "Rawlins wanted to talk to our covert ops detective. Well, I told him we didn't have one of those, nothing that fancy in Special Crimes Unit. Then Rawlins says, 'Oh, *shit!*'" Jack Coffey leaned forward. "Now, why should that make me think of you?" He paused a beat, allowing this remark to register with her. "So I said, 'You must mean Mallory.' Oh, yeah—now the guy's more relaxed. He thinks that stunt you pulled on him might actually be legal. So then he tells me this radio celebrity sent his company a huge retainer. Now Rawlins wants to know what they're supposed to do with the guy's check since—thanks to you—they're not doing any work to earn it. I said I'd get back to him."

"I'll tell him not to cash the check."

"That's *it?*" If he waited for her to defend her actions, he would wait forever, but she had no idea that his best shot was still coming. "I'm really worried about you, Mallory. You've never been this sloppy before. Such messy tracks." Did that get her attention? Well, no, but he pressed on anyway. "Two days ago, Ian Zachary calls Highland Security to set up an appointment. Five minutes later, you call Rawlins and tell him you're taking over, and he should keep his mouth shut. *Five minutes.* You should've waited longer, Mallory. Now I have to figure you intercepted Zachary's phone call. I don't remember asking any judges for warrants to tap a radio station's telephone. So, of course, you have some other explanation."

"I have a snitch at the station," said Mallory. "That's how I knew about the call to the security company." Nothing in her tone said that she expected him to believe this.

It was a lie, but it would do—in the event that Internal Affairs turned its eyes back to Special Crimes Unit. And now, for his next leap of inspiration, he said, "I'm guessing this all ties back to Riker somehow." He could see that she was not planning to elaborate on that, but there was no other explanation. She was good, damn good, even better than Lou Markowitz in the days when her old man had commanded this squad. It was unlike her to mess up so badly. Some personal aspect was affecting her judgment.

And now he allowed it to affect his own.

"Mallory, get out your damn notebook. That's an *order.* I've got a list for you, and I want every item to be perfectly clear."

Her expression said, *Yeah, right.* However, she produced a small pad of paper from her back pocket, as a token appeasement. "I'm on comp time. This might have to wait a few—"

"That's the first item—you don't get any more time off."

"I've got at least fifty hours of—"

"No comp time." He could see the next argument coming, and he put up one hand to prevent her from mouthing off. "You used your badge to muscle Highland Security. So now you cover your tracks. Open a case file for Ian Zachary. I'm guessing he wants security because of the Reaper. Those homicides belong to the feds, so make out paperwork for a celebrity stalker. Throw in some anonymous tips, and don't forget to backdate your file by two days." He slammed the desk with one hand. "I want to see you writing this down, Mallory."

She bowed her head over the notebook, and her pen began to move. A small victory.

"Next item," he said. "If there's an active phone tap at that radio station, make it go away. If that comes back on this squad, I'll fire your ass in a heartbeat. And the last little detail? Zachary thinks he has paid security, so you keep that son of a bitch alive. Officially, that's your new job."

"He thinks I'm his private investigator—not his babysitter."

"He better not die on your watch. Get out of my office."

For months, Riker had avoided saloons in the precinct of his old squad, and now a local bartender flashed a broad smile. "Long time no see," the man said, as he set down two drinks on cocktail napkins, bourbon and water for Riker, rye for Jo.

Another woman, one he had dated casually, had broken up with him in this same SoHo bar. There were many such landmarks in New York City. Over the past twenty years since his divorce, no relationship had lasted longer than a few months. Some of the women had left him in restaurants, and others had dumped him on street corners. Only now did he get around to wondering how he had erred in those brief encounters. It worried him that Jo might walk away before they even got started.

"I promised you a meal," he said. "There's a nice little place around the corner." A woman named Donna had dumped him there. "You like Italian?"

"No, thanks. Maybe some other night." She glanced at her watch. "I should be leaving now."

"It's early," he said. It was late. "Don't go." His feet were tapping a rung of the bar stool, and his hands were sweating. Neither of these symptoms had anything to do with the damage this woman had recently done to him.

Jo rolled up her sweatshirt sleeve, the better to see the bruise blooming on her right arm. She glanced at his crotch. "Does it still hurt?"

"Naw. Don't worry about it. I had it coming."

"You mean, you never *saw* it coming. My father's best advice—kick a man in the soft parts and run like hell."

"Well, I'm glad you stuck around, Jo. That took guts. Most women would've been unnerved to see a man cry like that."

An hour ago, she had kicked him in the testicles, and then, impressed by his suave fetal posture and groin clutching, she had shared the contents of a pharmacy bottle with him—pain pills, strong ones. Evidently, Jo and agony were old acquaintances. The lady had called it right—he *was* a jerk. But she was a good sport. Jo had suggested this pub crawl through SoHo for medicinal purposes.

"Your color's better," she said. "Not quite so pale. You're a very good patient."

"Better than Timothy Kidd? You were treating him, right?"

Now *she* was taken by surprise. If he had only thought of this earlier, he could have mugged her with words and saved himself a world of hurt. A few moments passed in uneasy silence. Did she regret coming out with him tonight? There was time in this lull to notice that she was wearing perfume. Though they had lifted many a glass at the end of a workday, he never had been so close to her, almost touching shoulders. He breathed deep and stared at the red stain on her glass. Her lipstick fascinated and flattered him, believing as he did that she had tricked herself out on his account, though she was otherwise her old jeans-and-sweatshirt self.

"You've been talking to Marvin Argus," she said. "He told you Timothy was my patient? Well, he lied. He does that a lot." She pulled the down jacket from the back of her stool, preparing to end the evening.

"Wait, Jo. So it was a different kind of relationship—you and Agent Kidd. You were close. I figured out that much. Lovers?"

"Would you find that hard to believe, Riker?"

He shook his head, and he must have done a fine job of communicating that he was not at all surprised that any man would want her—that he wanted her—for she seemed contrite.

"Sorry." She smiled, less anxious to leave him now. "Timothy was my friend."

Riker sometimes got lost in Jo's eyes, foolishly dropping the threads of his thoughts. He wanted to know if she had also worn lipstick for the murdered FBI man. Instead, he asked, "How did you two meet?"

"He came by my office asking for help on a case."

"The Reaper case?"

Her head moved slightly from side to side, more in wonder than denial. Perhaps, like most civilians, she assumed police omniscience, and now she was surprised by his ignorance. But how could he be wrong about this?

"Well, the fed was killed by the Reaper. Logical connection, right? And it's like you said, Jo—Argus lies a lot. So help me out here." That fed was not the only liar. Riker was already laying plans to hunt down Mallory, to back her up against a wall and find out what else she had held out on him, but for now he must wing it. "So that's not when you met Agent Kidd? When the murders—"

"No, I met him before the first juror died. No one had even heard of the Reaper yet. And Marvin Argus met Timothy after the second murder."

"They didn't work together?"

"No, Timothy worked out of Washington, D.C. Argus is based in Chicago, and he wasn't investigating the Reaper case either. Argus was only responsible for rounding up jurors and witnesses for protective custody. He probably thought Timothy was in town to check up on him. The second juror died in Argus's custody."

"So, Jo, in your professional opinion, which one of these agents was the most paranoid?"

She smiled. "Timothy. No contest. He cultivated paranoia, thought it enhanced his insight. And maybe it did. After two minutes, he could tell you your life story and how it would end. Or that's what he thought. I'll show you how he did it. Now remember, this isn't *my* style. My trade takes more time."

She nodded toward a lone patron between two vacant stools at the other end of the bar. "He's perfect for one of Timothy's stunts."

The young man's greasy hair was parted down the center and bluntly chopped off below his ears. He was smiling at some lame joke he had told himself, and one pudgy hand tapped out the rhythm of a tune that only he could hear. His polyester shirtsleeves were buttoned down and his collar buttoned up. Riker noted the pocket protector lined with pens and mechanical pencils. Without looking underneath the bar, he knew the pants would be black with shiny knees.

Jo colored in the rest. "I saw him walk in. He's wearing heavy correctional shoes, but there's nothing wrong with his feet. Trust me, I'd know by the walk. He's probably been wearing them since childhood. There's a whiff of smothering mother in that detail. He lives with her—that's why he still wears those shoes. And no barber cuts his hair that way. His mother does it, and she's always picked out his clothes. That's why he never fit in with the other kids at grammar school. All his life, she's destroyed any possibility of a friend his own age coming between them. He wishes he'd killed her while he was still in his formative years—maybe nine or ten. That's when the matricide fantasy started. When he finally gets around to murdering Mommy, you'll find him at the crime scene, probably the kitchen, knife in hand. He'll be very cooperative with the police—and very proud."

Riker was not impressed with what the FBI agent had taught her. It was only a parlor game compared to the real carnage, bloody and insane, that was the daily work of Special Crimes Unit. The profiler tricks had never solved a single case, never replaced solid police work. And, as Jo had pointed out, this was not her style either. He picked his next words carefully. "I have to wonder why you're doing Kidd's old act. Good job, though. I bet you've been practicing since he died."

She met his eyes, then looked down at her drink. "It's only a game."

"Yeah, and that's why your friend never would've made the cut for Special Crimes. I was a better detective."

Jo's head lifted slightly, and he could read her thoughts. Though she would never voice this aloud, she clearly had a higher opinion of the murdered agent's brains and talent.

"I didn't say I was smarter, Jo. But I was better. No tricks, no flimflam. I was the genuine article—a cop. I don't need to look at your hair and your clothes to tell where you've been and where you're going. I only had to read your notes on Agent Kidd and the liquor store."

And now those notes were ashes in his fireplace, along with the paper trail for her wine.

She started to rise. He put one hand on her arm to keep her with him. "You think you were close enough to that poor dead bastard to crawl inside his skin. You collect the Reaper's favorite wine because that's what crazy Timothy Kidd would've done. And that's why you only cleaned homicide crime scenes. It made you feel closer to his job, his life. You're actually hunting the freak who killed him. You're not a woman in hiding. That hotel is a damn goldfish bowl. It must drive the feds crazy trying to protect you, covering foot traffic and all the exits. And now you're really good at ditching those bodyguards whenever you like. You've been practicing that, too. Think you can actually finish Kidd's job for him? Am I close, Jo? I think I am—because you won't even look at me."

And here the conversation ended. Jo was done with him. She slid off the bar stool and moved toward the door, donning her jacket on the fly, long legs carrying her out to the street and away.

His gut was tied in knots. Prior to meeting Jo, he had no idea that it could physically hurt him to lose a woman's company. This was not the way he had wanted the evening to end. If he could have been any crazier about Jo, he would have shot her in the leg to prevent her from leaving him tonight.

And me without my gun.

Once the door had closed on Johanna Apollo, the bar became a desolate place. And then he remembered that she had worn lipstick—perfume, too. That fed him awhile as he followed her away from the bar. And down the deserted street they went, twenty yards between them, heading toward the glowing green balls that lighted the way down to the underground station. During the subway ride, he kept her in sight through the window of a trailing train car. And though he was right behind her as she made her way up the stairs to the Chelsea sidewalk, she had no clue that he was there and watching over her. He stayed with her as far as the hotel, where a nervous FBI agent was pacing before the front door. And then, sadly, Riker turned around and left, for his job was done; he had seen the lady home.

10

IAN ZACHARY WAS THOROUGHLY PLEASED WITH the young investigator from Highland Security. The tall blonde was beyond cool—sunglasses at night. Ah, but were those Armani shades a disguise or an affectation? His lawyers had warned him that he trod a fine line between freedom of speech and felony entertainment. The authorities would always be close by, waiting for him to trip over FCC regulations and federal laws.

However, this woman was not from any tribe of bureaucrats and hardly the type for undercover police work. Days ago, her bad attitude had made an excellent first impression. The expression of ennui, her tone of voice and stance, all said to him at their first encounter, *You're a cockroach. You know it, and I know it.* Now, that had attracted him to her, but it was the fabulous black leather coat that had actually sold him. On this criterion alone, he placed her at the top of her profession. The other investigators, hired and fired in quick succession, had been discount shoppers, every one. He also admired the more mundane aspects of his lovely private cop. By the dangerous bulge in the tailored line of her cashmere blazer, he knew that she carried a very large weapon. And he had sexual fantasies about this woman in handcuffs, but in all the most realistic scenarios, he was the one who wore them.

The investigator entered his studio while he was racking up a pretaped interview for his audience, not trusting his insane engineer to do this right. He leaned into a stationary microphone, saying, "Crazy Bitch, take a break." And now that they were guaranteed some privacy, he turned to the blonde from Highland Security. Wasting no time on civility, she handed him a fat manila envelope that bore the name of Johanna Apollo's employer, an ex-detective from Special Crimes Unit.

Over the past few months, her predecessors had failed to turn up anything in Riker's habits or his history that was even mildly dishonest. As Zachary perused her paperwork, he smiled, liking what he saw, the evidence of a man living beyond his means. And that would explain why NYPD had gotten rid of Detective Sergeant Riker.

"I've got another job for you. Can you stick around a few minutes?"

Just the barest inclination of her head passed for a nod.

He turned another page of the dossier. "My God, this is what he pays for rent? His apartment must be a palace. And what's the deal with Riker's first name?"

"He doesn't have one," she said. "I checked his birth certificate. Just the initial *P.* And it cost you five hundred dollars to have me wait in line for his records. You want to waste more money on that?"

"No, this is fine." There was contempt in everything she said to him, and he loved it.

She stared at the lighted screen of his laptop computer. "So *this* is your database?" Even that sounded like an insult.

"Yes, that's it," he said. "Couldn't play the game without it. Are you any good with computers?"

Without bothering to answer him, she sat down at his console and tapped the laptop keyboard, creating split screens to view two files at once. He watched all these images quickly flicker and change as she scanned his entire repository of fan sightings and personal information on the twelve jurors, living and dead.

"All the easy ones have been murdered," he said. "Those were the idiots who gave television interviews. So my fans had their names and photographs."

"I'm sure your lawyers had all the background stats on your jury. Addresses, too, right? So why didn't you give the fans—"

"I couldn't." He paused, wondering if he had just admitted to a crime. Legally, he had not been entitled to any of that information. "My lawyers won't let me. It's a technicality." He watched the file change to the related murder of Agent Timothy Kidd. Next, she scrolled the file on a national hunt for a major player. The Chelsea Hotel was the only highlighted address out of hundreds on the screen.

The investigator glanced in his direction. "So your fans located Dr. Apollo, but you never mentioned her on the air."

"She used to be in a witness protection program. The FBI got a gag order from a federal judge. If I just say her name on the air, I'm toast and the station loses its license. So I screen out all the hunchback calls."

"That's why you want her to do an interview? You think Dr. Apollo's going to expose herself on national radio?" Unspoken were the words *you fool.*

"You underestimate me," he said.

Her mouth dipped on one side to tell him that this was not possible.

"Next job." He handed her a sheaf of papers with the name and last known address of a surviving juror as well as drawings of the man's face. "I bought those sketches from a courtroom artist. I want you to find information on this man, but don't tell anyone the sketches came from me."

"Your attorneys wouldn't like that, would they? Cause and effect that ties back to you."

"Just a minor departure from the game format," he said. "The fans are a bit slow in developing solid leads. I want your report in the form of anonymous e-mail. And for God's sake, don't use a computer from Highland Security." His lawyers would go into cardiac arrest if they knew he was stepping outside the rules and gathering his own data.

She pocketed the papers, never taking her eyes off the screen and the latest sightings for fresh victims. "How stupid are your fans? You think they know what they're doing?"

"Well, it's pretty basic," he said, "tracking down helpless people so they can get their throats slit. But I don't think my fans give it that much thought. They call in a sighting, a juror drops dead. They never connect those two events. It's only a game, right? Now here's where I part company with the Reaper. He hates imbeciles, but not me. Without all these morons, I'd have no show. But the game's getting unwieldy—way too much information on the players. I can't tell good data from bogus."

"You're not really into computers, are you?" Her head turned his way, but the glasses were so dark, he could never be certain that her eyes were on him.

"I can open my e-mail," he said. "What more do I need?"

"More sophisticated software." She closed his laptop. "If I cross-index the fan reports by geography, date and time, I might get a line on the juror. But first I need to install my own programs." And now she was leaving—with his computer under her arm.

"Wait! You can do the installation here."

Her head slowly turned in his direction, dark glasses giving away nothing as she patiently waited for him to realize that they were going to do this her way.

She was barefoot, and her feet were dirty. At first, Riker had mistaken the strange young woman for one of the homeless insane. Her clothes were soiled, her hair was matted, and the odor of unchanged underwear was pungent. Yet she had identified herself as the sound engineer and personal assistant of the hottest radio star in America. As he trailed her through a maze of hallways, she said, "Everyone calls me Crazy Bitch." This nationally known victim of verbal torture and humiliation was the first show-business celebrity he had ever met.

"You're really mad, aren't you? Yeah," she said, "Zack told me you'd be mad."

"Lady, you've got a gift for understatement."

Crazy Bitch suddenly flattened against a wall, giving Riker a clear view of the tall blonde in sunglasses striding down the narrow corridor. He followed the example of his guide and joined up with the wall, for Kathy Mallory was not losing any momentum. This was why civilians always moved aside for her; she assumed they would want to save themselves before she could walk over them or through them. Riker had sometimes taken advantage of that, wading through crowds in her wake. Now she passed him by, never even glancing his way, as if they had never met.

"She's from Highland Security," said Crazy Bitch. "They cater to celebrities." The sound engineer continued down the hall, then stood to one side and gestured toward a doorway. "This is my booth." She nodded toward an adjacent door with a formidable lock. "And that one leads to the studio. Zack's just signing off. He'll buzz you in when the delivery guy leaves."

Riker walked into her own domain, a claustrophobic space of electronics and blinking telephone lights. On the other side of a plate-glass window, Ian Zachary was seated before a desk of dials and levers and one clear space for his catered meal. An apron-clad delivery boy laid out a late supper that no steak-and-potatoes man could identify: slimy round things covered with white sauce and garnished with the leaves of alien vegetables. Bubbling designer water was poured into a wineglass. For that alone, Riker would have disliked the man, but he had larger issues tonight—a message left on his answering machine in Zachary's voice and the words, *So what's it like to screw a hunchback?*

The radio host flashed a smile at the uninvited guest in the sound-booth window. Riker wondered if this man knew him on sight, or was he simply anticipating a fast reaction to his telephone message? Zachary tapped a button on his console. After the loud buzz, Riker entered the studio and slammed the door behind him. That made the other man jump, perhaps believing that his visitor was homicidally angry. He had no way to know that Riker slammed all the doors in the world all the time.

"Pull up a chair, babe. Make yourself at home."

Riker preferred to stand. He hoped his clenched fists would impart a strong desire to break the Englishman in half.

Unfortunately, Zachary was smiling again and taking no offense. "Have I got a deal for you—a fortune in free advertising."

"I don't give a shit about the advertising. Go fuck yourself."

"If that was possible," said Crazy Bitch, "he would've done it already. That's his big dream."

Ian Zachary stared at the woman walking toward him from the far side of the room. "I didn't buzz you in. How did you get past the lock?"

"Feeling a little less secure?" She leaned over the dinner tray and picked up a knife that was only good for slicing butter. After scrutinizing it, she pronounced it "Too dull." She picked up the fork and nodded her approval as she held it out to Riker. "Try this. Go for the throat."

"I think I might be in love," said Riker. "Are you married?"

"We're pretty sure she's a lesbian," said Zachary.

Riker shrugged. "I can work around that."

The woman bowed low over the dinner plate and deposited a glob of mucus on the food.

Her boss merely glanced at his ruined supper, then pushed it to one side. "Well, Riker, you might have some reservations about her table manners. You can't take her anywhere." He watched his assistant stalk out of the room, her bare feet slapping the floor. "She's totally nuts. How did she get past the lock?"

"Does it matter?" Riker had watched her jam the lock with a toothpick after the delivery man had departed, but he elected not to share this information. "If she wants to hurt you, she will. Just get used to the idea. But I'm first."

"I have a business deal for you. If the hunchback won't come on the—"

"She's never coming on your show."

"I think I guessed that. Now I want *you,* Riker. You could work with me on the Reaper murders, keep the show from getting stale. You probably wonder why I'd help that freak hunt down the people who set me free. You think I'm an ungrateful bastard, and you're right about that."

"No, I'm thinking you're a moron."

Apparently, Zachary enjoyed being insulted. Grinning, he held up a manila envelope with Riker's name printed in Mallory's neat block letters. "I know a lot about you." He dropped the envelope on the desk and pushed it in Riker's direction. "That's your dossier. No ordinary detective. I understand that Special Crimes Unit is an elite squad, and my fans just love hero cops with multiple gunshot wounds. I think we can work together. I'll give you access to everything I've got on the Reaper, and, babe, I've got plenty. My fans can get me anything I want."

"Your fans are squirrels," said Riker. "You've got nothing." He was leafing through Mallory's background report, a pack of lies. "And it would be a big mistake to call me *babe* one more time." Mallory's dossier had given him massive debts and a heavy mortgage for a summer house on Shelter Island, a place that he had never even visited. On the next page, she had jacked up his apartment rent to an amount that only a cop on the take could afford, thus painting him as a shady, money-hungry man with great bribe potential. He rolled the sheets into a paper truncheon. "I've got no idea why the feds don't shut you down."

"They tried. In fact, the FCC did suspend me for a few nights. Then a pack of ACLU lawyers beat up their lawyers on the issue of free speech. Oh, and then—you'll love this part—an idiot judge lifted my suspension before the matter even went to a hearing. I'm betting the Reaper kills the last juror before the government gets my case into court. Bless the morons. And back to my job offer. In addition to all that free advertising, you get paid a bundle just for—"

"No deal."

"Not so fast, Riker. I know what you do for a living these days. You clean crime scenes. That's a joke job. And I know you need money." He nodded to the dossier. "I have very good sources."

"So do I. The jury verdict was a farce. The Chicago cops say you committed murder. No mistake, hard evidence and eyewitnesses. And it was real cold."

"Well, this is what they didn't tell you—because they didn't know." Zachary flipped a lever on his console. "Listen. This tape was never been played on the air." And now the speakers carried the sound of breaking glass and a woman's voice screaming obscenities. "I recorded this in my old Chicago studio—the *first* time she tried to kill me. She broke the window on her sound booth to get at me."

Riker listened to the recorded voice of the shock-jock describing a woman who had gone mad, crunching broken glass underfoot as she rushed toward him with a broken shard in her hand. He even described a cut to his chest when she opened his skin.

Zachary turned off the machine, then unbuttoned his shirt to display a jagged scar. "It wasn't deep, not as bad as it looks. The station manager called in a doctor. I gave him a lame story about an accident. The woman was never charged. So you can't say I never gave her a break. They just took her off to a hospital. Ten days later, she was released from the psycho ward. That's when she started following me around. Have you ever been stalked?"

Riker nodded. It was a rare day when he did not have someone following him around, though sometimes it was only a feeling.

"Well, she came after me again on the day she died. I ran into that building to get away from her, but she caught up to me on the roof. It was a construction site, lots of workmen standing around. I'm guessing the sling blade belonged to one of them. Wicked-looking knife. It was in her hand when she backed me up to the wall. Then she rushed me. So, yes, I pushed her off that roof. I stepped to one side and helped her right over the wall. The knife dropped with her, but the police never found it, and the workmen didn't see it in her hand."

"And none of this came out in your trial?"

"I wouldn't let my attorneys use the tape. Incidentally, the prosecutor had her psychiatric history—years of voluntary hospital stays. She was always unstable, but the district attorney neglected to share that with my defense team. It would've ruined the case against me. You see, I wasn't the first man she tried to kill. So I had more than enough grounds for a new trial if the verdict didn't go my way."

"If all this is true," and Riker was skeptical, "why didn't you plead self-defense?"

Zachary leaned forward, smiling. "Tell me, Riker, what's more intriguing—a radio personality who killed a woman to save his own sorry ass—or a man who got away with cold-blooded murder?" He smiled. "Point taken? Good. After my acquittal, I was back on the air and my ratings were the highest in the history of Chicago radio. And then the major networks were calling me. New York City, every jock's dream, and national syndication."

"And now you help the Reaper kill off your own jury. You're getting away with murder . . . again."

"Only in America. I *love* this country. If you want fame, and you want it fast—well, then you've got to kill somebody. That's the American way."

"I'm out of here," said Riker.

"Wait! Just hear me out, all right? You could be the one to catch the Reaper."

"I'm not a cop anymore." Riker turned his back on the man and walked toward the door.

"Wait—three minutes, that's all I'm asking." Zachary raised his voice. "And I won't tell my audience about the hunchback, the prime suspect for the murder of an FBI agent. Just three minutes. That's the deal."

The man leaned far back in his chair, hands clasped behind his head, making himself an easy target for a beating.

Riker walked back to him, and Zachary sat up straight, perhaps believing that he was about to take a blow. But Riker only leaned over the console to push the lever that played the Chicago tape. He listened to the rest of the mad woman's murder attempt, her screams subsiding to soft weeping as she was strapped to a gurney and taken away. And now she was dead.

"You drove that poor woman crazy." Riker glanced back at the sound booth and the young girl behind the glass, Zachary's current victim. "I know your style. You're a damn psychopath."

"Actually, I'm not. At my trial, the prosecutor's shrink testified that I was a sociopath—not legally crazy. I'm also the nation's foremost expert on the Reaper. So work with me. I'll get you all the information you want. Would you like to see an autopsy picture, one of the Reaper's kills?" He opened the console drawer, pulled out a glossy photograph and handed it to Riker. "I got that from a fan who works in the Chicago morgue. Now this is what I have in mind. One of the jurors is in New York City—"

"I heard your show last night," said Riker. "Leave that poor bastard alone."

"There's something you should know about this juror, MacPherson."

"Your three minutes are up. Don't go near Jo, not on or off the air." He pointed to the crazy woman behind the window. "If she can get through that lock—*I* can."

After leaving the studio, he paused at the open door of the sound booth to speak with the young woman inside. She had freckles, and that broke his heart. "You should quit this job," he said. "Just walk away."

"I can't." Her eyes had a hint of gratitude, and mild surprise was also there. Kindness would be something rare to her these days. She was like a child on the verge of tears, though she was smiling when she said, "I want to be famous."

Riker nodded, silently responding with Ian Zachary's words in his head. *Then you've got to kill somebody.*

11

ON THE SIDEWALK OUTSIDE THE RADIO STATION, Riker was greeted by a small band of excited people. Their outstretched hands held pens and autograph books. Disappointment set in as they quickly identified him as a nobody, then turned their attentions back to the door, waiting for someone more worthy, somebody famous.

Mallory's tan sedan was not among the vehicles along the curb. Riker focused on the one parked some distance away. Nothing about this automobile would set it apart from the rest, but the suit and tie of the man behind the wheel was the standout feature of a security detail. After the midnight hour, this was no longer a neighborhood of suits. Riker approached the car at a blind-side angle, then ripped open the door and slid into the front seat beside a startled FBI agent.

"I wanna see Marvin Argus, right here, right *now!*"

While waiting for Argus, the time passed in easy conversation with the local FBI man, whose military service was thirty years behind him, though he still wore the crew cut and retained the hard body of his army days. Agent Hennessey was not much of a drinker and liked the early morning hours best, but the two men did find a common ground in their hatred of divorce lawyers.

From force of habit, Riker cultivated every contact with the New York bureau. Tonight, establishing rapport had been easy, almost instant—thanks to all the old newspaper headlines on his ambush by a psychotic teenager. So, quite naturally, the two men discussed the lighter side of getting shot in the line of duty. Agent Hennessey had a bullet wound of his own. He assured Riker that come summer, bathing suit weather, the scars would be magnets for bikini-clad cop groupies. More bonding occurred after discovering that they were both addicts. Two cigarette embers glowed in the dark of the car, and Riker learned that Hennessey's bureau chief was not a happy man these days, not since Special Agent Marvin Argus had blown into town from Chicago with his own crew. The man stopped short of making derogatory remarks about a fellow agent. But then, Hennessey had never met Argus.

"You're in for a treat," said Riker. "When he smiles, you'll wanna deck him, but you won't know why. I keep my hands in my pockets when I talk to the guy."

Finally, Marvin Argus arrived in a large white sedan with rental plates. He pulled over to the curb only two feet from the New York agent's front bumper. This earned him a slow shake of the head from Hennessey, for Argus had just parked his white elephant in the middle of a covert detail. The man from Chicago was broadly smiling as he approached the other agent's car, then leaned down to the open window on the driver's side. "So Riker spotted you, huh? Well, forget it, Hennessey. You're not in any trouble."

Many obscenities could be read into the grim, tight line of Hennessey's mouth, for he was not actually in need of this magnanimous forgiveness from an out-of-towner, an interloper with no authority over him.

Riker nodded his goodnight to the man beside him, then opened the passenger door and stepped out onto the pavement. "Argus, follow me." And because the Chicago agent did not appear to understand a direct order, he jacked up the volume, shouting, "Move! *Now!*" As they walked away from the car, Hennessey made a thumbs-up gesture. Riker had just earned some currency with this local fed.

"So," said Argus, "you got something for me?"

"Keep it down." Riker glanced back at the gallery of fans clustered in front of the door to the radio station. When they were beyond earshot, he turned on the man, saying, "You lied about Agent Kidd. He was never Jo's patient."

"Is that what she said? Tim had regular appointments with the lady—four times a week during office hours. That sounds like a doctor-patient relationship to me."

"That only tells me you were following Kidd—spying on one of your own guys."

"He was unstable," said Argus. "Everybody knew—"

"You think getting tailed by his own people might've made him a little crazier?"

Argus averted his face, signaling a lie in the making, but then he shook his head and looked Riker in the eye. "After Timmy Kidd was murdered, I questioned that woman for hours and hours, five, six interviews, and she'd never tell me what they talked about on those visits. She was keeping a doctor-patient confidentiality."

"Did she ever spell that out for you?"

"No, but I still say she was treating Tim."

Riker put more faith in Jo's story. Agent Kidd was always Timothy to her—his friend—never Tim or Timmy. Marvin Argus had hardly known the murdered man.

"Shrinks," said the lying fed. "They'll never give you a straight answer about a patient, not even a dead one. What else did Johanna say?"

Riker shook his head. He was here to get information, not give it away. "Kidd was based in D.C. I think he could've found a psychiatrist closer to home. Not one more lie. You got that? You still don't know why Kidd was in Chicago, do you?"

Argus shrugged this off. "He didn't report to me—not directly."

Not at all.

"And Jo was never a suspect," said Riker.

"Wrong, and the Chicago cops will back me up on this. She was the prime suspect for Timmy's murder. If I hadn't taken her into the witness protection program, she'd still be in police custody. Even the damn cops knew that Tim was nuts. This is the way they figured it before they lost the homicide to us. Only his own doctor—Dr. Apollo—could get that close to a flaming paranoid, close enough to slit his throat. And a little paranoia wouldn't hurt you right now, either. You couldn't play it quiet like I asked. No, you had to play cop. Well, you're not on the force anymore, so be real careful about who sidles up to you." He tucked his business card into the pocket of Riker's leather jacket. "And whatever Johanna tells you, bring it to me."

"Yeah, like that's ever gonna happen."

A black limousine sailed past them, then rolled to a stop in front of the radio station. The street door opened, and a lean figure in a hooded sweatshirt emerged from the building. The fans converged on him, and he signed their autograph books before climbing into the backseat of the limo. The long black car pulled away from the curb, followed at a discreet distance by Agent Hennessey. Marvin Argus ran toward his own vehicle, planning to join the parade. And the fans quickly melted away, leaving Riker alone on the sidewalk. Well, not entirely alone.

He stared at the pavement, watching a stealthy shadow coming up behind his own. Without turning around, he said, "Mallory, you're overpaid." As she came abreast of him, he held up a crumpled ball of papers, her falsified dossier on his life. "I found a few mistakes in this."

"So Zachary made you an offer? You're on his payroll?"

"No, but nice try. You might've run that past me before you set me up." He turned toward the street and the distant cavalcade of departing vehicles. "The FBI hates Ian Zachary. So how does he rate a security surveillance?"

"I arranged that," said Mallory. "I sent a few death threats to the local feds so they'd keep an eye on him for me."

"Mallory, you can't—"

"I can't be everywhere at once," she said. "Up till now, I've been playing the game by myself."

This rebuke was another reminder that he had abandoned her and left her all alone in Copland. So, if she had to bend the law a bit, well, that was clearly *his* fault. Her logic was flawed but consistent; she always came out blameless. And he had to smile because this policy of hers had not changed since she was ten years old. Here was his old Kathy.

"It's your turn," she said. "Wait for Zachary, then follow him. I'll catch up with you at the bar on Green Street."

Riker raised one hand to point the way Zachary's limousine had gone. His extended arm hung in the air for one foolish moment before dropping to his side. "He wasn't in that limo."

"Right," said Mallory. "He uses a double every night. You see? It's all coming back to you. Once a cop, always a cop."

She walked down the dark street, traveling almost the length of the block before he fully grasped what had just happened. She had sicced the feds on Ian Zachary, then duped them by letting them chase a doppelgänger. Before he could ask why, Mallory turned a corner and disappeared.

A truck with the logo of a janitorial service pulled up to the radio station. Five men in orange coveralls piled out and unloaded mops, machines and cleaning supplies. Riker backed into the dark of a doorway and waited the length of one cigarette. A man emerged from the building across the street and moved down the sidewalk at the pace of an elderly arthritic. He wore orange coveralls like the janitors, but none of those men had been stooped with age, nor had any of them worn the slouch hat that hid this man's face in shadow.

Following at a distance, Riker saw his target stand erect before descending a concrete slope to the lower level of a parking garage. Slowing his steps to give the man some lead time, Riker strolled down a ramp marked for one-way traffic. He was heading toward the lighted window of an empty ticket booth. At the bottom of the ramp, in place of a human being, an automated ticket machine extended its mechanical arm across the ramp to halt incoming vehicles with a bar of wood. Riker moved out of the way to allow a blue sedan to crawl past him. At the bottom of the ramp, the driver reached out the window and pulled a ticket from the mouth of the machine. The mechanical arm raised to let the car pass. Beyond that wooden barrier, all Riker could see were patches of light and empty parking spaces.

A gunshot exploded in the cavern below, quickly followed by the screech of the blue sedan's brakes and echoes of the bang.

Riker rocked on one foot, caught midstride and off balance. His body stiffened, his chest seized up, and he was dropping like a manikin. In an act of pure reflex, his hands shot out in front of him to soften his fall and save him from a broken nose, but now his arms had turned useless. He could not move them, nor could he breathe. This time, he thought his lungs would burst. The panic was ratcheting higher and higher, heart racing.

The gunshot had also panicked the driver of the blue sedan. The car was backing up, hitting the guardrail in haste to get out. Riker heard the crack of the wooden barrier, then footsteps and a tapping sound. His face pressed to concrete, all he could see was a dark coat and the white tip of a blind man's cane. No help was coming from that quarter.

Another gunshot sounded—and another.

The blue sedan moved forward, and Riker knew what would happen next. The frightened driver wanted distance before he reversed his gears and crashed backward into the wooden barrier that trapped him. The driver would not be checking for bodies in his rearview mirror.

Riker knew he was a dead man, out of breath and flat out of time. He heard the grinding of the gears reversing, the car engine revving, backing up, crashing through the rail, coming to smash his head like a melon. A warm body covered his own and rolled with him back to the wall and safety as the blue sedan sped past him in reverse. Riker's eyes were closing as his deliverer eased her body off of him to kneel at his side, but he was aware of Jo's hands on his chest, his face, and then her mouth was pressed to his as she breathed for him, filling his lungs with air. Panic and fear yielded to a lightness of the head, a floating sensation.

"Listen," she said. "It's like the day you almost wrecked the van. You won't die. If you lose consciousness, all the muscles will relax." And then she whispered, "Don't be afraid."

And he was not.

The paralysis had passed off, and what had begun as the kiss of life became a kiss for its own sake. Drunk on the euphoria of oxygen deprivation, that part of his brain where the thinking was done excused itself and stepped off a cliff. His hands were on the back of her neck, pressing her closer, his fingers tangling in her hair. Jo was life and breath and more.

She pulled back.

He tried to rise, and she put one hand flat on his chest to restrain him. "Stay here," she said. "I'll get help."

He had his breath back—and his mind had also come back to him. "Get out of here, Jo." He pushed her hand aside. "Go now! I need backup. Get to a phone." He was on his feet again and running down the ramp toward the thing that scared him more than anything else on earth. And he could not have done otherwise. This was a cop's job, running toward the sound of guns. Past the splintered guardrail and running on level ground, he rounded a thick pillar and came upon two men in a pool of overhead light.

Ian Zachary had lost the slouch hat of his janitor disguise. Unarmed, he squared off against the man who held the gun, taunting him. "What's wrong with you, MacPherson? A thirteen-year-old girl could've made that shot."

The other man, small and rail thin, raised his revolver and fired three shots at Zachary's chest.

Riker remained standing this time, fighting down the panic as bone locked with bone and every muscle constricted. He would not suffocate and die. This would pass; he knew it would because he believed in Jo. He was hyperaware of every detail to this scene: his banging heart, the sweat on his upper lip. And he could see that the gunshots had no effect on Zachary. The shooter could not have missed, but there were no holes in the target's orange coveralls and no ricochets off concrete walls.

Blanks?

Agape, Zachary stared at Riker, no doubt wondering why the frozen man simply stood there rooted to the cement. The paralysis passed off faster this time, and Riker relaxed into a casual stance, feigning mild interest in the stranger with the gun. When he felt steady and able again, he strode toward the shooter, rolling his body with all the old authority of the badge. He took the weapon from the man's trembling hand, saying so casually, "So you're MacPherson." He opened the revolver's cylinder and checked the chambers. "You're out of bullets. Tough break, pal."

Riker glanced at Ian Zachary and the bulk beneath the orange coveralls. Was the man wearing a bulletproof vest? Of course he was. All that bravado had come from a civilian's lame idea that the vest would take the bullet with no harm done. But getting shot in the chest was worth a ride to the hospital, vest or no vest.

"I have a carry permit." MacPherson's voice was shaky, and his eyes had the vacant look of a trauma victim. He was assuming that Riker was police, for now he unfolded a paper and handed it over, as if this might excuse him for this ambush of an unarmed man.

Riker held the document at arm's length to read the small print. Yes, this was MacPherson, one of the last three living jurors and duly authorized to carry a pistol for the purpose of self-defense. He handed the permit back, saying, "Okay, I guess you're licensed to shoot him."

Not seeing any humor in this situation, MacPherson actually seemed relieved that he was not in any serious trouble. Riker pulled back the man's coat to expose a metal cylinder hanging from his belt. He unhooked the speedloader and emptied its store of ammo into his hand. The cartridges were capped with wax to hold the charge of gunpowder, but no bullets.

"*More* blanks?" Riker was that rare person who *did* suffer fools gladly, for the criminally misguided had always been his chief source of entertainment. "So you thought you might need to reload in a hurry . . . with emergency blanks."

MacPherson nodded, then forced a smile because Riker was smiling.

"Imbecile." Ian Zachary shook his head slowly from side to side and leaned back against an old junker of a car, the perfect complement to his disguise of workman's coveralls. He was a portrait of New York élan, so blasé in the aftermath of his own attempted murder. He turned to face Riker, saying, "You're going to arrest him now, right?"

"Hell, no. How many ways can I say this?" Riker spoke slowly and carefully in the manner of talking down to a half-bright child. "I—am—not—a—cop—*anymore*."

"You could make a citizen's arrest."

"Naw, I'm gonna buy him a beer. Poor guy, he's had a rough day." Riker clapped one hand on MacPherson's shoulder. "C'mon, you're with me. I wanna know what the hell went on in that jury room."

There was no sound of sirens yet. He knew they should be gone before the first police car arrived. Jo would have located a public phone by now. However, he had a feeling that she would not leave her name as the 911 caller. Riker walked the incompetent shooter up the ramp in silence, and there was time to wonder who the lady had been following tonight. Himself? Was Jo taking the blame for Bunny's death? Was she worried that another friend would be the next target? Or was it Ian Zachary she was tailing? He glanced at the ashen face of MacPherson and decided to include him on the short list of men who so interested Johanna Apollo.

From the bowels of the parking garage, Ian Zachary called out, "Can *I* come? I'll buy!"

Riker sat back and enjoyed his favorite brand of bourbon—Free Booze—as Ian Zachary laid out more cash for the cocktail waitress. Turning to the small thin man between them, Riker said, "You're perfectly safe. This is a *cop* bar."

Once again, MacPherson failed to get the joke. He appeared not to understand that cops usually arrested people for waving guns around in a menacing way. Perhaps there was something to the Reaper's stupid-juror theory. But then he decided that this man had simply lost the ability to think clearly; he had spent too much time in seclusion, hiding from a maniac who wanted him dead. Riker could empathize with that, though he had never been a man in hiding. That was not his way. And he would never tremble so in public.

Upon entering this old SoHo haunt, he had made his usual scan of the crowd, checking out young males for signs of psychosis and concealed weapons. And now his gaze settled upon a blind man's white cane; it leaned against a bar stool draped with a black coat. Squinting for clarity, Riker decided that this man in the silly wig was young, but he could read no finer detail between the long red curls and the oversized dark glasses. The blind man dipped one hand into his coat, and Riker froze, waiting for a bullet. The man withdrew a wallet, set his money on the bar, and Riker began to breathe normally again. It was unlikely that this was the same white cane that had tapped past him in the parking garage twenty blocks away, but he wished he could see this blind man's eyes.

Two drinks had gone by, and he had learned nothing of the events that had led MacPherson and his fellow jurors to a not-guilty verdict. But he knew that something shameful had happened in the jury room. That much was in MacPherson's eyes as the man evaded every question.

"Well, what is a juror anyway," Ian Zachary was saying, pontificating to no one, for Riker had ceased to listen and poor MacPherson was sliding into shock. "A juror," said

Zachary, "is someone too stupid to get out of jury duty. Now, this man here, he was one of the rocket scientists in that courtroom. He's a math teacher."

MacPherson corrected him, saying in a small cracked voice, "*Was* a math teacher. I lost my job. I still have a wife, though." He looked down at his bony hands tightly folded in his lap. "But she always cries when I call home." He also seemed at the point of crying, and his last drink had done nothing to calm his nerves. "The jurors weren't stupid. Those poor people were only—"

"Hey, I was there, too," said Zachary. "Remember me? The defendant? When the prosecutor polled the jury in open court, one by one, they all voted not guilty. And you? You just tried to kill me with blanks, you fool."

"I only wanted you to know how it felt to be me."

"You mean you didn't have the guts to kill me. You're a coward."

"No, he isn't," said Riker. "He didn't run, did he? You and your fans set him up, nailed him down to New York City—even the building he lives in. And the Reaper's probably camped out at his front door right now. I say the man has guts."

However, MacPherson *was* an idiot.

Riker scribbled a brief note on a cocktail napkin, then pulled Marvin Argus's business card from his pocket. "It's time to call for protection, pal. You're naked now." Under the cover of the table, he pressed the napkin and the card into the man's hand.

"It doesn't matter anymore," said MacPherson. "I just want it to be over." He glanced down the note, then rose from the table, mumbling, "Men's room." He turned his back on them and walked toward the sign for the rest rooms at the rear of the bar.

"He's one scared rabbit," said Zachary. "Or maybe not." He slid along the seat of the leather booth, moving closer to Riker. "Wouldn't it be a kick if that was just an act? What if he turned out to be the Reaper?"

"Yeah, *right.*" Riker's attention was divided between the blind man at the bar and MacPherson, who stood by the pay phone, shaking his head and debating the wisdom of making a telephone call to the FBI.

The Englishman prattled on, oblivious to anything but the sound of his own voice. "No, he's not smart enough to get away with slaughtering all those people. And then there's the FBI agent in Chicago. Did you know he was one of the Reaper's kills? The newspapers never made the connection on that one. The Chicago cops wouldn't give reporters any details. But you may recall that one of my fans works in the morgue."

The blind man turned his head toward Riker, then quickly looked away and counted up his change from the bartender. Not blind? A fraudulent beggar, a con artist, in a *cop* bar?

Looking past Zachary to the window on the street, Riker drank steadily as he endured another ten minutes of crackpot theories on the Reaper. He was buying MacPherson some getaway time.

Now the shock-jock noticed that their drinking companion was still absent from the table.

"What's with him, I wonder? You think he's in the men's room slashing his wrists?"

"He's long gone," said Riker, though only a minute had passed since Argus's white car had pulled up to the curb and carried the juror away.

"He slipped out? You just let him go?"

Riker rolled his eyes up to the ceiling and said, "I'm not a cop any—"

"I know," said Zachary, "but if he dies tonight, it's on your head, isn't it?"

No, MacPherson would at least live through the night. The feds could not afford one more screwup on the Reaper case. And Riker could do nothing to save the man; he could not even protect himself—not with a gun, not when the mere sound of the shot could render him breathless and useless. He needed no more proof that his life as a cop was done.

"Maybe you're the one who needs protection." Riker ripped open the man's orange coveralls, revealing a bullet-proof vest of better quality than police issue. "Don't put all your faith in body armor. The next time that poor bastard comes after you, he might use real bullets—and he might make a head shot."

"Highly unlikely. You saw him," said Zachary, paying no mind to the broken zipper on his coveralls. "The man's harmless. But I still think the Reaper was one of the jurors. My favorite candidate is the jury foreman—the hunchback."

"Johanna Apollo?" No, this was not possible. Riker closed his eyes. *Bad dream, bad dream.* If Jo had been on Zachary's jury, Mallory would have—

"You really didn't know?"

When Riker opened his sorry eyes, Zachary had moved closer, and he was smiling.

"Fits, though, doesn't it? She makes a great suspect. Think about it, Riker. A unanimous verdict of not guilty. Was the jury really all that stupid, or did someone influence them? Only a psychiatrist could've run that jury room and turned all the ballots my way. That's why I sent her long-stemmed roses every day for a month. I figured her for a groupie."

"Shut up, you psycho."

What else had Mallory failed to tell him? Just as he was wishing that she was within strangling distance, he saw her seated at the end of the bar. All her attention was trained on the fake blind man in the red wig. And now Mallory slid off her bar stool to follow the little man out the door, leaving Riker to the job of tucking Ian Zachary safely into bed.

12

THE FAUX BLIND MAN WAS ACCUSTOMED TO BEING followed. Mallory had guessed as much when he changed trains three times, but she had remained with him, riding one car behind, though sometimes losing sight of the bright-red wig among the other passengers. He led her to Grand Central Terminal, almost deserted at this hour, and she watched him enter the downstairs men's room, a very suspicious act in itself. That public facility was a documented pesthole. Only vagrants did not avoid it, but he was not in that class. She had cost-estimated the black coat at something beyond the purse of a beggar, though his wig was cheap nylon hair and a very unnatural red. He must *want* people to notice him, but why?

She watched the rest room door and waited for him, guessing that he would change his appearance before he emerged. He would certainly lose the silly wig.

Mallory waited—and she waited.

Twenty minutes had passed. Only one man exited the men's room, but this was not the smooth-skinned youth, the fake blind man. This man was elderly, not aged with a white fright wig, but authentically wrinkled and peppered with liver spots.

She entered the men's room to make her own inspection, not yet willing to believe that she had been thrown off a surveillance detail by some rank amateur in a ridiculous disguise. This could not happen—not to her. One by one, she opened all the stalls, kicking open the ones that were locked, disturbing the slumbers of homeless men with authentic body odor and haggard faces, and definitely not her fake blind man in disguise. Angry now, she overturned the trash can on the floor, but found no sign of a red wig or a white cane. There was only one door, no other way out. A young man had walked into this room and vanished.

Mallory decided not to share this humiliation with Riker.

"Yes, Victor, I'm quite sure that she was police," said the elderly lawyer as he draped the black coat on a chair. The white cane came loose and crashed to the floor, startling his companion. But then, every little thing made Victor Patchock nervous. The youngster was in one of his silent moods, and so the old man carried on both sides of the conversation. "Yes, she followed me right to the rest room door. Well, actually, she was following the red wig. Commendable plan, my boy." He had finally come to appreciate the bizarre logic of a fugitive calling attention to his appearance.

The lawyer stood before the only unshuttered window and looked down at the quiet street below. The Upper East Side was such a good neighborhood, but what a dreary, tiny room. His last offer to move Victor to some better accommodation had been declined. The young man had even worsened his lot by removing the doors to the closet and bathroom, then stripping the place of all bulky furnishings which might conceal an enemy. From where the old man stood, he could see a razor on the edge of the bathroom sink, and the drain was clotted with hair from the younger man's clean-shaven head. Victor had always been boyish in appearance, but now the bald pate made him seem downright babyish—if a baby could sneer and go insane.

The old lawyer plucked his own camel-hair coat from a hook on the wall. "It's late, and I need my rest." He did love this fresh excitement of being followed by a pretty woman, a touch of after-midnight sex. The drama had certainly enlivened his golden years and deepened his sympathy for this young man who could not go home again. But, of course, there were limits. And now, as if in gentle rebuke, denying a toy to a child, he said, "I can't get you a new gun. Sorry."

Mugs's lips curled back over needle-sharp teeth as he crept toward the door, his ears flattened back and fur bristling. Whatever he sensed out there in the hall, he was planning to take it by surprise and make short work of it. The cat looked up at Johanna, pleading for her help in this venture, for he had never mastered the art of opening doors. Suddenly he was angry and hissing. She was opening the closet—the *wrong* door.

Johanna found her jacket, dipped one hand into the pocket and pulled out the small silver gun. In barefoot silence, she stepped up to the hallway door and stood on tiptoe to see through the peephole.

No one there.

Perhaps it was only a mouse after all, something small hiding below and beyond the perimeter of the fish-eye lens. She opened the door.

Riker had been sitting on the hall rug and leaning against the wood. Now he fell backward into the room and came face-to-face with the cat. "Hey, Mugs, ol' buddy."

The cat, somewhere between disgust and disappointment, padded off to his pillow basket, where he turned around three times, then curled into a ball.

"Hello, Jo," said Riker, still flat on his back and looking up at her.

Johanna's weapon was concealed behind her back. "Riker, I've got two FBI men watching me. So, thank you, but I really don't need more protection tonight."

"Argus's men?" He rose to his feet. "Sloppy bastards. I didn't see either one of them when I got here."

She waved him to the couch, and while his back was turned, she slipped the silver gun into the pocket of her robe. "What are you doing here?"

"I just found out that you were on Ian Zachary's jury. That was a shock and a half."

"But you had so much information—"

"Your notes? No, they never mentioned you as the jury foreman."

And now he surprised her one more time. He asked none of the predictable questions, like *How could you let that bastard get away with murder?*

Over the next half hour, they settled into an easy truce. Their pact was sealed with Johanna's hoard of precious goat cheese and a fine bottle of red wine pulled down from the rack on the wall. They sat on the couch, side by side, their feet propped up on the coffee table. Johanna had eased into a rare mood of happiness, so mellow, so peaceful. And she was the one who finally returned to the subject of Ian Zachary's trial.

"I didn't even try to get out of jury duty." She refilled Riker's glass with the last of the bottle. "I was closing down my private practice and referring my patients to other doctors—finding good homes for all my puppies. And I was almost done. So it was easy enough to clear my calendar. I didn't really think the defense lawyers would want a psychiatrist on Zachary's jury. But they never objected to me, never asked a single question. They didn't waste any time on the other two women either. After a while, I figured it out. They were using all their challenges to stock the jury with men who fit the demographics of Zachary's radio show. It was a local program then, just the Chicago area. You know the type of fans he has? Young males, badly educated and immature.

Most of them in going-nowhere jobs. Seven of the jurors fit that profile."

"That explains why the defense team didn't care about you. They only needed one of those bastards for a hung jury. So what happened in that jury room? How did they get a unanimous verdict?"

"I can't tell you any more, Riker. I won't lie to you, and I won't drag you into this."

He leaned down to pick up the leather jacket he had dropped on the floor, and now he pulled out a gun much larger than the one she had recently concealed in a cushion of the couch. With just a cursory understanding of his affliction, she knew it was madness for Riker to carry this weapon.

"Jo, I'm the one with the gun, and you're trying to protect *me?*" He looked down at the revolver in his hand. "I took this away from MacPherson tonight. Is he the one you followed into the parking garage?"

"Where is he now?"

"Marvin Argus took him away. That's his whole job in life, isn't it, protecting the jury? Maybe that's why he pulled his men off your surveillance detail. Well, I guess I'll be sticking around for a while."

Before he could ask any more questions about MacPherson, Jo selected an open wound that might distract him. "Does your doctor know what causes your seizures? Any physical problems?" She already suspected that the pathology was trauma related, but men were rarely open to this suggestion.

"Seizure," he said, as if the word might be new to him. "You mean like a *fit?* I don't throw fits. I'm thinkin' it could've been a heart attack." He seemed to prefer this more life-threatening explanation. Of course he did. Men had heart attacks, *women* had fits.

"Riker, you know I've seen it happen before. That day you lost control of the van."

He shook his head. No, he had not lost control; he had no frailties. All this was said with the set of his jaw, and then he turned away from her. Johanna was accustomed to this old obstacle, old as time. Men were the vainest creatures on the planet. Obviously, he believed that he had successfully concealed the previous episode.

Her first day on the job, training day, he had nearly wrecked a company van. There had also been a loud noise on that occasion, the sound of one car hitting another with the bang of two-ton missiles meeting head-on. The van had suffered no impact, though it had spun out of control and wound up with both front wheels on the sidewalk before Johanna could pull up the emergency brake. She had opened the passenger door and hit the pavement running to check on the other two drivers. Both of them had been in better shape than Riker. She recalled that awful moment when she had turned back to see him frozen behind the windshield. In the throes of a seizure, his lips had turned blue for lack of oxygen, and every cord on his neck had been strained to a rope of flesh. The seizure had passed off before she had time to climb back into the van. He was already breathing again, gulping air, and waving off her attentions, insisting that he was just *fine*. Riker had not driven a van since that day, and they had never spoken of the incident.

And there would be no more discussion tonight. He busied himself arranging couch cushions in front of the door to her rooms. Riker was planning to lay his body down as a human shield to protect her.

She stared at the revolver he had lain on the glove table by the door. This was fresh proof of her trauma theory. The cylinder chambers that she could see were empty. It was not loaded. Of course not—a gunshot would have paralyzed him. He had come to protect her with only the bluff of an empty revolver, and Johanna regarded that useless weapon with tenderness and great awe.

Special Agent Marvin Argus stared at the sleeping man on the hotel-room couch. He had tired out MacPherson with the argument for the witness protection program. Or perhaps the man was faking, escaping into feigned sleep. The runaway juror seemed to dislike him for no reason that Argus could fathom.

After packing up the meager belongings from his apartment, MacPherson had been willing enough to come to this hotel under FBI escort, but he stubbornly refused to leave town. Argus blamed Dr. Apollo for giving this fragile little man a backbone.

The doctor's guards were divided in their duties. One man was posted on the staircase between floors, and the other rode atop the only elevator in service tonight. This was not correct procedure for a stakeout. He should have had more men, but that would have meant answering too many questions. No requests would be made to the New York bureau. No local agents should learn about the captured juror until the Reaper had been taken into custody, dead or alive.

The agent thought better of lighting up his cigar in this hotel room. MacPherson had claimed to be allergic to smoke and probably lied about that. Little prig. However, Argus's future depended upon staying on good terms with this man for a while longer.

He turned down the volume on the radio, then pulled a curtain aside and craned his neck to see the sky. It was getting light. Dawn was only hours away. Dear God, how he wanted a smoke—and sleep. When had he last slept through the night? He had only dozed the night before. In the past hour, he had downed five cups of coffee—not enough, but there was more on the way. That bellman would take at least ten minutes more to fetch it, at least that long.

An infusion of nicotine might help to stave off the drowsiness, that and cold fresh air. The agent opened the window and stepped out onto the fire escape, then sat down on the metal grate and unwrapped his cigar. Leaning back against the wall, he exhaled the first blue cloud of smoke. His eyelids weighed ten pounds each. Argus glanced at his watch as if that would hurry the next pot of coffee.

The Chelsea Hotel was an inspired choice, now that he

was certain that the Reaper kept close tabs on Dr. Apollo. The death of the homeless man had proven that much.

He tried to pay attention to the news broadcast from the radio on the other side of the open window, but his head lolled to one side, and it seemed that his eyes had only closed for a moment. Surely it had been no more than a minute. The window closed behind him with an angry slam, and the cigar in his hand was still smoking when he started awake.

Damn you, MacPherson, you and your phony smoke allergy.

Argus could no longer hear the radio. The double-pane glass had cut off the sound. All he had to listen to was the sporadic static of cars passing by on the street below. He pulled out his cell phone to make sure that his men were in place and alert, trying the agent in the stairwell first, then the one on the elevator, who gave him two welcome pieces of news: Riker was visiting Johanna Apollo's floor—one less juror to worry about—and Argus's pot of coffee had arrived. There would be no more communication, no sound or movement, while they waited for a stone killer to walk into their arms. As Argus concluded his last call, his gaze was drifting down toward the street. It was a fight to keep his eyes open as he folded his phone into a pocket.

So tired.

He fixed his gaze upon the building directly across the street, determined not to let his eyes close one more time. And so he never saw the frantic shadow on the curtain behind him, arms waving. Nor did he notice a splatter of red dots appear in the next instant, staining the material with blood just beyond the glass. His eyes had closed before the drapes were pulled down from their rod, clutched in the death grip of a falling man, as the horror show was unveiled, blood on the walls, the furniture and the floor.

Argus would not wake for three more hours. A hotel maid would be the first to discover the body at nine o'clock, and she would call the police.

13

KEY IN HAND, CHARLES STOOD IN THE OPEN doorway to the reception area. For the third time in as many days, he was startled to see his new tenant, the former hermit. Or, rather, he saw Riker's back as the man walked down the hall toward the rear offices of Butler and Company—while Mallory, another unexpected sight at this early morning hour, was making a hasty retreat, heading toward the front door with uncommon speed and ignoring the fact that Charles was barring her way.

"Just a moment," he said, calling her attention to himself, the immovable object in her path, and it annoyed her that he would not step aside. Oh, how unfortunate. "I gather that Riker hasn't seen your recent additions to the wall."

"No," she said, still advancing on him.

Ah well, that would explain so much: her agitation, her strong desire to get the hell out of here. She never lost momentum, fully expecting him to get out of her way before they collided, but he had seen her do this trick too many times, and he stood his ground. Now he was looking down at her upturned face, such a lovely face, but definitely not a happy one.

"So Riker surprised you," he said. "You know he's going to have some questions about what you've done."

Mallory took the long way round him. Closing the door behind her, she said, "You can fill in for me."

Right.

Resigning himself to damage control, Charles walked down the hallway and paused by the open door to his business partner's private office. Riker was scanning the half of the cork wall that was all Mallory's work, a neat square composed of photographs all perfectly aligned and alternating with sheets of text. The overall effect was somewhat like a chessboard. Among the upper rows were candid shots of jurors who were still alive when captured by their photographers. Pinned alongside them were e-mails and letters from Ian Zachary's fans. In the lower region were pictures with the same faces, eyes closed this time, and the predominant color of their photographs was blood red. These were the postmortem portraits of people lying on morgue dissection tables. Previously, the only corpse pictured on the wall had been the murdered FBI agent, Timothy Kidd, Riker's own contribution from the suitcase of Dr. Apollo.

"'Morning," said Charles, trying to put a good face on what was already shaping up to be a bad day. He noted the man's paleness and ill-concealed anger. Well, this was no improvement in Riker's condition. Mallory's game plan had a nasty glitch.

"Where did she get all the photographs?"

"Most of them came from Ian Zachary's computer," said Charles. "Mallory hijacked it. Apparently, Zachary's fans are not above stealing things like morgue records to make him happy. And, of course, to win prizes."

The detective concentrated on the last row. Here were all the portraits of a surviving juror, Dr. Johanna Apollo. She was the only one on the wall to be represented from every angle. In the final shot, her deformed body was in clear focus, but the head was slightly blurred, turning in the direction of the camera click.

"The fans didn't send Zachary these pictures of Jo," said Riker. "Mallory took them."

"How did you know?"

"Years and years of looking at surveillance shots. Mallory's the worst photographer on the force."

"Ah, the center fixation. Yes, lots of wasted space around the subject's face. Not a very good sense of composition, is it?" Charles turned his eyes to the upper gallery of fan photographs representing nine other jurors, every one deceased. "To be fair, I think all of these pictures are equally bad."

"Yeah, but Mallory's shots are always *perfectly* bad." Riker tore a picture off the wall, and its pushpins went flying. "If I drew a gun sight on this, Jo's head would be in line with a bullet."

The metaphor was not lost on Charles. Riker was obviously questioning Mallory's intentions toward this woman. And now, in a face-off, the detective elicited a confession of sorts. It was all there, played out across Charles Butler's face in the red flush and the sorry eyes that would not meet Riker's own.

After ripping all of Dr. Apollo's photographs from the wall, the angry man slammed the door on his way out.

Chief Medical Examiner Edward Slope was seated behind his office desk, catching up on paperwork before cracking open the first corpse of the day. Without his uniform of bloodstained surgical garb, he might be taken for a graying general. His face was dignified, his expression set in stone, and his posture was perfect, even when he believed that he was not being observed. The pathologist looked up from his paperwork and almost betrayed a look of pleasant surprise.

Before Riker had gotten two feet in the door, he was subjected to yet another impromptu examination. Checking the mended bullet holes?

Dr. Slope's quick appraisal also took in the bomber jacket, flannel shirt and jeans. In lieu of hello, he said, "You look like hell, and I don't mean the wardrobe. I'm guessing that you're losing sleep while working undercover as a lumberjack." Slope had always fancied that he possessed a sense of humor. "And now you need a consultation, right?"

Apparently no one had told this man about the forced separation from NYPD, and Riker planned to take advantage of that. "It's definitely not a social call, Doc." He tossed a slew of photographs on the desk blotter. "What can you tell me about this woman?"

The medical examiner hardly glanced at the pictures of Johanna Apollo. "Since she's not dead yet, not one of *my* customers, I'm guessing you want me to tell you what's wrong with her. Got an X ray or a medical history in your pocket? No, I didn't think so. Well then, I'll tell you the same thing I told Mallory—just before I sent her packing. I can't do a diagnosis without the proper—"

"Mallory showed you *these* pictures?"

"Yes, two months ago, maybe three. At least *she* came in with a working theory. Based on her research, she decided the woman had Scheuermann's kyphosis. Wanted me to confirm it. Mallory seems very well versed on the subject of hunchbacks. Perhaps you two should talk more often, maybe compare notes. You're still partners, aren't you?"

Riker slumped down in a padded armchair in front of the desk. He was feeling all the aches of a night spent sleeping on the floor of Jo's hotel room, what little sleep he had managed, but anger was slowly dissipating exhaustion. Mallory had lied to him again. What a surprise. Her investigation of Jo was apparently not a recent thing, but dated back to the first encounter during a visit to Ned's Crime Scene Cleaners. He added this to the list of Mallory's deceptions, then turned his tired face to Dr. Slope. "I need information on this woman, anything you can—"

"She has a severe spinal deformity—that's all I can tell you with just a damn photograph."

"Not good enough, Doc. I once heard you do a twenty-minute spiel on the history of a corpse with no ID. That time, all you had to work with was a damn tattoo."

"*And* a corpse on the dissection table."

Riker gathered up his photographs, preparing to leave. "Well, thanks for all your help." As he rose from the chair, he thought better of taking the pictures with him and dropped them on the desk. "Keep 'em—a few souvenirs. If she shows up on your dissection table in the next few days, I want you to remember this conversation."

"Hold it." The doctor picked up one of the photographs and studied it with more care. "I don't believe I've seen *this* one. It shows a bit more of the pathology."

Riker sat down again.

"Mallory was probably right," said Slope. "Scheuermann's kyphosis is the most likely cause. The range, in layman's terms, is round back to hunchback. Hers is an extreme deformity. So I'm guessing there were other factors, maybe a childhood onset of osteoporosis or scoliosis." He pointed to the duffel bag that Jo carried in the photograph. "Do you know if this is a heavy load she's carrying?"

"Yeah," said Riker. "It's her job bag, all the gear to clean a crime scene, her moon suit, a respirator and—"

"So, in addition to heavy lifting and wearing a respirator on her back, she's doing a lot of bending and stretching."

"Sure. Goes with the job. But she only works three days a week."

"Then I can tell you that she spends the other four days recuperating. This woman is either a masochist or a very determined individual. How long has she been doing this sort of work?"

"Three months or so."

"By now, her pain medication is probably supporting three pharmacies—addiction levels. At one time, she might have controlled aches and pains with aspirin, but that won't help her anymore. I doubt if she sleeps through the night without pills, so you can add more drugs to the list. Heavy sedatives, anti-inflammatory medication, amphetamines to keep her going after nights when the pills don't work. She's probably under medical supervision. She can't get any of these meds without a doctor's prescription."

"She *is* a doctor, a psychiatrist."

Slope arched one eyebrow, and this was tantamount to an emotional outburst in his limited range of stone-faced expressions. "And now a *psychiatrist* is doing menial labor? I don't suppose you're planning to tell me why that—"

"Nope."

"Well—a psychiatrist—that's unfortunate. Then she also has a medical degree. She's probably prescribing her own medication. Doctors make the most dangerous drug cocktails for themselves, things they'd never give to a patient. That's why it's illegal to self-prescribe. But the law is so easily—"

"Back up, Doc. What about the masochist angle?"

"What? Pain for its own sake? Well, many people go into mental health professions because they've been treated for emotional problems of their own." Slope's eyes drifted back to the photograph. "That's a good possibility here. As a small child, her appearance would've been quite normal. Then—age ten to fifteen—she began to change—grotesque change. Hard to imagine a day in her life—curious stares, clumsy remarks. Now, given that teenagers are not the sanest, most stable peer group on the planet, try to picture this woman's adolescent years at the mercy of—"

"Pure hell."

Slope nodded. "At least a thousand arrows to the soul on a *good* day."

"Her father was a shrink, too."

"Then you can count on a history of long-term therapy. He would have put his daughter in treatment with a child psychiatrist."

"What about this angle?" said Riker. "You say the cleaning job brings on more pain. What if the job is like a hair shirt?"

"Penance? I suppose that's one possibility. Here's another. Given her choice of work these days, crime scenes, she might be coming to terms with death. She could be suicidal."

This last suggestion remained with Riker, riding with him on the subway back to SoHo. And the idea nagged at him as he walked the streets, heading toward an old familiar haunt, where he had agreed to meet Mallory for breakfast. She had a lot to answer for today. He was planning to make it a very short meal, perhaps their last one together. In addition to her other crimes against him, she had yet to mention tailing the fake blind man last night, though she had been given that chance earlier this morning.

Charles Butler had not remarked on Mallory's reappearance a convenient five minutes after Riker's angry departure. She had as yet not offered him any opportunity for conversation, but busied herself at a computer. Her fingers were flying across the keyboard. Her eyes were fixed on the screen, and she was stone-deaf to what he was saying—until he unplugged the thick gray cable from the wall and her screen went blank.

Good job.

Mallory's hands came to rest, but she would not look at him when she said, "It's better if Riker knows all of it now—all at once."

"Oh, well that explains everything, doesn't it?" And he knew, in Mallory's mind, it would excuse her for leaving him to face Riker's suspicions alone.

"Did he tell you where he was going?"

"No," said Charles. "I'm not sure we were on speaking terms when he left. He obviously thinks I was part of this scheme from the beginning."

"You didn't tell him how long—"

"Well, he's a detective, isn't he, Mallory? I'm sure he can figure that out. Just a warning." And this advance notice was more than she deserved.

"I'm meeting him for breakfast. I'll patch it up, okay?"

"No, that's not okay. All this deception—that's the least of the damage. He sees you as a threat to Johanna Apollo."

"He said that?"

"He didn't have to. It was—"

"Now that he knows she was on that jury, he'll do whatever it takes to keep her alive." As if this might pass for an answer to all present and future questions, she plugged in her computer, then resumed typing. "It's better this way."

Oh, of course. That, after all, had been her purpose in posing a threat to Johanna Apollo. And Mallory had done it so graphically, so deliberately in every photograph.

"You should have been honest with Riker," he said, "right from the start. Why can't you just sit down with the man and talk to him like a—" He had been about to use the words *normal person,* words that did not apply to her—nor to himself.

Charles Butler had been raised in an academic womb, entering Harvard at the age of ten, a freak, a thing apart from his peers. Mallory had matriculated to the streets at an even younger age and had also learned to survive on her own, absent any ties to other children. And, thanks to his own more elite education, Charles knew the cantos of *Paradise Lost,* but he was unable to recite the simplest line of a valentine to her for fear that it might strain their friendship or altogether end it. For her part, Mallory knew all the dimensions of hell on earth, having taken its measurements in her formative years, but she knew nothing about the human heart. And so they coexisted side by side, each in their own separate cell, business partners and prisoners who sometimes met for lunch or dinner, conversing but never quite touching one another.

And now he felt like a fool.

Why should it come as a surprise that Mallory could not sit down with Riker, all that she had left in the way of family, and tell him that she had created all this misery for him—out of love? He stood behind her chair, planning to tread more carefully with his remaining suspicion. "Riker doesn't know everything yet, does he, Mallory?"

She glanced at her watch as a pure distraction. Mallory always knew the exact time to the second. This was a gift, an odd quirk of her brain, and perhaps she made finer distinctions in increments of time for all he knew. Charles watched her quickly gather up keys and coat, playing out the charade of being late for her appointment, as if that could ever happen to one so pathologically punctual. And now, without further complaint, he watched her go. What else could he do? Mallory had taken hostages.

Riker walked into the din of conversation, clattering plates and silverware, with no hesitation, not pausing this time to examine every face with a wary eye, nor to check the patrons' clothing for the bulges of concealed weapons, for this was a haven, a safety zone, and most of the regulars carried guns. The rest were tame tourists with I-Love-New-York T-shirts and souvenir buttons.

Breakfast in this SoHo café was a habit that he had cast off during his extended leave from NYPD, not wanting to meet any familiar faces from his squad, and he had missed this place so much. The ritual meal had spanned twenty years, beginning with his oldest friend and continuing with that man's foster child, his partner—ex-partner—Kathy Mallory. It was nine o'clock, still crazy hour for the morning trade, but the small table by the front window was magically vacant, as if the third chair were still occupied by the late Inspector Louis Markowitz.

It felt like coming home again as Riker pulled up his regular chair. He nodded to a lean gray woman with a gravedigger's face, who stood five tables away. Her arms were laden with a juggling act of perfectly balanced trays as she distributed ten separate meals round a table of tourists, dealing out plates like playing cards. She astonished the out-of-towners, not asking who got what, but simply getting it right, each entrée, beverage and side order. Gurt was an actual waitress, not a starving actress or a painter. She had always waited tables for her living and knew all her regular customers and what they wanted, and she suffered no grief from anyone.

"You're early!" Gurt yelled at him across the room, as if the past six months of his absence were but a single day. "Planning to surprise the kid?"

Kathy Mallory had made no stronger impression on this waitress over the years. On her first day as a rookie cop, Lou Markowitz had brought his foster child to the café in uniform to show her off to Gurt, saying with great pride, "This is my kid." As far as the waitress was concerned, the young cop was then and now and forever—the kid. And, yes, even though this late breakfast date had been earlier arranged, the kid would be surprised. Mallory always walked in the door exactly on time, little punctuality freak that she was, and Riker was always late—but not today.

And he had other surprises for Mallory.

Gurt had no sooner placed his coffee mug on the table than he looked up to see Mallory hovering in the open doorway, and this could only mean that the second hand of the clock on the wall had struck the hour. It was rare to see her startled. As she crossed the room, her long black leather duster was swept back on one side, and she consulted Lou's old pocket watch tethered to her blue jeans by a gold chain. Reassured that her internal clock had not failed her, despite Riker's timely presence, she shrugged out of her coat, folded it over the back of her dead father's chair and took her customary seat at the table.

This café was also her own haven. She disliked change so much. Lou Markowitz might be gone, but his chair was still here. And, though she got no respect from Gurt, the waitress was a constant fixture in her life. Thus Riker knew with absolute certainty that Mallory had sat here each morning of his long absence, her head bowed over her plate, eating her meal in silence—all alone, and that realization caused him unexpected pain. Other cops, men she worked with every day, also frequented this place, but they would never sit down at this table with her, for she would do nothing to invite them. She would not know how.

Guilt and sorrow tempered everything he had prepared to say to her. All his stored-up accusations simply died.

This morning, Johanna showed some charity to Special Agent Marvin Argus, only opening the door by a crack. Mugs could not maul the man's legs, not unless Argus tried to force his way into the room.

"Got a warrant?"

"No." Having learned deep respect for the cat, the FBI agent stood beyond the range of swatting claws. His eyes were anxious and sunken in their sockets. His face was pale and bereft of the annoying smile. "I need your help, Johanna. There's been a murder—a man you knew."

She had a death grip on the doorknob as her head moved slowly from side to side, so deep in denial that she almost missed his next words. And now Marvin Argus's eyes were shocked wide by her inappropriate smile, for he had just put a name to the dead man, and it was not Riker.

The meal had arrived a few minutes after Mallory. Their waitress never bothered with the formality of menus since they always ordered the same thing. The past six months had dissolved, and it was as it had always been, two partners eating eggs over easy and drinking coffee black.

When their meal was done and the second cup of coffee poured, Mallory slapped a thick sheaf of papers on the table and said, "Sign it."

Riker looked down at the familiar appeal form to challenge his separation from NYPD. "How many of these things have you got?"

"I can print them out all damn day. I can keep this up as long as you can."

He pushed the paperwork to one side. "What did Lieutenant Coffey say?"

"He gave Commissioner Beale your field report."

"What field report?"

"I typed one up for you. It gives Special Crimes Unit all the credit for locating MacPherson and placing him in Argus's custody."

"And what about the other fed, the local man? Did you make him look like an idiot for losing Ian Zachary last night? That was your plan, wasn't it?"

"You mean Hennessey? I talked to him this morning—told him about what happened to Zachary in the parking garage.

Then I told him I wasn't planning to mention it to anyone." She handed a folded sheet of paper across the table. "Read this."

He took the report and held it out at arm's length, squinting at the text. There was no mention of the New York fed and his botched security detail, nor the shooting in the parking garage. Agent Hennessey was now in Mallory's debt. Clever brat. She had no gift for making friends, but she knew how to build up the favor bank. She was even better at this than her old man. He folded the report and gave it back to her, glad that he had misjudged her—though perhaps not entirely. What she had done for Agent Hennessey also had blackmail potential.

"Did he say anything about MacPherson?"

"No," said Mallory. "He had to ask me the name of the shooter. Interesting?"

"Argus isn't sharing information with the New York bureau."

"No." She smiled. "So we'll let the local feds find out the hard way."

"You're setting up a war between the Chicago bureau and New York?" Yes, Mallory would find that irresistible, dividing them, weakening them. There was no doubt left that she was plotting a case takeover. "So what happens when Zachary makes out a complaint on the shooting?"

"He won't," said Mallory. "I took care of that when he called me last night. I told him he'd look like an idiot with no corroboration—since the only witnesses hated his guts."

"And what about Jo?"

"*She* was there?"

And now he knew that Mallory had not stayed to watch the show, but he would always wonder if she had roughly predicted the outcome. Had she set him up to intercept MacPherson? No, that was crazy. He was giving her too much credit and pushing his trust issues over the edge. "No," he said. "Jo wasn't there. I just wondered if Coffey knows she needs police protection."

"Can't justify the manpower," said Mallory. "She's already got feds watching her round the clock."

Riker shook his head. "Argus pulled them off that detail last night. He's probably got them watching MacPherson full-time."

The next item of his agenda was the fake blind man Mallory had followed away from the bar last night. This was forgotten when he turned to the window, distracted by the sudden commotion on the street. Detectives were pouring out of the station house on the run, climbing into cars and peeling off down the street. Only Jack Coffey was still on foot and heading for the door to the café.

Trouble.

Riker turned to Mallory. "Any theories?"

Before she could answer, Lieutenant Coffey strode through the door and crossed the room to their table.

"Hey, boss," said Riker, forgetting for the moment that he was no longer a detective in this man's squad. "Who's minding the store?"

"Janos needs backup on a crime scene." Jack Coffey picked up the breakfast bill and laid down his own cash. "I need both of you. Now!"

"But, I'm not a cop anymore."

"Then you shouldn't be turning in field reports, Riker. MacPherson's dead, and you were one of the last people to see him alive." Coffey's thumb gestured toward the door. "Now get your ass in gear."

Mallory was already out the door and moving toward her car, running to catch up with the posse of homicide cops.

14

IT WAS A STANDOFF.

The crime scene was on the floor below Johanna Apollo's, and the front room was similar to her own, differing only in furniture and bloodstained drapes. The tension ratcheted higher and higher as men in suits and uniforms squared off against one another. Detective Janos, a large man with a thug's face, was flanked by two patrolmen, and all three were engaged in a quiet staring contest with an equal number of New York FBI agents. The police detective glanced at his wristwatch, and Johanna guessed that he was expecting reinforcements. The corpse on the carpet seemed almost incidental to this dogs' war over territory, but no one had yet pissed on the walls to stake a claim. The atmosphere was charged, and more energy was added with each person to enter the room. The outer hall, a contrast of noisy conversations, was filled with crime-scene technicians, men and women with nothing to do until this matter was settled.

The tension doubled when a fourth agent, Marvin Argus, returned from a hallway skirmish with a man from NYPD Forensics. And now the Chicago agent made a tactical error as he knelt down by the body—not *his* body, not yet. When

Johanna had first entered this room in Argus's company, the New York agents had given the man a dour reception. His own people considered him an intruder on this crime scene, and he had made things worse by assuming an air of command unsupported by rank. The local FBI men now seemed more closely allied with the police, all but spitting in Argus's direction.

An imposing gray-haired man with a military air and posture stood in the neutral zone near the front door, and he was looking her way. With the evidence of his expensive suit and a medical bag at his feet, Johanna guessed that he was no minion, but the chief pathologist himself. He towered over his own people, two men wearing jackets emblazoned with the initials of the medical examiner's office, and they called him Dr. Slope. Though this distinguished man was a stranger to her, he gave her a nod of hello. Earlier, his face had been expressionless stone, but fault lines of kindness had since appeared. She would not describe his gaze as simple curiosity. No, after fine-tuning her intuition, she decided that his eyes held merely deep sadness on her account, and there was more to it than pity for the hunchback. The aspect was closer to empathy. For the first time since entering the hotel room, Johanna felt that she was not alone. She smiled at this good doctor, who was wasted on the dead.

More detectives, a score of them all flashing badges, came barreling through the door to make a stand behind Janos. Mallory, the only woman, stood shoulder to shoulder with the men to form a wall of police, and, though none of them held a weapon, the room was electrified, as if all the guns had gone off at once, and real violence could only be moments away. Riker, the last to arrive, broke through the ranks and aimed his whole body at Marvin Argus. No one had time to stop him—assuming that they would want to. He took Argus down with one closed fist to the face. The hapless agent lay on the floor, staring at the ceiling and bleeding from his nose.

The sudden mayhem shook Johanna with revulsion—and it was also oddly satisfying. This latter reaction was shared all around the room. She might have expected the New York agents to close ranks around one of their own, but they stood very still with their hands in their pockets, perhaps as a precaution against spontaneous applause.

"You *stupid* bastard." Riker stood over the fallen Argus, shouting, "I handed that poor man over to you! You were supposed to take care of him last night—*all* night! Did you go to sleep on the job?" He pointed to the corpse lying near the window and partially covered by a fallen set of bloodied drapes. "And why would you bring him to this hotel? You *knew* the Reaper was following Johanna. You knew he was watching this place. It's like you invited that freak inside for a clear shot at murdering MacPherson."

Apparently, this detail was news to the agents from the New York bureau. The senior man hailed one of the police by name, saying, "Lieutenant Coffey—a word?"

When the two men returned from their brief conference in the next room, the dispute over turf had been settled. Possession of the corpse was yielded to the force with the greatest numbers.

Very wise.

Or had the police lieutenant purchased this crime scene with a promise of silence on the embarrassing matter of federal incompetence?

The three New York agents were walking toward the door, then suddenly turned back and, as an afterthought, picked up the debris of Marvin Argus, lifting him from the floor and removing him from the room before his own blood could confuse the evidence by mingling with MacPherson's.

"Guys?" A nod from Lieutenant Coffey cleared more people from the room. "Watch where you step—not like it'll help much. Jesus. Did the crime-scene techs get any time in here?"

"Yeah," said Janos. "Everything was photographed and diagrammed before the feds showed up." The detective accepted a large, clear-plastic bag from a man in uniform, then held it up so his lieutenant could examine the dark clothing inside. "This suit and cap belong to the bellman. We found the guy half naked and stuffed in a trash bin. The suit was thrown on top of him. He's still breathing, but not making much sense. So I figure the Reaper hit him from behind and used this suit to protect his own clothes from blood splatters."

"Maybe we'll get lucky with hair and fibers." Coffey turned to face Johanna. "Dr. Apollo, you saw Agent Kidd's crime scene. Notice anything different here?"

"The writing on the wall." She turned to the single line of block letters scrawled in dried blood: *Ten down and two to go.* Beneath these words was the trademark reported in the newspapers, a red scythe. "Timothy Kidd's murderer didn't leave a drawing or a message." She watched the medical examiner roll the dead man on his back. "I think you'll find that his trachea is cut. That's different, too. Mac was drowning in his own blood." She turned to the smudges of blood on the wall by the window. "See those fist marks? That's frustration and a call for help. He couldn't cry out. All he could do was bang on the walls, but no one heard him."

Coffey glanced at the medical examiner, who nodded in the affirmative. The lieutenant turned his attention back to Johanna. "Anything else you can tell us?"

She pointed to sections of wall on both sides of the front door. "No blood in that area. The killer didn't cut him right away, not the second he walked in. There was probably time for a few words of conversation." She walked ten paces along an adjacent wall and paused by the line of red spots across a framed painting. "That's the fly of blood from the knife. Mac was standing here when he was cut." And this was only one of the lessons from her months as a crime-scene cleaner. She stared at other areas marked by fountains of MacPherson's blood. "At least one carotid artery was severed. That would account for those splashes on the wall. A cut to the jugular vein would've been more like a leak—more like Timothy Kidd's murder. Mac's death was quicker."

She pointed to a corner that was free of bloodstains. "That's where the killer stood—watching Mac die." Her head bowed as she studied the drops and small puddles of blood on the floor. "Mac was moving in circles. I would've expected that. He was losing so much blood—so fast. The larger puddles have a different pattern. No focus anymore, just mindless ambling, spending his blood, dying in profound shock and absolute terror." She turned to face the lieutenant. "Forgive me. I'm telling you things that you already know. I didn't mean to—"

"No problem," said Coffey. "Be as thorough as you like." He stepped up to the unbloodied section of wall, then turned to survey the room from a murderer's point of view. "How do you know the Reaper stayed to watch his victim die?"

"She's right about that," said the medical examiner. He held up a plastic bag with a note inside. "This was stuffed in the mouth—most likely after he was dead or there'd be more blood on the plastic."

A gloved crime-scene technician took the bag from the doctor's hand, opened it and extracted the typewritten note with tweezers. He read the message aloud, " 'I'm too stupid to go on living.' That's all it says."

"I thought that was part of the message the Reaper always left on the walls," said Coffey.

"No, never," said Johanna. "But that's what the reporters were told. The note in the victim's mouth was the only detail the FBI could conceal from the media and Ian Zachary's fans."

Mallory stepped forward, eyes on Johanna, saying, *accusing,* "And now we've established that Agent Kidd gave you crime-scene details. Or maybe you—"

Riker caught Mallory's eye, and unspoken things passed between them. The younger detective fell silent and stepped back into the fold of police.

"Timothy thought I could help," said Johanna, "if I knew more about the ritual aspects." Head bowed, she stared at her clasped hands.

"Dr. Apollo?" Lieutenant Coffey touched her shoulder. "Does anything else resemble the crime scene for the dead FBI agent?"

"There was no note stuffed in Timothy's mouth," she said.

"Nothing in Bunny's mouth, either. The ritual elements were only for the jurors. And Timothy didn't panic and run around in circles like this. There was a single line of blood on one wall of my reception room, a light splatter pattern from the blade. But the rest of the blood was confined to a small area. When his throat was cut, he just sat down in a chair and died quietly." Glances went from cop to cop all around the room, and she knew that she had not been believed.

Lieutenant Coffey was incredulous. "The FBI agent never put up a fight?"

"There were no defense wounds," said Johanna, "if that's what you're asking. He just sat down and died. He would've lasted longer that way, less movement, less blood lost. Apart from that, Timothy's death had more in common with Bunny's. They were a different class of victims, more wary of their surroundings. Their jugular cuts actually did less immediate damage. If I can guess your next question—yes, those two could've been saved with pressure on their wounds and prompt medical attention. Given the aspect of heightened paranoia, the Reaper wasn't quick enough to do his usual thorough job on either of them. Bunny might have screamed, but I doubt that anyone would've paid any attention to him."

She heard the sound of the body bag zipper, but kept her eyes cast down as the medical examiner's men rolled their gurney into the hall. She might have expected the crime-scene technicians to take over now. Instead, she watched the shoes of detectives returning to the room and surrounding her. Johanna took shallow breaths and braced herself for a new attack.

"What about Agent Kidd?" Coffey's shoes were only a few feet away. "You're saying he could've screamed, too? So you figure he was just sitting there in your reception room—patiently waiting for help—*quietly.*" That last word carried the unmistakable tone of disbelief. "Was he waiting for you, Doctor?"

Mallory's running shoes stepped forward. "You were in the next room, isn't that right, Dr. Apollo?"

"Yes."

"But you never heard a thing." Janos's massive brogans lumbered toward her. "No screams, no scuffle—nothing."

All the detectives converged on her, all firing questions at once, enclosing her in a circle of bodies. One of Dante's outer rings? No. Johanna decided that hell was not a place after all, but an ongoing, endless event, a traveling creep show that followed her about.

She closed her eyes.

Her right hand was gently pulled away from her side, fingers intertwined with her own, and then—silence. She opened her eyes to see Riker standing beside her. The other police were backing off in a show of respect for this angry man.

Victor Patchock set his red wig on the dresser and surveyed his world of one room and a bath, bare walls and a patch of floor. Some time ago, he had removed the doors to the closet and the bathroom, and even the cupboard doors of the kitchenette, for they might also give cover to the enemy. But he could not remove the very walls to get at the smallest invaders, the mice. He could hear them tunneling day and night, the soft crumbles of plaster falling away under quick pink feet. Their movements inside the walls and the ceiling were constant, and he was alert to their every sound. They invaded his dreams. He dreamed them now, eyes wide open, staring at a bit of sky, all that he could see of it from the barred air-shaft window. The street window had been recently boarded up, lest he be seduced into exposing himself to the outside world on those shut-in days when the view of the air shaft was not enough.

His former life was so far removed in time and memory. It must have belonged to someone else. Victor wanted to go home again. He could not. And he was so changed, no one would recognize him. He ran one hand over his bald head, suddenly shocked, forgetting that he had mutilated himself by shaving off his hair.

He crossed the room to peer through a crack in the

boarded-up front window. The street below had sparse pedestrian traffic, but soon people would be coming home from work, filling up the spaces all around him, above and below him, a hive of people stressed out and strung out. But the mice were always with him.

Victor selected a white cane from the four in his umbrella stand and whacked one wall to scare the rodent army that he could hear but not see. He beat the plaster harder, making cracks and gouges, infuriated that he could not get at them. His cane snapped; his mind snapped. He walked back to the air-shaft window and looked upward to the small square of daylight. The walls crumbled around him as the sky grew darker, and this was his only proof of hours passing, for he no longer had any clear sense of time.

And now a new sound had been added. He could hear a thin stream of tinny music coming through the walls.

The mice had a radio.

Lieutenant Coffey stood beside the sound engineer known as Crazy Bitch. She had introduced herself that way, as if she had no other name. Detective Janos waited outside in the hall, for her sound booth was a small space. Jack Coffey wondered if she had bathed or changed her clothes in recent memory. Her bare feet were dirty, and the matted spikes of her hair stuck out at odd angles. She *sounded* rational. Speaking into the microphone of her headset, she introduced the police lieutenant to her boss in the studio on the other side of the window glass.

Though it was not yet airtime, Ian Zachary was interviewing a guest with a baby face, torn jeans and new T-shirt with the call letters of the radio station. If this was the SoHo fan, then Mallory's information had been correct. Coffey wondered if she really did have an informant at the station. Or had she planted an illegal bugging device in the studio? He was a long ways from collecting his pension, and it was best not to dwell on that.

The shock-jock held up two fingers to tell the lieutenant that he would have to wait a few minutes.

Not likely. Jack Coffey gently removed the headset from the sound engineer's dirty hair and boomed into the mouthpiece, "NOW!"

Zachary flinched with the sudden pain from his earphones, and the lieutenant could hear a buzzer sounding in the hall as the security door was unlocked. When Coffey and Janos entered the studio, the Englishman stood up to shake hands with them. "Hello, gentlemen. Pull up a couple of chairs."

Jack Coffey sat down. Janos remained standing, going with his strength, silent menacing via looming over small civilians like the man in the torn jeans, who was introduced as Randy of SoHo. The youngster had a vacant look about him, and the lieutenant wondered if he was high on drugs today, or was the boy bone stupid all the time?

Coffey glanced at a clock on the wall. "Zachary, you're here early tonight."

"I'm pretaping the interview with Randy here. I should've mentioned that, Lieutenant. You're on tape now, too. You'll be able to hear yourself on the air in three hours."

Randy leaned into the conversation. "I thought we were on the air right now."

A bemused Zachary pointed to the clock. "Can you tell time?"

"It's six o'clock," said Randy, taking no offense. "Almost exactly six o'clock."

"And when does my show start?"

"Nine o'clock."

"So I guess we can't be on the air—not right now—can we?"

Randy actually gave this a moment of thought, then grinned and shook his head.

Zachary shrugged as he looked from one cop to the other. "I wish I could tell you that he's an atypical fan. So, what's this all about? Do I need a lawyer?"

"Oh, yeah," said Jack Coffey. "We just had a few questions, but you should have a lawyer sitting in your lap around the clock. And the bastards even told you that, didn't they? They told you never to talk to cops, not without a lawyer checking every word that comes out of your mouth. They treat you like an idiot, don't they? But you're safer that way. Now, if you like," he pulled a small card from his pocket, "you can waive the attorney, and then we can get this over with. Or we can take you downtown, and you can just drag this out all night. Your choice." He tossed the card on the console. "That lists all your constitutional rights. I know you've seen it before. Just sign it."

He turned away from Zachary, assuming the attitude of a man who did not care one way or the other. And of course the shock-jock signed the card.

Coffey's smile was genuine as he turned to the interview guest. "So you're the famous Randy? You're the one who ratted out that poor bastard MacPherson?"

The young man nodded and smiled, so pleased with himself, just so happy to be here with Ian Zachary and the cops. "We live in the same building. He's a real nice guy. He fixed my busted radiator."

Jack Coffey was slightly discouraged to hear the boy use the present tense, the living tense for the latest Reaper victim. So much hung on the words of this moron. The lieutenant slid another card from his pocket. "This is called a Miranda card—just like Zachary's." He handed it to the younger man. "Would you like to sign one, too?"

"Oh, sure." Randy accepted a pen from Detective Janos and signed the card, not bothering to read it. And now Ian Zachary was having second thoughts as he stared down at the card he had just put his own name to.

Too late.

Janos whipped the Miranda card out of the man's hand, slid it into his coat pocket, then collected Randy's.

Coffey's attention was still focused on Zachary's guest. "Randy, you say you were friends with MacPherson. So now that your buddy is dead, how do you like your game prizes?"

"Well, I couldn't win the trip to New York City, could I? I mean, 'cause I already live here. I got a place in SoHo. But they put me up in a great hotel for the night. I *love* the minibar." He turned to Zachary. "I get to keep all that stuff, right? The candy and those little bottles of booze?"

"You earned it," said Lieutenant Coffey, answering for the shock-jock. "So the minibar made it all worthwhile?"

"Well, sure, but being on the show—hell, that's the best part. Can I say hi to my buddies at the carwash?"

Coffey held his friendly smile. "When you turned in MacPherson on the radio, did you know what would happen next?"

Before the younger man could speak, Ian Zachary shook his head, saying, "Don't waste your time, Lieutenant. The pinheads never make that connection."

Coffey ignored this and leaned forward in his chair, widening his smile for the fan from SoHo. "That's not true, is it, Randy?"

"Give it up," said Zachary.

Coffey swiveled his chair around to face the talk-show host. "I understand that Randy is the first winner to get on the air before the murder. Am I right?"

"A minor departure from the format," said Zachary, all but yawning. "Randy doesn't have anything quite as sophisticated as e-mail, or even a telephone. And he only had a bit of change left for the pay phone."

"So you couldn't afford to lose the connection. I understand." He wondered if Zachary's attorneys had been quite so understanding. "Your producer tells me you spend a lot of time at the station."

"Needleman? You *met* him?" Zachary's gaze was fixed on some point beyond the lieutenant's chair.

"We had a long talk on the phone." Coffey glanced back over his shoulder, but all he saw was a dark window like the one that spanned the girl's lighted sound booth. "Needleman says you spend twelve hours a day in here. He told me you had this studio built to specs for prison security. Are you afraid of the Reaper?"

"Hardly." Zachary was speaking to the dark window. "The Reaper only kills morons. Why would *I* be afraid of him?"

"And that's what I told your producer." Coffey smiled. "I said, 'Needleman, those two monsters are partners, buddies.'" He splayed his hands in the air. "Am I right?"

"In a manner of speaking." Zachary leaned back in his chair, so pleased, so smug. "I suppose you could say the Reaper is my biggest fan."

"So you knew he'd be listening," said Janos, "when Randy here told you MacPherson lived in his building."

"Yeah," said Jack Coffey, not wanting to give Zachary a moment to consider this. "That was real cute, not giving up the exact address. Instead, you just got Randy to mention the restaurant next door. Very smart." Actually—a huge mistake. A first-year law student would never have approved of that ploy. "And then MacPherson was murdered. The Reaper couldn't have done it without you. Have I got that right, Zachary? Did I miss anything?"

"I'd say you've got the gist of it."

"So that's a yes." Coffey turned to Detective Janos, saying, "Cause and effect. One down."

Zachary was half risen from his chair. "What the hell is that supposed to mean?"

Jack Coffey ignored the startled shock-jock and leaned toward the young fan, saying, "You never answered my question, Randy. What did you think would happen when you gave up MacPherson on the radio?"

"I told you," said Zachary, "the fans are idiots. They don't have the slightest clue—"

"Zachary, put a sock in it," said Coffey. Then, remembering that this man was British and slang-impaired, he added, "Shut up or I'll arrest you for obstructing an investigation. Clear enough?" The lieutenant turned all of his attention on the younger man, the dim-witted one. "Randy, when you made that call, what did you think would happen to MacPherson?"

With no hesitation at all, Randy raised his right hand. There was no malice in his face, only cheerful compliance, as he used one finger to make a chilling cutthroat gesture from ear to ear, the silent demonstration of a death.

And Jack Coffey said, "Close enough." He looked up at Janos, saying, "Cuff Zachary."

Janos moved behind Ian Zachary's chair and pulled out a pair of handcuffs, saying, "You're charged with the murder of John MacPherson."

And Zachary yelled, "This is insane! He tried to kill *me!*"

"Really? Did you report that to the police?" Coffey took the man's dumbstruck expression for a no. "Too bad. You were seen in a bar with MacPherson last night. We've got witnesses."

"He left before I did."

"So you're out drinking with a guy who tried to kill you." Janos slid the manacles over the man's wrists. "And you just let him walk away. No police report. You got a better story than that one?"

"The waitress says another customer opened your shirt that night," said Coffey. "You were wearing a bulletproof vest. That suggests another scenario for—"

"I always wear the vest. I get death threats. Ask the damn FBI!"

"Funny you should mention that," said Janos. "An agent named Hennessey called to tell us that he was assigned to your security detail. But you went out of your way to lose him last night. You wore a disguise and hired an impersonator to send him off in another direction."

Coffey smiled and shrugged. "So you can see why the feds don't exactly help your case."

The handcuff locks clicked shut.

"Ask Riker. He was with me."

Jack Coffey shook his head. "Not when MacPherson was killed. But even if you had a real tight alibi, it wouldn't help. You see, Janos misspoke. The charge is *conspiracy* to murder. You conspired with the Reaper—and your fans." He turned to look at Randy. "This one, for instance."

Zachary's eyes were rounding and his voice was louder, yelling, "You can't do this to me! I've got rights!" He sucked in his breath, then said more calmly, "Ask the damn ACLU. The law is on my side."

"Yeah, well, that was back in Chicago," said Coffey. "In New York City, we like to make up the rules as we go along. You and your fans aided and abetted a serial killer."

Young Randy had thus far been still and quiet in the rapt attention of one viewing this live action on television. He must have recognized himself in a criminal mention, for now he stood up and held out both of his hands, happily awaiting his turn to be manacled by Detective Janos—just like Zachary.

"No, not you," said Coffey to the youngster. "Morons are excused."

Randy nodded and smiled.

"Just kidding." Jack Coffey unhooked a pair of handcuffs from his own belt and did the honors himself, saying, "Randy, remember that card you signed? You have the right to an attorney during questioning. If you can't afford—Randy? Pay attention. This is the important stuff."

Charles Butler had a formal dining area, a waste of space in his opinion. Dinner guests invariably gravitated toward the kitchen, a warm and spacious room with rich ochre walls racked with spices and utensils that only a gourmet cook could identify. A red-checked tablecloth and a Vivaldi concerto created the atmosphere of an intimate bistro.

Mallory stood by the door, spying on Riker and Johanna Apollo in the front room. Charles left a pot of sauce to bubble on the stove and placed a glass of red wine in her hand. "So it's not working out quite the way you planned."

"No," she said. "Riker's not asking her the right questions."

"You mean he's not treating the woman like a criminal? Well, what a damn shame." Indeed, Riker was not behaving like a detective tonight, but more like a man in love. Charles knew all the symptoms. Obviously, Mallory did not.

She set down her wineglass and picked up a stack of dinner plates. He had thought it best to give her the chore of setting the table, since she would have rearranged anyone else's work. As she laid down the plates, napkins and silverware, he needed no ruler to tell him that every item was precisely one inch from the edge of the table.

He turned back to the stove and his task of stirring sauce. "Perhaps it was a mistake to expect Riker to work this out on his own." Oh, not likely that she would ever agree with that idea.

"Maybe you're right," she said.

And Charles lost his spoon at the bottom of the pot.

"He's too close to that woman." Mallory straightened the four chairs, then stepped back to survey her work, as if there might be a chance in hell that those chairs were not perfectly aligned with the table. "Riker's afraid to ask a question that might incriminate the doctor."

"In what crime?"

"She's holding out on me."

Oh, *that* crime. Well, from time to time, that would incriminate everyone Mallory knew. So the situation was not so serious after all, and he had hopes of getting through this dinner party without serious carnage. After retrieving his sauce spoon, Charles opened the oven, and the aroma of fowl roasting in its juices filled the room, mingling with that of garlic bread and the wine sauce. "Riker and the doctor look like they've put in a very long day. Perhaps we could put this business aside for the night."

"Don't you wonder how a smart woman could go along with that insane jury verdict?" Done with the table, hands on hips, she turned to face him. "You read the trial transcript. You know it wasn't an honest verdict."

"But Riker never read that transcript. He's taking the lady on faith."

"Faith? I'm talking about hard, cold facts. There's no way—"

"Mallory, if Riker set fire to a school bus full of nuns and children, then pushed it off a cliff, I'd have to assume that the nuns and children had it coming to them. That's faith."

She grappled with this for a moment, then rallied with a

better shot. "People are dying," she said, as if he might need that reminder. "I need to know if Dr. Apollo kept in touch with MacPherson. If she did, then she probably knows where the other juror is hiding."

"Nothing easier." He picked up an open bottle of red and led the way back to his front room, where Johanna Apollo stood by the far wall, admiring an original painting by Rothko while Riker admired her.

Seen from the back, the woman's deformity was hidden by her long cascade of dark hair; it was more apparent when she turned in profile, allowing Charles to refill her wineglass. He knew that Riker was seeing a different image of the doctor. From the detective's point of view, the lady was without blemish, her ordinary face without peer. And from Charles's perspective, Riker had unexpected good taste in women, opting for intelligence and large brown eyes with a remarkable depth that appeared to see all the way to the soul—the eyes of a healer. The wine had called out his poetic bent, and he carried it further, likening her to a bouquet of roses, though her floral perfume was discreet. Her warmth and presence filled the room as the scent of flowers would do.

Mallory appeared, and the flowers—shuddering—closed.

"My condolences," said Charles, "on the death of your friend Mr. MacPherson. Did you keep in touch with him after the trial?"

Dr. Apollo nodded.

Charles turned to Mallory, who was less than impressed with his interrogation style. She tipped back her glass. Riker, contrary to habit, had hardly touched his wine. Odd, that. And Mallory, with all her control issues, was drinking more than her careful allotment of precisely one ounce of alcohol. This promised to be an interesting evening.

Dr. Apollo excused herself and headed toward the kitchen. Of course, everyone wound up there eventually. However, given the example of the past hour, Mallory's mere presence was motivation enough for the doctor to quit any room. Charles topped off Riker's glass, then returned to the kitchen, where he found his dinner guest shredding lettuce for the salad. The doctor raised her face to his and smiled. Charles's own loony smile always had that happy effect on people.

They worked side by side, chopping vegetables in companionable silence, and then he took up Riker's cause, the complaint that her hotel was not safe. "My house is your house. I have two guest rooms, more than enough space, I assure you."

"Thank you, but it's better if I go back to the Chelsea."

"It's perfectly quiet here," he said. "Triple-pane windows, very thick walls. You could set off a cannon and never disturb the neighbors. So if you want some late-night distraction, music or television—"

"I'm just looking forward to a good night's sleep."

"I'm told you have a cat. If you're concerned about him, that's not a problem. I get along quite well with animals."

"No," she said. "Mugs isn't good with strangers. He's happier in familiar surroundings. We'll both be better off in the hotel."

"She's right," said Mallory from the open doorway. "Your walls might be *too* thick. If the Reaper was in your guest room, cutting the doctor to pieces, you'd never hear the screams. I'll stay in her hotel room tonight."

This was clearly not an offer on Mallory's part, but a hard statement of fact and no great favor to the doctor. Johanna Apollo was not smiling anymore.

Mallory stood by the spice rack, absently rearranging the bottles so that every label faced forward in perfect alignment, and the older woman watched with great interest. What would Dr. Apollo make of this show of compulsive neatness? Charles felt suddenly protective of Mallory, as though she stood naked, her vulnerability publicly exposed. He wondered what else had been observed and how close the psychiatrist might have come to a dangerous truth. And, if the doctor should guess right, how might she make use of that information?

Riker entered the kitchen wearing a happy glow that did not come from the wine. His glass was still full. "I'm hungry," he said.

Dinner was served quietly and without any more ceremony than the lighting of a single candle at the center of the table. Riker seemed unaware of any tension between the two women as he took his seat opposite Johanna Apollo, who might as well be the only occupant of the kitchen. He seemed—content. And this went deeper than his standard laid-back countenance; he was happy for the first time in many months. The cause could only be Johanna, and Charles's gratitude was boundless.

When the candle had melted halfway down and they were nearing the last course of dinner, the conversation turned to the subject of lawyers.

"It's a fascinating dilemma for the ACLU," said Charles.

Johanna nodded. "They always seem to pick the causes that paint them in a bad light, but this one is just too bizarre. The justice system is their raison d'être, and here they are helping Ian Zachary to dismantle it."

"One could almost feel sorry for them," said Charles.

"Hey," said Riker, "they're *lawyers.*" In his economy of words, this meant that, whatever their predicament, the civil-rights attorneys had it coming to them.

While Charles busied himself with setting fire to the bananas flambé, he wondered why Mallory was the only one not on a first-name basis with Johanna Apollo. As he set down the flaming desserts in front of his guests, in one frightened corner of his mind, he theorized that she was keeping a professional distance from this woman. Perhaps Mallory did not expect the doctor to survive. However, there was an alternate and equally good explanation, and now he chose to believe that Mallory simply did not like sharing friends with other people.

A beeping noise interrupted his thoughts, and only Charles, the confirmed Luddite, sat perfectly still as the others checked their cell phones. It was Mallory's, and she rose from the table to take her phone call in the privacy of the next room.

Upon returning to the kitchen, she said, "That was Ian Zachary. He's out on bail, and he wants to see me tonight."

This did not sit well with Riker, who checked his watch. "They're gonna let him go back on the air?"

"Not tonight," said Mallory. "He's suspended pending a hearing tomorrow. That should minimize the damage. Even if he gets a lead on the missing juror, he won't expose the man till he's back on the air. We've got twenty-four hours to find the Reaper or his next victim." She stood behind Johanna's chair, leaning down to ask, "Any ideas about where we should start looking?"

Johanna lowered her head and remained silent.

"Never mind, Doctor. We can talk about that later." Mallory turned her back on the woman and walked toward the kitchen door, saying, "Charles will drive you back to your hotel." Her hand was on the doorknob when she added, with just the suggestion of a threat, "I'll catch up to you later."

"I'll go with you," said Riker.

Slightly annoyed, Mallory turned around, obviously preparing to tell Riker that he was not invited. And now she discovered that he had not spoken to her; his eyes were on Johanna Apollo. Only Charles took note of Mallory's expression, for it was quick to surface but more quickly hidden, and he put a name to it—abandonment.

"Needleman's using an alias." Mallory inspected the door to the producer's booth and its premium lock hyped as pickproof. But this was nothing approaching the advanced technology for the door to the studio. "The address you gave me is bogus and so is the social security number." In anticipation of Ian Zachary's next question, she said, "Your producer's contract is still legal as long as there's no attempt to defraud. You can report the fake number to IRS on suspicion of tax fraud, but I promise you—ten Treasury agents will *not* show up to break down this door."

"You have to do something."

"Why are you whispering?"

Zachary turned his back on her and paced the floor in front of the producer's booth, occasionally glancing at the locked door.

Mallory sighed. This was going to be a long night. "Needleman never threatened you, right? So what's the real problem?"

"He watches me. I know he does." Zachary's voice was more normal now that he had been shamed out of the whispering mode. "The bastard gives me the creeps."

"*Needleman.* A man you've *never met.*" Could she make it more clear that he was wasting her time?

"His window is always dark," said Zachary, "but I can feel his eyes on me. I'm telling you this man is insane. Now, normally that's a prerequisite for my staff, but I'm not the one who hired him. He's under contract to the network."

"But your station manager knows Needleman, right?"

"Yes, but they only met once for the interview. My lawyer got me a copy of Needleman's contract. There's a clause that says he never has to personally deal with me."

"So that's the problem. He's outside of your control. Smart man." If not for the wine drunk tonight, she *might* have dialed back the sarcasm. No, probably not. "You think Needleman knows you killed the last producer? You only mention that murder every night on the radio."

Zachary faced the door to the booth. "You see this lock? It's relatively new. I didn't have it installed, and my contract's supposed to give me complete control of security. Needleman put that lock on his door, and he has the only key. How paranoid is that? He's the only producer at the station who locks the damn booth while we're on the air."

His jitters increased when Mallory rested her hand on the knob. She smiled. "He might be a fan. That's what you're thinking, isn't it? Judging by the calls you get, I'd say most of them are a little disturbed."

"What if he's the missing juror? You were supposed to find that man for me, remember? Well, suppose, after all this time and money, he was right here, hiding in this booth all along?"

Mallory decided to give Zachary a little thrill by pulling out a velvet pouch of lock picks and allowing him to watch her in the act of breaking and entering, thus giving him some value for the very large check that Highland Security would never be able to cash.

"It's illegal to carry burglar tools," she said. "If you ever rat me out, I'll have to hurt you. Understood?"

Perverse bastard, he seemed to like that idea.

The lock yielded, and the knob turned easily under her hand. And now, to give him his full money's worth, she pulled her gun from the shoulder holster, then opened the door—to an empty booth. She flicked on the light to see the same meager floor space as the sound booth on the other side of the hall. It also had a window spanning the length of one short wall and looking in on the larger area of the studio. The console of this small room had one pair of speakers, a headset and little else in the way of technical equipment. Clipboards with schedules hung from hooks on the rear wall, and the wastebasket held more than one man's debris. "How many people use this room during the day?"

"Two producers for morning shows. The rest of the jocks don't rate a staff, but sometimes sponsors come by and look in on their shows."

Mallory ran one finger over the surface of the built-in console. There was no dust. Evidently, the cleaning staff had no trouble getting inside.

"Well, this is progress," said Zachary. "You can dust this place for fingerprints."

"But I won't. There's no point." She did not plan to waste much time exploding the civilians' television mythology of fingerprints. "The prints can only be matched by cops, and they need a good reason to use the national database. Too many people have access to this booth. Some of these prints have been here since the last time the room was painted, a hundred sets, maybe more. Now—if you *die*—the cops might run all those prints, but otherwise—"

"So what's the problem? Not money. Just bribe a cop and run them all."

"No cop can run a hundred prints without attracting attention and losing his job. Half the prints won't even be in the database." Baby-sitting Ian Zachary was tedious, and now one hand went to her hip, sign language to tell him that this discussion was over. "Why not do it the easy way?"

She led him through the door to his studio. When they stood before the dark window of the producer's booth, she pulled out a camera the size of a cigarette lighter. "Tomorrow night, palm this in one hand, then jam it up against the glass. It's small but the flash is bright. He'll never see it coming. When you've got his picture, I can tail him for you. Satisfied?" She gave him the camera. "I'll put that on your bill."

He looked down at the small object in his hand, smiling at this elegant solution. "Great. So what about Dr. Apollo? Did you get me some good dirt?"

"Suppose I find something that forces her into an interview? Wouldn't that spoil the Reaper's game? She doesn't fit his criteria of too stupid to live."

"What if she's the Reaper? Think about it," he said. "A shrink is good at mind games. Didn't you ever wonder why Dr. Apollo voted not guilty with the rest of them? She could've hung that jury all by herself. And here's another thing. She's a hunchback, a cripple. She could walk up to those people and slit their throats before they even got suspicious."

"But why?"

He splayed his hands in a gesture of frustration. "That's what I need from *you.* A motive. It could be the other juror, too, but I'm betting on the doctor. If I could get her on the air for ten minutes—"

"You think she'd expose herself—to you."

"Yes. I'm that good."

"What if she didn't do it?"

"Well, I'd hardly be inclined to let that get in the way of a good show. And I've still got one more juror if the lady flops on the air. That's assuming that you can find him for me."

Mallory turned to the dark glass of the producer's booth.

"You're not coming with us." Johanna Apollo gently pushed Riker away from the car. "You can hardly keep your eyes open. Go inside and get some sleep."

Riker had no comeback for that. He was cold sober, yet his feet were dragging and so was his mind. He could only stand there and watch the Mercedes pull away from the curb.

When the car had reached the end of the street, a concerned Charles Butler looked back to see the man still standing there, as if he might have forgotten the way home—a door three steps to his left. "He's so tired. I hope he doesn't fall asleep on the sidewalk."

"It's my fault," said Johanna. "I'm guessing he never closed his eyes last night." She faced the windshield, and her voice was softer, lower now, in the range of conspirators. "All through dinner, I had this feeling that you wanted to talk to me in private."

"About Mallory," said Charles. "She tends to be a bit— Oh, how shall I put this?"

"Utterly ruthless?"

"I wouldn't have said that."

"No, you wouldn't. You're her friend, but that's her nature."

He began again. "There's a kind of purity in Mallory's character."

"And of course she's a sociopath," said Johanna, "but you already knew that."

They drove on in strained silence for a few blocks while Charles cast about in his great reservoir of words for exactly the right ones. "Mallory's foster parents were very sheltering people."

"And good people. That's what Riker tells me. He talks about the Markowitzes all the time. It's a pity they didn't get to that child sooner. I believe Mallory was ten or eleven when they took her into foster care."

He understood her meaning. Louis Markowitz had missed

the wonder years when his foster daughter should have formed her socialization skills—but never did.

"I'll tell you where Mallory departs from the sociopaths I've treated," said Johanna. "She doesn't make any effort to be charming."

"She wouldn't even know how." Charles had intended this as a defense, but the words had come out all wrong.

"However, she lies true to form," said the doctor, "and much better than most."

"That's a skill that goes with her job." Did that sound egregiously defensive on his part? He kept his eyes on the road and softened his next remark. "The lying, well, that's to a good purpose." Indeed, that was sometimes the case. "Here's another departure you may not have noticed. She never lies to increase herself in someone else's eyes." And that much was certainly true. "She doesn't care what the world thinks."

"But the world should care what Mallory thinks," said Johanna Apollo, and her voice was tinged with a sadness. "That young woman lives large, edgy, risky—and she's dangerous."

"Dangerous," said Charles. "Well, of *course* she is. She's the police." And she was so much more than that. "Mallory's also gifted. High aptitude for mathematics and computers. My job is career placement for very bright people with unusual gifts, so I can assure you she'd make a fortune if she quit her job with Special Crimes."

"But would she have a gun and all that power? Don't you think she'd miss frightening people?"

The Mercedes came to a gentle stop at a red light, and he turned his face to Johanna Apollo's. Her eyes held nothing but compassion, but this would not weaken his adversarial resolve, for friendship was everything to him, and his precious logic was sometimes warped to the best intentions. "Mallory frightens people when she has a reason to do so. You, for example. She thinks you're holding back something important. Her instincts are remarkable—and very rarely wrong. And I've never found any false notes in her basic code. She's a cop, and a good one. She *is* the law."

•

"I'm sure she knows exactly what she is."

Charles nodded, understanding these words on every intended level. "But don't be too sure that you have an easy diagnosis for Mallory. Even if you were right about her, I'd never have her trade places with someone—"

"Someone normal? Less dangerous perhaps? You *do* understand her, and you wanted to warn me about her. Thank you. I'd be honored to have Mallory for an enemy. But I think she looks at me like a broken piece of machinery that won't cooperate in her scheme."

"If you know who the Reaper is—"

"I'd never tell Mallory. Why ruin her game? She's beautifully equipped to work it out on her own. Oddly enough, I admire her. She makes no apologies, takes no prisoners."

"Actually, she does," said Charles as the Mercedes rolled forward again. "That's not just a figure of speech. She takes hostages. That was . . . the warning."

Riker watched the taillights of the Mercedes until they winked out with the turn onto Houston. He sat down on the front steps, preferring this to falling down. The cold air was doing him no good. Had he ever been this tired before? Jo was right. Tonight he would be useless to her. But he had no worries about the Reaper while the giant Charles was in her company, though Mallory would actually make a more formidable opponent, and she was the one he counted upon to keep Jo alive through the night. With any luck, the lady would sleep through the changing of the guard when her second watcher arrived at the hotel. And he could only hope that Jo had the presence of mind to lock up Mugs before the cat could annoy Mallory and die.

It was at times like this, when he was at his weakest, that unbidden memories flooded his mind. He covered his eyes, as if that would help him block out an image of the wild-eyed teenager sitting on his bloody chest. The young psycho had been so disappointed that there was not one bullet left so that he might shoot out Riker's eye. In the mornings, in that small space of time when dreams were not yet shaken off, he could feel the cold metal pressed to his eyeball and hear the click.

His head tilted back, and he stared at the sky where the stars ought to be. There were none. Chains of thought on the subject of heaven led him back to Mexico and starry nights in Cholla Bay. If he could only make it back to that place, that summer. He had finally found a way to kill his waking nightmare, replacing it with a picture of his younger self standing on the beach under a Mexican sun. This boy was waiting for the man to wise up, to come back to the only place where he had been truly happy. If Jo would go with him, he might save himself. A cop's pension would buy a life for two.

He shook his head.

No, you damn jerk. That's a pipe dream.

The boy with the guitar had had his chance and blown it, thrown it all away and gone home to New York. And the man, full grown and going gray, would surely die in this town. Falling short of salvation tonight, Riker thought he might settle for a drink or ten. He rose to his feet and headed down the street to a bar.

Hours later, closing time, he was home again and entering the apartment building, feeling insufficiently smashed and counting on a quart of bourbon in his kitchen cupboard to finish the job. Riker was off to his bottle and his bed, and, with any luck, a blackout night with no dreams.

When he stepped out of the elevator, the hall was pin-drop quiet. Pausing at the door, he fumbled with a ring of keys. Unlike most New Yorkers who only bothered with one lock out of three, he had lately picked up the habit of locking them all. The process of opening them took longer when he was drunk. Finally, after all combinations of keys and locks had been exhausted, he opened the door and felt along the wall till he found the switch and flicked it.

No light.

The door was slammed shut, but not by his hand, and Riker only had time to track the sound of an intruder's quick shuffling footsteps in the dark. The gunshots were four explosions in rapid fire, and he did not stiffen this time. He folded to the floorboards, hitting with both knees and feeling no pain. Kneeling now, he faced a wall of blackness and never saw the light from the hall when the shooter opened the door behind him. Riker closed the door himself as his body completed its fall to the floor, toppling backward and slamming into the wood. Dust motes drifted down to settle on the lenses of his open eyes.

He never blinked.

15

Mrs. Ortega's rolling wire arsenal was armed with liquids, powders, pastes and every tool of her trade. Intent on braving a cleaning woman's vision of purgatory, she walked toward Riker's apartment with grim resolve and squeaking cart wheels. Her apron pockets jingled with quarters for the laundry machines on the floor below, wagering that Riker's sheets had not been changed in months. She planned to root him out in this early morning hour, while he was half asleep and helpless to prevent her from completing her mission. The real beauty of her strategy was Riker's heavy drinking. All she had to do was fire up the vacuum cleaner and jack up the pain of his hangover to drive him out so she could get on with her job. This was going to happen.

Her attitude abruptly changed.

Riker's door was not quite closed, and this was enough to set off a siren in the breast of every New Yorker. In this town, locking up was such a primal instinct that dogs would do it if they only could. A sage voice inside her head screamed, *No, don't go in there!* Yet she put out one tentative hand and pushed the knob inward by a few inches before meeting resistance from an obstacle blocking the door. She could see a revolver lying at the center of the rug, and now she knew what the obstacle was. Using all her slight weight, she pushed hard against the sturdy oak door, then slammed herself into the wood, again and again. Riker's inert body slowly, grudgingly moved inch by inch. Dead or alive, he would yield to Mrs. Ortega's great will.

When the telephone rang in Johanna Apollo's hotel suite, it was Mallory who answered. First she heard the voice of the excited cleaning woman. Then Charles Butler was on the line, and he was only marginally calmer.

"Listen to me," said Mallory. "Mrs. Ortega is absolutely right. Don't touch his body. Don't do anything till I get there. I'm only a few minutes away." After hanging up the phone in the middle of Charles's protest, she rapped on the bathroom door, shouting to be heard above the sound of running water, "Doctor, we have to leave! *Now!*"

Mallory stood before the open closet, reaching for her coat, then suddenly turned to see the small animal just released from the master bathroom, where he had spent the night. He had been softly creeping up behind her when a tiny squeak of excitement gave him away. Now he paused as their eyes met, and they mutually agreed that she could kill him any time she liked.

Mugs, wise cat, retreated to his basket pillow.

"She said not to touch anything," said Mrs. Ortega, "and that includes him."

"Mallory says a lot of things." Charles could no longer bear to see Riker lying there, eyes wide and staring, seeing nothing. He lifted the man's body in his arms, then laid him down on the couch. "I can't think why I let you talk me out of calling—"

"No phone calls." Mrs. Ortega came running from the bedroom with a blanket to cover Riker. "Trust me on this one.

He wouldn't want anybody to see him like this." Her only betrayal of emotion was the way she tucked the blanket around the still body, then smoothed out all the folds in the material. If she could not mend him, she could at least neaten him up a bit.

Charles glanced at his watch. Just as he was thinking that Mallory should be here by now, given the reckless way she drove a car, the detective came striding through the open doorway.

"I *told* you not to move him." Mallory only glanced at Riker, then turned her back on him, as if he were a piece of evidence at a crime scene instead of the more obvious victim of a life gone terribly awry. She drew her gun, opened the doors to the closet and the bathroom, then disappeared down the hall to the bedroom. Reappearing a moment later, gun holstered, she said, "Tell me you didn't call anyone else."

"No," said Charles. "But I should have. He needs a doctor."

"I brought one." Mallory nodded toward the front door.

Johanna Apollo stood in the hallway, gladstone bag in hand. Her wide brown eyes were fixed upon the gun on the floor. "You didn't say he'd been shot."

"Not a mark on him," said Mrs. Ortega, suspiciously eyeing the medical bag in the hunchback's grip. "You're a *doctor?*" Her tone implied fraud, quackery.

Apparently, Johanna Apollo was not satisfied with a cleaning woman's assessment of Riker's bullet-free status. She ripped the blanket away, then shifted him onto his side and checked for overlooked bloody holes. Finding none, she rolled him on his back again.

"He doesn't blink much," said Mrs. Ortega, "but he's not dead."

Taking the cleaning woman's arm, Mallory led her away from the couch, saying, "Show me where you found the body."

The *body?* Charles winced.

"He was right there." Mrs. Ortega's pointing finger made the vague outline of a prone figure on the rug in front of the door.

Mallory stared at the weapon on the floor. Beside it lay a round metal object ringed with deep bullet-size chambers. The cleaning woman had earlier identified it as a speed-loader, this intelligence based on extensive television viewing.

Johanna Apollo was bending over her patient, shining a light into Riker's eyes and finding no one at home in there. "Profound shock."

Heedless of this, Mallory stood over the weapon on the floor and pulled on a pair of plastic gloves. "That's not Riker's gun." She picked up the weapon, opened its cylinder and emptied two unspent bullets into the palm of her hand.

Charles lacked his cleaning woman's television expertise in weaponry, but he was quite sure that these were not normal bullets. They would be more accurately described as the bottom halves of bullets sealed with wax.

"Blanks," said Mallory, somewhat incredulous. "Someone broke in here and shot him with blanks."

Mrs. Ortega and Charles sighed in unison. So ended their only line of speculation, the theory of a suicide gone wrong.

"So it was a robbery." The cleaning woman was almost cheerful, much preferring this less personal crime. "*Blanks.* Go figure." She returned to the couch and leaned down to pick up the cast-off blanket. "These criminal types get dumber every year. That's what Riker always says." She rearranged the blanket over the man's body, saying to the doctor, "You have to keep him warm."

"You're right. Thank you." Johanna Apollo moved aside to allow the cleaning woman more room, then patiently waited out the manic tucking and smoothing of the blanket, as if Mrs. Ortega's ministrations were more important. Charles was deeply grateful for this small act of grace. Johanna had rightly intuited that this little stranger with a Brooklyn accent was in a bit of trouble herself. Mrs. Ortega was tightly reining in emotions that would only humiliate her should they spill out.

And now he studied Mallory, the only unaffected person in the room.

She was utterly focused on the weapon in her gloved hand. "This has to be the revolver he took away from that idiot juror. Riker said the man emptied this gun in the parking garage. So the perp who broke in here took the ammo from MacPherson's speedloader." In Mallory's other hand, she hefted the remaining truncated bullets, as if they might have real weight. "The shooter was already inside. He was standing here in the middle of the room. When Riker opened the door, the lights were off. He was facing the dark and backlit from the hall." Her gun hand was rising, the muzzle pointing toward the door. "And the shooter fired exactly four blanks."

Charles closed his eyes for a moment. Her picture of events was all too clear. Turning to the prone figure on the couch, a man twice proved to be unsafe in his own home, Charles hunkered down beside the doctor, who was sorting through bottles in her medical bag. "Johanna, you should know his history. A psychotic teenager shot him four times. All the wounds were to the torso, all life threatening. It happened in his old apartment back in Brooklyn."

"He nearly died," said Mrs. Ortega.

"He *did* die," said Charles. "He was clinically dead for three minutes before the paramedics revived him." And, in a sense, the man had died again, for the gunshots had obviously seemed quite real to him.

"Four bullet wounds," said the doctor. "And now four blanks. He must have thought the boy had come back to—"

"No," said Mallory. "The shooter's dead."

"Extremely dead," said Charles.

"Yeah," said Mrs. Ortega, "you wouldn't believe how dead that kid is." The cleaning woman turned to Mallory. "So let me get this straight. When Riker fell down, the freak left him for dead 'cause he didn't see any holes in the body. And that's how you know the lights were out. Yeah, that's it. Poor guy. Didn't even have time to reach for the wall switch."

It was Mallory's mildest form of contempt, something bordering on courtesy, to simply ignore the cleaning woman's observations, though Charles thought the logic was rather good. However, now he had time to notice that the wall switch was in the on position, but the lights were off. Perhaps crime detection was something the layperson should *not* try at home.

"If the freak cased this apartment," said Mallory, "he'd know the only other tenant on this floor was out of town. No risk."

"And thick walls," said Charles. "No one would hear the gunfire and come running."

Mallory shook her head. "I don't think he planned to make a lot of noise. He came here with something else in mind. Finding MacPherson's gun in the apartment—that was a bonus."

"So Riker surprised a thief," said Charles, having learned nothing from Mrs. Ortega's last foray. "Well, that fits. I expect it would've taken an experienced burglar to get past the locks on Riker's door."

"You never felt that draft?" The young detective nodded toward the bathroom she had checked upon her arrival.

The door was slightly ajar. Charles opened it a bit wider, and now he was staring at the broken window overlooking the fire escape.

"Not a pro," said Mallory. "Only amateurs do that."

"But breaking that window should've set off the alarm. I had a security service install it before he moved in. They assured me the police would be notified the instant—"

"No," said Mallory. "That would only work if Riker bothered to pay the monthly service fee." She was facing the open door to the kitchen, wherein lay a mountain of unopened mail. Mallory had recommended bars for the bathroom window and even offered to pay for them. But Riker had declined the bars, arguing that he had nothing to steal.

Charles looked around the room of wall-to-wall debris. Yes, jewel thieves and the like so seldom broke into places like this. His gaze settled on Johanna Apollo as she tied a rubber tourniquet around Riker's upper arm to plump up a vein. She was unaware of the younger woman stealing up behind her.

Mallory bent low to Johanna's ear, saying softly, "The Reaper likes to play with people, doesn't he, Doctor?"

Johanna froze, as if Mallory had screamed instead of whispered. The doctor quickly recovered her poise and, with a steady hand, filled a syringe from a thin bottle. "Yes, he does." She shot a trial spurt of fluid into the air, then filled Riker's vein with the rest of her chemicals. "I'm going to need a few more things from the pharmacy."

When Mrs. Ortega had quit the apartment with a handful of prescriptions to fill, Charles was given the task of putting Riker to bed, and Johanna was left alone with the young detective, whom she had come to regard as her jailor. At least there was no doubt about who was in charge.

"How long will this take?" Mallory might as well have been asking when her dry cleaning would be done.

"He's in shock," said Johanna. "I can bring him around in a few hours."

The younger woman advanced on her with a slow shake of the head to say, *No, Doctor, that's not what I mean, and you know it.* "How long will it take to *fix* him."

"The state he's in now—that's only a symptom of his core problem." Johanna sank down on the couch, taking her cues from animals in the wild, not wanting to give the appearance of challenging Mallory's authority in this room. She did not regard this young woman as less than human, but somewhat more dangerous. "A cure could take years. Long-term therapy."

Judging by Mallory's sudden anger, Johanna knew the detective had no clue to the extent of Riker's infirmity. He would not have shared the entire experience in the underground parking garage. He would never have mentioned the paralysis brought on by gunfire, not to the police, and certainly not to this one.

"You know what happened to him," said Mallory. "It's a simple—"

"The problem goes beyond hearing those shots and thinking he'd been ambushed again." That effect would have been temporary. Twice now, she had seen it pass off very quickly. "I interned at a city hospital. I've seen my share of trauma victims. There's more to this than a single event." Johanna found herself preaching to the walls.

"You're wrong." The detective was shaking her head. "I need him back on his feet by the end of the day, and fully functional. He's on the Reaper's radar now. Or did you really think that firing exactly four blanks was just a coincidence?"

Johanna deferred to Mallory on the subject of psychological terrorism. She wondered if this young sociopath was what Timothy had in mind when he wrote the words, *Only a monster can play this game.* No case would ever be proven against the Reaper and no justice obtained for the dead, not by normal human means—but perhaps by Mallory's. Johanna's sidelong glance caught her own profile in the full-length mirror hanging on the open bathroom door. She studied the hump on her back without bias and fairly deemed herself the lesser monster in this room.

"There's no one I care about more than Riker," said Johanna. "I would've died before I'd let this happen to him. But you—you pushed him into this confrontation. You might as well have shot him yourself. The game means more to you than he does."

Mallory sat down at the extreme edge of a chair, creating the nerve-jangling illusion of hovering there like a cat set to spring. "You like him so much? Good." She brought one fist down on the coffee table with the force of a hammer. "Then *fix* him!"

Much could be read into that small gesture of violence. It was no signal of a runaway temper, but deliberate and manipulative. The young detective had a freakish containment of emotion, and this control had come from long practice at trying to pass for normal.

"A quick fix?" Johanna settled into a calm, absolute certainty that Mallory would not physically harm her, and, hence, had lost all power over her. "Riker's not unconscious. I'm sure he's aware of what's going on around him." She nodded toward the hallway that led to Riker's bedroom. "Suppose you go in there, hold him very close and tell him you care if he lives or dies. Or you could shoot him with a *real* bullet. Either way, there might be a beneficial shock value." And she wondered which of these alternatives Mallory would be most comfortable with. "But I still recommend therapy."

"*Years* of therapy." The detective's tone was not mere sarcasm but malice. She stood up suddenly, the better to look down on her opponent. "No time, Doctor." Mallory pulled a velvet wallet from her back pocket and plucked out a thin piece of metal. She crossed the room to stand before a small desk. After diddling the lock on a drawer, she opened it and pulled out another weapon. "This is Riker's gun. Six months ago, I cleaned it for him. He's such a slob. He'd never do it himself." She carried the revolver back to the couch and held the muzzle close to the older woman's face, close enough to see that all the exposed chambers held lethal bullets. Had the young police been hoping for a cringe or a tremor? Yes, there was a flicker of annoyance in those green eyes.

"Breathe deep," said Mallory. "Smell the oil? This gun's been cleaned every day since he left the hospital. He's got a new oil can under the sink and three empty ones in the trash—the trash he only takes out once a month."

Johanna wondered if Mallory had been systematically breaking into this apartment to check up on Riker. Of course she had. She passed through locks with such ease.

The detective's body slowly revolved, and her eyes wandered over the chaos of the front room. "So it didn't take me years to figure out what was wrong with him. Look at the mess in this place. But what a nice, well-oiled, *spotless* weapon." Her fingers curled tightly round the handle of the revolver. "It's *insane* how many times he cleans his gun." One white hand slowly drifted down to the back of an armchair, touching it lightly, almost a caress. "He sits here with his cigarettes, his bourbon and his gun. The next morning, the ashtray's full, the bottle's empty and the gun is perfectly clean. That's how I know what he's thinking about every night. He's setting up habits, planning his own crime scene—*staging* it. That's why the empty bottle and the gun oil are so important. They're props. The night he finally decides to do it, I know there won't be a note left behind. He'll want me to believe it could've been an accident. Riker thinks that'll make it easier for me to lose him."

Stunned, Johanna resolved never to underestimate this woman again. She would not be tempted one more time to find Mallory a convenient slot in the range of sociopathic behavior. This creature was standing alone in a category all her own. Whatever she was, she was one of a kind.

The young detective stood at the window. Something on the street below had distracted her. There was a sudden tension in the rising hand that held the gun. She laid the weapon down on the desk blotter, saying, "It's fully loaded, so don't touch it. Just think of it as a bomb. You still think he's got *years?*" She crossed the room quickly and the door closed behind her with a bang.

Johanna stared at the revolver, then looked up to see Charles Butler standing on the far side of the room. He must have heard a good part of the conversation, for his face was sad and sympathetic.

"Riker does that, too," said Johanna. "Always slamming doors."

Charles strolled over to the desk, picked up the gun with obvious distaste and shut it up in the drawer. "Mallory only does it when she's irritated."

"Or to intimidate."

"That, too." He joined her on the couch, easing down on the cushion and giving her a foolish smile as he hunted for some way to arrange his long legs.

Mallory took the stairs at a dead run, feet touching down on every third step and landing in the hall. She ran to the door and pushed into the street. The man she had seen from the window was heading for the subway. She followed at a distance, descending the stairs to the underground train, following the red wig, the black coat and white cane. The man's movements were quirky as he turned to see her coming up behind him. She made no attempt to hide. He dropped his cane, and she stood very still, patiently waiting for him to retrieve it. He backed away, and she took two steps forward. He turned and ran, pausing at the stairs to the lower level, then clutching the rail in his stumbling descent. Cat and mouse, they rode the trains uptown and down.

Johanna stared at her hands. "I thought Mallory was using Riker to get to me . . . so she could play the game."

"And now," he said, "you realize that it was quite the other way around. Riker needed help. Her dragging him into this mess, that was brutal—and necessary. I couldn't have done it. Neither could you."

She nodded. "I'm wondering if Mallory might be the better psychiatrist."

"Oh, hardly. What she did to him was dangerous. Though I don't think anyone could've predicted this outcome. But Riker's still alive, isn't he? You know, it was Mallory's idea to move Riker in here. You might say that was for her convenience—so she wouldn't have to drive all the way to Brooklyn to check up on him." Charles's eyes slowly took in the entire room. "This was the only safety net she could devise for him. Now, this is a bit of a stretch for you, given what you think of her, but—"

"She saw Riker's breakdown coming."

"Yes, and long before I did. She always knew how much trouble he was in. Her instincts are superb, and that's quite a compliment to you. She seems to have great confidence in your ability to—"

"She thinks I can fix him in a day. Impossible. There's more to this than a single frightening incident. It could take months just to uncover his history before I could even begin to deal with the anger issues. That's why he slams doors. On some level, he's angry all the time."

"But that's a recent thing with Riker. I agree there's a complex problem here, but you might want to consider the idea that it all began six months ago. Before that—"

"Before that, he drank too much. That's been going on for years, hasn't it?"

"Well . . . yes."

She studied the room, the signs of depression spread in long tentacles of debris, a tangible malaise. Just looking at this clutter made her tired. "Charles, I recall him saying that he's known you for four or five years. In all that time, has he ever been a particularly tidy man?"

"No, but his old apartment wasn't nearly as bad as this." Charles's foot nudged an open carton containing an object that was only recognizable as pizza by the wedge shape of the fungus. "And all the really moldy food? That was kept in the refrigerator." His hopeful smile wavered. "All right, granted Riker has other issues, but he was never unbalanced. Nothing about him indicated an unstable mind. And he *never* slammed doors."

Johanna nodded, for this supported Mallory's theory. Riker's anger was tied to recent history.

Mallory's mouse in the red wig had learned quickly. She never came closer than twenty paces. Now he actually stopped to place a phone call from the Wall Street station. And then they were off again, more trains, more stations, all around the town. And all the while he was showing more signs of being rattled, dark glasses sliding down his sweaty little nose. The next time he looked back at her, she smiled, and he stumbled. She knew with a certainty that his next stop would be Grand Central.

Johanna leaned forward, already forgiving Charles Butler as she laid one hand upon his arm. "Now, tell me what you're holding back. Something intensely personal?" Yes, she was right. His face was flushing, apologizing for him even before he spoke.

The man's words were hesitant at first. "This has to be in confidence."

"One doctor to another," said Johanna.

"I heard this story from a third party, Louis Markowitz."

"Mallory's foster father."

"Yes. Louis was also the commander of Special Crimes Unit, and he was rather worried about Riker." Charles paused, perhaps realizing that he had just supplied her with more evidence of a man in trouble long before the day he had been shot. "This wasn't an actual consultation. You see, I don't treat patients. It was more like a conversation to put Louis's mind at ease. He couldn't handle this problem internally. He described the police psychologist as a hack and somewhat less than discreet. So I was the only one Louis could talk to. It seems that Riker had been fixated on his former wife. At the time, they'd been divorced for fifteen years or so. As obsession goes, I thought it rather mild."

Charles smiled as he accurately read her mind. "I know. Given the time frame, you're thinking I must be mad. But there was no overt behavior problem. Riker took an apartment a block away from his ex-wife. He kept close tabs on her routine, knew where she'd be on any given day—so that they might pass one another on opposite sides of the street. Oh, and this is what got Louis Markowitz's attention. Riker used police privileges to track down all her parking tickets, scads of them. And he paid them for her—anonymously. That was the extent of his obsessive behavior. He never approached his ex-wife, never even wanted to talk to her. And I don't think he loved her anymore—just the idea of her—of their life together."

"A romantic ideation?"

"Yes. Despite appearances, I believe he's a deeply romantic man. Now, if you were to repeat that, I think Riker might shoot me. So his ex-wife merely represented a part of his old life, and he simply couldn't move past it."

"His old life, when it was *good.*" She had made her point, for Charles lowered his eyes as he nodded. After a moment of uncomfortable silence, she prompted him, saying, "And then?"

"Well, then he *did* get past it. Riker was talking about moving out of that neighborhood even before he was shot. Before that happened, his frame of mind was improving. Hardly a man in decline. And that's why I believe Mallory's diagnosis is correct." He smiled apologetically. "Sorry. That's jarring, isn't it? But I don't think this problem requires burrowing years into his past. And Riker wouldn't want you to know the history with his ex-wifc . . . not you . . . of all people."

He held her gaze a moment to be sure that she understood the import, the very reason for this disclosure. And there it was, inescapable, as if Charles had writ the words within a heart carved upon a tree, *Riker loves Johanna Apollo.*

16

THE JANITOR HAD FINISHED SWABBING THE FIRST toilet bowl when he realized that he was not alone. A sign had been posted to close the men's room while he cleaned it, but a patron had slipped silently past him when his back was turned. He watched the stall door at the end of one row slowly, softly closing. And he detected a scent unrelated to cleaning solvents, piss and defecation. It was not cologne, for he knew all those smells. Odors were his life. Perfume?

Well, if there was a transvestite back there, he was a quiet one. And, absent the sound of a zipper, what might the pervert be doing? Shooting drugs of course—so predictable. He also knew that the addict would be a newcomer to this downstairs rest room. All the permanent residents, homeless men who made their beds in the stalls, would know better than to enter this place while his cleaning cart barred the door.

After ten years in Grand Central Terminal, the janitor was never taken by surprise. His job had gone stale; he had seen it all and sometimes saw it ahead of time. He could even roughly describe the next person to enter the facility by the light tap of a cane on the floor beyond the door. A blind man was an easy guess—too easy. It was hardly worth the trip around the corner to the section of urinals and sinks. The door opened, and, surprise (yeah, yeah), a white cane preceded—a blind woman? Oh, no, the janitor was not so easily fooled. That was definitely a man behind those dark glasses. Apart from the long, red hair, everything was masculine. So what he had here was a blind drag queen dressed for a day job from the neck down.

But not a redhead.

The wig disappeared into a pocket of the black coat, and the blind man's own snow-white hair was mussed. Leaning toward the vaguely shiny metal that passed for a vandal-proof mirror, the old geezer ran his gnarly fingers over his scalp to smooth down the wild strands.

Not blind either.

But this was hardly surprising. Grand Central was a mecca for bogus beggars. The janitor leaned on his mop, bored by the ongoing striptease, but this was all the spectacle he had. The old man's dark glasses were now secreted in the breast pocket of a very fine suit that really belonged in the posh ticket-holders' rest room upstairs, and the white cane was hooked in the crook of his arm, then hidden beneath the folded black coat.

When the crazy old bugger had closed the door behind him and the janitor believed that the rest room held only one drug-shooting, cross-dressing occupant, he turned in the direction of the toilet stalls. His mouth fell open, and his heart banged against the wall of his chest. A tall, green-eyed blonde blocked his way to the stalls. He quickly stood aside as she marched across the tiles, heading for the door in hot pursuit of the old man. And she was no transvestite, no sir—no Adam's apple on her. This one was all girl and strictly uptown in that long, black leather coat that must have cost the world.

The janitor's heart calmed down. He smiled. Life still had a few surprises for him.

Mallory glared at the old man's back. He stood at the center of the great hall and the crisscrossing traffic of commuters. Once again, she had followed a fake blind man with a long red wig. He had led her back to this same place. But this time, she had passed the young man by, entering the men's room well ahead of him—only to watch him grow old before her eyes. Somewhere along the route of changing subway trains, this elderly man had donned the disguise of the younger one, and she planned to make him pay for that deception. Mallory reached out and clamped one hand on his shoulder, then spun him around. A cellophane-wrapped cigar flew from his hand, and he could only stare at her in bug-eyed surprise.

"Where is he?" She grabbed the old man's arm in a tight grip. "Where?"

"You'll have to be more precise, my dear. I know so many people." The cultured tones of an educated man were a good match to his tailored suit. She had counted on a little stammering, signs of frayed nerves, the typical response of civilians in sudden encounters with police. So why was this man smiling?

"The guy who gave you the wig and the cane—the *young* one—where is he?"

"Oh, I really couldn't tell you. Sorry," he said, though his grinning face put a lie to that. "Well, I expect you'll want to arrest me now. Obstruction of justice or some such thing? As if the city doesn't have enough lawsuits for false arrests." He put out his hands awaiting the manacles, entirely too gleeful.

Mallory regarded him as she would a bag of snakes and cockroaches, for she suspected him of being a lawyer. Near his feet was the cigar he had dropped, but littering was only worth a ticket. She stepped closer to him and feigned a swoon, eyes closing. He reached out to break her fall, grabbing her by both arms.

"That's assault!" Her voice was loud. Heads turned all around the hall. "You just assaulted a cop!"

The old man's eyes were bulging, and he lacked the presence of mind to take his hands off her shoulders. He was staring at all the faces turning his way. People were slowing down, then stopping to watch, and two young policemen were running toward him.

Johanna Apollo opened the door to find Mrs. Ortega standing in the hall, clutching a large plastic bag with a pharmacy logo. The cleaning woman wordlessly moved into the room and dumped out the medical supplies on the coffee table. Then, breathless from running all the way, she hurried down the short hall to the bedroom. Johanna followed, intending to approach this wiry little person with greater caution than she had taken with Riker's other protectors.

In the bedroom, Mrs. Ortega was fretting over the sleeping man, tucking the blanket under his chin and smoothing stray hairs from his brow. Such simple services—and done so awkwardly. Clearly, acts of tenderness were outside the character of this rough-spoken New Yorker. The cleaning woman exuded anxiety, and she no longer had her mask of bravado to disguise the fact that she was coming undone.

"He's in deep trouble." Mrs. Ortega continued to fuss with the blanket, picking off tiny wadded balls of wool as she spoke her piece. "All the drugs in the world ain't gonna help him."

"I know," said Johanna, and not in any condescending manner. "But the prescriptions always make the friends and family feel better."

"Gotcha." Mrs. Ortega nodded as one conspirator to another, but her sorry eyes remained concentrated on Riker. "I should've got to him sooner. I seen this kind of thing before." The cleaning woman waved one hand in the air to say that she had borne witness to the whole sorry range of humanity. "Riker's got nothin' and nobody. Holes up like a hermit since he got shot. I mean the time he was *really* shot, *real* bullets. Now look at him. I seen it before—maybe not this bad. Say one of my customers loses his job. Well, life gets a little crazy, sure, but *that* guy's still got his nice clean home—*real* clean." She pressed one hand to her bosom and said with great pride, "*I* do windows." She turned back to the man on the bed. "Most people in trouble, they still got friends, family—something *normal.* You know what I'm sayin'?"

"I know," said Johanna.

"Riker's home was in Brooklyn." Mrs. Ortega pulled a rag from an apron pocket. "He can't go back." She absently polished an uncluttered corner of the small table by the bed, the rag running round and round as she spoke. "So how does this happen—gettin' ambushed again?" She wagged one finger at Johanna. "I'll tell you how. He cut off his friends, lost his job. He's off his game. If he'd gotten one piece of his life together just a *day* sooner, nobody could've taken him down this way. Not Riker. No, ma'am. If I'd only got to him sooner." She sat down at the edge of the bed, slowly folding her lean frame, as if deflating, losing air and will, and her voice was smaller when she said, "I could've fixed him."

"How?"

Mrs. Ortega looked up, suspecting derision. Instead she found compassion in Johanna's eyes and also the encouragement to keep going, and so she continued. "It's like everybody's life sits on three legs. You got your home—that's a big one. And then there's work, then friends. Well, say one thing goes wrong, maybe two—you can still stand on one leg, right? But what's Riker got?" Mrs. Ortega's eyes were unfocused, looking inside where the guilt was stored. "No wonder he fell down. I should've got to him sooner."

"He's still fixable." Johanna pulled a wad of money from the back pocket of her jeans. "I'd like to rent your cart of supplies for the rest of the day."

"Naw." The woman waved away the proffered money. "This is my day off. That's why I stopped by to finish up with my charity case here." The old New Yorker attitude was creeping back into Mrs. Ortega's voice, and her face showed the more normal state of contempt as she threw up her hands. "You think this slob would ever pay for a cleaning woman? Never. So I'll stay and finish the job—for free."

"I've got a better idea," said Johanna. "You'll like it."

And Mrs. Ortega did like the plan. She loved it. It reeked of the pop-psychology cures found in her self-help books and television programs. For Johanna's part, it was merely an entrée, a means of walking around inside Riker's head.

The elderly lawyer stood in the company of policemen and a hundred other people.

He was not the focus of everyone's attention, for the most dedicated travelers, obviously out-of-towners, were bent on catching trains of overground rail and underground subway, and selectively blind to the show. But a hardcore New York crowd was assembling in a wide circle, maintaining the distance of an experienced audience for live theater.

The old man waited with great trepidation as the two young officers spoke with the pretty blond police who had accused him of assault. Detective Mallory smiled as she turned his way, and he took this as a good sign that their recent misunderstanding would be presently and pleasantly resolved.

She looked down at one of her black running shoes, and her face was somewhat petulant when she said, "You scuffed it. Do you have a handkerchief?"

"Ah, yes." What a small price to pay for freedom, a very small price indeed. With a courtly bow, the old man pulled a folded square of monogrammed Irish linen from his pocket and handed it to her. She held it for a moment, her eyes meeting his with a cold stare. When she opened the handkerchief, a twenty-dollar bill appeared in the fold of material. He stared at it aghast. There was no way it could have—

"A bribe?" The young woman held up the handkerchief and the mysterious twenty-dollar bill. She handed the money to one of the men in uniform. "The bill is evidence. Bag it."

"That's not my twenty," said the incredulous lawyer. "I can prove it." He opened his wallet. "See? I don't have anything smaller than a fifty."

"So now you're trying to bribe *all* of us?" She turned to

the officers. "That's probable cause for a search. Pat him down for weapons."

The brief foray into his clothing turned up the odd contents of his pockets and what was hidden under his folded coat. A red wig, a white cane and dark glasses were confiscated as the audience of civilians stepped closer. This show kept getting better and better.

The detective had a very unnerving smile. "This better be a good story. What are you up to, old man?"

It was the tapping of the blind man's cane that woke Riker.

No, not that.

Jo was lightly rapping the floor with her soles, a sit-down tap dance, an old soft shoe to the rhythm of *Wake up, wake up*. He opened his eyes a bit wider when he saw the long tube that began with a needle in his arm and led up to a bag of fluid hanging from the bedpost.

"That's a Valium drip," she said.

Valium? How humiliating—the drug of choice for old ladies and other sissies. A cluster of pharmacy bottles on his nightstand completed the image of an invalid's sickroom. He looked down at his chest, where four new bullet holes should be, and saw that his clothes had been changed. He wore a black T-shirt. His pants were also black, part of a suit that he seldom wore, and that accounted for the lack of stains and cigarette burns in the material. And his feet were bare. He was all laid out like a corpse at his own wake.

"So, Jo, who picked out my ensemble?"

"I did. That's your shroud. You're dead today." She smiled, as if this might be a good thing. "It's a trick I learned in college. Remember final exams? Those days when you didn't want to get out of bed—ever again? Playing dead can actually cheer you up. Nobody expects anything of a corpse. Life gets so much easier after you die. Oh, did I mention that I'm the one who dressed you? And now that I've seen you naked, shouldn't I at least know your first name?"

"I told you the day I met you, Jo. I don't have a first name, never did." He fished in one pocket and found it empty. "Go get my ID. Check it out."

"I already looked at it. There's an initial, a *P.* What does that stand for?"

"That's all it says on my birth certificate." He watched her remove the needle from his arm, then noticed the puncture wounds of other injections, a chemical soup. He felt docile but not dopey, no fog in the mind, and he needed no help to get out of his bed. Had he known what Jo had in mind for the day, he would have rolled over and gone back to sleep.

Lieutenant Coffey had a comfortable front-row seat in the shadows, but the show on the other side of the one-way glass was over. In the next room of bright lights, an elderly prisoner sat with his baby-sitter, a great hulk of a cop, whose facial features suggested that he might be prone to bone-snapping violence. Detective Janos was under orders not to speak, for his soft and gentle voice was evidence of a benign soul adored by dogs and children. So he merely stared at the old man, sometimes grunting a reply. The prisoner was smiling, apparently enjoying Janos's company and chatting amiably, not caring that the guttural responses were somewhat limited.

Lieutenant Coffey turned to the young detective seated beside him in the dark. "What possessed you to arrest a lawyer?"

"Always wanted to," said Mallory.

Jack Coffey nodded. This was every cop's fantasy.

"What the hell?" Riker would have decked anyone else for trying to wrap him in an apron, but since it was Jo, he was helpless to untie the bow she had fashioned behind his back.

"We'll start with the kitchen," she said. "It's a pit."

A good description. The floor was so sticky with spilled food and beer, he sometimes got stuck like a bug on flypaper when he walked through the room barefoot. She led the way down the hall to the kitchen, where a familiar object was waiting. Riker had never seen Charles's cleaning woman separated from her wire cart of tools and supplies. "Don't tell me what you did with Mrs. O.'s body. It's better if I don't know."

Jo pulled a garbage bag from a box on the cart and handed it to him. "I supervise. You do the work." She sat down at the table and watched him bundle junk mail and beer cans into the bag. After the floor had been cleared, she handed him a plastic bottle. He struggled with the concept of a spray nozzle as she explained that the liquid would cut through the grease on the tiles, then asked, "So what did your parents call you when you were little?"

After spraying the floor, he pushed the mop around in silence. Jo's foot tapped to an impatient rhythm, and he said, "My dad called me Hey Kid. My little brother's name was You Too."

"You never asked what the *P* stood for?" *Highly unlikely,* said the tone of her voice.

"Okay, I'll tell you the story my old man told me." Riker pretended interest in the floor tiles emerging from the dirt. "Dad's name was Phillip. He said I was named after him. But he didn't want me to get stuck with a tag like Junior for the rest of my life, so he just put the *P* on my birth certificate. He said it was a secret, just between us, and even my mom didn't know. Well, I loved that story, and I never told it to anybody, not ever. Not having a first name—that drove the other kids nuts. It was great."

"But when you were older and less gullible, you asked him for the real story, right?"

17

THE ODOR OF RANCID FOOD WAS FOUL, AND SO Johanna supervised the cleaning from a distance. Riker was stalled. He stood barefoot in the light of the refrigerator's grease-splattered bulb, his hands filled with small packets of mustard and ketchup salvaged from take-out containers, and now he debated the value of his condiment collection.

"Oh, get crazy," said Johanna. "Just toss it. Every time you throw something away, your load gets a little lighter."

Mrs. Ortega's philosophy of clutter was carried through all the drawers of the kitchen, repositories of empty matchbooks, dead batteries and metal parts that had fallen off of appliances that he no longer owned. One broken swizzle stick was tied to a memorable binge, and he was allowed to keep it. Out on the street, Johanna watched him load the garbage cans with bags of trash and throwaways, including socks with holes that could not be mended, not even with the yarn of entire socks. The effect of her drugs was wearing off. He objected to bare feet on cold pavement, but she would not let him put on shoes, arguing that dead men had no need for them, but socks might be all right. He found one hardly used pair beneath the bed, and she stood over him as he sat on the rug and put them on.

"So how old were you when you knew your father lied about your first name? When did he tell you the real story?"

Instead of answering her, he lowered his head to take on the next task, foraging under the bed for the wildlife of spiders and dust bunnies. And now it occurred to her that the story of his first name was not the small, easy confidence that she had counted on to open his mind to the healing process and the toxic secret that poisoned him.

"All right," she said, spilling pharmacy tablets into her hand. "Never mind."

The meds, a chemical cheat, would destroy his resistance. Jo held out the pills in one hand and a glass of water in the other. He took them willingly enough, trained from childhood to follow the doctor's orders with absolute trust. She planned to render him defenseless so that she might crack his mind wide open before this day was over.

"Let's try something easier," she said. "Why do you always slam doors?"

Lieutenant Coffey sat in the dark, irritated beyond belief. In the interview room on the other side of the one-way glass, his detective was not faring as well. To some extent, the silent treatment had worked, for the suspect was certainly talkative. However, the elderly lawyer was winning the day, slowly wearing down poor Janos with endless prattle about the great game of cops and killers, and displaying ignorance of both.

Jack Coffey turned to Mallory. "You got his stats?"

She nodded. "Old and rich. I'm guessing he got fed up with retirement. He thought I was going to arrest him for obstruction of justice."

Perversely, Mallory had arrested him for everything but that. Jack Coffey scanned the list of charges against the old man: littering, assault on a police officer and two counts of bribery. And she had no less than twelve corroborating statements. God bless eyewitness testimony, worthless as it was, and the power of suggestion. Though the evidentiary twenty-dollar bill was certainly Mallory's own money, eight of her witnesses had come to believe that they had actually seen the old man hand her the bribe. But all the lieutenant had really needed to know was that the elderly lawyer represented a young man with an obsessive interest in Detective Sergeant Riker.

"I guess this'll hold him for a while," said Coffey. "But he'll never give up his client. And now he's going to sue the city just for fun."

"Wrong," she said. "He's going to fold after a few hours in a lockup cage. The old man was a probate attorney. No criminal practice—only wealthy law-abiding clients. I'm betting this is his first visit to a police station."

"Let's find out." The lieutenant pressed the intercom so his voice would be heard in the next room. "Janos? Book the old bastard. And take your time. We got all night to dick around with him."

Jack Coffey smiled, for the attorney's expression of shock was worth the threat to his pension. It was slowly dawning on the old man that his incarceration was going to be dragged out a bit longer than he had previously supposed. He might be looking forward to lockup time in the company of prisoners with satanic delusions and head lice that were all too real.

It was during a field trip to the downstairs laundry room that Riker made his first confession. While waiting for the washing machine to finish the spin cycle, he sat beside her on a bench by the window, his face bathed in late afternoon light, eyes in soft focus, looking inward.

"Insanity goes with the job," he said. "All the people in this town are smashed in together, stacked up like cordwood. I'm surprised they don't go nuts more often. And the things they do to each other, Jo. It's a horror show every night. And here's the scary part. Sometimes police go nuts, too. I'll never be a cop again."

"Because of what happened in the parking garage? And that day with the van?"

"Yeah, I froze. And those weren't the only times."

She waited out the silence as he loaded the wash into the dryer. When he sat down again, he would not look at her. He spoke of all the details to his waking nightmare. While the dryer ran round and round, she sat beside him, holding his hand and listening to the symptoms of his trauma, the paralysis of loud noises, the suffocation and panic that followed. It was a replay of his own death, replete with the weight of a psychotic teenager sitting upon his chest, making it impossible to breathe. Worst was the feeling of shame.

"That's what the burnouts do," he said. "They freeze up when guns go off. And then some other cop gets shot because they can't—" He lowered his eyes. "Every day, I wake up scared."

"And this is what you've been living with," she said, "every day for all these months." Johanna knew he was still holding back. The worst thing in his mind was still locked away from her. But this was a promising beginning, and she had come to share Mallory's concern for a quick solution—else she might lose him.

They sat there for a quiet hour. Her hand rested on his knee to anchor him to the solid world of the laundry room. His hand covered hers, holding on to save himself, holding on to his sanity by touch and force of will. The laundry in the dryer went round and round. The sun went down.

The elderly lawyer was pressed up against the wall of the lockup.

He was in fear of his new cellmate, a man much smaller than himself. Mallory sat at a table a few feet away and watched the performance of the perp who shared the lawyer's narrow cage. Another precinct had contributed the

Central Park flasher, a bona fide pervert reportedly too shy to talk. The sex offender was wearing nothing underneath his overcoat, and now he exposed himself to the lawyer. According to the rap sheet, the man's gender preference ran to heterosexual liaisons, but a few dollars had inspired him to blow the old man a wet kiss.

"Did you see that? He spit on me," said the attorney.

"He must like you," said Mallory, though that little gesture would not get the flasher's charges dropped, and she did not intend to pay any more cash for anything less than skin contact.

They were folding laundry at the kitchen table when Johanna said, "You look ten years younger. Mrs. Ortega said that would happen."

Riker smiled against his will, liking this compliment from her. He was highly suggestible now, the lingering effect of her drugs. He took her orders and put his back into the work when they moved on to the gross problem of the tub and the shower stall. There he wiped away months of lethargy and sorrow with a sponge. The broken window glass had been replaced by a glazier, and Jo had swept the floor herself so he would not cut his shoeless feet. Next, she planned to teach him how to turn on a vacuum cleaner. By day's end, Riker would be tired and ready for a long and natural sleep, but she had yet to break down the rest of his walls.

Johanna resorted to a touch of shock therapy. "Your bouts of paralysis are a form of panic disorder."

He turned to her with a look that said, *No, anything but that.*

"Sorry," she said. "That sounds like a woman's affliction, doesn't it?" Ah, men—bigots every one of then. "When you hear the bang of a gun, you're always waiting for the next bullet, and the—"

He was shaking his head, not wanting to discuss this anymore.

Well, too bad, Riker.

"Last night, you opened the door on a dark room, you heard all four bullets—and you shut down. You were dead—*again.* That's what your mind told you, but the body rebelled. It *demanded* air. Your lungs filled up and you came back. This time, your brain was slow to catch up with what the body already knew. How much do you remember about last night?"

More head shaking. Riker did not want to remember. He opened the medicine cabinet and carefully examined a bottle of aspirin with an expiration date from the previous decade. To toss or not to toss? He never noticed that he was standing alone.

Treading softly into the living room, Johanna went to the closet and pulled the small silver pistol from the pocket of her jacket. She had never fired a gun in her life. She held it in both hands, bracing for the shot as she glanced toward the bathroom. Riker turned away from the medicine cabinet, and now he watched her through the open doorway. His jaw had gone slack, then he mouthed the word *no.* She squeezed the trigger and the bang stunned her as she felt the recoil of the weapon. She would have dropped the gun, but Riker was beside her and taking it from her hand.

"What the hell are you doing?" He pushed the heavy couch to one side and inspected the floorboards. "We got lucky. The upholstery stopped the bullet." He looked down at the gun in his hand. "Well, that figures—a peashooter. If you'd fired my gun, you could've taken out two tenants on two different floors."

"Riker, you didn't freeze up that time."

He looked down at the wonder of his body in motion. "So I'm cured?"

"No. I'm good, but I don't do miracles. If it was that easy, I would've dragged you to a firing range. The drugs in your system dulled the panic response. And I should probably give some credit to the Reaper. He gave you what you've been waiting for since the day you left the hospital. He took the pressure off, the pressure that was killing you. Even without the drugs, you might've bypassed the paralysis this time. But a few visits to the firing range could be . . ."

She could tell that Riker was not listening to her anymore. His concentration was somewhere else as he stared at the silver gun in his hand.

"You know," he said, "most people think a small-caliber pistol is next to useless. But this little twenty-two of yours is a Mafia favorite. It's an executioner's gun. The bullet shatters and it stays in the body. No messy holes in the walls to mark a crime scene. But, Jo, if you want to kill a man with this, first you have to tie his hands. Then you force him to his knees, put the gun to the back of his head and squeeze the trigger." He glanced at the new hole in his couch. "That was the first time you ever fired a gun, wasn't it? Now, let's say your guy is on the loose and coming at you. If you can't place the shot in his head—and you can't—then you might just piss him off. But I'm betting you won't even get off one round."

He removed the clip from her pistol, then turned his back on her. He walked to the closet and placed the clip and the gun in the separate pockets of her jacket. "And it wasn't the Reaper who fired those blanks. He's a slasher, not a shooter. It was the same psycho kid who ambushed me six months ago." He gathered up a stack of clean sheets and walked off down the hall to make up his bed.

But that boy was long dead. A worried Johanna picked up the telephone and dialed the number on Charles Butler's business card.

Mallory edged her chair closer to the lockup cage and its two occupants, the pervert and the old man. She lightly rubbed the back of her hand, feigning an itch. "Damn." She gave the flasher an angry look. "I think I picked up one of your fleas."

The elderly attorney began to squirm and scratch his own hands and face, agitated by the power of suggestion. He pressed his back to the cage door and put up both arms to ward off the smaller man, who slowly extended one hand for the promised skin contact that Mallory had bargained for.

"Don't let him kiss you on the mouth," she said. "We don't know where he's been, and he hasn't been checked for TB yet." This was the flasher's cue to cough.

She smiled as the old man slid into shock. Ah, germs. She had found his soft spot, and she could read the lawyer's thoughts, *No, this can't be happening to me.*

"This is just a holding cage," said Mallory. "I can move you downtown to a bigger lockup if you like. You'll have more room, more people to talk to, maybe twenty or so—all a lot like him." She shot a warning glance at the coughing pervert, a reprimand for overacting.

Riker pushed the vacuum cleaner across his bedroom rug, drowning out the sound of Johanna's worried voice. She leaned down to the wall socket and pulled out the machine's plug.

"If that psychotic was still alive," said Johanna, "you'd be under police protection right now."

"I am." He dropped the vacuum hose and turned on her. "There's always cops following me around. What's the problem, Jo? Does that sound a little crazy? What about that dead FBI agent? Did Timothy Kidd sound crazy, too? He was paranoid, wasn't he? Did he think he was being followed?"

"But there *was* somebody following him."

"Yeah, and I know that feeling. Poor bastard—always looking over his shoulder. So now I have to wonder, how does the Reaper get so close to a paranoid fed—close enough to slash his throat?"

"Well, maybe I am a miracle worker. You're all cop now, aren't you? Isn't this how you talk to suspects? You're just trying to evade the subject. This idea of yours that the shooter—"

"How did Agent Kidd lose his edge, Jo? He knew he was being followed—followed by his own people, for Christ's sake. Here's a guy armed with a gun, and his nerves are so shot, he hears pins dropping in other rooms. How did his killer get close enough? According to your own notes, he knew that bastard on sight. So how does a thing like that happen, Jo?"

"The same way it happened to you—twice."

The little flasher was more sympathetic than Mallory. He was listening with rapt attention as the elderly attorney rambled on about the death of his wife and the long bout of depression that had followed her funeral.

Mallory's fingernails rapped on the table, just a hint that he should speed up his story and get to the good part, the identity of the young man who owned the red wig and white cane.

A uniformed officer opened the door and leaned in. "Detective? You've got company, the chief medical examiner."

Mallory was immediately suspicious, for she had done nothing to merit this kind of service. Dr. Slope preferred to have cops come to *his* shop.

Johanna sat on the edge of the bed, tired and feeling the need of support. Though she had not done any of the physical work, this day was wearing on her.

Riker, however, was showing no signs of all the chemicals she had used to fine-tune his body and his mind. He loomed over her, arms folded, waiting for her to say something—to defend herself. Yes, that was the sentiment, and she could not understand the change in him.

"I've already told this story so many times," she said. "It was all in my statement for the Chicago police and the—"

"And now you can tell it to me."

How did this turnaround come about? Riker was growing more remote in every passing minute. She stared at the floor as she spoke to him. "It had to do with comfort zones. Timothy had one place where he felt safe. My waiting room was very private and secure. Patients were buzzed into that room.

When the sessions were over, they left by the back door of my office. Coming or going, they never encountered one another. It was Timothy's habit to come twenty minutes early for appointments. He said my waiting room was like a decompression chamber—his safety zone. I never buzzed anybody into that room after he arrived. I'm guessing the Reaper came up behind Timothy when he opened the door. His throat must've been slit instantly. So that's how it happened—in the one place where he wouldn't expect to be assaulted. And you, Riker—you never expected anyone to shoot you in your own apartment. Not the first time, not the second time."

Riker would not allow the subject to come back to him, not yet. He stepped to one side, exposing the small surprise he had prepared for her on the bureau. It was the packet of letters she had carried in the torn lining of her jacket. He must have found them when he had returned the gun and the clip to the pockets. And while she had been on the telephone with Charles Butler, Riker had been sitting in this room, reading all of them.

He picked up the packet and held it high as a tangible accusation. "Agent Kidd was working full-time on the Reaper case."

"Eventually, yes. But not when we met. I didn't lie to you."

"And you didn't tell the whole truth either. He was looking into the jury murders while the first one still belonged to the Chicago police."

"I know it looks that way."

"And you were lovers," he said. "You lied about that."

"I suppose the police might've thought so—if they'd found those letters the day they searched my rooms."

"He touched you."

"Timothy? He never did."

"He *touched* you."

"Oh, I see." She had not expected Riker to use that sense of the word. "I suppose he did, but Bunny touched me, too, and he wasn't so talented—only a schizophrenic."

"Timothy Kidd loved you." He tossed the letters onto the bed beside her. "And he died because of you. No defense wounds. That's what you told Lieutenant Coffey. The guy just sat down in a chair and bled out—quietly. He wouldn't put up a fight because you were in the next room. So he was bleeding, dying in your reception room. And you—a damn doctor—help was just on the other side of a door."

"I didn't know," she said. "He never made a sound."

"You said his trachea wasn't cut. He could've yelled for help, but he never did, and you know why. If you'd walked into that room, the Reaper would've killed you, too. That's how you knew the freak stuck around to watch his victims die. Because Timothy loved you so much, he never made a sound. He died for you."

"That's not why I kept his letters." She gathered them up from the bedspread and held them in both hands, suddenly realizing that she had betrayed their precious value to her. "He was my friend. This is all that's left of him, his personality." And she should have burned them long ago, for she knew every line by heart. "I didn't encourage Timothy's feelings for me. I thought he was too vulnerable and—"

"Too crazy? He thought his own people were following him—and the Reaper. And even though it was all true, he knew you didn't believe him. And why should you? He was a freaking paranoid. But what about me, Jo? Do you believe me? Cops *do* follow me around, Jo. And why? Because the psycho who shot me is still out there—still *alive.* And sometimes it's not cops. I know that boy's watching me, Jo. Do you believe that?"

Paranoia would also go with Riker's job, the half-turned stance to see over his shoulder, the bit of business caught in the corner of his eye as he paused to listen for odd noises, singling out one from the rest. He thought a teenage psychopath was coming to steal his life, and this was his fear every day since he had been shot.

Yes, she believed him—and she cried.

He sat on the bed, close beside her and a different man when at last he spoke again. "You feel everything, don't you, Jo? Everybody's pain."

Johanna dropped the letters to the floor and placed one

hand on his chest over the worst of his scars, the one perilously close to his heart. She had seen all the wounds while dressing him. It was miraculous that he had survived, and she knew what it had cost him to live with his memories of that event and the crushing weight of stress in every moment of his day.

He gently moved her hand away so his scars could not hurt her anymore.

When Mallory entered the private office, Jack Coffey rose from his desk and quit the room, most likely sensing the tension between the two men who remained and guessing that he was best left out of this conversation.

Chief Medical Examiner Edward Slope was seated with his back turned on Charles Butler, who slumped against one wall in abject misery. Mallory only glanced at him, posing a question with her eyes, no doubt wondering what he had given away. Charles shook his head to tell her that he had made no admissions, but she was not reassured, for his unhappy face said so much. He could not hide a thought and never attempted to lie, which explained why Edward Slope took all of his money in a weekly poker game.

Mallory folded her arms against the medical examiner, demanding, "What's going on?"

"That's what I'd like to know," said the doctor, "but Charles won't confess. Tell me, Kathy, how is Riker these days?"

"Mallory," she said, correcting his forbidden use of her first name. "I haven't seen Riker lately. Why are you here?"

"Charles wants to know if I botched the autopsy on the boy who shot Riker."

"I never said anything of the kind." Charles turned toward Mallory, helpless now, because he was not adept at misleading people. That was *her* forte.

"I bet Dr. Apollo put that idea in your head," said Mallory. "Am I right? She's the one who thinks the autopsy was rigged?"

"Right," said Charles. "Not *my* idea."

"That fits." She circled around to the back of the medical examiner's chair and leaned down to speak to him. Her voice dropped into that low range for telling secrets. "Nothing I say goes beyond this room. Deal?"

"Knowing you as long as I have, I'm hardly going to promise that."

"You asked about Riker." She moved behind the desk and sat down. "He's in a bad way." This unpredictable truth telling was truly disarming, and she engaged the surprised man in a staring contest. "If Riker had to take the psych evaluation today, he'd fail it. So don't help me. Rat him out. See to it that he never gets his badge back." And now, assured of the medical examiner's allegiance, she faced Charles. "Dr. Apollo got this idea from Riker, didn't she?"

"Johanna wouldn't say. She only asked if there was anything odd about the autopsy report. Something withheld."

Mallory nodded. "Every time Riker walks into a room, he's checking every stranger for concealed weapons. That's been going on for a long time. Now I'm guessing he thinks the shooter is still alive. His concentration is split. He's looking for the wrong suspect, and that's going to get him killed. I told him the perp who shot him was dead. I told him that six months ago. But I guess he didn't believe me."

"Hard to imagine why," said Edward Slope, perhaps leaning a bit too hard on the sarcasm.

"I don't understand," said Charles. "How could Riker believe a thing like that? Didn't the police shoot this boy quite a few times? *Thirty* times?"

"Well, we shot *somebody*," she said.

Charles's lips parted to speak, but mere words would not suffice, not just this minute, nor could he get them out, for his mouth had gone suddenly dry.

Edward Slope leaned back in his chair, then graced Mallory with a rare smile. "And people say you have no sense of humor."

18

"THE PARENTS IDENTIFIED THE WRONG BODY." Riker paced the bedroom floor, working off his anger. "And they *knew* it wasn't their kid. That's why they never filed a wrongful-death suit against the city. Happens every time a suspect gets shot by the police. The relatives always do that. But not this time."

"There must've been blood tests on the body," said Johanna.

Riker shook his head. "What for? Thirty bullet wounds made the cause of death pretty damn clear. And the next of kin identified the corpse. That satisfied all the requirements for the state. So why run the blood tests? Why fool with a good thing?" Weary now, he sat down beside her at the edge of the mattress. "It all worked out so nicely for everybody. NYPD looks good for closing a major case in record time. The city avoids a megabucks lawsuit for shooting the wrong suspect. And that psycho kid goes free. I'm sure the parents loved that part."

"Then this is just theory. You don't actually—"

"There's more. I got all the proof I need. The parents went to Europe after the shooting. Probably got their kid settled in with a new identity. Maybe four weeks later, they came back to town. So I go by their place and talk to the doorman. This is around the time I started picking up on the shadows, people following me everywhere I went. Sometimes it was Mallory. She's easy to spot. Thinks she can do surveillance. She can't. But one of them wasn't a cop. It was a little freak in a bad wig, not your basic undercover outfit. He was young, and his size was right." He turned to Jo. "So—still think I'm sane? Or am I as crazy as Timothy Kidd?"

And now it was Johanna who needed a change of subject. She took his hand, interlaced her fingers with his and said, "Tell me your damn first name. Tell me . . . or I'll make you clean the toilet."

Janos found Mallory alone in Jack Coffey's office. "The old guy wants out."

"He knows the conditions," said Mallory. "Did the pervert kiss him yet?"

"No, the lawyer bought the little guy off with a gold watch." Janos held up a slip of paper. "But the old guy gave up the name and address for your phony blind man."

Great! Just great!

Riker was on his knees, wearing a damn apron, and his head was deep in the toilet, though not on some philosophical mission to see where his life had lately gone; he was brushing stains that required close-up squinting. Oh, and this was the best part of his big dream: into the bathroom walks Edward Slope, the chief medical examiner himself, all decked out in a three-piece suit.

"A house call? From a *body snatcher?*" Riker sat back on his heels, then slumped against the tiled wall. "Can't you wait till I'm dead?"

"I want you to see something." Slope opened an envelope and pulled out a batch of photographs. One of them wafted to the floor. It was the picture of a body on the doctor's dissection table. "That's the well-bred young man who tried to kill you six months ago. I did the autopsy myself. As you can see, he's quite dead. It only took the police a few hours to track him down. He was shot to pieces before you got out of surgery."

Another photograph joined the one on the floor. The corpse was full of holes, the face was gone. Riker remembered this particular picture as the one Mallory had liked best. She had brought it to his hospital room and held it up like a trophy. At the time, he had been surprised that she had not brought in the actual body, bronzed and nailed to a plaque for her wall. He looked up at the medical examiner and smiled with only half his face to let the man know that he was not buying any of this. Never had, never would.

Edward Slope hunkered down and papered the floor with the rest of his evidence. "This psychotic little geek is as dead as roadkill. It was a very thorough job, nine cops and precisely thirty bullets. You were told about this. Did you think your own people would lie to you?" And now, perhaps recalling that one of these people was Mallory, he amended this query. "*All* of them liars? Every cop in Special Crimes Unit?"

"Well, that's what cops do," said Riker. "Every day, we lie to suspects. Goes with the job. Yeah, they'd all lie to me, especially after pumping thirty rounds into this poor bastard—whoever he is." He picked up one of the photographs and tore it in half. "He's not the kid who shot me."

Dr. Slope produced papers from his coat pocket. "These are the lab results. I ran all the tests, Riker. You know me. I never leave anything to chance. You have to believe in fingerprints, in blood and DNA. And there's the gunpowder residue on the boy's hand. And there's more."

"Oh, yeah?" Riker removed his hausfrau's rubber gloves. "Well, here's the kicker, Doc. The proof. There were guards posted in my room the whole time I was in the hospital. They only do that to protect crime victims from *live* suspects. Nobody, and I mean *nobody else* gets twenty-four-hour bodyguards, not *ever*. But every time I opened my eyes, there was a cop watching me, and I could always hear more of 'em out in the hall."

Riker saw a painful surprise in the doctor's eyes.

Edward Slope was now the saddest man in New York City. "Not all of your guards were cops. The first few days, your doctors only allowed medical personnel to see you." He reached out to retrieve some of his pictures from the floor. "Sometimes it was me sitting in the intensive care unit. That was right after your surgery. You weren't expected to survive. So—if you went sour—well, I thought someone should be there, someone you knew." On hands and knees, he gathered up the rest of the photographs, then made a show of neatly stacking them and avoiding Riker's eyes.

"Later on," said Slope, "there were so many drugs pumped into you. I'm not surprised that you can't recall this—one of those guards was your father. That old man put in a lot of hours taking turns with Kathy Mallory. They were there through all the days when you were swacked on painkillers that only worked half the time. And the others—patrolmen, detectives, they came out of the woodwork to sit in your hospital room—on their *own* time, *willing* you to recover. After you were on the mend, they still came, so many of them. My fault. I got the hospital to rescind visiting hours. I wanted someone in your room round the clock. The distraction would keep you from reliving the event when you were most vulnerable. And—Dr. Apollo will back me up on this—most trauma victims have an irrational fear of being alone. So those cops all turned out for you—so you'd always know that you weren't on your own—that you were at the head of a damn parade, the whole police force, thirty thousand strong. Those cops, your guards, they all thought it was important for you to know that. But . . . obviously, you . . . got the wrong message." He stood up, preparing to leave, then leaned down to place one hand on Riker's shoulder. "Believe me *now.* I'm sorry. I never realized . . ." Rising slowly, stiff and awkward—add on shamefaced—the pathologist turned sharply on his heel and quit the bathroom.

Riker had no sooner recovered from the shock of an emotional Edward Slope than he wandered into the front room and met another unannounced visitor.

Trouble.

He should have told Johanna to bolt the door against the cops.

The commander of Special Crimes Unit was definitely not here on any sentimental errand, not a well-wisher or a cheerleader, not a *happy* man. Jack Coffey was holding a thick bundle of papers. This could only be Mallory's form to appeal the separation from NYPD. Yes, he could see that now as the lieutenant held up the paperwork within four inches of his senior detective's face, saying, "Don't fuck with me, Riker. Just *sign* it."

And sign it he did.

Jack Coffey departed without another word said, and Riker closed the door behind him—gently—no slamming.

"So you're a cop again." Jo sat on the couch by the dim light of a single lamp, her body sunk deep in the cushions. She seemed tired and pleased. When he sat down beside her, she rested her head on his shoulder, and they passed a little time this way in companionable silence.

Peace—perfect peace. That was Jo's present to him.

He wished he had something to give to her, and perhaps it was natural to be thinking of flowers, though she deserved something more exotic than the bloom he had settled upon.

"My old man was tough," said Riker. "It took years to get him to talk, but he finally gave up the whole story. My mother was dying the night I was born, or that's what Dad thought. She was only nineteen, and he wasn't much older. They were dirt poor in those days. They had nothing. Well, Mom wanted to leave me something—something *just grand.* That's the way my dad put it. So she made him promise to—" He glanced at Jo's upturned face and smiled. "It helps if you know she was really drugged up that night, lots of heavy medication. So Mom was stoned when she made him promise to put Pimpernel on my birth certificate."

"My God. She named you after a flower?"

"Yeah. Cruel, isn't it? But it could've been worse. *The Scarlet Pimpernel* was Mom's all-time favorite movie. But, crazy as she was that night, she knew she couldn't name me Scarlet Pimpernel. Everybody would've called me Scarlet, right? And that was a girl from *Gone With the Wind*—wrong sex and a whole different movie. So she settled for Pimpernel. But you can't raise a little boy with a name like that, not in Brooklyn. My old man argued with her for hours, even though he thought she was dying. Finally, the poor bastard caved in when she cried. One damn tear. That's all it took to break him, and he swore he'd name me Pimpernel."

"And then your father saved you by only putting the initial on the birth certificate."

"Yeah. Sometimes I forget how much I owe him for that. Well, Mom didn't die, not for another fifty years. When she got home from the hospital, her brain was good as new—almost. She agreed with Dad. It would've been a rotten thing to do to a kid growing up in a rough neighborhood. But she wouldn't let him change the initial on my birth certificate. Now my old man won the second round. When the next baby came along, they named him Ned. Nothing fancy—just plain old Ned."

"A pimpernel," said Jo. "I don't think I'd recognize that flower."

"I would." He still had the lieutenant's pen in his hand, but now that all the clutter was gone, there was no scrap of paper within easy reach. "Half the house was wallpapered in damn pimpernels. My bedroom, too—now *that* was child abuse." He took her right hand in his. "I still have dreams about that wallpaper." Riker drew a little flower on her open palm. "It's small, not much to look at. I'd rather give you roses."

He loved her smile.

The door was kicked open, breaking the chain before Victor could bolt it again. He was crying when they entered his apartment.

"Victor Patchock?" asked a large man with a thug's face and an incongruously soft voice.

He nodded, believing that he was about to die. When the pair advanced on him, he reached out to the umbrella stand and plucked out a white cane. He waved it high and wide. This was the last stand of a righteous man, whose eyes were scrunched shut. All he could hear was the swish of his cane slicing the air and hitting nothing.

He dared to open his eyes again.

The large man seemed astonished, and the tall blonde at his side was also taken by surprise. She had a gun in her hand, but the barrel was pointed toward the floor. Tilting her head to one side, she seemed genuinely curious when she asked, "How stupid are you?"

Earlier, upon opening his front door, Charles Butler had been pleased to see the chief medical examiner standing in the hall, for this was an opportunity to smooth out the ragged edges of their friendship. Edward Slope had announced that he was making the second house call of his career. What an honor.

Charles's mood was more somber now that he had come to understand the true purpose of the doctor's visit. He placed a drink in his guest's hand, then joined him at the kitchen table and continued his perusal of the crime-scene photographs. The corpse depicted here was no longer recognizable as a seventeen-year-old boy. "I see most of the shots are to the head."

Edward Slope nodded. "That would've been enough to make Riker suspicious." His eyes were less focused now that he was feeling the anesthetic benefit of twelve-year-old single-malt whiskey, but he was not finding sufficient solace in his glass. "You probably noticed. The shots to the torso seem almost . . ."

"Like an afterthought? Yes, I agree." It appeared that the detectives of Special Crimes Unit had thought it unseemly to blow the boy's face away. And so they had added more shots to the torso for the sake of decency.

Dr. Slope set down his empty glass and pushed it away. "They're not trained to make head shots, you know. Cops usually aim for the widest part of the body. Less chance of bullets going wild . . . and their targets frequently survive."

"No chance of that here," said Charles. He examined the last photograph, then quickly scanned the postmortem report. "But it *was* self-defense? The newspapers all—"

"If that's what it said in the newspapers, then it must be true." The pathologist covered his tired eyes. "Sorry. That was unfair. The boy fired on them first—one shot before they killed him. I was on the scene when the techs dug his bullet out of the wall. It was a justified shooting. No question."

No question? Ah, but the doctor's face was saying something entirely different.

Charles pulled the X rays from the envelope of autopsy materials. These pictures of naked bone told him so much more than the boy's blown-away flesh could reveal. And he would undoubtedly have to fetch Edward Slope a new whiskey bottle before the evening ended.

"All these bullets." Charles turned to his friend. "I imagine you found it impossible to determine which one killed the boy."

"That's what it said in my report." The doctor emptied the bottle into his glass, then quickly drained it. "None of the police bullets went wild. That was the truly odd part. A shootout is a terrifying experience for cops. Fear gets in the way of their aim—but not on this occasion." And now, fortified by alcohol, he found that he could look at the photographs one more time as he replaced each one in the envelope. "What a mess. All those bullets. All on target."

Charles held the X ray up to the light, fascinated and horrified. Among the massive damage of shattered facial bones was the one remarkably symmetrical hole in the boy's skull. It lay between the orbits of the eyes, not one hair off center.

Symmetry, thy name is Mallory.

She might as well have signed her work. Other, *later* holes and grooves at the top and sides of the skull told the rest of the story. He envisioned the other detectives firing shots at a falling target—a dead one—to obliterate the evidence of Mallory's remarkably cold and steady aim, until the final effect appeared less like an execution.

"I suppose it's better for all of the detectives," said Charles, "if none of them knows which shot was fatal."

The doctor's sudden relief betrayed him. Obviously he was assuming that the omissions in his report were less transparent than he had supposed. Edward Slope could not fail to believe that his secret was safe. His proof of this was sitting right there on the other side of the kitchen table. Charles Butler's face showed no signs of a tell-all blush; he had learned how to lie.

Riker stepped out of the shower as a new man and donned his best suit, the one least stained. When he walked into the living room, he found Mrs. Ortega surveying the new-and-improved state of his apartment. He lightly kicked her rolling cart of supplies. "Get this thing out of here, okay? It's ruining the damn ambiance."

She ignored this, turning her back on him to inspect the rug and run one finger over the surfaces of tables and chairs, checking for dust. "So this is what you've been doing all day?"

"Yeah. Not bad, huh?"

"Amateurs, the both of you. I'll take it from here. Just stay out of my way." The intrepid cleaning woman marched toward the tall windows that bore the streaks of his own attempted washing.

"I love you, too," said Riker, but he said it low, almost a whisper, so she would not feel obligated to insult him in return. "Where's Jo?"

"Gone. She said she had to go feed some *cat*." Mrs. Ortega spat out this last word with great contempt. In her philosophy, the only good fur-shedder was a dead one.

Riker stood before his desk, staring down at the small drawer where he kept his weapon. It had been opened, though the key was still hidden in a crack behind one wooden leg.

And the gun was gone.

He wasted no time on this little mystery. The perp who had broken his bathroom window would not have known how to finesse this excellent lock, and there was no sign of forcing the wood. Mallory was the only thief who had recently visited his apartment, and she traveled everywhere with lock picks in her pocket.

So the brat had not trusted him with his own gun.

Regulations required him to report a missing weapon, but that would only create more trouble for both of them. And now he wondered if he should demand its return. Or should he wait for Mallory to break into his apartment and put the revolver back in the drawer?

Yeah.

That would be the polite solution.

All but the cat's head was swaddled in a white cloth binding so that he could not win this fight to stay alive. The veterinarian's hand hesitated with the needle. All the pity in the doctor's eyes was for the woman and not the animal. "You know it's the best thing for him, Johanna."

But not for your reasons.

"You don't have to—"

"Yes, I do." She held Mugs gingerly, minding the phantom nerve that so agonized him. "*Now,* please."

The needle was injected into Mugs's neck, and minutes passed before it had any effect. His personality was still intact when he met her eyes, looking there for mercy and asking, *Why?* She cradled him until he was lulled into a drowsy stupor by her slow rocking motion and the sedative. At last he was well beyond pain in real or imagined realms. She wanted to believe that he was not beyond love, that he could luxuriate in the feeling of her arms about him now that it did not hurt him anymore, not in his body or his mind. She kissed him, then held him close until he went limp. Though the poison would come later, this was not like sleep; this was good-bye.

"He's at peace, Johanna," said the doctor. "He'll never feel the next one." The second shot would wrack the cat's body with a violent seizure, a prelude to death. "It's for the best."

"I *know* that," she said, but a long time passed before she would cease her rocking and open her arms to release Mugs.

19

JOHANNA APOLLO HAD TAKEN THE LONG WAY home from the law firm on Madison Avenue. The zigzag journey had led her from evening into dead of night as she revisited the favorite streets of her adopted city.

She was hungry and cold, and she needed her meds to ease the pains of the day. One of her watchdogs awaited her in the hotel lobby. The young FBI man's face was washed with relief that she was still alive and his job was secure. Now he backed away from her, maintaining the discreet distance of a court order. She felt guilty, though she had never consented to this bodyguard service. No matter how the night might end, this young man and his partner would have some explaining to do come the morning. Too bad. Not their fault. They must wonder how she always managed to evade them, when she should be so easy to follow in any crowd of normal upright people. During the brief elevator ride, she consulted her wristwatch twice.

Less than an hour to go.

It was a short walk from the elevator to the door of her room, but the hallway elongated in a side effect of weariness. She had a pill for that, but nothing to cure the dread of this homecoming, the awaiting quiet and the sense of no one home anymore, no Mugs.

She put her mind to other things, arrangements still to be made, preparations for the night ahead. She entered the hotel room and flicked on the wall switch. Everything was as she had left it. Mugs's pillow still held the impression of his small body, and the object inside remained hidden. The suite was perfectly quiet for the first time since she had moved in, and yet she knew that she was not alone. The bedroom door was wide open. It had been closed when she left, and the hotel maids did no cleaning in the evening hours. Every detail of the room beyond the door was lost in the dark, and this moment would have held less terror if she had seen the sudden flash of a knife. She might have welcomed that. Instead, she heard the cat cry out.

The dead cat.

Mallory slowly emerged from the darkness, cradling Mugs's limp body in her arms. The cat lifted his head a bare inch, softly mewling, so enfeebled by heavy sedation.

"You followed me to the animal hospital."

"And I saw you run out of there crying," said Mallory. "Took me six seconds to work it out."

"So you intercepted the second shot."

"The deadly one." The detective walked into the front room and sat down in an armchair. The cat, reduced to a rag of fur, was now casually draped over her crossed legs. Mugs lifted his head once more, and his half-closed eyes struggled to focus on the one he loved, Johanna.

Mallory's slow smile was disturbing. "You think the cat knows you tried to kill him?" Her long red fingernails absently grazed Mugs's fur. "You're very good at ditching your FBI bodyguards, Dr. Apollo. That has to stop. I think we understand each other."

Oh, yes, Johanna understood terrorism, small scale and large. Mind games were her stock-in-trade. Mallory would have done well to remember that.

"And how much does Riker understand?" She was mentally squaring off against the young police. "Does he know how you manipulated him, calculated his every move—nearly cost him his sanity? Does he understand any of the damage you've done? Suppose he'd died that night in the parking garage."

"So you *were* there." Mallory's composure was eerie; she had missed the implication of some fault within herself—or *dis*missed it. Her voice was a cold monotone when she said, "Riker always knew what I was doing, but it didn't matter to him. He played the game for your sake—not mine—not his."

The silence was filled with awe and wonder, for Mallory had successfully transferred the blame for all that had gone before and whatever might happen before this night was done. She had neatly shifted past and future blood onto other hands, Johanna's. The psychiatrist, out of her depth, sank down on the couch and merely watched, helpless to do otherwise, as the younger woman, the ruthless one, reached behind the chair and pulled out the plastic pet carrier. Mugs was placed inside with only slightly more care than might be given to a stuffed toy. However, Johanna made no protest, for the box would hold no fears for Mugs while he was sedated.

"Putting the cat to sleep," said the detective, "that fits with the last meeting of your little therapy group in Tribeca."

"You bugged that room?" There could be no other explanation, for she had given that news to the group this evening.

Mallory ignored the accusation as her eyes roved over the furnishings. "This hotel room—so temporary, such an easy loose end to tie up. I know your type, Dr. Apollo. If you were going to kill yourself, you'd be one of those nice polite people who slit their wrists in the bathtub—so they won't leave a mess behind. But you'd never have the guts to do it. You can't even kill a cat. I've seen your drug cabinet. You've got enough stuff right here to put down a hundred cats, but you had to pay someone else to do it to him. So I know you're not planning suicide. You just can't count on living through the night." Mallory picked up the carrier and walked to the door. "Well, I can't force you into protective custody."

"Where are you taking my cat?"

The detective silently stepped into the outer hallway, heading for the elevator, and Johanna followed, saying, pleading, "You won't like Mugs when he's fully awake."

Mallory stood before the elevator, one red fingernail on the call button, when she turned her head with the slow swivel of a machine, and that disturbing smile was back. "Are you afraid I won't be *nice* to the cat?"

Johanna hurried to board the elevator as the doors opened and the detective stepped inside with her living cargo stirring, faintly crying inside the box. "Why are you doing this to me?"

"Nothing personal," said Mallory. "The last two jurors have to survive. It's my game now, *my* rules. I'm the *law*." She watched digital numbers changing, numerals descending as they sank through all the floors of the hotel. "Riker thinks the feds are using you for bait. He hasn't put it all together yet. He can't. He's too close to you. Oh, I found the gun."

Johanna was so unsettled that she nearly asked *which* gun. She looked down at the small silver twenty-two in Mallory's hand. It was a lady's pistol, purse size, and that description alone would explain the look of derision on the detective's face.

The doors slid open, and the two women crossed the lobby in tandem. Johanna was pulled along by invisible strings, lured by the pet carrier in the detective's tight grip. Mallory paused at the cluster of armchairs by the window, then nodded to the FBI agent standing on the far side of the room. She turned on Johanna, saying, *commanding,* "Sit down."

And Johanna obediently sank into a chair.

"Stay here," said Mallory, "where that fed can see you. Stay until I come back for you. And *then* I'll give you the cat."

The surprise visitors just kept on coming, but at least Charles Butler had brought a six-pack of imported beer. Riker had no theories on what Mallory might be up to. She had yet to divulge anything about the night she had followed the fake blind man from the cop bar on Green Street.

"Damn, Mallory."

Speak of the devil, and she will come.

When he responded to the next knock at his door, Mallory stood in the hallway, holding Jo's pet carrier with all the familiar scratch marks. He could see the cat's fur behind the wire opening, but Mugs was not in his usual bloodcurdling voice tonight. Riker bent low to open the small door, suddenly concerned that Mallory might have killed the poor critter. "Hey, Mugs, buddy." No claws, no hissing or threats of any kind. Well, this was a bad sign. He withdrew the small limp body and checked it for bullet holes.

Riker looked up at Mallory, but before he could ask what was wrong with the cat, she said, "I didn't do it."

Charles Butler entered the room from the kitchen with two cold bottles of beer in hand. "Ah, the famous Mugs. What's wrong with him?" And now he also turned to Mallory.

She was definitely on the defensive when she said, "Dr. Apollo's *vet* drugged him."

Riker smiled at Charles. "You don't want to be around when this cat wakes up. He'll take an arm off you." He stroked the cat's head, enjoying the novelty of getting this close to the animal who maimed him on the day they first met.

"You *like* that cat." Mallory's tone of voice said that this could not be a good thing, not a *normal* thing.

"You could say I admire his style." Riker folded the animal into his arms. Mugs lifted his head, saw a familiar face and closed his eyes again. "So what's the deal?"

"Just keep him here for a while." She looked around the room, appraising the gleaming surfaces of furniture. The windowpanes were so clean that the glass had virtually disappeared. This was the trademark of a little cleaning woman from Brooklyn. "Put him in the bathroom. If Mrs. Ortega spots one cat hair, you'll never see her again." Mallory walked toward the door, saying, "I'll be back. I've got a litter box out in the car."

She had one hand on the doorknob, but Charles's larger hand pressed flat against the wood to delay her. He glanced back at the cat when he said, "Still taking hostages, I see."

Mallory glared at him, angry and biting down on her lower lip until sympathy pains forced him to step aside.

Johanna doubled over, as if the pain were sudden and not something that had been building for hours. Predictably, one of her bodyguards came on the run, defying the court order to keep his distance.

"My meds," said Johanna. "They're upstairs in my room."

"All right, Dr. Apollo, hold on." The agent pulled out his cell phone. "I'll get my partner. He's watching the rear exit."

"No need to bother him," she said. "I can walk." She rose from the couch. "Perhaps if you'd help me." She took his arm as they moved toward the elevator and rode up to her floor without exchanging another word until they entered her hotel suite.

"I have to take the pills on a full stomach," she said, "but I can't wait for room service. It takes too long. There's a restaurant across the street. I'll just get a warmer coat, if you don't mind waiting."

A minute later, she emerged from her bedroom wearing a hooded black poncho over her down jacket. While crossing the street with her escort following at the usual unobtrusive distance, she had a change of plans and led him instead to the subway. It was a simple matter to separate from him, hiding herself behind a staircase, but only for a few moments, time enough to hand off the poncho to an old woman bent with age, a fixture in this place. The elderly vagrant accepted the customary twenty-dollar bill. Johanna boarded a train and watched from a window as the agent spotted the black-hooded figure and followed the old beggar to the lower level and a southbound train. Johanna traveled north, unmolested.

"The feds are watching her right now," said Mallory. "They won't screw up again." She carried the litter box into the bathroom where Riker was making a nest of towels for the cat.

He was wondering what Charles had meant by hostages. "So keeping the cat here—that was Jo's idea?"

"Yes." With that single word trailing off to a hiss, she managed to upbraid him for doubting her. And when that failed to work, she added, "The cat's sedative should wear off in another hour, and the doctor needs a good night's sleep." Unspoken were the words, *And that's the truth.*

There *was* a distinct ring of truth in there somewhere, though he was still planning to call Jo's hotel—but not just this minute. He could see that Mallory had something else in mind.

She shifted into attack posture, hands on hips—confrontation time. "I know Dr. Apollo was at the parking garage the night Zachary was ambushed. You *lied* to me about that."

"Mallory, don't get me started on the subject of lies."

"Did you know the doctor had a gun? A little twenty-two." She read his face and smiled. "You *did* know. You held out on me." She hunkered down beside him. Her voice was almost taunting. "And you never asked her what she was doing at the garage that night, did you?" Hands braced on the floor, as if set to spring, Mallory leaned over the body of the sleeping, helpless cat, saying, "I've got a fake blind man in custody." She pulled back. "You know the one I mean. And he's another little detail you forgot to mention."

Riker was staring at the bathroom tiles, wondering how she had managed that turnaround when she was the one who had—

"Time for the interview." Mallory rose to her feet and left the bathroom. He could hear her voice drifting down the hall. "Coming, Riker? Or don't you want to know what happened in that jury room?"

Johanna was admitted to a studio with the configuration of a large dark cave. Ian Zachary stood beside a tall Japanese folding screen that partially hid a console of light and dials. He waved her to a chair.

"Good to see you again, Doctor. It's been a long time since the trial. I can't talk you into waiting another hour?"

"It's now or never," she said.

"If you wish." He raised one hand to the young woman in the lighted window and spoke into the microphone of his headset. "Crazy Bitch? Rack it up." He turned back to his guest. "I can't change your mind?"

"No, I have other plans for later." She watched his eyes travel back and forth between herself and a square pane of glass, a dark twin to the brightly lit window of the sound engineer's booth. If this had been a police station in Chicago, there would be a watcher behind that glass.

When Ian Zachary sat down at his console, the Japanese screen cut off his view of the dark window, but the sound engineer's booth was still visible to him, and the girl held up one finger to indicate one more minute to go, though it was the middle finger.

Interesting.

"So, Doctor, what name are we using tonight? Johanna Apollo or the alias?"

"My own name." And now she was also captivated by the dark window, for the screen did not cut off her own line of sight; it only hid Ian Zachary from a watcher who might or might not be there. She tried to gauge his level of paranoia, a key element for every player in the game.

20

THE SQUAD ROOM OF SPECIAL CRIMES UNIT WAS ghosty and quiet tonight. All the action would be in the back rooms used for interviews and lockup. By the dim lights burning at vacant desks, Riker could count three detectives working late, and another light burned in Lieutenant Coffey's office. Mallory switched on Riker's own lamp, then stood to one side so that he could see how ruthlessly she had taken advantage of his absence. The old desk gleamed like a brand-new one. Gone were the familiar landmarks of grimy smudges, fossilized coffee spills and the scorch marks of abandoned cigarettes. Riker was also suspicious of the chair and its unrecognizable upholstery, but when he flopped down on the cushion, he was happy to discover that it still conformed to the shape of his rear end, though it reeked of the chemicals used to restore the leather.

Raising his eyes to Mallory's, he picked up the threads of their interrupted conversation—more like a confession. "I thought I was being followed around by cops." He swiveled his chair to face the window and looked down on the dark SoHo street. "Everywhere I went, I could swear I saw a cop behind me. Nuts, huh?"

"No," said Mallory. "That was real. Some of them were Zachary's rent-a-cops, but the rest were from Internal Affairs."

"IA was on my tail?" Slowly, his chair spun round to face her. "What the hell for?"

"They got an anonymous tip." Mallory examined her perfectly manicured fingernails, as if one of them might be flawed or chipped—as if his desk could sprout wings and fly. "Some citizen told them you were doing a lot of heavy lifting for a cop on full disability. They followed you for months with cameras. They wanted something incriminating on video. Nobody told them you never cashed the city's checks."

"But you knew, didn't you?" Mrs. Ortega could have supplied her with that information, but long before the cleaning woman's discovery of the checks, Mallory had known that he was not opening his mail. Her invasion of his private life was tabled, for he had a larger issue with her just now. "So it was an *anonymous* tip?"

Something in his voice—oh, perhaps the heavy sarcasm—gave away his disbelief, and he could see that old look in her eye. She was getting ready for the grand denial. And this told him that his own partner had turned him in to Internal Affairs. It fitted so well with her stealing his gun tonight. Mallory had not trusted him to stay alive, and so she had sicced the IA watchdogs on him, cops to keep an eye on him when she could not be there. In his alternate theory, she had used the Internal Affairs fumble to embarrass the commissioner, just a dab of blackmail to grease the forms for Riker's appeal. It had taken less than the usual ninety days for his reinstatement; it had taken one hour. And now it occurred to him that his partner had also diddled a computer to send out those bogus disability checks, for he had never asked for any assistance from the city of New York.

He lit a cigarette and waited for her to lie her way out of this—and he waited.

Unpredictable brat, she sat on the edge of his desk, legs dangling in the old familiar manner of Kathy the child. And, though a clock hung on every wall, she pulled out her pocket watch and pretended interest in the hour. It was Lou Markowitz's gold watch, handed down through four generations of police. Mallory was reminding him that she was Markowitz's daughter, the only child of his oldest friend. This was such a clumsy tactic, for she had little understanding of sentiment or sympathy; she had none of her own. Offense was her best game. Her crippled idea of defense only saddened him. He had no more heart for this. Thus wounded, he pocketed all his questions and accusations. An hour would pass before he realized that Mallory's *inept* ploy had been a roaring success, that she had expertly distracted him by creeping up on his sentimental blind side and slaying him with sympathy.

"We should get moving." She slid off the desk and turned her back on him. Heading toward the hallway, she said, "Your friend Agent Hennessey is waiting in the interview room. I picked him for the token fed."

"Good job." As Riker rose from his desk and followed her down the narrow hall, he was only beginning to appreciate Mallory's long-range planning. Her best scheme had begun with Agent Hennessey following a doppelgänger while Ian Zachary was ambushed in the parking garage. The next piece of FBI incompetence, MacPherson's murder, had only sweetened her deal. In exchange for files on the Reaper and a clear field for NYPD, all federal foul-ups would be overlooked during press conferences, and New York agents would share the spotlight at endgame, hence the "token fed."

Riker knew that Lou Markowitz would have approved of his foster child's work. She was manipulating the system even better than her old man. Lou, in his prime, had outwitted the FBI—but never actually extorted them.

The partners talked as they walked, and now he learned that the fake blind man was undergoing a psychiatric evaluation at Bellevue Hospital at the insistence of a lawyer. The public defender would not believe that his client could competently waive the right to representation. And while they awaited the return of Victor Patchock, another interview subject was being held in the lockup cage. This one was an elderly attorney named Horace Fairlamb.

"So you busted a lawyer," said Riker.

That's my girl.

They entered the larger of the two interview rooms, the formal one with the long table and a one-way glass for covert observation. Riker shook hands with Agent Hennessey, then suffered a bear hug from Janos. The detective had just heard the news of Riker's reinstatement and greeted him like a returning prisoner of war. While Janos made the introductions to Horace Fairlamb, retired attorney at law, only Riker was positioned to see his partner pirating paperwork from cartons piled at one end of the table. Each box bore the stamp of the FBI. Thick documents and manila folders from the Reaper file were now disappearing underneath Mallory's blazer.

Suspicious brat.

Riker had no doubt that Hennessey would honor the deal of full disclosure, but Mallory trusted no one. And now she excused herself from the room after stealing all that she could covertly carry.

The men took their seats at the table, law enforcement on one side and Horace Fairlamb on the other. The old man was asked to repeat his story, what he had told of it so far. Detective Janos, showing the wear of this baby-sitting detail, pleaded with the elderly lawyer to stick with the pertinent facts, then rolled his eyes as Fairlamb insisted on beginning his story at the beginning. And so they all listened to the drawn-out details of a beloved wife's death, culminating with the funeral. "That was the day I gave my New York law practice to my son." The old man had then traveled to Chicago to live with his daughter and grandchildren.

And now three men with grim smiles admired his wallet photographs as they were passed around the table.

"But after a few days," said Horace Fairlamb, "I could see that it wasn't working out. I spent most of that time staring at the walls and crying—quite a burden for my family. So one day, I left my daughter's house, checked into a hotel and stepped out on a ledge."

Janos raised his head, interest renewed. Evidently, he had not heard this part before. "A jumper."

"A would-be jumper," the attorney corrected him. "One of the hotel residents was a psychiatrist, and that was the day I met Dr. Apollo."

Riker leaned forward. "So she always lived in hotels, even in Chicago?"

"As long as I've known her—three years. Anyway, I became her patient. She treated me for depression. Part of my therapy was studying for the state bar exam. At my age—imagine if you will. But I passed the exam. Well, I was back at work and somewhat useful again. Then one day, I had a breakthrough in therapy. I finally admitted to myself that I had never cared for the practice of law." He sighed. "Half a century wasted in utter boredom. And probate is about as boring as you can—"

"So that's when you took on the little freak with the red wig?" Riker was not quite so patient as Detective Janos. "Then life got interesting, right?" And this was his euphemism for *Speed it up, old man, or I'll shoot you.*

The lawyer was mildly surprised. "I never had an attorney-client relationship with Victor Patchock. Is that what you thought? Oh, my word, no. I performed *other* services for Victor—things of a covert nature. I arranged for his move from Chicago to New York, him and another fellow."

"MacPherson?"

"I never knew the other man's real name. He was even more distrustful than Victor. So I got them both credentials with fake names, credit cards, passports and the like. Lodging them in New York was simple enough since I own several buildings here. Then there were the disguises and running around as a decoy in the middle of the night. Oh, I must say it was miles more fun than lawyering. Then I procured firearms for them, and that's not as easy as you might think.

You can't just walk into a gun store, you know. There are forms to fill out, serial numbers that can be traced. So there was no legal way to proceed. I went through a dozen bartenders before I found—"

"Wait." Riker had a sixth sense for lawyerly fiddles, and this attorney had already confessed to several crimes. "Janos? You read him his rights?"

Detective Janos held up the signed Miranda card that listed every constitutional perk, including the fact that anything said could be used against the old man in court. "Mr. Fairlamb's representing himself. He did his own plea bargain with the DA's office."

"Indeed," said Horace Fairlamb. "I have complete immunity in exchange for cooperation. So there won't be any charges for procuring firearms, document fraud or obstruction of justice. Oh, and all those other charges? Bribery, littering and such—all gone. Now, I want to make it perfectly clear that getting weapons for Victor and his friend—well, that was not Johanna's idea. In fact, she was horrified when I told her—somewhat after the fact, I'm afraid."

All heads turned in the direction of an irritating rapping noise. It came from the other side of the one-way mirror that concealed a viewing room. Riker stared at the glass. "Who's in the box tonight?"

"That's an assistant DA." Janos stared at the mirror, then raised his voice for the benefit of the man behind the glass. "He's reminding me that he's a busy little prick with big plans for the evening. I suppose he thinks we're wasting his time."

Riker banged one fist on the table, and the annoying rap abruptly ceased.

Horace Fairlamb put a cigar in his mouth, Cuban of course, and Riker would bet that contraband was also included in the deal with the district attorney.

Damn every lawyer ever born.

Agent Hennessey leaned across the table to light the old man's cigar, saying, "So let's get on with the good stuff, all right?"

"Yeah," said Riker. "Let's start with the murder trial. What happened in that jury room? Why did they all vote not guilty?"

"I have no idea," said Horace Fairlamb. "I never discussed that with my associates."

Janos's head snapped back, as if the lawyer had stunned him with a baseball bat between the eyes. "Hey, we had a deal, old man."

"Oh, yes . . . the deal." The old man exhaled a cloud of smoke. "As I recall the terms, I agreed to tell you everything I knew about the Ian Zachary jury. So now I've told you all I know. And, if I may anticipate your next question, I have no idea who the Reaper is."

Weary Janos laid his head on the table, and Agent Hennessey slumped in his chair, muttering, "We've all been scammed."

Well, not all of them, not Mallory. And now Riker understood why his partner had not bothered to sit in on this interview—this worthless crumb she had thrown to the FBI.

Behind the lighted glass sat young Crazy Bitch, eyes glistening, fever-bright. The girl gave the impression of a cat on tenterhooks, forever trapped in a conflict of fight or flight.

Johanna Apollo stared at the other window on this studio, the dark one, and this unsettled Ian Zachary. She smiled.

Paranoia, my old friend.

It had been childishly simple to suss out the Englishman's weakness. She looked down at the carpet and noted the impressions left by the console's former position. He had turned his desk sideways so that he would not have to face the booth window when he worked his telephones, his levers and dials. However, that had not ended his discomfort. His next solution had been the Japanese folding screen beside his chair. It sheltered him from the window's view, making it easier to lose the idea of a watcher behind that dark glass.

Crazy Bitch must be a mind reader of sorts, for she caught the doctor's eye and made a thumbs-up gesture. Johanna was uncertain about the words this girl was mouthing, but she thought the context might have been *Go for his balls.*

Noting Johanna's interest, Zachary stared at the Japanese screen, as if he could see through it to the dark window on the other side. "That's Needleman's booth—my producer. Did you see something?"

"Not yet."

He lost his charming smile for a moment, but then he rallied, turning to the lighted window and his assistant, who instantly ceased to clap her hands. "Crazy Bitch? You screwed up the voice level again."

The girl behind the glass extended one finger from a closed fist, an obscene gesture to tell him how much his criticism meant to her.

He flicked a lever, then leaned far back in his chair. "I could run the whole show from this console. But my assistant has a certain entertainment value. You may have noticed—she's insane."

"Eccentric, perhaps," said Johanna. She had found the younger woman's survival instinct was still intact, always a good indication for hope, but yes, Crazy Bitch was definitely in trouble. Johanna's sudden smile was directed at the producer's booth, and this had a telling effect on Zachary.

Once more, he turned to face the screen blocking his view of the dark glass. "So, Dr. Apollo, do you know Needleman?"

Though no sound escaped the lighted booth, Crazy Bitch was laughing hysterically and nodding with wildly exaggerated bobs of her head.

"Everyone knows Needleman," said Johanna.

Riker had invited the FBI man to the second interview of the night, the one that might actually break the case. They entered a small room with a lockup cage and no mirrors—no witnesses. Mallory was clearly surprised and unhappy to see Hennessey, not liking this change of plans—her plans.

The fake blind man had finally been returned from Bellevue, and his public defender had just finished reading the psychiatric evaluation, slapping it on the table in disgust. Though the court-appointed lawyer was still not satisfied that his client was competent to waive legal counsel, and he said so for the record, he now left the strange little man in police custody and quit the room with a secretive smile, so happy to finally end his long workday and happier still to be rid of this lunatic.

Victor Patchock sat with his arms folded. His white cane had been taken away from him, but he stubbornly insisted on wearing his wig and dark glasses, and neither would he remove his overcoat. "In case I have to leave in a hurry."

"You're not going anywhere for a long time." Mallory snatched the dark glasses away. Patchock raised his hands, anticipating a blow to the face, and the overcoat fell open to expose drops of blood on his shirtfront. A surprised Agent Hennessey stared at these bloodstains.

Riker and Janos turned in unison to stare at Mallory.

Before she could utter her trademark line, *I didn't do it,* the little man quickly closed up his coat, saying, "I have nosebleeds when I'm under stress."

Now that Mallory had been cleared of mistreating her prisoner, she reached toward the little man once more. One white hand, five sharp red nails, flashed out to touch the nylon strands of the red wig and to make the little man flinch. "Why the costume, Victor?"

"That was Dr. Apollo's idea," said Victor Patchock. "She told me no one would look for me under a neon sign—if you take my meaning. Before she bought me the wig, I couldn't bring myself to leave my room."

"So she was treating you?"

The little man nodded. "Getting out of my room was a big part of my therapy. You know, taking back my life. So I spent my time following other players around, MacPherson, Johanna and—"

"And Ian Zachary." Mallory touched his arm, making him jump a bit. "That's how you knew he'd be in the parking garage the other night."

"Yes. It took me a while to figure out that his limo was picking up an impersonator. After I caught on, I followed him to that garage lots of times." Victor Patchock smiled at Riker, but it was not a happy smile, more on the sly side. "I followed you around, too—all those nights you went out drinking with Dr. Apollo after work. You never saw me, did you? No, you only had eyes for the doctor." He wagged one finger at the detective. "I would kill for that woman. Just you remember that, you bastard." Now he turned his suspicious eyes on Mallory.

"Victor?" Riker slapped the table to regain the little man's attention. "What happened in that jury room? Why did you all vote not guilty?"

"Andy," said the man in the red wig. "It was his doing."

"Andy Sumpter?" Agent Hennessey was startled. "The juror?"

"The first one to die," said Victor Patchock.

Johanna Apollo continued to glance at the dark window from time to time. This had the desired effect of rattling Ian Zachary, but never for more than a few seconds. Now he relaxed into a self-satisfied smile. "You have a lot of explaining to do, Doctor."

"I know," she said. "It would be easier to understand if we start with the voir dire, the jury selection. Your lawyers dragged out the process. There was lots of time to get full background checks on everyone in the jury pool."

"Stacking the jury isn't a crime, Doctor. It's a science."

"Oh, I agree," said Johanna. "It only seemed insane at the time. Your lawyers didn't care about biases. All the physically small people, the frail ones with the most retiring personalities, they were never challenged by your defense team. And then there was me, the hunchback, the cripple—so vulnerable. Andy Sumpter was the lone exception, a man with the emotional maturity of a child and the body of a weight lifter. The prosecutor loved him, didn't he? Andy came off as such a law-and-order freak. I'm sure you coached him every step of the way."

"Now *that* would be a crime." Zachary's smile was unaffected by this accusation. "Let's stay with the facts for now, Dr. Apollo. We can talk about your unsupported theories later on."

"Andy slept through most of your trial. That's a fact. But when we retired to the jury room for deliberations, he was suddenly wide awake. The first round of ballots were for a guilty verdict—except for Andy's. The judge wouldn't accept a hung jury. Day after day, he kept sending us back to that little room to work it out, and every day more votes swung over to Andy's side. The first two crossover votes were easy. Those people just wanted to go home. But the rest stood firm—even while Andy sat there, glaring at them one by one and punching his fist into his hand, over and over."

Victor Patchock was off to the men's room, escorted by Detective Janos. In addition to nosebleeds, he had announced that frayed nerves also affected his bladder.

The moment the door closed, Agent Hennessey discovered that he was Mallory's new interview subject. She stood beside his chair, preferring the advantage of looking down at him. "Jury tampering," she said. "The feds were investigating *before* the first juror died. That's what brought Timothy Kidd to Chicago after the trial. He wasn't working the Reaper murders." Unspoken were the words *You liar.*

"But that can't be right," said Riker, answering for the stunned FBI agent. "Wrong department. Timothy Kidd was a profiler—murder cases."

Mallory shook her head. "Kidd was never a profiler. He was a garden-variety field agent—just like Hennessey here. And he was also a flaming nutcase."

"She's right, and she's wrong," said Hennessey, speaking only to Riker's friendlier face. "A year ago, Agent Kidd had a nervous breakdown. He was pulled from fieldwork and transferred to an office job. All he did was shuffle papers and make out reports on obscure complaints. So one day, Dr. Apollo's charge of jury tampering lands on his desk. No one else took it seriously. A hung jury might've gotten some attention, but you can't buy a whole jury, can you? The verdict was unanimous, and her claim was unsupported." He glanced up at Mallory, to say, "You were wrong about the tampering charge," then quickly looked away, not even willing to meet Riker's eyes anymore. "There was no federal case before the first juror died. But Dr. Apollo papered every agency, local, state and federal."

Riker nodded. "And crazy Timothy Kidd was the only one who believed her."

"That's right," said Hennessey. "So Agent Kidd went to Chicago for a follow-up interview, and that was on his own initiative. He was never assigned to any criminal cases. A few days later, the Reaper slaughtered the first juror. There was a message on the crime-scene wall, written in the victim's own blood. One down and eleven to go. That's what it said. We never got that detail until the second juror died. Then the Chicago bureau stepped in and placed the rest of the jury in a protection program. Agent Kidd was using sick days, commuting between D.C. and Chicago. So he *did* investigate the Reaper murders, but he did it on his own time."

"Argus didn't know that," said Riker. "He thought Kidd was in town to check up on his work."

Their conversation ended when the door opened. Detective Janos and his charge had returned from the men's room. Victor Patchock sat down, adjusted his wig and continued his story of the jury deliberations. "Well, Andy comes up to me one night when we're all eating dinner in a restaurant with the bailiff. On my way to the toilet, he boxes me into a corner and whispers, 'Number four Ellery Drive.' That's where I live—*used* to live."

"But we never had any paperwork on you," said Hennessey. "Why didn't you support Dr. Apollo's complaint?"

"I was the one who went to the judge," said Johanna Apollo. "But the other jurors wouldn't back me up, no corroborating complaints. The judge asked if I might be hysterical—all the pressure of a televised murder trial. He loved the whole circus, actually used makeup in court. And he didn't want a mistrial. So the judge sent me back in there with all those frightened people."

"And Andy Sumpter," said Zachary. "So you were afraid."

"I'm not immune to intimidation," she said. "Andy was angry with me, and he let me know it. He glared at me for hours. He was so quiet—except for the sound of his fist punching into his hand, and every punch was for me. Obviously, Andy knew about the complaint, and that would've been your work."

"But I had no contact with the jurors," said Zachary. "Can you prove otherwise? No, I didn't think so. Well, maybe the judge was right. Are you prone to hysterics, Doctor?"

"Actually, you're the one who seems on edge tonight." She turned her chair to face the dark booth, and this had the predictable effect of jumping up the man's anxiety. "I'm going public with my story because—" And here she paused to borrow a phrase from Mallory. "I can't count on living through the night."

Riker was slowly shaking his head from side to side. "Okay, Victor, let me get this straight. Jo went to the judge to save all your sorry hides, and none of you backed her up?"

"No," said Victor Patchock. "Not then. Andy was a crazy bastard. We had to deal with him eight hours a day."

"What happened after the verdict?" asked Riker. "Did anybody else come forward to back up her complaint?"

"No. When Andy got killed, I never thought anything of it. I'm sure no one else did, either. He was the type you'd expect to get his throat slit. I never heard anything about a note written in blood. Nobody told us a killer was threatening the rest of the jury, not then."

Agent Hennessey looked up from his perusal of the Bureau's Reaper file. "That call was made by the Chicago police while they still had jurisdiction. The cops had a real short list of people who wanted Andy Sumpter dead. They figured the crime was staged to look like a psycho killing—to draw attention away from his loan shark."

"So Andy needed cash," said Mallory, who loved money motives best.

"Andy was your most insanely loyal fan," said Johanna. "But I'm sure he had other incentives. He wouldn't settle for a hung jury. Did you tell him the verdict had to be unanimous?"

"More accusations? Once again, you're all alone, Dr. Apollo. No support for your story. And let's not lose sight of the fact that you also voted not guilty. Would you like to explain that? Because right now you look like the prime suspect for jury tampering. Swaying an entire jury—well, that would be child's play for a psychiatrist. Andy was just an overgrown brain tumor."

"A good description. So you *did* get to know him."

Zachary sighed. "I can't see that moron convincing an entire jury—"

"He terrified them. And you told him how to do that. He wasn't smart enough to work it out on his own. He was so close to blowing his temper and hurting those people."

"But he didn't. And that was your doing, wasn't it, Dr. Apollo? And yours was the only complaint. That's interesting, too."

"If the other two women hadn't died, I think they might have come forward. It would've been easier for a woman to admit what happened in that room."

"You make it sound like a rape."

"The assault took place in the jury bathroom," said Johanna. "But you already knew that. You planned it."

"It was like a rape," said Victor Patchock. "You lose your manhood the first time he makes you back down. None of the men in that room would admit that Andy had them cowed. The votes changed with every ballot, one or two a day, till he had them all."

Hennessey looked up from his notebook, pen hovering, "But you say Andy never touched anyone?"

"Well . . . yeah, he did. It was MacPherson. Poor Mac. He went into the bathroom. It had two stalls. So nobody thought it was odd when Andy followed him in there. But then Andy slid under Mac's stall door. Oh, Mac, he was scared shitless—speechless, never called out for help. I always wondered how Andy knew he wouldn't scream like a woman."

"Practice," said Riker, who could see where this story was going. "He'd probably done it before."

Victor Patchock lowered his head. "Then Andy jammed this stinking, dirty snot rag in MacPherson's mouth. He spun the poor guy around and spread his legs. So Mac had to lean both hands on the wall to keep from falling. And that poor bastard still didn't know what was coming—not till he heard the sound of Andy's zipper coming down."

The little man squeezed his eyes shut. "Outside in the jury room, there wasn't much to hear—grunts, Andy laughing—and thumps—when his rear end hit the stall door." Victor Patchock beat his closed fist on the table, over and over, saying, "Thump, thump, thump," in the rhythm of a rape.

"So Andy comes back to the jury room with this big sloppy grin on his stupid face. MacPherson was in the bathroom another twenty minutes. When he finally came out, he wouldn't look anybody in the eye, just stared at the floor. He was shaking all over, dying inside, trying so hard not to cry. But then he did cry—real quiet, just tears. There was blood on the seat of his pants. Everybody knew what happened to him in there. Nobody ever used the bathroom again—except Andy. MacPherson changed his vote."

"Andy Sumpter wasn't gay," said Ian Zachary. "This man was paying child support on three children."

"The rape wasn't about sex," said Johanna.

"Ah, the feminist party line. I know this cliché. Rape isn't about sex—it's about power. Is that the way you see it, Dr. Apollo?"

"No," said Johanna. "I thought it was probably about money. Or did you promise to make Andy famous? Oh, the things your fans will do just for a few minutes on the radio."

"Maybe Andy was *your* bitch, Dr. Apollo. You were always in control of that room. That's one thing the jurors agreed on when they talked to the media. They took their cues from you."

"I did my best to keep Andy from spinning out of control. He always wanted to use his fists, and it was a fight to keep him from hitting those people. So, in hindsight, he probably wasn't your best choice for intimidating that jury—always a second away from exploding. And this is what comes of amateurs like you dabbling in psychology."

"But you claim this no-neck moron thwarted the entire justice system. Stupid Andy swayed the whole jury."

"Andy came from the cave," said Johanna. "But you're right about one thing. It was my fault. Now I wish I'd just let him explode in that jury room, a room full of witnesses. He might've hurt one of them badly, maybe a few broken bones. But you never would've walked away from that trial as a free man."

"And, without that unanimous verdict, without *your* vote, Doctor, the Reaper would've had no motive to kill the jurors. All those people would still be alive."

"When the other jurors were dying, Dr. Apollo kept us alive, me and MacPherson," said Victor Patchock. "She paid for everything. And she kept us from falling apart. But then—"

"Something happened," said Mallory prompting him. "Something changed?"

"I found out who the Reaper was. That damn lawyer, Fairlamb, ratted me out to Dr. Apollo. She was waiting for me in that underground parking garage. She took my gun away, but she was too late to stop MacPherson." He turned to Riker, saying, "I waited outside on the street, and then I followed you guys to that bar on Green Street. And there's poor Mac, a prisoner, jammed in that booth between you and Zachary."

"Who is the Reaper?" asked Agent Hennessey.

"He is," said Patchock, pointing to Riker. "He followed Mac to the garage that night. Later on, when I was leaving the bar, Riker was still waiting for Mac to come back from the men's room. Arrest him!"

Riker glanced at Mallory. She was not the least bit annoyed with the little man for wasting her time. And he knew why, or so he thought, but then she surprised him.

Mallory put one hand on Victor Patchock's shoulder, nails embedding in the material, just a gentle reminder that she was in control of him. And her voice was a monotone when she said, "I know you're holding back. Big mistake, Victor. Don't fool with me."

"I have to go to the toilet again."

When the door had closed upon the little man and his warden, Hennessey turned from one cop to the other. "Did you guys believe any of that?"

"The rape happened," said Riker. "I believed that much."

"No way," said the agent. "Dr. Apollo never mentioned an assault in her complaint."

"Of course not," said Riker. "Who would've believed her? You didn't. There were ten people on the other side of that bathroom door and a bailiff out in the hall. How could Andy Sumpter be stupid enough to risk it? The plan is so stupid it's damn smart."

"It did happen," said Mallory. "Andy needed cash, and some people will do anything for money." She turned to Riker. "But Victor did lie."

"I heard the noise in the bathroom," said Johanna. "The other jurors had gone selectively deaf. So I went to the door to get the bailiff. The hall was empty. That's when I realized that you'd bought him off. He was the one who carried your instructions to Andy Sumpter. You not only arranged the rape, but you timed it with the bailiff. You wanted him gone while that assault was going on." Johanna addressed all her words to the dark window.

Even the girl in the lighted booth was a believer now, turning that way as if peering through the solid walls that separated her booth from the producer's.

"Excuse me, Doctor." Zachary rose from the console, walked around the Japanese screen and jammed a small camera up to the glass, illuminating the booth with a bright flash.

No one there.

He returned to his chair, behaving as if that had been a perfectly normal thing to do. "Go on, Dr. Apollo. You were giving me credit for suborning the entire jury."

She studied his more relaxed face. He was enjoying himself again. What a pity. But she could fix that. "You won't get away with jury tampering. And you won't be a media star anymore."

"Let's talk about *your* crimes, Dr. Apollo. After the trial, I sent you roses every day for a month. I'm sure you know why. I never doubted that the verdict was your work. By your own account, you kept Andy Sumpter from beating up those people. You, more than anyone else, helped to sway that entire jury. Oh, and one other thing—you voted not guilty. I'd say you earned your roses, Doctor."

"You won't get away with it."

He smiled and threw up his hands. "Bring on the police. Let's have another trial. No, wait. What was I thinking? You have no proof."

"You misunderstood," she said. "I was alluding to all the people who want you dead. Those jurors you and your fans hunted down, they had husbands and wives, parents and children. Lots of wounded survivors. This is your new trial, right here, right now. If I'm believed, then you're a dead man."

"Just one moment, Dr. Apollo. If I understand you correctly, you're openly soliciting my murder on the radio."

Johanna's eyes turned back to the dark window of the producer's booth, and she sucked in a breath, startled by the image on the other side of the glass. What malicious creativity. She would never have anticipated anything on this level of sophistication.

"Fascinating."

Zachary lunged for the Japanese screen, knocking it down with his fist so that he could see the producer's booth. A sheet had been draped across the window glass, and two holes had been slashed in the fabric, two dark eyes slanting upward. And though there was no third hole to indicate a mouth, Johanna would later remember a complete face with an evil smile.

Upon the return of Victor Patchock, it was finally established, to the little man's satisfaction, that an FBI agent, not Riker, had been the last one to see MacPherson alive. And then Hennessey left the room to respond to a cell-phone call in private. Without missing a beat between words, Mallory picked up the rhythm of the interview. "Let's talk about the parking garage. What were the two of you planning that night?"

"MacPherson and me were going to scare the living shit out of Zachary."

"So your gun had blanks, too?"

"No, I was gonna shoot the bastard for real. *Real* bullets. I wanted to hurt him so bad, him and all his moron fans. I hate him more than the Reaper."

"You wanted revenge," said Mallory, "that much is true. But you told us a few lies, Victor. I warned you about that. You said Dr. Apollo was the last one to change her vote."

He lowered his eyes as he nodded, reaffirming his statement.

"You're lying to me," she said. "And such a stupid *little* lie." Mallory held up an old newspaper clipping. "This is an interview with one of the jurors. According to this, the last holdout on that jury was a man. So it wasn't Dr. Apollo, and I'm damn sure it wasn't you. If you lie to me one more time . . ." Her words trailed off, and she let his imagination do the work of frightening him.

"It was Mac," said Victor Patchock. "He was the last one to change his vote."

"And he's not the one who got raped in the bathroom," said Riker. "That was you."

"No! It wasn't me!"

"You're lying," said Riker. "That night in the parking garage, MacPherson only wanted to scare Zachary. Payment in kind. He wanted Zachary to know what it felt like to be scared. But you wanted a different kind of payback. You brought real bullets. Andy Sumpter was dead, killed by the Reaper—no satisfaction there."

"So you went after Ian Zachary," said Mallory, "your rapist by proxy. I warned you not to hold out on me one more time."

Riker leaned toward the little man. "Did you plan to shoot the bastard's balls off? You think you could've made a shot like that—while you were hiding in the dark?"

Victor Patchock's head rolled back, and he stared at the overhead lights. His nose had begun to bleed, and he wiped it with one hand, smearing blood across his face. "I was the first one to change my vote to not guilty. Not that I was scared. That wasn't it. I just wanted to go home. So I don't know why Andy did that to me. Why? I already voted his way." He used his coat sleeve to wipe the blood from his hand. "I'm a *little* man . . . I know that. Dr. Apollo kept voting guilty. It was just her and MacPherson. But after . . . I came out of the bathroom . . . Andy demanded another ballot. He stood next to my chair, one hand squeezing my shoulder—not hard, more like I was his girlfriend or something. And he was staring at Dr. Apollo. Everyone else, except maybe Mac, was looking the other way—if you know what I mean."

"So you were Andy's hostage," said Riker. "That's why Jo voted not guilty."

"He knew where I lived," said Victor. "Suppose I'd pressed charges? Who would've believed me? Nobody backed up Dr. Apollo. What chance did I have? The stupid ones were clueless, and the smart ones would never go up against Andy."

"Except for Jo and MacPherson," said Riker. "You could've—"

"Okay! All right! But what then? I'm a *little* man. And you damn cops, you can't keep criminals in jail for six minutes. Andy would've been back on the street in an hour. You know he would've . . ."

Raped you again?

"So the lady changed her vote for you," said Riker. Jo would have internalized all of Victor Patchock's fear and pain, then sought to end it.

"Dr. Apollo voted not guilty," said Victor. "When she caved in, Mac did, too. He couldn't make a stand without her. He just couldn't do it alone."

Riker lowered his eyes. There was guilt enough to spread around this table in equal shares tonight. He had his own regrets on MacPherson's account and took on a share of the blame for that death. A good man was gone, and this coward, this self-described *little* man, had survived. Victor Patchock was about to become famous. The news media would make him a symbol for the American justice system, proof that it was still alive and well. Or was it?

Crazy Bitch could only stare at the blinking phoneboard lights, too afraid to pick up any of the calls. It might be a curious fan or maybe an angry station manager. The relentless digital clock on her console was counting down the seconds. Not a moment's peace, hardly time to draw a breath. She dumped her purse out on her desk and rummaged through the mess, hunting for a way to keep the entire world at bay, and she found it in a paper bag with a hardware store logo.

She was *saved.*

She laughed and laughed while tears streamed down her

face, tears brought on by a joy so exquisite that it was almost unbearable. The mike was dead, and her voice could not be heard outside this room. She clenched her fists, then filled her lungs and screamed to no one, "I'm gonna be famous!"

Hennessey had not yet returned when Mallory decided to reconvene the interrogation in the larger interview room, the one that allowed covert observation from behind the mirror on the wall. Riker guessed that this was for the benefit of the assistant district attorney. If that man was still waiting behind the glass, he would see Mallory end a brief interview with a willing statement from Victor Patchock—absent any duress. She pushed a pad of yellow paper in Victor's direction, and the little man began to write down all the details wrung out of him in the smaller room. His face was free of tears now, and the evidence of his last nosebleed had been wiped away.

"Write it all down." She turned to the one-way glass, saying, "It's a wrap. Let's go collect the doctor."

On the other side of the mirror, Jack Coffey's voice was slightly sardonic as he spoke into the intercom. "The boys from Chicago lost Dr. Apollo again."

"No way!" Mallory stood up and faced the mirror and her boss who stood behind it. "All those idiots had to do was—"

"It's not a problem." Agent Hennessey stood in the doorway. He was smiling as he folded his cell phone into the breast pocket of his suit jacket. "My guys found her. She's a guest on the Ian Zachary show. We've got men at the radio station right now. As soon as the show is over, we'll make the arrest for jury tampering."

Betrayal.

Riker leaned his tired head upon one hand. The moment Mallory turned on the FBI agent, he decided to let her rip the man's head off. Hennessey did not know her well enough to be forewarned as she walked toward him, her words carefully measured. "When did all of this go down?"

"My bureau chief's been monitoring the show for twenty minutes. He says the lady makes a good case. So Zachary's going away for jury tampering, and he won't be feeding the Reaper any more helpful information." Hennessey patted Victor Patchock on the back. "And now we've got your corroboration for Dr. Apollo's complaint." He turned to smile at Mallory, as if that would help him. "The doctor and Mr. Patchock go back into protective custody whether they like it or not. They're material witnesses now." He turned away from Mallory—a huge mistake—to see Jack Coffey enter the room.

Riker thought the boss was curiously calm.

"So thanks for all your help, Lieutenant," said the agent, "but we'll take it from here."

Mallory was silently coming up behind Hennessey's back when Riker had second thoughts about the impending violence. He grabbed her by the shoulders as her nails—call them claws—were on the rise, then whispered in her ear, "Let Coffey go off on the bastard. Trust me on this one." His tip-off was the lieutenant's composure.

Jack Coffey was actually smiling when he pulled up a chair at the table. "Hennessey, here's a little something your boss probably didn't mention. It happened three minutes ago. Somebody called 911 for a disturbance at the radio station, and six patrol cops responded. The FBI agents tried to stop them from going up to Ian Zachary's floor. Well, the uniforms don't take orders from feds." The lieutenant propped his feet up on the table, and the FBI agent stiffened his own posture, bracing for more bad news.

"Sorry, Hennessey. It seems one of your guys is losing a little blood. But the good news? Our guy didn't break his damn jaw. It's just a split lip. A few stitches, he'll be fine. And that disturbance call?" Coffey shrugged. "Turned out to be a false alarm."

Normally, Riker would have suspected Mallory of making that bogus 911 call, but she had an alibi for the time frame. Evidently, the lieutenant was picking up her bad habits.

Jack Coffey turned to Detective Janos. "Those uniforms belong to the midtown precinct. Keep an open line to their sergeant. They have orders to hold that floor. Make sure that's *all* they do. I don't want anybody rattled till we're ready to make an arrest." And last, but with the greatest satisfaction, he turned back to the FBI man, saying, "We'll take it from here."

"You have no jurisdiction on a jury tampering charge," said Agent Hennessey.

"Oh, that's all changed," said Coffey. "We have a few charges of our own." He glanced at Mallory. "You didn't tell him about that yet? Sorry, I ruined your fun."

Hennessey would have left the room with his document cartons, following in Jack Coffey's wake, but Riker was now blocking the door. "Not so fast, pal. You made a deal with Mallory. You're going to keep it." He looked down at the boxes of Reaper files. "Or maybe you'd rather leave all that stuff here."

Over the next thirty minutes, Dr. Apollo's voice was heard on radios all over New York City and the portable set in the interview room.

Riker turned down the volume as he faced the one-way mirror. "What's taking so long on that arrest warrant?"

Jack Coffey's voice came over the intercom, saying, "We're shopping for a judge who isn't afraid of the ACLU. Shouldn't be much longer."

The contents of the Reaper file were spread across the long table, and Agent Hennessey could only watch this invasion of his paperwork. His fingers lightly drummed the table to advertise a bad case of arrogance withdrawal. The FBI man's detainment had not been formalized, though a strong suggestion was made by the massive bulk of Detective Janos leaning against the only door.

Mallory owned the agent now, and she was in the early stages of toying with her food. After scanning the contents of an FBI folder, she looked up from her reading. "So Dr.

Apollo was always on the shortlist for the jury murders." She crumpled a sheet of paper, and Hennessey watched, fascinated, as the wad rolled between her palms, compacting into a perfect ball the size of a marble.

"That's destruction of government—"

"It's bogus," she said. "And you knew it when you padded out the Reaper file. Now I want the good stuff, the personal notes that never made it into your database. How many screwups were purged from the computer?"

Hennessey hesitated too long. Her paper marble shot past his right ear and bounced off the wall behind him.

"If I have to find those mistakes by myself," she said, "then I add them to the rest of the mess your people made of this case. I might hold a press conference—all the major networks—national publicity, all of it bad."

And those were the magic words.

Hennessey retrieved the wadded paper from the floor. "This sheet isn't total crap. When Agent Kidd was murdered, Dr. Apollo was our prime suspect for a copycat killing. She had her own history with psychiatric treatment, long-term therapy as a child and a teenager. Maybe our man said the wrong thing and she snapped. It happens. Or maybe he was the one who snapped, and the doctor killed him in self-defense. But we know the Reaper didn't murder Timothy Kidd."

"You're wrong," said Riker. "And that's one more screwup for the feds." He looked up at his partner. "Mallory, are you keeping score?"

Agent Hennessey might be on the defensive, but he was showing no signs of backing down from this theory. The FBI man was adamant when he said, "Timothy Kidd's murder didn't have the elements of a Reaper killing except for the penknife, and that detail was in the newspapers. There was no scythe drawn in blood, nothing written on the wall of the doctor's reception room. There was no note stuffed in his mouth. And even the cut to the throat was different, less damage and not as deep."

"But then that homeless man was killed with a penknife,"

said Mallory. "The same sloppy cut as the one that killed Timothy Kidd."

"Right," said the agent. "We figure the doctor killed Bunny, too. Argus misread the whole thing. He thought Bunny's death meant that the Reaper was keeping tabs on Dr. Apollo."

Mallory seemed genuinely offended, for the agent was putting no earnest effort into any of these lies. "You *knew* they were both Reaper victims, Bunny and the fed. Argus was tailing her long before that. He was using her as a lure for the Reaper, and then he did the same thing to MacPherson, hanging him out as bait."

"Argus wasn't on the Reaper investigation," said Hennessey. "His only job was coordinating juror protection, and he screwed that up. No one was authorized to use the jurors as bait. The agents in Behavioral Sciences were making a case for—"

"The profilers?" Mallory nodded. "Not a decent psych credential between them. If it hadn't been for their interference, the case would've been closed by now. You never asked the right question, the one that begins every cop's investigation—who benefits?"

"It's not that kind of crime," said Hennessey.

"Sure it is," she said. "You messed up because you were all trying to think like psychiatrists. Dr. Apollo was the only one thinking like a cop."

Jack Coffey's voice came over the intercom. "We've got the warrant. Let's move, people."

Hennessey was rising, perhaps believing that he was invited to go along.

A uniformed officer entered the room and set a formidable power tool on the table before Riker. "Big enough for you?"

"That'll do me. Thanks."

"What's the drill for?" asked Hennessey.

Riker plugged it into a wall socket to test it. "Ian Zachary's studio has a world-class security door, three inches of metal and an electronic lock. Can't force it, can't pick it." He switched on the drill for the full effect of a squadron of dentists from hell, then cut the power. "So we go right through the lock."

"Let's do this the smart way," said Hennessey, sincerely deluded in the idea that he might have some influence in this room. "We wait till the show's over. We'll let the doctor play it out, maybe collect more evidence that way—*recorded* evidence."

"Bad idea," said Riker. "She's locked in that room with a stone killer." He turned to the one-way mirror. "Ready when you are, boss."

"The Reaper can't be Ian Zachary," said Hennessey. "The man has an unbreakable alibi for Timothy Kidd's murder. Agents were parked right outside his door round the clock."

"Yeah, right," said Mallory. "He could never get past one of *your* guys."

It was rare and wonderful to hear Mallory's laugh, even if it *was* slightly evil, and Riker smiled as he followed the sound of her laughter through the door. Hennessey was right behind them when he met up with the immovable obstacle of Detective Janos.

Mallory's tan sedan took a corner and took his breath away. The car hung on two wheels for exactly four of Riker's heartbeats. Tonight, she had grudgingly used the siren and the portable turret light, thus giving civilian motorists fair warning before she climbed up their tails and scared them out of their minds.

"It was a great plan," she said. "Almost flawless."

Riker hefted the weight of the drill in one hand. "You know he'll be out on the street an hour after we book him." He watched the cityscape flying past the passenger window of Mallory's tan rocket.

"I promise you, we'll nail Zachary," she said. "But it *was* a good plan. The feds were always looking for some sick, twitchy law-and-order freak hiding in a dark room. But there he was, hiding right out in the open."

"And we'll never make a case against him. He'll never do any time for murder."

"We'll nail him cold."

"You mean—in the act, right? With Jo for bait."

"That was the doctor's plan," said Mallory.

Riker turned up the radio and Jo's voice saying, *"Did I do the right thing? No, and I regret my errors every day. All those—"*

Mallory reached out and turned down the volume. "What do you think she's doing? She's calling him out. He's rattled enough to go after her right now, but he won't. First, he'll want to set up an alibi. Maybe he'll try to use the feds to—"

The car stopped short of the curb, slinging Riker's body forward as his partner ripped open his suit jacket to expose the empty shoulder holster.

"Why aren't you wearing your gun?" She dug her nails into his arm. "Your gun, Riker! Where is it?"

And only now did he realize that Mallory, for all her crimes, was not the concerned thief who had made off with his weapon. "So you didn't pick the lock on my desk drawer?"

"Well, yeah, I did. But I didn't take your revolver."

His eyes closed as he recalled his lecture on the stopping power of a smaller caliber firearm than his own. "Aw, Jo. It had to be her. She's got my damn gun." He handed Mallory the drill. "She's planning to shoot that bastard, and she wants to do a proper job of it. You go. I'll wait here and cover the entrance."

Mallory had not expected that, not from him. Her hand froze on the door's handle and her eyes narrowed, so suspicious, unable to come up with any logical scenario where he would volunteer to remain behind, gun or no gun. Mallory did not trust him anymore, yet she opened the door. She had no choice but to leave him here. Upstairs in that building, there was a gun in play, and she was the only cop who knew about it. Time was precious; bullets traveled so fast. She broke off this conversation of the eyes and ran for the door.

When she had disappeared into the radio station, he slid into the driver's seat and put her car in gear. As he nosed it out into the street, he turned up the volume on the radio, confirming his suspicions. Words chopped off at the end of one segment were now repeated in the next, and this was the mark of an amateur at the switch. He watched the radio station recede in his rearview mirror.

At best, he could only count on ten minutes of lead time. It would not take long for Mallory to discover that she had been scammed. He headed the car toward the Chelsea Hotel, then glanced at the clock on the dashboard as he listened to Jo's prerecorded voice taunting a serial killer, calling him out for a showdown. There was no other way to read her intentions.

Calling for backup was not an option. Neither feds nor local cops would approve of Riker's plans for their material witness, Johanna Apollo. He intended to grab that woman, to rip his stolen revolver from her hands, then run with Jo to Mexico. No baggage, just her very life was all he wanted, all he needed. But first he must have his gun back so that no one would ever make it past him to get to her—not even Mallory.

21

THE OUTNUMBERED FBI AGENTS HAD BEEN CONtained on the floor below, and Lieutenant Coffey stood outside the door to Ian Zachary's studio. He had lost his satisfied smile. According to Mallory, there was a lethal weapon in play, and the game plan had radically changed. The narrow corridor was crowded with police, and yet the only sound was the tap of Mallory's foot.

Special Crimes Unit had never used the lower ranks for cannon fodder, and so they waited for a uniformed officer to fetch two bulletproof vests, one for the lieutenant and one for his detective. With a wave of his hand, Jack Coffey motioned the remaining uniforms to move back down the hall. The metal studio door was thick enough to offer protection from a .45-caliber bullet, but the surrounding wall might not. Prescient Mallory had known that this arrest would not go down nicely. She had brought her own drill to the party, and she handled it like a gun. In her other hand was a wiring diagram of the electronic door lock.

Coffey stared at the power tool. "You're sure you can't electrocute yourself with that thing?"

"No electricity," she said. "The lock has its own circuit

breaker." Her voice was testy. She obviously resented having to play this out by the book *and* respond to silly questions. "The body armor should have been here by now."

"Maybe we shouldn't bore out the studio lock." Ian Zachary's door could only be opened from an interior control panel. The doors to the booths had locks made to open with keys, but they had both been fused shut with a glue that had hardened to the temperance of steel. The studio door was Mallory's own preference for the first strike. The lieutenant was not yet convinced. "Zachary might not hear the drill if we go through one of these side doors. They've both got windows on the studio."

"And the glass is four inches thick, unbreakable." Mallory looked up from her reading to glance at the ruined lock on one of the flanking doors. "You know why those locks are glued shut. One of them doesn't want any witnesses—probably Dr. Apollo. We can't wait for the body armor."

"Lieutenant?" A uniformed officer was monitoring Zachary's show on a pocket radio. As he walked toward them, he removed his earpiece and turned up the volume on the noise of violent breakage. "It sounds like he's taking the place apart."

Without waiting on orders, Mallory put the drill to the lock, knowing that the sound would alert the people inside. Jack Coffey stayed her hand before she could power up the tool and give them away.

"Cover me," he said. "I'll drill the lock."

"It's *my* drill." She held it tightly in both hands.

The lieutenant could only stare at her. What a hell of a time for this silly kid stunt. However, it *was* her drill, her case—her show all the way. Jack Coffey removed his hand from the tool. Stepping back, he drew his gun, demoting himself to Mallory's backup, then waved the uniforms farther down the hall. "Okay, Mallory, *now!*"

He had not expected so much noise. The loud squeal of metal grinding on metal made all his nerve endings stand at attention. Zachary and Dr. Apollo would know they were coming, but which of them would be holding the gun when the door opened? He trained his own gun on the door, ready to kill whoever pointed a weapon at Mallory. She was halfway through the lock, and a death might be only seconds away.

His detective looked up from her work, saying, "We'll never make a case if you shoot my corroborating witness."

"Mallory, *later* you can remind me to fire your ass." He turned to the sound of footfalls pounding down the hall at his back. Two uniformed officers came on the run. Instead of the requested flak jackets, they carried two large bulletproof shields.

Johanna Apollo was startled to hear her own voice on the radio. She had not expected Zachary to play that interview tape on the air. How could she have guessed wrong about that? If he thought he was impervious to an investigation, he might not come tonight.

Or was he already here?

She turned off the radio and held her breath, standing very still in the dead quiet of the front room. Had she actually heard a noise in the hall? Or had she intuited a presence out there—sensed it in the fashion of Mugs or Timothy Kidd? Tonight there would be no buffer of FBI agents downstairs in the hotel lobby. The federal bodyguards were looking for her elsewhere.

No interruptions, no witnesses.

Gun in hand, Johanna settled into an armchair and braced her elbows on the upholstery. The recoil of Riker's revolver would be stronger than Victor's smaller gun, and she would not risk it falling from her trembling hands, for one bullet might not do the job. After turning off the table lamp, all that illuminated the hotel room, she could see the shadows of two shoes in a crack of yellow light below the door. The narrow foyer's walls seemed like an extension of the gun's barrel.

A knock. How polite—and unexpected. Johanna called out, "It's not locked!"

The door opened slowly, and this was something she

should have anticipated. She could see that now—her error. Ian Zachary would pride himself on theatrics. His dark silhouette filled the door frame, backlit by the lamps in the hall.

She had rehearsed this moment inside her head so many times. It had always begun with immediate violence, a body barreling through the door, rushing in with a view to unbalancing her with cold, paralyzing terror. That had been Timothy Kidd's imagined re-creation of the juror murders, but that was not to be—not here and now. And what else might she get wrong before this night was over?

The room suddenly flooded with light from the ceiling fixture. Her eyes were still adapting to the brightness when she saw his hand on the wall switch and heard him say, "I should come inside." His voice was in the range of seduction, and this was another surprise. "If you shoot me in the hall," he said, "the police might not buy the idea of self-defense."

During her training days as a crime-scene cleaner, Riker had told her that hesitation should be listed as the cause of death for most homicide victims. Educable Johanna raised the gun. She must kill Ian Zachary *now.*

He closed the door behind him—and locked it.

The gun was so heavy.

"There, that's better," he said. "Now you have privacy for a murder—and a better story for the police." Zachary strolled toward her, smiling, all but laughing at the gun in her hands, only sparing it one glance. He stopped a few paces from her chair, then raised his arms to show her the spread of his empty hands. "I don't have a weapon, but here's a thought—maybe you could plant one on my dead body." He lowered his arms. "You might have time to run to the store, some all-night bodega where the clerk won't remember a distraught hunchback buying a penknife."

The gun barrel wavered. Her finger touched lightly on the trigger, and he became an easier target as he closed the gap between them. She fancied Timothy inside her head, screaming to the rhythm of a banging heart, *Kill him, kill him, kill him!*

Her script for this event was already in shambles. It

should not have surprised her so when Zachary leaned down and simply plucked the gun from her shaking hands, saying, "Not quite the scenario you had in mind? Too civilized for a cold-blooded killing? You don't know what you're missing, Dr. Apollo." He pressed the gun to her forehead an inch above her eyes. "What a rush. Better than sex."

She looked down at her hands, limp useless things, and waited for the shot.

Riker sailed through another red light, avoiding collisions by the grace of providence, for his eyes kept wandering to the rearview mirror, expecting Mallory to climb up his taillights at any moment. She would have discovered by now that Jo's interview was on tape, and it would only take her six seconds to steal another car.

A fire engine beat him into the intersection, stringing its long body across the entire width of the street. He slammed on the brakes, but not before he had done some damage to the other vehicle and crumpled a fender of Mallory's car. He reversed gears and backed up by ten feet as an angry fireman climbed down from the driver's seat and walked toward him. Now the driver was joined by other men dropping down to the pavement like combat troops parachuting in for a battle. They were all moving in tandem, and the strategy was clear: they were planning to surround Riker and take a little satisfaction out of his hide—slow torture by paperwork and forms filled out in triplicate. Flashing his badge would not save him, and he could not spare the time to do even that much.

Taking a tip from the Mallory School of Bad Driving, Riker aimed the car at the walking wall of firemen. Brave bastards, they waited until the last possible moment to jump aside. And now the small tan sedan was running round the long red truck, using all of the sidewalk to do it, and civilians were diving into the street. Move or die—that was the message.

Mallory would have been proud.

"If I wanted you dead," said Ian Zachary, "I could have killed you months ago. You were the easiest one to keep track of." He ran the gun barrel lightly along the deformity of her spine. "Such a distinctive profile. Tell you what. Let's do a trade—your life for Victor Patchock's." He reached out to a small table, picked up the telephone and carried it to her chair. "Call him over here."

"You'll kill us both."

"No, no, no." Zachary wore a condescending smile as he knelt down before her. "The last juror standing takes all the blame. I thought you understood that, Doctor. *That's* why people keep dying in your vicinity. First Timothy Kidd, then poor Bunny. When the police find Victor bleeding all over your rug, I think they'll have enough to close out the case."

"And no witness to back up the charge of jury tampering." Johanna nodded her understanding. One of the surviving jurors must die tonight. "But if I'm supposed to be the Reaper—if I die, you have no show left."

"You *do* understand." He rewarded her with his widest smile, then patted her hand. "Good girl. Yes, ideally there would be another trial—yours. A long, drawn-out affair. You're wealthy, Dr. Apollo. You can hire the best legal team in the country. I promise you'll never do a day in prison for all those murders. You'll buy your way out with legal talent. It's the American way."

"And then we start over?"

"Right. A fresh jury. And, next time, all twelve of them die."

"And then another trial? Do you get all your plans from comic books?" Ah, she had disappointed him. This was not the response he had expected. But she knew he would not kill her—not yet. First, he must make her into a believer—a fan of sorts. She was all the audience that he would ever have. He wanted—applause.

He set the telephone in her lap. "You see? I *do* have an interest in keeping you alive. So you know I'll keep my word." He pressed the receiver into her hand. "Call Victor Patchock."

"You have a famous face," she said. "How many people spotted you downstairs in the lobby? How many of them saw you get on the elevator?"

"Oh, I don't need an alibi tonight. This time, I'll be the one who discovers the Reaper's next victim." He held up her old business card and flipped it over to show her a personal note. "Recognize your own handwriting? I took this off the corpse of Agent Kidd. The wording is ambiguous, no names or dates, just a reminder that the appointment's been changed from ten to eleven o'clock. I'll say you invited me over, lured me here with the prospect of interviewing Victor. But then—what a shock—you killed him right before my eyes." He looked down at his watch. "It's close to eleven o'clock."

"I don't know where Victor is." And this was true. She had been unable to reach him tonight.

"What a pity." He pulled a small silver penknife from his pocket and opened the blade. The honed metal edge gleamed bright. "You can split hairs with this thing—razor sharp." Zachary smiled in mock chagrin. "Oh, I lied about not having a weapon."

Removing the telephone from her lap, he set it on the floor. "Fine, don't call Victor. I'll just have to make do with you." He rose to his feet and backed away from her. "More fun this way. Make me chase you around a bit. Up you go." With a lifting gesture of the small knife, he urged her to rise. "How fast can a hunchback run?"

Crazy Bitch sat behind Ian Zachary's console, leaning into a stationary microphone and saying, "They're coming, boys and girls." She had cut off the pretaped interview to give the fans a moment-by-moment account of an unknown invader drilling out the lock on the studio door. "Is it the cops? Is it the Reaper? Stay tuned." She laughed too loud, creating an electronic feedback squeal that drowned out the sound of the drill. Hysteria was toned down to mere giggles.

"Yeah, like you're gonna turn me off before that door opens. Oh, here they come."

There was an unintentional moment of high drama in the silence that followed. The door swung open, and Crazy Bitch had lost her voice, unable to adequately describe the scene before her eyes when tall Mallory strode into the room, wielding a wicked-looking drill and carrying the shield of a medieval knight. The blonde was moving forward with grim resolve.

Could this woman be any more pissed off?

Crazy Bitch thought not.

•

Ian Zachary could not yet bear to part with his audience, or this was Johanna's thought as she watched the small blade dip and rise to punctuate his words.

"You have no alibi for any of the jury murders," he said. "I was very careful about that. Curse of the grotesque. Poor baby, you spent all your evenings alone. And then there was Timothy Kidd, murdered in your reception room. Now Bunny's crime scene was a piece of luck. I was counting on the neighbors to lead the police back to you. I never expected you to be there when they found the body."

Zachary turned away from her, thinking so little of her ability to fight back. After plumping up the couch pillows, he sat down and stretched out his legs on the coffee table. "Standing trial for murder isn't the worst that could—"

A knock on the door was followed by Riker's voice yelling, "Jo, it's me! Open up! I know you've got my gun!"

Zachary, vaguely amused, pulled the revolver from his pocket. "This is *his?* You stole a *cop's* gun?" He inclined his head in the manner of a complimentary bow. "You're an interesting woman, Dr. Apollo." He waved the revolver in the direction of the door. "Let him in."

Johanna smiled, and he didn't like that. "You're afraid of Riker," she said. "You're the one with the gun, but you'd never open that door yourself. You don't want to get that close to him."

The knocking was constant now and louder.

"You were hoping he'd just get tired and go away?" Zachary crooked one finger around the base of a ceramic table lamp. "I think this might get his attention."

The lamp toppled to the floor, smashing to pieces. Riker's knocking escalated to the bang of a closed fist, and he yelled, "Jo!"

Zachary took aim at the door. "I can drop him from here if you like. Let him in, or I'll shoot him right now."

"It's a big gun," said Johanna. "Powerful." She stood up and moved between the door and the couch, blocking his aim. Behind her back, she could hear the savage kicks to the wood, but the dead bolt lock was holding. "You could get both of us with one bullet—if you're lucky. But you won't risk a shot through a closed door—not you, the pathological planner. What if you miss Riker? What happens to all that careful scheming? Improvisation is not your forte."

"It's a moot point, Doctor. Look at what he's doing to that door."

She turned to see the wood splintering on one side of the lock. The frame was cracking, yielding, and there was only time to open the bottom drawer of the armoire before the door banged inward and Riker crashed into the room. He had one instant to register the weapon in the other man's hand, and then Johanna made a mighty swing to bring the wine bottle across the back of his skull.

Riker dropped like a stone.

Crazy Bitch played the tape for a commercial break during the police-enforced interlude. Her eyes were trained on Mallory, who was evidently not Zack's own private cop.

One of the uniformed officers carried the drill into the hall and knelt down before the lock on the producer's door. Inside the studio, the two police in street clothes stood before the booth's window, admiring the sheet spread across it. Far from the effect of a cartoon ghost, the black slashes that stood for eyes were eerie. The thick glass was scratched but intact, and the remnants of a broken chair lay on the floor below.

Detective Mallory walked toward the console, intractable as a slow train wreck in the making. She wanted an explanation—*right now.*

"Zack did it," said Crazy Bitch, so easily prompted by a vision of Mallory's footprint on her face. "He left before the show started." She affected a deep frown as she turned to the producer's booth. "At least I *think* Zack's gone."

Was she overdoing this? Yes, she must be, for the blonde had one hand on her hip, and, in the other hand, the drill was slowly swinging like a pendulum.

"I've been playing pretaped interviews. You can't have dead airtime. I could lose my job for that. So how do you like the show so far?"

The drill crashed to the floor. The blond police braced both hands on the top of the console, leaning forward to communicate that Crazy Bitch should not to try her patience for one more minute.

Lieutenant Coffey interceded, calling out, "Hey, kid, what happened here?"

"I'm pretty sure Zack wanted to kill Needleman."

"The producer?" Coffey turned to face the draped window. "Is he in there now?"

"Who knows? Well, Needleman's door is always locked," said Crazy Bitch, "so Zack tried to break through bulletproof glass. And that was *really* nuts. He even knows the glass is unbreakable, but there he is, red in the face, banging that chair against the window. Then he racked up a few hours of old canned interviews and ran out the door. But I really liked the tape he made tonight. So, after he left, I changed the—"

"Shut up," said Detective Mallory.

The lieutenant was more polite, but just barely. "When Zachary left, was he carrying a weapon?"

"No, not that I could see, but I wouldn't take chances if I were you. I mean look at what he did to that chair." She stared at the sheet covering the producer's window. "Zack might be in there. If you kill him, can I still finish the show?"

Ian Zachary stood over the inanimate body of Riker. "Well, that solves the immediate problem. Is he dead?"

"I'm a doctor." Johanna knelt on the floor, checking life signs and finding them strong. "I know how to place my shots." The blow had split the skin of Riker's scalp, and his blood was on her right hand.

Zachary leaned into the hallway. "I love this town. All these people behind their closed doors. They don't want to get involved. Ah, New Yorkers."

"They probably didn't hear anything. The walls are very thick—just like Riker's place. I know what you did to him, and that was a mistake. He had no idea you were the Reaper."

"Oh, the blanks? Yes, I suppose it was a pointless plan—but great fun. He actually fainted."

Johanna shook her head. "He scared you, didn't he? Riker caught you by surprise that night, but you'd never go up against *him* with a knife. So you picked up the first weapon that came to hand, Mac's gun—Mac's bullets. No, that wasn't planning, Zachary. That was just another mistake."

She looked up at him, only a glance to gauge the fall of his confidence, then her eyes were cast down as she stared at her hand, at Riker's blood. "You can still walk away from this," she said. "My fingerprints are on the bottle that hit him."

"He saw me point the gun at him."

"That's not a problem. Side effect of concussion—it can wipe out ten or twenty minutes of memory, and Riker only saw you for a second. But what if he did remember? So what? He knows I'm the one who stole his gun. You can say you took it away from me, that you saved him from the Reaper—*me*. Don't you see? You don't need one more dead body to make the case. Just pick up the phone and call 911. The story's more believable if you're the one who makes that call."

"You're good, Doctor. And you're right. Your little plan might work. But that would still leave the loose end of Victor Patchock."

"He won't make a credible witness in court."

Zachary was no longer listening to her. His smiling eyes were lit with some new inspiration. "You have a much more interesting choice now." He pointed the gun at Riker. "I can kill him—or you can get Victor Patchock over here. Pick one." He waved the gun from side to side. "Who lives? Who dies? Up to you."

"I'll think about it," said Johanna, as if Riker's life meant very little to her. She rose from the floor, the bottle still gripped in one hand. "First, I'm going to wash up. And then I'm going to pour myself a drink." She turned toward the bathroom, fighting down the impulse to look back at Riker and see which way the gun was pointing now.

"Dr. Apollo? Hold it! I'll tell you where you can go and when."

"Then shoot me." She turned around to face him. "No, you can't do that, can you? A gun—that's not the Reaper's style." She took one step toward him and raised the bottle as a reminder that she had just brought down a bigger man, a better one. "*Now* how do you like your chances with that tiny knife? Like I said, Zachary, you're no good at improvising. And there's another flaw in your plan. That business card with my personal invitation? That note is in my secretary's handwriting," she lied. "I haven't seen that woman since Timothy died. Do you want the police to find that card in your pocket? No, I didn't think so. While you're burning that little piece of evidence, I'll be washing up." Bottle gripped tight in her right hand, she left him standing there and closed the bathroom door behind her.

"No, I said Zack *might* be inside." Crazy Bitch stared at the recently opened door of the producer's booth. "He really wanted to get in there."

"But you're the one who glued the locks shut," said Mallory.

"Yeah, just in case he was in there. Well, he's crazy, isn't he?"

"And you didn't want anybody to know that you were running the show tonight." Mallory inspected the interior, then pointed to the sheet spread across the window. "Is that your work?"

"How could it be? The producer's door is always locked."

"But you had a key, didn't you?"

Crazy Bitch gave her a wobbly smile as she backed up to the door of the studio. "The commercial break is over. I have to get back to my show. It's my show now."

"Just a minute." Jack Coffey appeared behind her, blocking her backward exit. "Where can we find this guy Needleman?"

"Probably home in bed. It's a school night."

Mallory loomed over the shorter woman, willing her to make sense with a glare that promised unspeakable violence if sense was not immediately forthcoming.

Crazy Bitch hurried to explain that Needleman was the station manager's nephew. "He's only fourteen years old."

"A payroll scam," said Mallory. "So the station manager pockets the extra paycheck?"

"You didn't hear that from me, okay?"

"Tell me how you know," said Coffey.

"Well, the station manager goes home at six. So it was my job to unlock the producer's booth after Zack left for the night. A couple of real producers use it for the morning shows. I was told it was a joke, just a way to get back at the bastard and drive him nuts. And that was fine with me, but I didn't believe it. If that was true, why not just give the other producers keys of their own?"

Lieutenant Coffey seemed smug as he turned on Mallory, saying, "Good reasoning. I might give this kid *your* job." Crazy Bitch sensed a note of payback in his voice as he rested one hand on her shoulder, saying, "Go on, kid. Tell us how you cracked the payroll scam."

"I screwed the hundred-year-old bookkeeper. He gets a cut from the producer's paycheck—and *he* told me."

Mallory missed the moment of the lieutenant's disappointment. Her head was turned, listening to the whispers of a policewoman. And now she ran down the hall. Lieutenant Coffey turned to the officer. "What did you say to her?"

"I gave her a message from Detective Janos," said the police officer. "Her car was stolen. Some firemen got the license plate number after the car hit their truck. They saw the thief driving south."

Johanna stood before the sink, looking down at the pimpernel Riker had drawn on the palm of her hand. She washed away his flower and his blood.

After leaving the bathroom, she walked into the kitchen, pulled down a wineglass from a rack on the wall, then rummaged in a drawer. The noise attracted Zachary. He was at her side when she pulled out the corkscrew.

The muzzle of the gun was pressed to the back of her head, yet her voice was perfectly calm. "Sorry," she said. "Looks dangerous, doesn't it?" She held up the twisty metal and made a show of inspecting it. "So sharp." Johanna walked past him, pretending that the gun did not exist. She sat down in an armchair and plunged the tip of the screw into the cork of the wine bottle. "Your plan is falling apart." She twisted the corkscrew by a full turn, driving it deeper. "Wondering how many other mistakes you made?"

And now she noticed her crime-scene bag open on the floor by the couch.

Zachary pulled on one of her disposable gloves, then picked up a rag and proceeded to clean Riker's revolver. "Tell me what you think of my *new* plan—my improvisation. First I shoot *you* in the head. You see? I can be flexible. Then I put the gun in your dead hand and shoot poor Riker in the heart." He held up his gloved hand. "When the police arrive, yours are the only fingerprints on the weapon. A clear case of murder and suicide. That works so nicely with all your guilt for those dead jurors."

"You're making this too complicated," she said, twisting

the screw deeper. "More mistakes." She pulled out the cork. "I washed Riker's blood off the bottle. I hope you don't mind me tampering with your evidence."

He made a long reach across the cocktail table and ripped the bottle from her grasp. "No problem. There's still a bloodstain on the label. I think that's enough to point the way for the police. How dumb can they be? Incidentally, you have excellent taste in wine. The last time I saw this vintage—"

"Was the night Timothy saw you in the liquor store. That's when you thought he'd pegged you as the Reaper. And *that's* why you killed him." She gave him a benign smile. "You can't fob that off as just another detail in your great plan. You killed him because you panicked. One more murder might be dicey. You've botched so many things."

He leveled the gun at her face. "Are you sure you want to piss me off?"

"Not my intention—just a symptom of something called the Stockholm syndrome."

He nodded. "Hostages bonding with their kidnappers. I don't see the—"

"There's more to it. The hostages actually work with the kidnappers. You see, it's in their best interests to help the kidnapper get the result he wants so the victim can survive. That's why I'm going to help you fix your errors—like the one with the business card."

"No, you're stalling for time. Waiting for reinforcements? Do you actually believe that Riker would tell another cop he'd lost his gun to a woman? Absurd. No one is coming to your rescue. Time to make a decision, Dr. Apollo." He walked to the kitchen and pulled another goblet from the rack on the wall. On his way back to the couch, he paused to nudge Riker's body with his foot, then moved on to pour some wine into Johanna's glass and more into his own.

"Are you sure you want to drink that?"

"Are you insane?" He held the bottle high. "It's impossible to find this vintage anymore."

That might well be true. She had inadvertently cornered

the market with her collection. "What if the wine is poisoned?"

His glass hovered in midair, and his face was also frozen.

"You're not sure, are you? Lost your edge?" She sipped from her wineglass and assumed what she hoped was a Mallory smile.

Perversely, he found that reassuring, and tipped back his own glass for a long draught. "You still believe you can talk your way out of this?"

She nodded and drank her wine. And he drank.

"Just as I remember it—fabulous." His gaze fell on Riker's body. "Too bad. I actually liked that man."

"He's not dead yet," said Johanna.

"He'll be dead soon enough, Doctor. And it's all your fault, you know. All those murders. If only you'd hung that jury when you had the chance. It would've taken one vote—yours. If you'd voted guilty, my plan would have died right there in the courtroom. You see that now, don't you? All your fault. And now poor Riker has to die."

"You're making everything too complicated. That's how they'll catch you."

"You'll never know, Doctor. You'll be dead. Or . . . one phone call to Victor Patchock and you get to live." He perused the bottle's label. "So Timothy Kidd put you onto this wine. That night in the liquor store—was he following me?"

She sipped from the glass. "That's been driving you crazy, hasn't it? How did Timothy know it was you? What did you do wrong?"

"He found me in the neighborhood of a fresh corpse."

"That wasn't it. The body hadn't been found yet. No, the odd note was when *you* recognized *him*. In hindsight, it's so simple. You haunted your crime scenes. That's part of the kick, isn't it? The police activity, the media frenzy. That's how you knew Timothy was FBI. Forgive me—I'm digressing. Of course he recognized you. Your face was on the news every night. But he had to wonder why you'd be surprised to see him, a man you'd never met. And then you disappeared so quickly. Details like this are food for a paranoid personality. He was only suspicious that night. When another juror turned up dead the next day, that's when he—"

"Still trying to buy time? You really think the cavalry is coming over the hill to save you. Now, that's odd, because you're the one with the rescuer complex." He yawned. "Let's get this over with, shall we?" He aimed the gun at her face.

"Actually, I was just about to pay you a compliment."

He lowered the gun. She knew he would.

"The idea was brilliant," she said. "And you almost pulled it off. You nearly disemboweled the justice system."

"With a little help from the ACLU."

"Yes, a nice touch." She watched the rise and fall of Riker's chest, and found comfort in this.

"I don't have to kill him, Doctor. Choose. Riker or Victor." His gun hand warred a moment with the hand that held the wine. The revolver was left to rest on the couch cushion. He drained his glass, then filled it again. "Perhaps I shouldn't rush you. As victims go, you're miles more entertaining than the rest of them."

"Even my friend Timothy?"

"Oh, absolutely boring. Though, to be fair, I suppose it's difficult to be scintillating company once your throat is slashed and you're bleeding to death." Zachary lifted his wineglass again, then watched, surprised and helpless to prevent it from tipping forward. His fingers could not close around the crystal. The wine spilled across the couch cushions in a wide red stain.

Johanna was reminded of Timothy Kidd quietly bleeding his life away in an armchair.

Zachary gave her a foolish smile. "I'm drunk."

She shook her head. "No, that's not it." Johanna looked down at her glass. "Such a poor wine. That's all you had in common with Timothy—neither one of you had a discriminating palate. I think my chemicals actually improved the taste."

It was a struggle for him to keep his eyes open. There was

a high color in his cheeks and his eyes were those of a dullard, slow to focus. But now, as he began to understand what she had done, he made a clumsy attempt to rise from the couch. Panic worked against him. "You drugged me." His fingers wormed around the handle of the gun, but he could not lift it from the cushion. "You put me to sleep."

"I considered that option," she said. "I have a high tolerance for these drugs, but you have greater body mass. So I couldn't count on outlasting you. And you might've been the first to wake up. No, I didn't sedate you . . . I killed you. A syringe in the cork. It's the simple plans that work best."

"But you drank—"

"I killed us both. There was no other way." Johanna sat quietly, finally coming to terms with Timothy Kidd's last moments and sharing them. She sipped air and life, what measure was left.

The more Ian Zachary struggled, the faster he died. The red wine stain spread across the upholstery, just like the bloodstains on Timothy's chair. She had not anticipated the justice of this tableau. She had not dared to think so far ahead, lest she falter with the syringe while poisoning the wine.

Zachary's head rolled to one side, and he stared at her in dumb surprise. The muscle spasm, a preview of her own death, made his body go suddenly rigid. Then came the violent shakes, and then nothing at all. He had ceased to exist.

And she was alone.

There was no euphoria to numb her own panic while she separated from the solid earth. Johanna Apollo, the recalcitrant suicide, grieved for her lost life as she careened away from it. This was the moment after the leap from a mountain, the knowledge that she could not scratch her way back to the ledge, and the experience of free fall was intense. There was such cruelty in this long descent from grace—so much time for regret.

The final spasm came. The wineglass fell from her hand. And, in the ether of her dying brain starved of oxygen and blood, regret, tenacious thing, remained.

Riker was bleeding from a head wound, always a good indication of ongoing life, and his pulse was strong. Mallory was still holding on to his wrist as she spoke to the 911 operator, saying the words guaranteed to get the best service, "Officer down."

His limp hand fell back to the floor. Mallory rose to a stand and moved on to examine other elements of her new crime scene: Riker's blood on the wine bottle, his stolen revolver in the loose grip of Zachary's gloved hand. So the doctor had lost the gun to this man before she could get off one round; no surprise there. The Reaper's trademark, a honed penknife, lay at Zachary's feet, and one case was closed. What else? Spilled wine on the couch and a shattered glass on the floor by the doctor's chair. In the absence of visible wounds, poison was such an easy call—a murder-suicide.

No, it was not quite that simple. There were a few outstanding details.

And now the scene was all too easily read, and here her mind made a bruising stumble, slamming up against her own mistake: she had underestimated the doctor's feelings for Riker.

He moaned, and she turned around to see other signs of Riker's awakening, subtle movements of his face and limbs. Before the real horror show could begin, she turned out the light so he would not open his eyes to see the dead white face of Johanna Apollo.

After dragging his body into the hallway, the young detective returned to tamper with the crime scene. In her limited rule book for a cop's life, this was an act of heresy.

She could not remove Riker's stolen gun from the premises; Jack Coffey knew who had taken it, and he would expect to find it listed on the crime-scene inventory. She settled for hiding the revolver in a drawer of the armoire, and now it was less clear that suicide had been Dr. Apollo's *second* option. Next, with one hand, Mallory wiped the wet face of a corpse, formerly a woman who had loved her life and proved it, leaving behind the irrefutable evidence of tears.

All gone now, perfectly dry.

Riker would never know and never blame himself.

When the ambulance arrived, Mallory was on her knees, holding Riker tightly in her arms, rocking him and lying to him, telling him that everything was fine—just *fine*.

EPILOGUE

"A WAKE FOR A DEAD CAT." RIKER'S FATHER SHOOK his head, mystified that he should be invited here on such a foolish pretext. The old man had been the first guest to arrive. Mugs's real friends would come later to view the remains, possibly to spit upon them, and be reassured that the cat from hell was finally out of their lives. The ever skeptical Mrs. Ortega would prefer to see the dead body, but ashes would do.

Riker lifted his beer can in a toast. "To a great scrapper."

Over the months since Jo's death, the cat had declined, day by tail-dragging day, finally succumbing to old age and grief, but not without one last fight, a good one by Riker's account. Though Mugs now resided in an urn on the fireplace, Riker still bore the scabs of long scratches. His own fault; he had tried to cradle the dying animal in his arms, though he always omitted that part from the story of the cat's final brawl.

However, he had invited his father for another reason. He wanted to tie up one last loose end. A question had nagged at him every day since Jo had been gone. Without being asked, the old man had taken charge of her funeral arrangements, and Riker's gratitude ran deep. Had the matter been left to himself, the turnout would have been pathetic, not filling one pew of a small church. Dad had called in a lifetime of stored-up favors to fill a cathedral with cops, a grand affair that had made the front page of the *New York Times.* What power the old man had. Even high command officers had come out that day in dress blues as a tribute to the lady, a stranger to them all.

Father and son so rarely spoke, it was difficult to ask how Dad had known about this woman's terrible importance to him. No one could have mentioned it to the old man. Riker had not even told Jo. And so he had to ask.

Dad's reply was predictably brief. "I read your statement and the police report." He glowered at his son, for this evidence was so obvious. Why was he being asked to waste words upon it? That was not his way, and his own son should know better than to expect this of him. All of that was in the old man's eyes, but no more words were forthcoming.

"Not good enough, Dad." Riker slugged back his beer, then crumpled the can in one fist to tell the old bastard that he was dead serious. "Now, why did you go to all that trouble for a woman you've never met?"

"I *told* you. It was all in the paperwork and her fingerprints. When she clubbed you with that wine bottle—well—what that woman did—" This was a strain on him, so many words and all in a row. He paused to read his son's expression, which said, with quiet resolve, that there must be more. And so his dry cracked lips pressed into a line of resignation, for Dad wanted it known that he spoke under duress.

"You went in there that night—without your gun. You loved her." He tilted his head to one side to ask his son if this was clear, the connection between these two things, or had he not raised a detective after all. "She died for you," the old man said. And thus he owed an enormous debt to Johanna Apollo, for his son was precious to him; that was also in his eyes, and he lowered them lest any more nonsense should leak out in this manner.

Rising from his chair, Dad reached out one bone-dry hand and let it rest a moment on his son's shoulder, just a light tap that stood for a kiss. And now he took his leave of this ridiculous party for a dead cat. That last sentiment was conveyed by the subtle shake of the head as he walked toward the door. His hand was on the knob when he spoke again without turning around, and this was one of his longest speeches. "The day of the funeral, you asked me about Johanna's gravestone. Well, it was finally installed. I went out there this morning to make sure they did a right job of it. They followed the attorney's instructions—the ones she gave him the day she died." And now he quickly departed, sparing himself the emotional response of a simple thank you from his son.

The stone had not yet been carved on the day when Jo had gone into the ground. A wooden marker had sufficed for the burial. Riker had been told that a more permanent monument had been ordered by the recent codicil to her will. And this had been more evidence of a suicide planned in advance of the Reaper knocking on Jo's door.

He kissed his last hope good-bye.

Thanks to the concussion, his memory of that night had ended on the wrong side of Jo's door. He could not recall breaking it down. And now he knew that his father had not been privy to any more evidence beyond the reports and statements.

Riker could not stop thinking like a cop, even on this his day off. Why had his father, the miser of words, found it necessary to repeat the gravestone story? And why did the old man prefer his own fable to the truth? Both father and son had reviewed the same evidence.

But only his father had seen the instructions for the stonecutter.

Had Jo left a sentimental passage on her tombstone, some message the old man had mistaken for Riker's but actually meant for another man? On his black days, Riker believed that Jo had died for the love of Timothy Kidd, that she had always planned to kill herself to end the grief and buy a little justice for a dead man.

On his good days, all he had left was pain.

Mallory slumped down behind the wheel of her car and waited for Riker to emerge from the apartment building. She knew it would not be long. He had been too eager to end the only party he had ever given, the dead-cat celebration.

She passed some time studying the pocket watch handed down from her foster father. The cover bore a gold engraving of an open field beneath a heaven of roiling clouds; a lone figure, bent and bowed, was walking against the wind. Once it had conjured up memories of home and the people who had loved her. That old connection was lost to her now, for every time she looked at the watch, she thought of Johanna Apollo.

Everything had changed.

Mallory looked up to see Riker standing at the curb, waving one hand to stop a taxicab. She put her tan sedan in gear and edged out into the street, following at a distance of several car lengths. When the yellow cab stopped at an intersection, she saw Riker's arm extend from the rolled-down rear window, holding out money to buy a bouquet of flowers from a sidewalk vendor. The red roses could only be intended for a woman.

She followed his cab across the bridge to Brooklyn, and now she knew where he was heading, for that way lay the cemetery. Twenty minutes later, the cabbie left his passenger at the gate. Mallory took her own time finding a parking space some distance away. She had no fear of losing him among the many paths that wound through acres of grave sites.

When she found him again, his body blocked her view of the tombstone. From her hiding place behind a larger monument, Mallory could only tell that the grave marker had been recently installed. The workmen's tracks had disturbed a light covering of this morning's snow.

Riker's felt hat went flying off in a strong gust of frigid air. When he dropped his bouquet, the wind took his roses, too, nudging them along the cold ground, picking at their petals—destroying them. And what damage had Dr. Apollo done to Riker? Had the woman left some little bomb of words engraved in granite? He was bending, folding, as if the doctor had reached out from the frozen ground and gutted him.

Mallory had said nothing to alter his theory of the murder-suicide as a long-planned event, nor had she discouraged him from casting himself in the role of an unwanted intruder on that scene. In her rationale, Riker would not grieve if Johanna Apollo had never been his to lose. But now that plan was unraveling, and her frustration was escalating by the second, for there was no way to get even with the dead.

She need not have worried that Riker would catch her watching over him. When he finally turned around, he was as good as blind, tears blurring his eyes and streaming down his face. After he had disappeared over the rise of the gravel path, an angry Mallory approached the gravestone to see what the dead woman had done to him. But there was nothing written there that could break a man in half, no words at all beyond the doctor's name and the dates of her life and death.

Understanding came swiftly as a hammerfall.

The man had come to a boneyard, of all places, looking for love, and he had gone away without it. Johanna Apollo had died for him, and, for a little while, something very rare had belonged to Riker—until Mallory had destroyed the only evidence.

In her own inimical, violent style, her own version of remorse, she slammed one closed fist down on the gravestone, wanting the pain, wanting to feel *something*. Mallory turned toward the path, intending to hunt Riker down before he reached the gate. She planned to hurt him with the certain knowledge that Johanna Apollo had loved him more than her own life. This fresh agony would be her gift to him—all the details of the altered crime scene.

But she could not move.

It was as if a wall had suddenly sprung up about her, surrounding her with invisible bricks of irony. Riker would never believe her—not her, a liar and a manipulator extraordinaire, though he would nod and smile, thanking her for her trouble. Then he would pour himself a shot of bourbon, dismissing her gift as some new trick to fix him one last time.

Riker had lost everything.

A family of four came along the path, crunching gravel underfoot and bearing flowers for a nearby grave. They gave a wide berth to the young woman who stood there so quietly, all of them believing that her sorrow must be recent and profound. The mourners departed. Night fell. And Kathy Mallory was left in the cold company of stone.

The marker was a plain one of deep red granite, and its only ornament was modest. The flower carved within a heart was not a rose, nor any bloom that one could readily identify. It was small, not much to look at—a common pimpernel.

THE HOUR WAS LATE. THE TRAFFIC WAS SCARCE. A few cars crawled by at the pace of bugs attracted by house lights, five flights of electric-yellow windows.

The narrow mansion was not a rarity in New York City, home to millionaires and billionaires. However, its nineteenth-century facade was an anachronism on this particular block of Central Park West. The steep-pitched roof was split by a skylight dome, and attendant gargoyles were carved in stone. Wedged in tight between two condominium behemoths, this dwelling was in the wrong place at the wrong time and regally unrepentant, though the police were at the door.

And in the parlor, up the stairs and down in the cellar.

So *many* police.

Nedda Winter sat quietly and watched them pass her by on their way to other rooms—and they watched her for a while. Soon they came to regard her as furniture, but she took no offense. She turned on the antique radio that stood beside her chair. No one reprimanded her, and so she turned up the volume.

White-hot jazz.

Benny Goodman on the clarinet and other ghosts from the

big-band era flooded the front room and infected the steps of people in and out of uniform, passing to and fro.

Lift those feet. Tap those toes.

Miss Winter repressed a smile, for that would be unseemly, but she nodded in time to the music. The house was alive again, drunk on life, though the party revolved around the dead man at the center of the floor.

Miss Winter was well-named. She had the countenance of that season. Her long hair was pure white, and her skin had the pallor of one who has been shut away for a long time. Even her eyes had gone pale, leached of color, bleached to the lightest tint of blue. She was so well-disguised by time that the police continued to ignore her, demanding no apologies, nor any explanation for her long absence. They had even failed to recognize this house, an address that was infamous when the music on the radio was young.

Fifty-eight years earlier, in the aftermath of another violent crime, which remained unsolved, a twelve-year-old girl had vanished from this house, and now the lost child, grown up and grown old, had come back home to live.

The medical examiner's vehicle was parked at the curb, and behind it was another van with the CSU logo of the crime-scene technicians. The front windows of the house were all alight, and the silhouettes of men and women moved across pulled-down shades and closed drapes.

A warm October breeze of Indian summer rippled the yellow crime-scene tapes that extended down the stone steps to include a patch of the sidewalk. The tape did the restraining duty of a velvet rope for theatrical productions, though tonight's audience amounted to only three stragglers, refugees from a saloon in the hour after closing time. Happy intoxication was in their stance and in their badly-sung song, which was grating on the nerves of a uniformed officer. The spinning cherry lights of police units made the officer's face alternately beet-red and pale white as he waved off the drunks with a loud, "Get the hell outta here!"

Charles Butler parked his Mercedes behind a police car and stepped out into the street, unfolding and rising to a stand of six feet four. Smooth grace in motion served as compensation for his foolish face. Bulbous eyes the size of hens' eggs were half-closed by heavy lids and pocked with small blue irises that gave him a look of permanent astonishment, and his hook of a nose might perch two sparrows or one fat pigeon. Otherwise, the forty-year-old man was well-made from the necktie down and well turned-out, though he had omitted the vest from his three-piece suit.

He had dressed in a hurry. Mallory was waiting.

Two uniformed policemen stood guard before the house, barring all comers from the short flight of stone steps leading up to the front door. As he approached these officers, Charles inadvertently smiled—a *huge* mistake. Whenever his features were gathered up into any happy expression, it gave him the look of a loon—a second cousin to the three departing drunks. Before he could be driven off, Charles pointed upward to the worst-dressed man in America, Detective Sergeant Riker, who slouched against a wrought iron railing, cadging a light from another man, then exhaling a cloud of cigarette smoke with his conversation.

"I'm with him."

At the sound of a familiar voice, Riker turned around with that crooked smile he saved for people he liked. "Hey, how ya doin'?" The detective descended the short flight of steps to the sidewalk and gripped the larger man's hand. "Thanks for coming out. I know it's late."

Indeed it was, and Riker had the appearance of a man who had slept away most of this night in his suit. But then he always dressed that way, pre-wrinkled at the start of every workday. The yellow light at the top of the staircase had the flattering effect of minimizing the creases in the detective's face, making him appear somewhat younger than his fifty-five years.

"My pleasure." Charles looked down at his friend of average height, feeling the need to apologize for looming over him.

"Did Mallory tell you anything useful?"

"No, nothing at all."

"Maybe it's better that way." Riker motioned him toward the stairs, then led the way up. "Two women live here. One of them killed a man tonight. Simple enough?" He flicked his cigarette over the railing. "Check 'em out. We'll talk later."

When they passed through the open door, Charles heard music, vintage jazz, and he would not have been surprised to hear the clink of ice in cocktail glasses as they entered a din of conversation in the large foyer. They walked by a cluster of men wearing badges clipped to their suit pockets, and Detective Riker nodded to them in passing. "Those guys are settling a little problem of jurisdiction." He led Charles through a louder dispute between a woman in uniform and a man in a suit. Riker explained this one, too. He pointed to the young man with the folded stethoscope squeezed tightly in one raised fist. "Now, that's one pissed-off medical examiner. Mallory won't release the body. She's using it to rattle the ladies who live here."

At the threshold of the front room, Charles had only time enough to blink once before entering a spatial paradox. The inside of the house appeared to be much larger than the exterior—a trick of cunning architecture. And some of the magic was done with a score of mirrors in elaborate silver frames ten feet tall. They created a labyrinth of rooms and flights of stairs and corridors where none existed. Thus, a dozen people were transformed into a mob, and each reflection added its own energy to the fray.

The grand staircase was the focal point, a tenuous bit of engineering that seemed to have no secure supports as it curved up to a partial vista on a floor above the cathedral ceiling. Though the rest of the stairs spiraled out of sight, in mind's eye he was swept along with them, rushing round and upward through all the dizzying flights.

Back to earth—a corpse lay on the floor, partially obscured by upright people, and Charles Butler, unaccustomed to crime scenes, was caught in a quandary of manners: perhaps he should have admired the dead man first, and maybe he should not be tapping his feet in time to the music of a clarinet.

An even less reverent police photographer stepped over the body to speak with Detective Riker, who directed the close-up shots of the deceased. After snapping pictures in quick succession, and in time to the beat of a snare drum, the photographer departed to another room, giving Charles his first clear view of the victim.

He had been prepared for something brutal and grisly, given that this case had attracted so much attention, but the man on the floor seemed to be merely resting—if one could only discount the pair of scissors protruding from the chest. The victim did not belong in this neighborhood of wealth. His pants were shapeless and dirty, the T-shirt stained with more sweat than blood, and a pointed object lay near one open hand. Thus laid out was the simple story of an ice-pick-wielding intruder felled by a homeowner who favored shears.

What could possibly interest all of these—

Following a cue of upturned heads, his attention was drawn to the second-floor landing and the slender young woman standing there in blue jeans and an attitude of privilege. Blond curls, cut by a virtuoso, grazed the shoulders of a tailored blazer worn over a silk T-shirt. Arms folded and long legs akimbo, she affected the pose of one who owned all that she surveyed, even the people in the room below and, most particularly, the corpse.

Mallory.

More formally, she was Detective Mallory and never Kathy anymore. She preferred the distancing surname even among those who knew her best. And, though Charles was her foremost apologist, he found the background music fitting. Louis Armstrong was belting out the lyrics of Savannah's hard-hearted Hannah.

—pouring water on a drowning man—

One cream-white hand with red fingernails—call them

talons—lightly touched the banister as she slowly descended the grand staircase, circling in a wide arc, her eyes fixed on one face in the crowd.

But not *his* face.

Two crime-scene technicians moved out of Charles's way, and now he could see the object of Mallory's fixation.

A child?

Detective Riker had told him that two women lived at this address. There had been no mention of this little girl shivering like a whippet, that nervous, tremulous breed of dog that can never quite get warm, no matter what the temperature. No—wait. This was no child, but a tiny woman with a few silver threads in her dark brown hair, someone closer to his own age. Eyes cast down, this person presented herself at the bottom of the staircase in the manner of a penitent—or a volunteer for human sacrifice.

Tall Mallory literally descended upon the smaller woman, rapidly closing the distance and causing the little householder to shrink even more. Before the small head could turtle into the cowl of a white robe, Charles noted one charming detail: the short brown hair was angled across the ears, creating the illusion that they were pointed in the elfin way.

"That's Miss Bitty Smyth." Detective Riker raised one eyebrow, as if expecting Charles to recognize the name.

He did not.

"Bitty? That's a nickname?"

Riker shrugged and splayed one hand to say, *Who knows?* "That's how she introduced herself. If she's got another name, we can't get it out of her. We can't get *anything* out of her."

"She might be in shock." Charles watched on in helpless fascination as Mallory reached out to Bitty Smyth and gripped the woman's thin arm. He was about to discount the possibility that Miss Smyth was the scissor-wielding homeowner when he turned to see the other resident of the house, a woman with long white hair and a green silk robe. She was barefoot and seated beside an antique radio, the source of the music. How amazing to find this old piece in working order.

By the detail on its cabinet, he could date the radio back to the middle nineteen-thirties—the woman, too. He guessed her age at seventy or thereabouts. Her hand was on the dial, raising the volume.

"That's Miss Nedda Winter," said Riker. "She's Bitty's aunt." Again, something in Riker's manner suggested that Charles should also know this person.

She caught Charles staring at her, and he could only describe her expression as one of curious recognition.

The old woman turned off the music. Her attention had quickly shifted to the young homicide detective who had hold of Bitty Smyth's arm. Nedda Winter rose from her chair. She was taller than many of the men in this room, and her strides were long as she rushed toward her niece with an obvious plan of rescue. Riker, moving faster than his usual mosey, headed off Miss Winter. And now Charles was treated to a display that simply did not fit the man he knew. Playing the consummate gentleman, Riker extended one arm to the lady, as if she might need his support, then dazzled her with a broad smile and smoothly led her out of the room.

Star treatment. Perhaps he *should* know that old woman.

Charles turned back to the interrogation of Bitty Smyth, who was now facing in his direction. A bible was clutched to the tiny prisoner's breast, and her large brown eyes rolled back as her lips moved in what he took for whispers of fervent prayer.

Well, Mallory had that effect on people.

His next impression was that Miss Smyth had disconnected from the solid earth and might fly upward if not restrained. As Charles drew nearer, he heard Mallory say that, no, she had not found Jesus and had no intention of being saved. The smaller woman's head wobbled and nodded, perhaps in a fearful palsy, or maybe agreeing that this young policewoman was beyond salvation.

"Charles." Mallory quickly dropped her hold on Bitty Smyth's arm, as if caught in the act of beating a suspect. Supporting this illusion, Miss Smyth sank to an armchair, still nodding and trembling on the verge of a smile, so greatly relieved.

The long slants of Mallory's eyes were always the first thing one noticed—a strange bright shade of green not found in nature. She did not smile upon greeting him, and he had not expected that. Her expressions were usually deliberate or absent, a chilling idiosyncrasy.

She had others.

Though Charles Butler possessed a vast knowledge of abnormal psychology, Mallory sidestepped every attempt to classify her with any sense of confidence, as if she belonged to a separate species of one, a denizen of some unsentimental planet of perpetual cold weather.

"Hello," he said, smiling and standing back apace to take her in, as if he expected her to have grown over the weekend.

Her hand was on his arm, and, with the lightest of pressure, she was able to drag him down a narrow hallway and into a small boxy room all decked out like a tailor's shop with the tools and machines of the trade. Racks of thread spools lined one wall, and a basket of mending sat on the floor near a dressmaker's dummy.

"A sewing room," she said, "without a single pair of scissors."

"I think I noticed them back in the parlor." And here, wisely, he stopped, for Mallory's eyes widened slightly to tell him that she did not appreciate him pointing out the obvious thing—the shears planted in the dead man's chest. And neither did she care for being interrupted. Arms folding across her chest was all the warning he would ever get.

"So," the detective continued, "this woman comes downstairs—in the *dark*—sees the burglar. Then she runs to the other end of the house to look for the sewing shears. And the perp just stands there in the front room, waiting for her to come back and stab him to death."

Charles hesitated—always a good idea to tread carefully with her. There was only one logical conclusion, but he sensed a trap in the making. "Then it's not a case of self-defense?"

"No, that's exactly what it is," she said, somewhat impatient. "Self-defense. That much I believe."

"Right." Charles needed no mirror to tell him that he wore the comical face of a fool who has just discovered that it was not night but day. Hands in his pockets, he stared at his shoes. "I gathered from Riker that you wanted a psych evaluation of those two women."

"No, that was just an afterthought." She closed the door, then leaned her back against it, as if to block his escape. "What can you tell me about those people?"

He shrugged. "Only their names. I just got here."

She put one hand on her hip, a sign that she did not entirely believe him, but then it was her nature to be suspicious of everyone who did not carry a badge—and everyone who did. "You've never met them before?"

"No," said Charles, "I don't know either of them."

"Well, they know *you.* And they've known you for a long time." Her eyes were asking, accusing and demanding all at once, *And how do you explain that?*

Detective Riker liked the kitchen best. Unlike the rest of the house, this room was built to human scale. The low ceiling made it cozy, almost cottage-like. He declined an offer of alcohol but allowed Nedda Winter to make him a glass of ice tea with thanks.

She selected a lemon from a bowl of fruit. Knife in hand, she stood at the butcher block and smiled at him. It was almost a tease, as if to ask—did he object to her holding this dangerously pointed object?

Riker's mouth dipped on one side to say, *Yeah, right.*

He made a cursory inventory of the room, his gaze passing over a meat cleaver, then traveling onto a cutlery block of knives. A case bolted to the far wall contained a fire extinguisher and a small axe. With all the lethal weapons in this kitchen arsenal, a pair of scissors had been an odd choice to bring down an intruder tonight.